Praise for
The Ghost Daughter

"O'Leary's book is a mystery full of surprises, but at its heart it's really a story about the meaning of family and the long-lasting damage that mental and physical abuse has on a person. I loved the way the story is revealed slowly and the changing points of view drew me in and kept me emotionally attached to the lives of the three women. Violent at times, emotionally charged, and sometimes invoking tears, a gripping story."
—Diane Ferbrache for the *Unshelved Book Club*

"The West Coast has always been the last best place, a region equal parts Eden and earthquake. In Maureen O'Leary's hands, that landscape is charged with mystery, disaster, and a wealth of drama, all headed by a cast of irrepressible woman. *The Ghost Daughter* is that rare and fabled beast: the literary page-turner."
—Christian Kiefer, author of *The Animals*

"Two parts thriller, one part meditation on the nature of love and motherhood, and one part poem, *The Ghost Daughter* combines masterful storytelling and artistic language to create a breathtaking work of literary suspense. Reading it was like riding a roller coaster overlooking an ethereal canyon. Intricately woven twists, turns, and plummets abounded, inducing a sublime mental whiplash. And yet, in spite of my hunger to learn what happened next, I found myself slowing down, craning my neck to absorb O'Leary's rich, haunting language and gripping narrative voice. Peopled with human monsters, mortal ghosts, and lost maidens, *The Ghost Daughter* plays out like a modern fairy tale, a linguistic aria written in praise of the power of reinvention, resurrection, and redemption. As eviscerating as it is lovely, *The Ghost Daughter* is not to be missed."
—Tawni Waters, author of *Beauty of the Broken*

"In the fragile landscape of Northern California, Maureen O'Leary excavates her characters' hearts with precise honesty, exploring the ways connections between mothers and daughters, friends and lovers stretch, break, endure. A beautiful and moving book."
—Karen E. Bender, National Book Award finalist and author of *Refund*, *Like Normal People*, and *A Town of Empty Rooms*

Dear Terri,

How lovely to have you for a reader. I hope you enjoy!!

Love,
Maureen

The Ghost Daughter

The Ghost Daughter

Maureen O'Leary

coffeetownpress

Seattle, WA

coffeetownpress

Coffeetown Press
PO Box 70515
Seattle, WA 98127

For more information go to: www.coffeetownpress.com
www.maureenolearyauthor.com

Cover design by Sabrina Sun
Cover photograph of the beach by Evan Hartzell

The Ghost Daughter

ISBN: 978-1-60381-287-0 (Trade Paper)
ISBN: 978-1-60381-286-3 (eBook)

Library of Congress Control Number: 2015954721

Printed in the United States of America

For Ciara

Acknowledgments

I AM GRATEFUL TO Catherine Treadgold, Jennifer McCord, and Melissa Rouse of Coffeetown Press for their brilliant insight and careful attention. It has been an honor to work with them.

Thanks go to Tricia Ireland-Stirling and Vanessa Diffenbaugh for the criticism, encouragement, and help getting this novel to the world. Thanks to Sally Wofford-Girand for lending me her guidance as I found my work a home.

I am grateful to the Squaw Valley Community of Writers, and my teachers there, Elizabeth Rosner, Glen David Gold and Janet Fitch, whose work will always inspire in me a diligent attention to craft.

Thanks to my students, who show such courage in their own writing. Thanks to my parents Jack and Honey O'Leary for the encouragement. This story was deepened by the inspiration of Rachel Libby-Gensler, who knows a mother's grief more than most, and continues with grace anyway.

As always, a deep bow to Lora Schoen, Laura Alvarez, Evan Hartzell, and Andrew Kjera for their friendship and example of integrity, forgiveness, art, and love.

From my deepest heart I am grateful to Jim, Ciara, and Margaret, the epicenters of my life, the reasons for everything, the ones who remind me of why on the day when an indifferent Earth shrugged her shoulders, I was the one by the big oak desk and so was spared.

Chapter 1

October 17, 1971
Arcata, California

Crystal

~~~

THE LITTLE GIRL clasped the giant's neck as he carried her through the forest. He ran and ran and she was falling.

"Hold on, little one," he whispered.

Blood came out of his head. The bad men chased them. They shouted from the darkness. She had been sitting in the backseat while he was driving when another car bumped them from behind and they crashed into a tree. The girl had hurt her arm. The tall man scooped her out of the car and ran fast on his long legs.

Her stomach felt funny. It was night but the stars were hiding. All she had was Angel Bear crushed in the giant's jacket. He carried her book in the inside pocket too. It knocked against her legs.

They stopped and leaned against a tree. The tall man couldn't breathe very well. After he removed her shirt, she hugged herself in the cold air. He was worried about her hurt arm and her blood. He looked at the cut and she knew not to cry. She always knew not to cry.

The voices got closer. The giant swooped her up and the trees rushed past like nightmares. His hands were rough on her bare back and she was afraid of the shadow men. She felt sick but she knew not to say it.

They slid down a hill and it felt like crashing again. He put her down. The moon made a blue light and shadows. She clutched for him and almost cried when he gave her Angel Bear to hold instead. He turned her away and pointed to the path through the forest.

"Run, Crystal!" he said.

The men shouted. The giant's hands were hot on her back, pushing her. "Right down that path. Run!" he said. He sounded sick. He dropped to his hands and knees and crawled like a dog. His blood was black in the moonlight. It dripped on the ground.

"Run!" he said. She knew not to cry. She followed the path and she ran without a sound.

Chapter 2

October 17, 1989
Del Rio Beach, California

Angel

~⌣~

N OTHING IN ANGEL'S college sociology classes had taught her how to persuade a schizophrenic man to give someone else a turn in the shower. The sibilant sounds of the running water quieted his demons and gave him his only peace. Getting him out would require a magic touch.

Within Jerry's matted head churned awful worlds. The other shelter residents called him a priest of devils conjuring evil with his constant muttering that nobody understood. His inner voices had taken over all circuits. To the residents Jerry was a living symbol of the worst that could happen.

Angel Kelley didn't fear him. Her professors lectured about case studies and textbook examples of schizophrenia but she recognized Jerry's kind from fairy tales. She knew all about heartbreak and lost travelers alone in haunted woods. Jerry's was a very old story.

To tell the truth, she felt a kinship with him. She was so sad these days and so mixed up that maybe they understood each other. Jerry certainly knew the kind of loss that would take a fairy tale to explain. He and Angel were both the lost children in the woods as well the monsters that chased them. Monsters did not fear other monsters.

This wasn't to say Jerry did not have fears. There weren't any free clinics in Del Rio Beach for people like him and anyway it was nearly impossible to get him to go inside. He hated buildings. He took his meals in the courtyard and slept there too. Angel rigged a tarp for him when it rained and called it shelter.

One hot Tuesday morning in mid-October, the story on the street was that Jerry got over his phobia of the indoors long enough to go into the Ace Hardware, grab a machete from the gardening tools, and hack a fellow's head off. The tellers of the tale streaming in for the dinner hour granted that the story was probably at least partially fiction. No one had seen it happen. There was no bloody head rolling in the gardening tools aisle for proof.

Yet when Jerry hunkered down in the outdoor shower stall, only Angel dared approach. The other residents spat on the patio cobblestones. They snatched at their misery with curses, too spooked to say his name.

Angel's boots slipped on the redwood deck. She'd helped build the structure and it didn't drain well. She entered the world of white steam in which Jerry stood naked and the color of dirt. Water dripped from the point of his beard. He was an earthen castaway. He was the spirit of a tree.

"Did you use soap?" Angel asked.

"Yeah I used soap. You're not my mother."

"Okay," she said, backing out. "Hurry up."

The afternoon sun dried the wet beads on her eyelashes. The sun crushed the courtyard with an unrelenting heat that was putting everybody in a bad mood.

"He's on his way," she said to the other guys.

"You're too soft on the freak." This from Gene, who smelled of gasoline and used his enormous stomach as a battering ram. His size worked to his advantage with everybody but Angel. She intimidated Gene like a mouse did a cartoon elephant. He said she was too small and she made him nervous. He never knew where she would turn up.

Angel also had the management authority to dump troublemakers into the street. A man Gene's size had a hard time hiding from the night patrols looking for sleepers on the beach and along the river. She'd expelled him before for being belligerent and she'd do it again. She had to think of the safety of the group.

Gene was lucky Angel believed that everyone deserved a fresh start. Redemption was always possible, even for Big Gene. "Give him a minute, brother," she said. "John is ahead of you anyway."

John gripped the ends of the towel around his neck. A trim sandy mustache as tight as a toothbrush twitched over his ravaged lips. He was twenty-two days clean, a record among the men. He tossed Gene a half nod.

Jerry slammed the door open and loped past them, his long whiskers jumping around as he murmured incantations. His clothes clung to his wet skin. He padded across the hot stones on bare feet as gnarled as roots. The other men stood off some yards just in case he was in a hacking mood.

Gene used the distraction to jump the line. He moved fast, leading with his belly like a toddler proud of his body. After he disappeared behind the door, he slid the bolt with a neat click. John hurled himself against it. He cursed. He beat his fists. He was going to drag Gene out and kill him, the fat son of a bitch.

Russell jumped down the kitchen stairs. Flour and sugar streaked his jeans and puffed from his boots. He leaned in for a kiss but Angel ducked. Not in front of the residents. Not in front of anyone. That was the deal and she wished he'd stop forgetting it.

"I need help with the guys," she said.

"Since when?" Russell looked over her head at the ruckus. He smelled like vanilla cake.

"It's a weird day," she said.

"I'll look after this," Russell said. "You go on inside. You're needed."

"Why?" She whipped around, scanning the courtyard for Jerry.

"Just go," he said.

Gene started up with a Lynyrd Skynyrd tune in a solid baritone, singing about how he was a simple kind of man.

Now the guys who hadn't even been waiting in line rushed the shower stall. They pounded on the thin walls. Russell hollered at them to back off. Luckily Russell was bigger than most. He would handle it okay. Goddamn Gene.

Angel steeled herself for a new crisis, but within the kitchen all was at peace. The new college volunteers chatted while a box fan whirred in the window. They were two young hippie-style girls with long shiny hair and flowing skirts. Joni Mitchell crooned out of the tape player and Jerry stood in the corner by the dry goods pantry, pointing one snaggle-nailed finger at the plank floor.

"What are you doing inside, man?" she asked.

He raised his head. The clouds from his eyes fell away and just like that, there was no more underworld king. He was just a man.

"Jerry," she whispered. Her heart lifted. She'd heard of this, moments of clarity in a schizophrenic mind. She'd never expected to have one with Jerry. "I'm so happy to see you," she said.

"Go outside," he growled in the back of his throat. No time for niceties. "Sweet Angel. Get out of here now. Go outside now."

"Why?" she asked.

His face twisted with the effort of a person trying to speak a foreign language. "Danger," he said. "Danger Will Robinson." He waved frustrated hands, then bowed out the door. She moved to follow but one of the volunteers called her back.

"There's a man in the lobby asking to see the permits," she said. "I told Russell and he said to tell you."

"Goddamn," Angel said. Jerry returned to his regular spot under the elm tree in the corner of the courtyard by the fence. He was agitated, the darkness having descended once more. Angel felt as helpless as if someone she loved had disappeared in fog.

"Hey, is that guy Russell seeing anybody?" the other volunteer asked, tomato sauce dripping off her flowing sleeve. Polished pink candy toenails peeped from brand new Birkenstocks. Angel did not have time for Jerry now.

"No sandals in an industrial kitchen," Angel said. "Next time wear shoes." They got these volunteers once in a while from the university. They cost training time yet rarely lasted more than one night. Angel tugged at a knot in her own tangled, caramel-colored hair. She did not need to compare herself to a couple of college kids pretending at peace and love.

Her boot heels echoed on the stairs down to the basement office. The light flickered. One manager on duty was not enough. Without Russell around she'd be in real trouble tonight. He was only supposed to be there to lead the Narcotics Anonymous meeting, not keep the peace. Keeping the peace was her job. One of her jobs.

The city council sent an inspector almost every day. Behind her back the mayor called her Queen of the Trolls. This tidbit came from a former classmate who worked in his office. The bigwigs had it in for the shelter. They said it attracted the homeless to the city, and bums were bad for business. Angel thought that was a terrible way to think about human beings in need. Somebody had to stand up for poor Jerry out there circling the elm tree. She wished she could have spoken with him just a minute longer in that moment when he'd stepped free of his mind's haunted forest.

She scooped the paperwork from the big desk into an envelope and turned to climb the stairs. She didn't have time for disappointment. She would throw the man the permits and run outside before Russell with his good intentions and Gene with his bad ones broke the shower stall down. If the city council thought they were going to discourage her by relentlessly searching for code violations, then that was funny. Fighting for the shelter made her happy. It was the only thing that did anymore.

She paused on the stairwell. Shelter noise thumped overhead. Dinnertime. Footsteps fell as heavy as a succession of tired soldiers. A plate shattered. Russell must have ordered people inside to help set the table for supper. Good for him. The thought of the city man stampeded by twenty-seven grumpy homeless guys made her smile.

Then the world ended.

A deep rumble of sound followed by shaking. The light bulb popped in a shower of filament and glass.

Shoved by invisible hands, Angel fell to her knees. The floor rocked on a furious sea. She groped for the desk and crawled beneath it. Her forehead rammed the wood as it jumped around her shoulders.

Choking dust exploded in her nose. She cupped her face and breathed into her hands. There was no room to run. There was rumbling and crashing on top of the rumble and another wave slammed the massive oak desk against her head.

A greater sound thundered underneath the crashing. A tsunami. A freight train driven by angry gods.

The shaking stopped. But it didn't stop. The concrete floor writhed as if infested with worms. There were no borders in the pitch blackness. She did not begin and she did not end. She was the desk, she was the bricks, and she was the ceiling coming down.

The desk cracked in a muffled sound. Then silence.

Angel could not move. The space under the desk now contained her body and a pile of hard things, splintery things. Grit covered her fingertips, lips, and teeth. A scream erupted in her throat but she swallowed it down and thought there was not enough air for that.

She was no Queen or Angel. She was a shut mouth. She was a closed eye. She was a crumpled page in a book of tales the earth did not want told.

Chapter 3

October 17, 1989
Palo Alto, California

Reese

REESE HATED THE barbecues at George and Linda's house. It was all IBM talk and drunken do-si-dos in doorways with everybody flirting with everybody else's spouses. Last weekend they ran the neighborhood parcourse with George and Linda before brunch. Linda's enormous breasts strained the seams of her t-shirt and she wasn't capable of any of the exercises. There were two sets of bars at the chin-up station and Rod and George got into a pissing contest over how many they could do. Rod won and the tiny veins on his bumpy cheeks flared red and Reese was embarrassed. Then the men jogged ahead of their wives on the trail, slicing their elbows in the air like roosters.

That meant that Reese had to walk with Linda. Linda wasn't interested in running. She meant to walk languidly, limp as a hothouse flower.

"I'm like a total blonde," she said. "It's my trademark, you know?"

The smell of Obsession wafted from her cleavage when she pulled Reese close with one arm. Reese leaned in like a plank. She knew what these people wanted from her. They wanted easy conversation and flirting and boy versus girl banter. Reese was pretty and blonde enough to fit right in. If she was getting tired of the game nobody had to know.

But Linda irritated Reese with a boredom that made her bite the inside of her mouth to taste the blood. She swore that she would never go out with them again. Still, she found herself three days later at Linda's house on a Tuesday night, waiting for George to finish burning the hamburgers so they could watch the World Series on their new big TV.

Rod didn't even like George. George was fat, he said. His spare tire had a spare tire. That was true, but at least George talked like a grownup. Reese did not want to spend one more minute in conversation with Linda. She kept poolside and focused her attention on her daughter.

Madison sang to herself while she kicked in the water. She clung to the side of the kidney-shaped pool, up to her armpits in a pink floating ring. Reese wished she'd brought her own bathing suit. It was the kind of hot and dirty late autumn day that made her thirst for rain.

Rod stood on the deck holding a drink. He watched Madison with more attention than usual. He was posing for their hosts because in the fatherhood aspect Rod was the clear winner. Maybe their wives were neck and neck in the beauty department but George didn't have a kid.

Resentment bubbled in Reese like prehistoric tar. Her husband's eyes were red rimmed already and it was barely five o'clock. He drank every night until the alcohol puffed up his feathers for display. She couldn't control him. She could barely look at him. His drinking was a hungry monster that was going to ruin everything. Real damage was on its way. Her own prehistory had taught her how to recognize impending disaster but not how to stop it.

In Reese's past there was another daughter, one named Crystal, and she had lost her. If she thought on Crystal at all, it was to tell herself that she had never existed. Her ghost daughter had almost no substance anymore. The memory of that child was the color of glass.

Her daughter Madison was a brand new story. When it came to this daughter, Reese's heart was full of rising heat. Her ardor was terrifying but also gave her a tiny private hope that maybe she was a true person underneath the lacquer and layers and broken pieces. In the process of losing Crystal, Reese had also lost herself. In the eighteen years since she'd last seen her first child, Reese had become an exoskeleton of a woman. She was brittle and hollow in all matters except with Madison. There was such a thing as being born twice. It was her second daughter who gave her life, not the other way around.

Madison stopped kicking and leaned back so her hair floated like seaweed. Reese imagined her in ten years at fifteen and then in another ten as a full-grown woman. The girl had the looks of a beauty pageant winner with her pointy chin and little bow lips. She would be safer out of the woods of childhood. It would be better when her dimpled cheeks flattened into hard planes and her hands didn't look so much like a baby's. It was too much to be that small. Anything could happen to a person that small.

"Put your face in the water, Maddy," Rod said. His self-conscious smile made Reese chew poison between her back teeth.

"She's okay doing what she's doing," Reese said. Rod squinted under a visor he made with his hand. Without sunglasses his face looked as raw as a hammered thumb.

Reese sipped Diet Coke and silently listed plausible excuses for leaving early. Stomach pain. School night.

Then the air itself shimmered. In the distance rolled the noise of approaching thunder or maybe trains. The ground jerked with the motion of a pulled rug. Reese braced herself as gravity itself jumped up and down.

Quick peaked waves swung back and forth over the edges of the pool. The hot air expanded and contracted and for the space of fifteen long seconds the whole world shifted under a hot and turbulent sea.

Rod and George staggered around holding their drinks aloft. Linda shrieked while the backyard bucked and rolled. Flung to the deep end, Madison clutched the floating ring around her chest with both tiny fists. She bobbed on the surface of the stormy waters, her lips pursed in a pink knot. She didn't cry. She didn't make a sound. The water chopped as though it were filled with ten kids. With limbs of stone, Reese watched her daughter cling to the float, her legs pedaling under her body. She made it to the end and clutched at the stair rail. Still, she didn't cry.

The shaking stopped. Madison dropped the floating ring and ran into Reese's arms. Reese grabbed her as though she were the one who had been awash in a chlorinated sea. Rod and George babbled over each other. The thing to do was to see if the electricity worked. Turn on the television for the news. This was the Big One for sure. They ran into the house. Linda, her robe flying open to expose soft white flesh spilling over the top of her bikini, approached with a towel for Madison.

"Are you all right, honey?" Linda asked. Madison dug her face into her mother's shirt. "Let's go see what's on the news. That was the Big One, right?" Her hips wiggled when she walked away in her high heel sandals.

"You're prettier than her, Mommy," Madison said, like someone splashing water on a grass fire. "A lot prettier."

"Thank you." Reese pulled her daughter closer. She flashed on a momentary thought that it would be possible to engulf Madison into the emptiness of her body and hold her there for safety.

"That was scary. What happened to the pool?"

"Earthquake. Had to be." Car alarms hooted down the street.

They kept their arms around each other as they stared into the pool. Reese conjured the old trick of concentrating on her breath to quiet her strange mind. The earthquake unsettled her. A crack split across the white expanse of the underwater bowl of the pool. They watched mud ooze from the fissure and bloom in a mushroom cloud while people turned off their cars one by one until it was quiet.

Reese handed Madison her hat. The little girl's angel face was stoic in the shade of the brim. The ground shivered again, as though it had made itself nervous with such a big display. A string of car alarms exploded in renewed ringing. Reese tossed Madison the bag with her clothes in it. They had come from home in a separate car. Reese's shirt was wet and see-through from Madison's wet body, and besides, she needed to get home to make sure everything was all right there. An earthquake could not have come at a better time. It was the perfect excuse for leaving.

"I'm still drippy," Madison said.

"Dry off all the way," Reese said. "I'll take you to get frozen yogurt."

Inside the house the TV roared. Linda held the remote, her eye makeup a smudge of oily ash from the heat and the drinking. She was crying.

"Are you hearing this?" Linda asked. Newscasters spoke in excited voices.

Shake, rattle, and roll, folks. Seventy thousand people were stuck at Candlestick Park for the World Series. No game tonight and good luck getting home.

Untold numbers dead in San Francisco. Preliminary reports rolled in. A hunk of the Bay Bridge's top level broke like a ramp to the bottom. People were jumping off and swimming in the drink. Reporters spit and buzzed the bad news from helicopters.

Reese laughed and felt mean.

"This is like so not funny," Linda said. Water plopped from her bathing suit and hair onto the rose-colored carpet. Reese was sorry she made Madison get dry before coming inside. Nobody cared about a rug at a time like this. She sometimes thought the wrong things were important.

There were reports of hundreds dead in downtown Santa Cruz. Blood flowed in the streets from people crushed in the old brick storefronts built on marshy landfill. Less than half an hour in and they already had an expert engineer on hand to explain. The mortar crumbled with age, see. The bricks couldn't hold. In an earthquake the water shimmied up through the dirt and that was that. Liquefaction, it was called. Basically what you had there was dirt Jell-O.

Reese laughed again. Dirt Jell-O.

Linda rolled her eyes. Chocolate-colored moles splotched her creamy skin. She reminded Reese of a dairy cow.

"What's happening?" Rod had a fresh drink from the bar.

"Reese thinks it's a big joke," Linda said, telling on her like a third grader. "I for one do not think it's funny. I mean, people are *dying*."

"For Christ's sake, Reese," Rod said. "Is there something wrong with you?"

His words slurred together in a mush. He made Reese think of dirt Jell-O. He knew something was wrong with her. This was an old conversation, not some idle put-down to make himself the big man in front of Linda.

"I'm getting dressed now," Madison said. She padded through the room.

"Don't leave without me." She went into the guest bedroom down the hall.

"You're leaving?" Rod asked. "You can't leave. They invited us."

"School night, Rod," she said. "Wet shirt. Earthquake. Stomachache. You can stay though."

Onscreen a helicopter flew over the Cypress Highway in Oakland. Black smoke poured from between two levels of road sandwiched together in wide steps of collapsed asphalt. Cars full of people were wedged between the slabs. Nobody knew how many dead. Maybe thousands.

The air conditioner kicked on. Reese shivered. She called for Madison to hurry up. In the bathroom she wiped at her shirt with a hand towel. Someone rapped on the door. She opened it, expecting to find Rod, pleading with her to stay.

"Hey, you okay?" George. He stank of charcoal and beer. His head popped in before the rest followed, the spare tire taking up a lot of space.

"Yeah," she said. George shut the door with his foot. He smiled into the mirror, lowered his hands to her shoulders. He snuffled at the side of her neck.

She jerked away. "What are you doing?"

"You're beautiful, Reese." His breath was steamy at her throat. "I mean seriously."

"But what about Linda?" As if Linda were the reason why not. "Come on, George. Stop fooling around." She tried for the regular light banter, hating the sound of her own weakness.

"What do you think they're doing out there right now?" George asked. His stomach pressed against her back. Panic filled her mouth with the taste of metal. He laughed.

"Please," she said. He took it the wrong way, as an invitation, despite her pained face. She caught their reflection as he slid his meaty hands down her arms and gripped her wrists like bike handles. He pulled her hands out from under her. She bent forward under his weight, pain shooting through her hipbones where his weight shoved them against the marble countertop edge.

"What is it with your fucked-up hands, anyway?" he asked, distracted. He pressed her palms against the mirror, her fingers splayed like the legs of white spiders.

Spread your fingers. Ray's voice had been velvet. His lips curled. He knew what he was saying. *Spread them.*

Just as suddenly, she was pinned like an insect under the casual violence of another man. She had mistaken George for a soft man. For a dumb one. He grinned at her from behind, his brow a furrowed mask of corruption. She had thought there was power in her disdain. But as always it was only about who was bigger.

Reese sucked in her stomach to gain the few inches of space she needed to escape. She squeezed out from beneath the hard flesh of the man's belly and moved fast down the hallway.

George followed. "That fucking pool is going to cost us a fortune to fix, I'll tell you," he said, his voice full of throaty cheer. "Want cheese on your hamburgers, anybody?"

Reese huddled against the wall as he passed her. She stood in the opening of the living room and felt like throwing up. Rod called for cheese and raised his glass. Earthquake or no, they had to eat, right? Linda kept her face to the TV but still managed to wave for cheese. Reese was caught in someone else's banal nightmare. Her hips hurt and she knew she would have bruises where the skin stretched tight over bone. She wrung her hands, sickened by the popping of her freakish knuckles.

Then while she watched, Rod rested his hand on the small of Linda's back and stroked her there. In the space of a breath, he dropped it and stumbled through the open sliding glass door. Linda looked over her shoulder at Reese, raised an eyebrow, and smiled.

The tectonic plates that covered the surface of things shifted. The layers that took eons for her to build split and broke apart in moments. The primordial mud had been rippling beneath all the time, waiting for a breach. Reese's heart galloped in fury and she raced to meet it. Rage filled her with a hot comfort that washed away the weakness she'd felt pinned by George's insistent body in the bathroom.

Her façade of normalcy tore away in sheets that she couldn't stop. She wasn't one of the group. She wasn't one of any group. There was nothing normal about her. She forgot to concentrate on her breathing. She balled her crooked fingers into fists.

The screen flashed with the World Series commercial loop. Women in bikinis washed cars and mobs of happy men drank beers. George and Rod outside at the barbecue clinked their glasses together and acted like television commercial friends.

There had to be a hammer in the garage. Everyone had a hammer. The television and framed Nagel prints and glass-topped coffee table cried out for smashing. She could break Linda's fingers one by one. She knew how that was done. She knew how to wipe the smugness from Linda's face and turn it into something else altogether.

The news started again with footage of an apartment building in San Francisco that had leapt off its foundation. Sewage burst through the cracks of sidewalks in brown geysers. Smoke billowed from the rooftops.

A reporter on the street asked questions of the passersby. *I was driving when it happened*, someone said. *I was driving and I didn't feel a thing.*

She went into the kitchen and put a glass under the faucet, but the pipes groaned and the water came out dusky and full of particles. Something caught her eye on the counter. A candle flickered next to the toaster. It was a Mexican Virgin Mary devotional filled with red wax, the Mary figure draped in a nun's blue habit and standing on a bower of roses. Reese put down the glass of cloudy water and stared at the candle.

Linda didn't go to church. The women in their social circle of IBM wives kept their bodies, faces, and decorated houses as their true altars. They all played the same transparent game in a tiny world that Reese had thought she understood. St. Mary didn't belong in such a place. Seeing her there was like finding an Easter egg in a litter box.

Mary of the candle lifted her eyes to Reese. *We share a secret*, Mary said. *I know what you are.* Reese grabbed the candle. The hot glass seared her palm. Cursing, she flung it into the sink where it shattered into pieces.

She picked up a shard of the waxy glass between two of her fingers that were bent as twigs. Our Lady of Broken Things. She'd thought she had everything under control. Meanwhile the rest of them mocked her. She never had anything under control.

From a snarled, forgotten place in her mind, a thought whispered that she would take Madison with her as she headed south on the 101. She would take them to where the road wound by the coast and veer right until they tumbled into the sea. Then it was more than a thought. She felt the accelerator under the ball of her foot, and the stomach dropping fall to the rocks. The whisper became a shout. Her palms burned with the comfort of the steering wheel as she wrenched it with neck-snapping certainty toward death.

"Go home with Daddy," she yelled. Terrified, she threw the piece of broken glass like shaved obsidian onto the floor. Maybe Linda would step on it. Reese hoped so, but it wouldn't be her fault. She was in a window of time that she felt closing on her like a guillotine's blade. If she slipped away now, she could escape with doing minimal harm. If she left in that second, nothing would be her fault.

"Mommy, wait!" Madison was frantic behind the door.

Reese grabbed her handbag. Her pulse slammed against her eardrums. Rage flared hot as white flame that did not care who got burned or smashed or lost. She had to get away from Madison. Madison wasn't safe with her. This was as certain as plate tectonics.

Reese talked herself down as her sandals flapped against the stones of the walk leading away from the house. Let Rod take care of her. He wouldn't be able to stay late, groping Linda when he thought nobody was watching. It was a school night. He'd have to sober up quick to get Madison home by bedtime.

An aftershock rocked her car from side to side. She gunned the engine to the fresh cacophony of haywire alarms. She burned past the rows of oversized creamy stucco houses lining the street like molars on an open jaw. None of these buildings had toppled in the quake and that was too bad.

The steering wheel thumped free from under Reese's misshapen fingers as she turned onto the freeway. She drove straight on. She passed the exit to the 101 connector. At least she would avoid the temptation of the winding coastal road.

The road stretched in a long ribbon of unmarked asphalt. No cracks broke this highway but a fault line ran under it nonetheless. All of the smooth surfaces of Reese's life held a secret weakness that could split open at any time and let out all the filth.

Reese twisted the radio dial. No channels played music. Only earthquake news. She turned it up to match the noise in her head.

In her early twenties she'd had an older lady therapist named Eleanor who didn't buy Reese's assertions that she was "fine."

"You're not fine," Eleanor said. "You're a nuclear warhead about to go off any minute."

Reese remembered Eleanor now as she wove through rush hour traffic. She never liked Eleanor but never forgot what she said, either. That was one therapist who knew what she was talking about. Rage glowed in Reese's belly like a chip of plutonium with a shelf life of a thousand years.

She had no control over Rod or George or her father Ray Hamilton, or any man for that matter. But she would have control over herself. She took a deep breath. She would drive for a while and then return to her daughter and leave Rod. Rod and Linda could have each other. They could fuck each other silly in the backyard while George watched and flipped cheeseburgers to eat by himself. Reese had survived worse than this. She wiped her eyes with the heel of her hand and slipped on sunglasses against the glare. She might have been going crazy again but there was no need to panic.

Her finger joints echoed an ancient pain. She blasted the radio to drown the memory of her daughter's voice crying out for Mommy. First she thought she heard Madison. Then it was her first daughter Crystal crying out from the crushing weight of eighteen years of abandonment.

But that wasn't real. She had to focus on what was real. She had to focus on nothing but the present moment. Reese would drive until she knew she could return powerful and unafraid. The trick was to just keep on driving until the quake was over so she would no longer feel a thing.

Chapter 4

October 17, 1989
Del Rio Beach, California

Judith

〜✺〜

H OT LATE-AUTUMN DAYS brought supplicants to the beach no matter the state of the waves. The ocean lay flat as glass under the sun's lidless eye. The sky spread out in blue with not even a whisper of mist. Surfers sat on their boards with bowed backs, staring toward the horizon as though marooned. Judith didn't bother with her surfboard on such a quiet day. It was enough to dip in the ocean, lie on the sand, think.

Judith was thinking of leaving her daughter.

Angel had grown into a strong young woman. The stories Judith told her of the witch mother and good lady didn't make sense anymore. Angel deserved a whole, real life apart from Judith and the stories she wove from a child's nightmares.

Only Judith knew that memory made up the true fabric of the stories she told Angel about her own beginnings. The night Judith found Angel alone in the woods was the night of her own rebirth. Angel's animal eyes glinted in the darkness. Her cheek was hot and greasy with blood. She clung to Judith's neck with monkey strength. The child's naked back burned under her palms.

She and Angel had grafted to each other like tree and vine for eighteen years. They had different roots but inseparable fortunes during that long time, but now Angel was grown. She managed the homeless shelter downtown and did good work there. Judith suspected that Angel and the young man from the bakery were a thing now, which was good. It had looked like Angel would never date again after breaking up with her boyfriend Sundullah. *Boyfriend.* The word was so light for the heaviness his absence left in their lives after they split. Angel had lurched around like a train wreck for months, and two years later, still wasn't the same. Life could do that to you. Judith knew.

She closed her eyes. Meditation could help with the answers. Where to go next. What to do there. How to tell Angel that the vine yearned to unwind from the trunk. She hoped Angel understood that Judith was never the tree.

"This spot taken?"

Judith started, an old trauma response, though the danger was long in the past. A beach towel snapped across the sand and her landlord Albert slumped down upon it.

"Beautiful day," he said. He laced his hands behind his head.

Albert's body hairs were silky and black and long as doll hair. Drops of paint clung to streaks on his forearm. He must have been working on something before coming out for the last hours of sun.

Her heart stuttered when she looked at Albert. He was just a sweet artist man wishing someone would love him. He was nice-looking, too. It wasn't his fault that she was dust inside when it came to men. Her ability to love had been a fragile thing to begin with when it was ground to dust in the back of Ray Hamilton's Cadillac a very long time ago.

"Thinking of barbecuing steaks tonight," Albert said. She saw her own reflection in his sunglasses. The slanted sun made her long white hair a witch's halo. "Would you like to join me for dinner?"

"Going into town to see my daughter," Judith said. Now she would have to make it true. Poor Albert wasn't wrong to want company for dinner. She knew she had a certain kind of beauty, with her muscles and tan. She spent time in the water almost daily and her body showed it. Despite her white hair, she was only in her forties. She felt tenderness toward Albert and his doomed tendrils of hope. What he didn't know was that whole parts of her were dead.

Since Angel's break with Sundullah when the girl was still in college, Judith had feared her daughter would grow comfortable with loneliness as she had. But in the past year Angel seemed to finally be coming back to life. She wouldn't talk about why she'd left Sundullah. Her cave-eyed silence reminded Judith of the nearly mute child she had been in their first days together. At least she was seeing someone new. At least her voice no longer carried the hopeless quality of someone who had fallen to the bottom of a well.

Judith wouldn't tell Angel so, but she missed Sundullah too. For seven years he was her daughter's best friend, her only love. Yet the time when the three of them made a kind of family of the heart lay shrouded in the fog of decades, not the mere three years it had been. It seemed very long ago that his guitar music filled their tiny house. He wrote music in an almost offhand way, the notes making the rooms beautiful somehow. It didn't matter that they were poor, living in a small in-law unit in the backyard of a grand house. Sundullah's guitar made them forget the lingering urine and sandalwood smell of the old woman who had vacated the space by dying. His music made it a privileged place. A home. Even then Judith knew he would be an even greater talent than his father.

Now Judith only saw her daughter's old love on television interviews. Since his first album went gold he appeared there, both familiar and strange. Silver, gold, platinum. The measures of his new world were cold and hard. Even his face had grown out of its softness, revealing cheekbones like continental planes.

Despite the deep brown of his skin, Sundullah resembled his white mother in the ways that Hollywood seemed to like. Judith distrusted Sundullah's parents from their first awkward meeting, taking photographs of the young couple before their ninth grade Homecoming dance. Sundullah's mother had been a model in the sixties. She had reptilian features, Judith thought, and the regal posture of a Scandinavian ice queen. His father was a local rock musician of some renown. He was an older Black man with years on tour carved into his wrinkled face like a map of roads. Though Sundullah's father was friendlier than his mother, neither of them seemed to appreciate their son. The two traveled together on band tours, leaving Sundullah alone in their fancy house in the hills with its view of the Bay and cathedral ceilings.

Sundullah hated being alone. Judith handed him a key to their cramped place so he could come and go when he wanted. He slept on their threadbare couch so often that the cushions flattened under his lanky bones.

The television appearances reminded her that Sundullah was more beautiful than any child she ever knew. He looked like a Rastafarian boy god. He had long dreadlocks, full lips, and even through the screen she could see eyes that were still kind. Their sadness made it obvious, however, that he was burning in Hollywood without Angel's love. There were canceled concert dates, reports of "exhaustion," and rumors of drug use. Judith had recognized in him even as a young teenager that he had musical genius and beauty, yes, but also a deep sensitivity bordering on neurosis. He was born with a golden voice but no armor. No toughness.

It was wonderful that they'd stayed together even after Judith and Angel moved to Del Rio Beach when Angel started at the university nearby. Judith found yet another in-law unit behind another big house. Sundullah would come to visit and stay with them between recording sessions and tours. He sat at Judith's table and ate the vegetarian soups she made to make up for his bad nutrition on the road. His shoulder blades stuck out like wings as his head hung low. When Angel rubbed his temples with her fingertips, he would relax like a child. He would pick up his guitar and pick out a new song for them near the window that caught the warm evening sun. Under Angel's love, Sundullah was safe.

Judith's daughter had received Sundullah's adoration with the same nonchalance with which she took breath. When she started college, she showed no interest in the boys she met there. She put Sundullah's poster from his first tour up on the wall of her room in the cottage and devoted herself to her classes in between phone calls from the road. Then it was over for no reason that Judith could see. After failing for months to get Angel to open up about it, Judith finally realized that her purpose in raising Teresa's little girl was through.

Judith knew how to hide and she knew how to be alone. She knew how to survive. She was no use to a young woman learning to live in the world. She was less than no use to a young woman who needed to learn how to love. She was afraid that she had done some damage. It was time for her to go before she could hurt Angel further.

The sun hammered her face despite that lateness of the afternoon. It was a violently hot day. She should have brought sunscreen. Albert sat up to join her contemplation of the sea. He smelled like turpentine and clean sweat. She liked that smell. She would miss Albert.

Maybe she would head to New Mexico and find a colony of artists and painters in the desert. She could cook meals of black beans and mole sauce for them and take a vow of silence. She could find a habit to wear like she once did. She could become invisible as water if not quite as necessary.

She would find a doctor wherever she landed. Her lymph nodes harbored growing seeds of tumors. She'd had a consultation that morning with Dr. Henry, who loved talking about her recovery. He lived for cancers caught early enough to cure. The insurance she got through the textbook company she worked for would pay for the bulk of the treatments. There would be nausea, hair loss, and long waits while the healing poison dripped into her system, but she would recover if they started now. They should have begun months ago, but Dr. Henry liked her chances.

Judith hated small rooms. After an entire life of craving nothing as much as freedom, she looked upon long stretches of immobility as a prison sentence. She knew as soon as Dr. Henry explained the diagnosis that she would never tell Angel. She would not chain Angel to worry and obligation, not now. Maybe she'd go through treatment in her new place or maybe she would not. Judith wasn't afraid of death. She knew better than to fear eternal quiet and solitude. It was life that required caution.

The glaring surface of the ocean shimmered like a pond in a stiff breeze. Judith thought the offshore system must have finally broken. She lifted her chin for the wind to hit her face but none came.

"Whoa," Albert said, "did you feel that?"

Judith's stomach fluttered like a dip on a roller coaster. "I don't know," she said.

The water beyond the breakers undulated. People on the beach looked around at one another. Someone down the shoreline shouted a word that turned Judith to stone.

"Earthquake," Albert repeated. "Mother Earth is letting us know."

Judith grabbed her things and ran up the beach, hot sand kicking out from beneath her bare feet. Only one thought went through her head with the pure hot focus of the sun in a cloudless sky.

My daughter. I have to find my daughter.

Chapter 5

October 18–20, 1989
Del Rio Beach, California

Angel

~ ~ ~

MAYBE THERE WAS a place beyond the needs of the human body, beyond pain. Angel could not find it. She tried to sleep. Her back curled so that her chin dug into her chest, and her forehead pushed against her knees. As long as she lived she would suffer. She would live a long time. She would live a short time.

Angel did not know how long she would live. She was not sure she was living now. She waited as long as she could and then emptied her bowels. It hurt. Everything hurt. She closed her eyes and slept.

SHE WAS A twisted and corroded root. She was a caterpillar in a cocoon that dried out before having a chance to form wings. She was a baby chick dead in the shell, festering slimy and rotten within the dark walls. No light entered. She opened her eyes wide to nothing. This was blindness or this was the dark of non-existing things. Sometimes she was numb. Then numbness wore off to electric pains that shot through her spine into her jawbones. She parted her teeth into a rictus. A silent plea.

Get me out get me out get me out get me out.

TIME PASSED OR didn't pass. Angel's body spasmed and then prickled to numbness again. Sometimes she slept. Sometimes she woke. Sometimes she could not tell the difference.

She dreamt. Angel walked in the forest. The duff snapped under her sneakers. She held the hand of a tall angry woman who pulled her so that her elbow strained in its ligaments.

You're hurting me.

Shut your mouth.

Angel's mouth was shut.

They practiced for their escape with Michael. They had to make it seem normal, the woman said. So walking in the woods Saturday night won't be such a big thing. If Ray notices us he won't care because we'll just be taking our walk. We just want to see the stars.

Who is Michael?

The woman smacked her on the cheek so hard she fell. Sticks dug into her palms. *Don't say his name. You don't know his name. Never say his name out loud again. If Ray hears it he'll kill us. Do you understand me?*

This witch haunted her childhood dreams. Always the same dreams playing on an endless loop like a memory. Angel chewed this over. At first she tried thinking of other things for comfort such as someone coming to the rescue. But no one knew she'd gone downstairs except the volunteers, and they had not survived this. The abyss of that certainty threatened to suck the breath from her lungs forever.

So she pondered the witch woman with the heavy hands. She pondered the familiar stinging of her cheeks. That time in the woods wasn't the first time she'd felt the weight of the witch's gnarled hand. It wasn't the only time.

Angel's mother had always invented fairy tales out of her childish nightmares. She sat on the bed and talked of a witch with twisted fingers who lived in a tiny house behind the castle of a monster. She read the real fairy tales for bedtime stories and then spun new ones out of the terrifying silk of Angel's dreams. *The witch lived too far away to matter and the monster died a long time ago,* her mother said as she rocked her. *Anyway, dreams can't hurt you.*

This wasn't a dream. She wasn't sleeping. The tall woman was a complex knot to pick at and observe. She had once known this person but not everything about her was real. The stinging hands were a memory, but the color of her eyes was a dream. No one's eyes could be the lapis blue of a gem. Her gnarled hands were also the stuff of impossible nightmares. No one's hands could be crooked as twigs.

But the tall woman's voice was real memory. Angel remembered the unhappy timbre of it—like the flapping of a crow's wings against glass.

ANGEL RESTED AGAINST her mother and listened to her heartbeat. When she woke to the dirty blackness of under the desk, she cried. Her tongue caught the moisture of her tears as they fell. Then more sleep.

Conscious sometimes, other times not. Compressed lungs would only hold so much air at once. The brain required oxygen for her body to come fully awake.

Her mother told stories about fairies, witches, and good ladies. Angel loved the good ladies the best. They lived in the forest in lonely houses. They waited for children to come to them. One good lady named Judith looked after a little ghost daughter who was lost and hurt. She became the girl's mother and she hid the girl away and protected her from the bad witch and the monster.

I love you, my Angel.

With one fingernail Angel tapped time against the wood under the desk. The sound made her think of scratching against a coffin lid. So she stopped.

She wanted her mother.

A SMELL WAFTED THROUGH the gaps in the bricks. It was the smell of toenails and bad meat left out on the counter. It was the same smell as a neighborhood cat that was hit by a car and lay dead two days in the gutter before she found it.

Death coming, the air said.

Bring it on, Angel thought. *Bring it the fuck on.*

Then her anger collapsed, a paper accordion fan crushed by bricks. She began to cry again. Then she stopped.

Bring it on.

When she said things out loud she sounded like a jack in the box coiled deep and waiting for the lid to pop. The lid wouldn't pop.

HUNGER. PAIN. CHILL. Breathlessness. Stench. Sleep.

More asleep than awake. Maybe this was dying. Boring, slow, and uncomfortable.

She was not alone. A girl child with enormous eyes rested against the C of her belly.

"What do you want?" Angel asked. Her throat ached with the effort of speaking; her tongue was rough as wool.

The child's eyes glowed in the dark. Angel held her tight in the cradle of her middle.

ANGEL'S EYES OPENED. Angel's eyes closed. She opened them again. It made no difference. She scratched at the haphazard bricks walling her in until her fingers bled and then she sucked on the tips for the taste. She rolled tighter until she became antimatter and ceased to exist at all.

YOU ARE ADOPTED, her mother said. Her hair had been long and white for as long as Angel could remember.

Who is my real mother?

I am. I conjured you out of my heart. That is much more powerful.

Did you find me in the forest?

That's just a story, Angel. I wanted a child so I visited a place called an adoption agency. They place babies with mothers who can care for them.

Angel saw why her mother reverted to the fairy tales whenever she could. Haunted forests made more sense by far than agencies and signed papers and a forgotten babyhood with people neither of them knew.

In a moment of clarity, Angel thought, *This is where my story ends.*

In a childhood full of fairy tales there were many girls locked in towers, but none buried under rubble and left to die alone. One of the cruelest of the tales told of a selfish rich woman who refused to help her poor sister's children dying of starvation. When she cut into the fresh bread she had bought for her husband's supper, blood flowed from the loaf in rivers. The message of the story was that it was important to be a good person who helped the poor. The gory bread was the rich woman's punishment for greed. Good people met good ends in stories. A fairy tale would have a good woman meet an enchantress who would make gold coins spill from her mouth when she talked.

Good people didn't die like this.

Under the desk the world was silent as stone. The air smelled rotten.

In the quiet of the tomb Angel blinked at the truth in the dark.

She wasn't a good person.

She'd killed the baby who had been growing inside her. The baby who now would be nearly three.

No one knew about the dead baby but Angel and the strangers at the clinic. She thought she could erase death from ever having happened by keeping it a secret and doing hard work and good deeds. But managing the shelter had never been penance. There was no need to lie to herself about it now. The homeless men needed her and she was good at fighting the city. The shelter made her happy.

College was lonely. She'd been surrounded by people drinking and taking mushrooms and running naked in the meadows spanking the butts of the mule deer who just wanted to be left alone. People flopped into new beds every night without so much as buying each other a cookie first. Angel had no place in any of that. In the ways that mattered she was a married woman. Sundullah was her love. He had been her reason for everything.

Between classes and writing papers she sat in her room in her mother's rented cottage and watched her boyfriend's rise to fame on MTV. Her Sundullah became everybody's Sundullah. One VJ called him America's Baby Bob Marley. When she tried to talk about their relationship with people in her classes, they didn't believe her so she just shut up about it. Meanwhile he called her in the middle of almost every night and his voice was growing thinner and thinner until he sounded like someone calling from a ghost town. His uncle Eli was his manager, and Angel knew for a fact that none of Sundullah's family understood about how nervous he could get or how sad. His own parents barely knew him. She was his comfort from the time they met in ninth grade. She was the only one who made him feel strong.

An artist's soul, her mother had said. She had labels for Sundullah that helped explain why he would get so nervous and sad. *Genius. Gifted. Highly sensitive.* And sometimes, *depressed.*

Her mother didn't know why Angel broke up with him. She swallowed the secret and it rested inside her like a jagged stone. She never meant to date again or fall in love. There was no such thing as anything but Angel and Sundullah unless it was just Angel missing Sundullah and wishing things were different. For almost a year she lived like a nun in the tiny room above the shelter kitchen, every day seeking redemption through her work.

Russell was an ex-addict who worked in a bakery and brought the Narcotics Anonymous meetings to the shelter twice a week. He started coming earlier and helping with dinner prep. They worked side by side, cutting carrots for stews and slicing long baguettes into circles to serve the residents.

In the truth under the desk she had to admit that she looked forward to seeing him like she looked forward to putting on sweatpants at the end of a day. With Russell she wasn't concerned with nurturing a wounded genius. With Russell she laughed at dirty knock-knock jokes and listened to Led Zeppelin tapes. Then one day in the dry goods pantry Russell set down the tray laden with stale donuts from the bakery and kissed her. His shaggy brown hair smelled of yeast and sugar and she had let him move his warm hands up her shirt. In fact, she liked it. She liked him. She didn't love him but she liked him and she let herself kiss him back.

IN THE PAST month she'd had Russell in her room a few times after lights out. But being with Russell only made her want Sundullah more. When she was with Russell, sleeping desire winked awake inside her and ripped the Sundullah yearning freshly open. None of that stopped her from seeing Russell. She still let him sneak upstairs. She let him share her Spartan twin bed and she tried to forget what she'd lost. She didn't even bother to take the Sundullah poster down from the wall. She looked up at his face while she lay in the bed with her new sort-of boyfriend. When she kissed Russell, she felt like a child biting down on the razor-edged root of a loose tooth. It hurt. So she bit harder.

Under the desk she could smell her own excrement and piss. She could smell whatever meaty thing was on the other side of the brick pile poisoning her pocket of air. Her back erupted sporadically into the buzz of pins. Her kidneys ached but nothing came out of her anymore.

No, she wasn't a good person. And this was how she would die. She opened her eyes wide. She stretched out her fingers in the blackness.

The little girl laced her fingers with Angel's. Her palms were rough and dry as monkey's paws.

We loved you. I am sorry. Angel's voice was a raven's croak.

The little girl's eyes made two pinpoints of light. They disappeared. They came back.

Are you my daughter? Or are you me?

There was no answer. Angel's love for her lost child overflowed and she hummed a Sundullah song through a throat filled with needles. The lyrics were simple. They'd written them together during a study hall in high school, four years before she made a horrible decision by herself in a clinic that smelled of bleach.

We'll run hand in hand through the streets of this city. We are the two musketeers so handsome and pretty. We'll remember this time when I first was your man.

We'll remember this time as the time we began.

A BOOMING AS FAR away as the moon vibrated through the bricks. This was either happening or not happening. Angel's thoughts collided in pieces like the collage of a mad child. She imagined bulldozers overhead, tamping the earth down. Sealing her tomb. This had been the Big One. There was none bigger, no chance for life after this kind of death. Aftershock tremors irregular but strong shook her half world under the desk. Despair took less courage than hope. The noise went away. It came back. Or maybe she did. She could not ascertain the real from the dream any longer.

Awake. The act of blinking scraped sandpaper over her eyes so she just kept them shut. Her rattling teeth made a percussion that rang down the frozen curve of her spine. Then they stopped. Another boom she felt more than heard. And another. A ribbon of warmth spread throughout her arms and legs. She exhaled in tiny puffs. The ghost baby rested against her breast and touched her face as if to say that it wouldn't be long now. After this kind of pain, death didn't hurt.

Angel was the fossil of a sea creature trapped under sediment. Her epoch was over. What was left was a shell and the pain inside of it. Then not pain. Then nothing.

Chapter 6

October 18, 1989
Palo Alto, California

Reese

⌒⌒⌒

REESE SAT IN one chair in a row of chairs in a hospital waiting room. The top of her head tingled with the closeness of the low ceiling. Every part of her craved to be out from under it. She took in a breath and let the air out in jagged pieces that serrated her lungs.

The doctor wore a white jacket and a name badge. Dr. Hendricks of the gray hair and vast experience in giving this kind of news in this kind of way. Reese hated him. The hospital's doctors and nurses tried to bring Rod back to life with all of their machines and hard work and expertise. But there was only so much anyone could do for a man wrapped around a tree. His back was broken in three places.

The doctor talked in slow motion. Reese waited. He already said that Madison was alive. Madison was alive and in the operating room having surgery while Reese sat in the row of chairs and the doctor ground through the details. Somewhere in that great big hospital, strangers cut into her child and pried her open like an oyster on a shell, her soft inner parts giving way under scalpels and knives.

Reese sat in the chair and gripped the armrests so hard her fingers hurt.

Jocelyn appeared at the doorway with her hair a mess and purse falling open. This was how a distraught sister behaved. Dr. Hendricks turned his attention to her. Jocelyn's face crumpled as a totaled fender when he told her the news.

Rod was dead. No more Rod. Blood alcohol level really fucking high.

If Rod had not died then Reese would have had to kill him herself. She was glad to be relieved of the responsibility.

Jocelyn cried in great wracking heaves. She clutched Reese's shoulders and cried into her chest as though Reese were her real sister or as though they'd ever been friends. Reese, for her part, sat straight as a statue, writhing within.

Madison might live. The *might* was a crevasse and the winds that blew from the bottom of it froze her solid. If Madison lived, the road to healing would be long. But kids were surprising in their resilience. Maybe she would walk again. If. But. Maybe.

The doctor shook his head because he was sorry. His face was a mask of tragedy.

Reese watched Dr. Hendricks with a critical eye. Bad performance. The doctor didn't care about Rod or Madison. He didn't care about any of his patients. This doctor was in it for the money and why wouldn't he be.

Jocelyn wept as though she and Rod hadn't been quietly estranged over the past six years. Jocelyn didn't want Rod to marry Reese. In the beginning Reese listened in on the other line whenever Rod's sister called.

"There is something about that girl I don't trust, Rod," Jocelyn had said, her disapproval hissing through the wire. Reese held a finger on the mute button as Rod defended her to his sister. Reese was just quiet, he said. She was beautiful. She understood him in a way no one else did. If he had to choose between his family and Reese, he was sorry but he would have to choose Reese.

The respect Reese had for Jocelyn's powers of observation had long since worn away. Jocelyn was fat and stupid, built like a truck driver. She was yet another boring cow of a woman, her brother an irritating chicken of a man who had almost killed their daughter.

Almost. There was a whole world in the word *almost*.

Jocelyn blew her nose into a tissue from a neat pack she carried in her purse. "Oh my God. Poor Maddy," she said. She blustered all over again and reached for Reese a second time.

Reese's mind burst upon a strange image. Falling beams and loose bricks rained down around their heads. The ceiling of the waiting room really did feel too close. In the corner the television blared relentless facts about the earthquake. The Bay Bridge had broken so that a slab of the upper deck bisected the lower. A woman crashed her car into the gap and died. The levels of the Cypress Structure in Oakland were death for most of the people stuck in between.

Reese interrupted the doctor's litany of injuries. "Is there anything I can do for my daughter here?" she asked. The doctor clamped his lips.

"Just pray," he said. "If that has meaning for you."

Jocelyn began to do just that out loud. Reese gathered her things. She had to get out or she would kill someone for real.

Reese moved to the door, but two police in dark blue uniforms stopped her. They were men—one black, one with pale yellow hair. They were tucked in and armed and padded as cops always were, their faces like walls. She started and stepped backward, back into the waiting room. Her throat dried up. They stood blocking the only exit.

Police. She was always sure they hated her, that they could smell criminal on her. Her brain whirred in panic.

They've caught me now.

Even after eighteen years of being a completely different person than she'd been when she was arrested, Reese still dreaded cops. Her rational mind knew that no one from her old life cared or thought about who Reese used to be for a single second. Reese herself never thought about the long nights she'd spent in jail when she changed herself like a larva in a hexagonal cell. She had forgotten those days the way she'd forgotten her own time in the womb. No one remembers when she was formed and born. The fear of police was a primal remnant of those very old days. Her rational mind suppressed the panic that arose the time a motorcycle cop pulled her over for speeding, or when she spotted one of the neighborhood safety patrol cars cruising through the neighborhood. On that day, however, her rational mind was drowning in disaster, its voice barely a whisper from under waves of chaos.

"Reese Camden? We have some questions about your husband," the blond one said. "We need to know exactly what happened prior to the accident."

Somewhere above their heads in ICU, surgeons cut into Reese's daughter as Reese stood there with strangers in uniforms talking about nothing that mattered. The cops' questions were about as relevant as water pistols at a nuclear apocalypse.

"Please have a seat," Yellow Hair said. The walls grew closer, the ceiling lower. Reese's breath became short. A weight crushed her chest. If the surgeons turned their knives on her they would find in her guts only gray and white beads of light like the bug races on a dead television channel.

Something was going wrong with her. Something much worse than a long drive could cure.

"If you'll just sit here …." A hand pinched her elbow almost to the edge of pain. Cops could move a person. They knew all the secret judo. Reese sat down hard on a chair across the room from Jocelyn. The doctor lingered to watch the show. Hate acted on the rising static of panic like a bullwhip. Down. Reese focused on the hate. She slid on her mask.

Grieving widow. Sad wife. Disbelief. What? He's really dead? The surprise wasn't a lie. The grief was.

"What time did you leave your husband and daughter at the residence of George and Linda Harris?" The officer had a notebook and a stubby pencil with no eraser.

"I don't know. About six I guess."

"After the earthquake?"

"Yes," Reese said. "After the earthquake." She answered the questions. She was not drinking. She never drank or did any drugs. She was sober. No, she was not in recovery, she just chose not to drink. She was the designated driver between them, yes. This was all true.

They questioned her further. She diverged from the truth on a frontage road of lies. She did not know that Rod was drunk, she said. Her face to the cops remained earnest despite red shame crawling up her neck. She did know Rod was drunk. She never should have left her precious daughter alone with him. She said she did not think that Rod would try to drive home drunk with Madison in the car beside him. The truth was, she had not been thinking at all.

She wasn't lying out of a fear of the police. She knew enough of criminal behavior to be sure she wasn't guilty of it here. She was lying because she liked the story of her ignorance better than the truth. She was lying out of fear of herself. She bounced her legs on the balls of her toes. Madison was dying and the truth that she was to blame was an eel slithering in murky places. She had tried to evade harming Madison by leaving her alone with Rod. It was hard to believe she could have been so stupid.

The police exchanged information for information. Madison had the presence of mind to buckle herself in. The seatbelt probably saved her life. Reese imagined her daughter's soft body in the twisted metal hell that used to be Rod's BMW. The firemen needed to use the Jaws of Life to pry her free.

The police asked the same questions again and again like amnesiacs. Reese grit her teeth and answered, her lies unfurling like paper ribbons catching fire and trailing smoke.

No, Rod did not have a history of DUI. *Not getting caught, anyway.*

The real trouble she was facing was in the shattering forest of her mind. There would be no coming back from madness if Madison died and it was her fault.

Reese shook her head when speaking to the police. She did not know that Rod planned to drive drunk. *He was always drunk. The alcohol stank off his skin like pickle cologne when he sweated.*

She did not know he was drunk. He hardly ever drank.

"You liar," Jocelyn finally said from across the room. "He was an alcoholic and you knew it."

"He was fine when I left them." Reese spoke only to the police as if Jocelyn was a raving madwoman it was best to ignore. As if Jocelyn were the one losing her grip.

"You killed him when you let him get in a car," Jocelyn said. She moved so that she was right in Reese's face. "This is your fault."

Reese slapped Jocelyn hard across the cheek with a quickness that spoke of easy conscience and years of practice.

"Okay," the blond cop said. He was a big man and wedged himself between them. As soon as Jocelyn got over the shock she started crying again. A nurse poked her head in to see what the fuss was about. The doctor waved her away.

"I want to go to my child now," Reese said. The doctor shook his head. Madison would be in surgery for hours longer.

Reese's face stung as though she was the one hit. Jocelyn blubbered in the corner telling her story to the cops as though they had asked for it. The cop talked into his radio. There was a lot going on that night. They had to go. They brought Jocelyn into the hall. They were probably warning her to give her sister-in-law a wide berth. It was good advice.

On the television an apartment house in the Mission District in San Francisco tilted off its foundation. A fire raged by the marina. There were people crushed under collapsed buildings in Santa Cruz and Del Rio Beach. They didn't expect to find anyone alive but that didn't keep rescuers from staying up all night to try.

Reese's mind upended and chaos jammed the circuits. Her brain swarmed with a billion insects crawling on jagged electrical legs.

A nurse in pale blue scrubs ran into the waiting room. "Mrs. Camden," he said. He motioned for her to follow him and she and the doctor had to jog to keep up with him down the hall.

"Madison has gone into a crisis," he said as they neared the elevator. He guided her inside and punched the buttons. "The surgeon will explain more. He wanted me to get you in case this is—"

"Shut up," Reese said. "Just shut the fuck up."

When the nurse patted her back, she jolted at his touch. "She better live," Reese said. She bit the inside of her cheek until she tasted the hot copper of her own blood.

The nurse and doctor nodded as though they had seen her kind of sadness before. They didn't understand that Reese meant that Madison had better live or she would come back and kill them. She would release the hard radioactive pebble she carried inside of her until it expanded and exploded, wiping the doctor's face from his skull. Her rage would shatter the building in a storm of dust and debris that made Loma Prieta look like a warm embrace from the earth mother of them all.

Chapter 7

October 21, 1989
Del Rio Beach, California

Angel

～～⌣～⌣～

FAR AWAY A metal bell clanged. Would it be heaven or would it be hell? A skinny arrow of light sliced into Angel's underground den. Through the half opening of her eyelids she watched it grow.

Her finger bisected the light. Tiny dust motes floated in the beam. Angels. Demons. Heaven. Hell. Soon she would find out which.

A dog barking. Voices.

Voices of men calling the name of God.

IS SHE ALIVE?

A masculine voice in her ear, a rough hand at her cheek. Her head was heavy at the end of a rubbery neck.

Her jaw clenched. Her eyes would not close. They would not open. *Do not bury me again.* She couldn't talk to tell them she was alive. They might leave her in the ground if she didn't let them know she was alive. Her limbs shook, her bones loosened in their sockets. She was a skeleton, a doll on a garbage heap. Someone pulled until the bricks expelled her. Chunks of brick, dirt, splintered wood and plaster fell into the hole where her body had been. Her head flopped back so that her chin pointed to the clouds, her neck bared to the cold air. Paramedics bustled around her with hands that moved with authority. They placed her limbs here and there. They secured her neck in a brace. A man's voice barked orders. They lifted her as if she were weightless. The stretcher was not soft. Oxygen mask. Blanket tucked tight around her shoulders. The whole world erupted in sharp edges. A needle jabbed her hand for an IV tube. Fine white silica dust cut her lungs. She imagined they bled with every breath. She would be scoured from the inside, slashed to pieces on the outside.

The voice of Angel's mother rose above the directives of yelling men. There was a fluttering at her shoulder like a dove trying to alight there. She turned to the pleading voice, the frantic hand. Longing pressed at her ribcage, leaving no room for air.

No voice to say *I can't breathe.*

I'm not breathing.

More yelling. Black curtains descending.

ON THE TELEVISION, workers in masks pulled dead bodies from under mountains of bricks. The cameras did not show the faces of the dead. There was a limp hand streaked with blood. It could have been Jerry or one of the volunteers, the city council man or Gene. The bodies went into white opaque bags zipped to the top.

Angel lay on a field of white as well. She lay on white sheets under a white blanket. Painkillers dripped into her bloodstream through a tube fastened with white tape to the back of her hand.

Russell sat with his knees pressed together in a chair too small for him. He held her tapeless hand like a giant tending a fairy's bedside. Gray dust coated his boots from the days he worked to dig her out. The nurses slipped on the silt that pooled on the floor.

City Council got their wish after all. The St. Francis shelter was closed. In fifteen seconds God and Mother Earth did what the mayor could not accomplish in the two years of his tenure.

Angel held her fingers in front of her eyes. Waved them. Light. Then covered her eyelids. Dark. How strange to have that freedom of movement.

The morphine took away her concerns, but sadness remained a cold underground aquifer. She did not feel it so much yet, but she would. The drugs did not take away her power of reason. Eventually grief would pull her under. She couldn't stay high forever.

"Where's my mom again?" Her mouth was lacerated. Made it hard to talk.

"I think a friend of hers died or something." Russell kept his eyes on the screen. "She had to go to a funeral."

"What friend?" Angel asked. She'd never heard her mother talk of a friend.

"She wouldn't leave without good reason, I'll tell you that," Russell said. "She stood on the sidewalk for four days straight, Angel. Never left once."

That was impossible. No one could stand for four days straight. It was impossible but nonetheless true. It seemed the whole world bent to the will of some random perverse storyteller so that things that could never happen were happening. The Bay Bridge had broken in two. Double highways had pancaked flat with people driving on them and under them. The ground had split open in trenches deep enough to swallow houses.

Russell ran his thumb over her knuckles. Angel's school picture from senior year of high school flashed on the television. They kept showing the same footage of Angel carried on a stretcher, her mother running alongside and Russell following behind.

They called it the Miracle of Angel. She was one of the last of the catastrophe's buried people found alive. She had survived three days without water.

They'd found a kid in the Cypress Structure in Oakland that morning. Angel was obsessed with the story. She switched channels to skip commercials. They had to cut through the body of the boy's dead mother in order to rescue him. She craved the details of that excavation. She imagined the rebirth of a child emerging through the barrier of his mother's bones and muscles and skin. How did the first breath of air feel after something like that?

"I want to go home," Angel said. She did not know what home. She meant she wanted her mother.

"I don't think they're letting you out for a while," Russell said. He turned off the television. She was too weak to protest. She was falling asleep again. "It should have been me under there. Not you."

"You would not have fit," she said. Her tongue wrestled with her mouth. The morphine made thinking and talking a labor. Yet despite her fuzzy brain she was the world's expert of under the desk and Russell would not have fit. But he wasn't listening. He leaned forward and swished his palms together like a penitent man.

"I was in the courtyard," he said. "I made everybody else go to the dining room while Jerry hid in the shower. Did you know that? He wanted to watch the water spin down the drain. I sat outside thinking I could wait for you so we could talk in private."

He bowed his head. She wanted to hold his face and kiss his craggy cheeks. She would absolve him of his sins. Her mind pulled at something he said. He was with Jerry. Maybe the tree king lived. She meant to ask him. Then forgot the question.

The nurses entered and Russell had to leave so she could empty her bladder into a catheter tube. It hurt but the morphine took away the humiliation of it. Her body didn't mean anything anymore.

Russell returned. He talked more, the sad words floating to the ceiling. His grief flowed through her. She was sleeping awake. She'd lost her body. The body that she used to have disappeared when the earth started shaking at 5:04 p.m. on October seventeenth. The news got it wrong. She hadn't survived the quake.

"The earth shrugged her shoulders and I happened to be near a big oak desk," she said. The act of speech brought to mind cactus spines in deserts where it never rained.

A doctor appeared and made her sit up. Her hips crackled like bleached sticks. He listened to her heart through her back. He asked her to take a deep breath.

"Thank God you're alive," Russell said.

"There is no reason why them and not me," she said.

"I need to hear," the doctor said. "Will you both please be quiet."

She obeyed and shut her mouth. Had déjà vu. Her jaw dropped like a skeleton's and she began to cry in great dry sobs. The doctor ordered an increase in meds. One nurse pressed on the syringe while another held her down.

She slept.

WHEN SHE WOKE Sundullah held her hand. Her skin looked deathly pale next to his. He smelled of clove oil and the nag champa that clung to his dreads. His hair was longer than the last time she saw him. She freed her hand and rolled the ends of one lock of his hair between two fingers. This was her thread to the world. This was the proof she needed that she'd survived.

He stared into her eyes as if he wanted to see if she was truly alive. She had forgotten how strange his eyes were. They were green like sea glass with swirls of orange next to the pupils. He was a supernatural creature made from fire. The lower part of his face was hidden behind a paper half mask. No one was allowed in her room without one. Her lungs, the doctor had said. An infection. It would take time to recover. She pulled it down under his chin. His face had grown thinner, his jaw and cheekbones cutting their hard lines with no trace of the young boy in his features.

"Was that you singing just now?" she asked.

"Yes. I wanted to wake you. I was afraid you were dead."

The oxygen tube in her nose chafed. She pulled it out. "I lived," she said. "Or so they say." He pressed his face into the white blanket and her hand was a tiny yellow bird resting in the nest of his black mane.

"Happy birthday," he said. "I've missed you." His crying jag was short. He wiped his eyes on the sleeve of a faded denim jacket. It was something Jerry would wear—worn and softened by sea air and sun.

"You're famous," she said. The drugs formed clouds that shifted and thickened where complete thoughts used to be.

"You're beautiful," he said. It was the same Sundullah but with sharper edges and bigger somehow. He filled the room. He squeezed her hand and that was when she knew it wasn't a dream. His fingertips were as callused as horns from playing his guitar. They always had been.

"You were mine," Angel says. "Now you are everyone's."

"Still yours."

"Do you have a girlfriend?"

He smiled with his mouth closed—like a sphinx "Do you have a boyfriend?" he asked.

Her mind drifted from these impossible questions. When they were teenagers she had not known where she ended and Sundullah began. They tore down the school hallway whooping like movie Indians in matching knee high suede moccasins with fringe. The ringing echo in the old building was awesome.

Angel made her hand flat and beat it over her mouth and made a weak sound so that he would remember. He smiled right away.

"We got in trouble for that," Sundullah said. A deep dimple appeared at the side of his mouth. At least he hadn't outgrown the dimple.

"The American Indian Club got offended and we had to apologize," Angel said. An old story but a good one.

"We were so racist." His laugh was like warm honey. She remembered that though they thought it was ironic to be called racist, they had been sorry. They had never meant to do to the American Indian Club kids what people had been doing to them since they were in kindergarten. Angel's parents had been Mexican and white. Sundullah's mother was white, his father black. Looking at them, it was hard to tell which ethnicity box to check. Mixed race made people uneasy. It invited questions about a person's hair or the color of a person's father.

Angel tried to laugh along with him but choked instead. She fumbled for the oxygen tube and Sundullah gently placed it back into her nostrils. From his jacket pocket he pulled out a tin of bee pollen lip balm. He rubbed his finger across the top of it and smoothed the wax over her shredded lips. She took the sip of water he offered from the cup and straw on the bedside tray.

When they were Angel and Sundullah, her body had been a strong place. It was a new place, belonging wholly to herself but also to him. She loved how she felt running, dancing, making love, or just sitting behind Sundullah with her ear to his back listening as he played his guitar and sang. Now her body was a shell of tinder. Now she was either in pain or numb. If a wind blew through the room she would disintegrate. She was too weak to take in air and retain it in her lungs. Purple spots spattered in her vision. It was urgent to speak before she passed out.

"I saw her," Angel said. "I saw our daughter."

"What are you talking about?"

"I was pregnant before. I didn't tell you."

"Angel," he said. His voice deeper and rougher than she remembered. He was pleading with her to stop but she had to say it. A machine at the end of one of the wires on her body started beeping.

"She was with me. While I was trapped. She was there when I was dying."

A young nurse walked in and saw Sundullah sitting on the bed. She stopped as if she'd hit an invisible wall, a blush crawling up her neck. She backed out. Sundullah did not see the nurse, but Angel did. She did not know how Sundullah could survive a world where he could neither hide nor be seen for who he truly was. He would not survive this world unless he had someone to love and look after him. Her heart rose in a painful hope that he had found someone who could replace her.

Sundullah opened Angel's fingers. He pressed his face into the inside of her open hand. His lips were full and soft and she knew just what it was like to kiss them. Her stomach burned at the thought of some other girl knowing it too. This loneliness was what she deserved.

"I had an abortion before we broke up. That was what I did. And I think about it every day."

"None of that matters now." He waved a long-fingered hand as though pain could be warned away so easily.

Her mouth was sour with the truth but the morphine loosened her tongue and she needed to confess. "I killed it. Her." She gasped for air. Thorns lined her ribs and dug into her lungs. "I always think of the baby as a her. I know it was a her. And I killed her."

"Come back to Los Angeles with me," he said.

"I can't."

"When I'm done with this tour, I'll come get you myself," he said. His lips moved in a prayer against her palm. "Please come back to me. I can't do this without you anymore."

"Did you hear what I said, Sunny? We made a baby. I was pregnant. Then I wasn't. My choice. I didn't even tell you about it. I don't belong in your world. I thought I was a good person, but I'm not. I don't deserve you."

He shook his head and squeezed his eyes shut. His eyelashes tickled her fingertips. "Come back to me," he said. He wasn't listening. "Come on tour with me. I'll make my uncle understand. People know I'm losing my shit out there. They say I'm on drugs but it's only stuff the doctors give me so I can get out there every night. The managers will be glad I have someone. Believe me. Come back to me."

"Show me that you heard me," she said. "Show me you understand what I did."

He buried his face in Angel's side. Pain bloomed from the pressure. "How could you?" he said, his voice muffled in her gown. She dug her fingers into his dreadlocks while he cried. She wished she could join him, but her eyes were dry. Her mourning for their baby had already occurred in lonely places.

"I couldn't take care of you both," she said. "So I couldn't take care of either of you."

She rubbed his scalp the way he liked. She knew what to do to calm him. She made him feel safe. She was the only one who ever could. She wished it were enough to make her good. She wished it were enough for her to forgive herself for what she had done.

He caught his breath and wiped his face on the bed sheet. "I brought you this," he said. From a canvas messenger bag he pulled out the *Children's Fairy Tales* she loved as a kid. She'd given it to him the last time they met with the stupid idea that leaving Sundullah such a powerful charm would keep him safe and soften their goodbye.

A brown stain covered the top of the pages. When she opened it the scent of vanilla bloomed from the paper. It loosened a memory that had once been tucked much deeper in her mind. There was a man with huge hands, giving her this book to hold. He pushed her into the darkness and told her to run.

Her throat closed. She wheezed for air. The machine rang like a car alarm tripped by thieves. With a swing of her arm, she swept the book to the floor.

Personnel rushed the bed, including the timid nurse who snuck peeks at Sundullah. "Mask on," the doctor said. He pushed Sundullah out of the way.

Without Sundullah's weight on top of her Angel was untethered to the earth. Without love she was a floating lantern heading for the sky. She would burn and she would die.

The doctor took her pulse. The ghost man from her memory had wanted her to run so she had run. She gasped for air as though bad men were chasing her. The doctor gave orders in a steady stream but not to her. She had no idea what to do. More nurses filled the room from the hall. Angel reached for Sundullah, but he wasn't there. The machines emitted a long robotic scream. *Code blue*, the doctor yelled. Respiratory distress.

She isn't breathing.

A flash of white.

Then black.

Chapter 8

October 21, 1989
Cupertino, California

Reese

R EESE'S LIFE HAD been reduced to a series of chairs. First there were hospital chairs that looked soft but were slippery with steel armrests that made rest impossible. Then there were the squeaky leather padded chairs in the funeral home for the wake. This afternoon she kept to the hard Queen Anne chair in the corner by the curtains in her own living room.

Her family had never used this room. They were never a family. They were never living. From this perspective her whole life felt as false as her name. Without Madison she had nothing.

Reese concentrated on sitting as straight as possible with her legs crossed at the ankles, like a woman in a magazine from the 1950s. She would have enjoyed those days. She would have thrived in the social structure. Games with obvious rules were easier to play. She would have looked good in the dresses. There would be no attacks from fat men in guest bathrooms. It would be easier to get and keep power if people would just play their roles.

People wandered in and out and offered words that had no meaning. They treated her like an altar. Some brought starchy baked casseroles. Others brought flowers or books of inspirational quotes. She might have liked some jewelry or gifts of money. If she were a goddess she would demand diamonds, gold, and cash. She would demand thick steaks so rare they were bloody and for a side dish an unlimited supply of painkilling drugs.

Reese had spent the two days of Rod's wake and funeral in a tomb of thought. The house was grave silent without the noise of Rod's game on television and Madison's tuneless singing while she played. It scared her the way a coffin might if she woke to find herself inside. She was dead and buried. If Madison's life wasn't a sure thing, neither was hers.

As Reese sat by the blue-curtained window, Linda leaned forward and air-kissed her on the cheek. Her black dress clung to her sloppy body, riding up her thighs as she walked. Rod would have liked it. She'd probably bought it to impress him.

Reese watched the people come and go. They brought potato dishes and round cakes with black poppy seeds in them that crunched between the guests' teeth like beetle shells. She sipped water from a glass. She was deeply thirsty, but as for hunger, she might never eat again.

Jocelyn scuttled around the food table and accepted hugs from visitors. Her husband Carl stood around looking awkward as large men do in crowded rooms. He offered people drinks which Jocelyn served. He patted her shoulder whenever she passed him. She didn't know how Jocelyn could stand it. Rod's sister and her husband were desperately unstylish and confusing people. They made Reese want to break things. So much of her life was reduced to controlling her urge to break things.

The clock said two more hours remained of this meaningless game. The charade didn't matter, but still Reese played. She had some power as the grieving widow. People were too afraid to look her in the eye and she liked that.

The visitors spoke in hushed voices, like dead people whispering from inside their own graves. Someone said that at least Madison was alive and wasn't this a blessing. The visitors who whispered Madison's name sounded like snakes.

Nobody expected Reese to talk. That was the only true blessing. That Madison was in a coma at the hospital was not a blessing. That was just a fucked up fact and Reese had nowhere to put her rage.

Jocelyn's rear end pushed the seams of her skirt. A greening bruise flowered on her cheek. This was the damage of Reese's hand. Jocelyn kept custody of her eyes and pretended Reese wasn't there. There was no faulting Jocelyn's awareness as to how high and thin the wire Reese walked was. How close she was to falling free of sanity or decency.

The afternoon sun filtered through the blue curtains, casting everything in cold diffused light. Reese was aware of what she looked like in the gloom. She arranged her legs just so. She was a gorgeous grieving widow. People gave her space, and not just because she'd hit Jocelyn and everyone knew it. No one could think of what to say to a beautiful woman with such horrible luck.

A studio portrait of Madison hung over the piano that she had been learning to play. Reese had taken her into the photo studio before the first day of kindergarten. She wore a red dress and smiled at the camera from under teased bangs. When the photographer finished clicking, her face had returned to its usual seriousness.

Reese often watched her daughter in the playground before coming forward to collect her. Madison's mouth was set in a grim line as she played the chasing games with the other children. It was a myth that kids laughed all the time. It was a myth that kids were happy. They were weak and small and they knew it damn well.

It would be months before the doctors let Madison out of the hospital. Reese needed to sell the house. Cash out on Rod's stocks and options. He had been worth a lot of money. Now she was worth a lot of money.

She ran the numbers in her head. There was enough in the joint account for a big change. It would be a total shape shift for both of them. She would never come back. She would change her name again. She would take Madison with her. They would move far away from Jocelyn and Carl and their sentimental bullshit about family sticking together at a time like this. Reese and Madison needed only each other.

Someone new was at the door. Reese crossed her ankles and rested her high heels to the side like a perfect lady. It was uncomfortable and she liked it that way.

She'd had no idea Rod had so many friends. The funeral had been packed. The priest didn't know what to say about Rod, a man he'd never met. They never went to church. Reese watched the mourners from her place in front of the casket. Closed, of course. She sat in front of it during the services and thought of nothing but the urge to unzip out of her skin and run around in her bones.

Quiet female voices hissed in the foyer. Jocelyn returned to the kitchen. The new guest, a woman with tanned skin and long white hair, stepped onto the thick carpet sea. Reese's heart raced but she did not move from the chair.

The woman smiled with a closed mouth as she pulled a chair to sit beside Reese. She dragged it across the carpet so that it dug grooves into the pile like a trail. Reese was highly strung . Fight or flight. She couldn't decide which.

"Do you remember me?" the woman asked in a whisper that shrunk the room.

Reese felt a crack break in spider lines down her forehead. Parts of her past and present rearranged themselves in a disjointed tableaux. Scenes of her life blocked themselves like her own private Stations of the Cross going backward through time. Reese and the funeral. Reese and Dr. Hendricks. Reese leaving Madison with Rod.

Then a tremendous leap backward into her pre-life, a time she often believed never existed, back to when she was a teenager named Teresa Hamilton and this woman sitting in her living room was her high school teacher, the nun Sister Judith.

"I know your face well," Reese said. Her index finger tapped a rhythm on her knee.

"Teresa. I am so sorry for your loss," she said.

"I'm Reese Camden."

"I know who you are."

They looked at each other.

In the kitchen a timer went off. The oven creaked open.

Judith craned her neck to see the portrait of Madison on the wall. "Is that your daughter? It must be."

Don't look at my daughter. Reese's leg twitched. She said nothing.

"I hear she was hurt in the accident." Reese could not read her tone. "She looks nothing like her sister."

"Madison's father is white," Reese said.

"*Was* white." Reese remembered Judith's blunt truths from her year as a student in her high school chemistry class. Nuns ran the St. Rose Academy for girls, but Sister Judith was the only one she had liked. It was impossible to have ever been that young, at the mercy of adults. Madison's smile in her photograph hurt Reese's chest.

"Why are you here?" Reese asked. "How did you know where I live?"

"I always know where you live."

Reese stuck out her chin and thought about that. Before dying, her own mother had never looked for her once. Reese hadn't thought that anyone knew where she was. She thought she had kept where she was and who she was a secret.

But one person knew. It was another little earthquake, finding out that she had not disappeared the way she had thought.

"I failed you," Judith said, "but at least I always made sure I knew where you were."

Reese looked into the kitchen. She could call out. She could announce an intruder in the house and Jocelyn would make Sister Judith leave. Jocelyn lifted a hot tray with thick mitts while her silly friends leaned their fat butts against the counter. They were no help to Jocelyn or to her. They were birds on a wire, chattering about nothing. They had no idea that Reese was being eaten alive in the very next room.

"I'm here to say I'm sorry about what happened to your family," Judith said, "but that isn't all. The truth is I'm here to warn you."

The clock on the mantel whirred in the quiet. Dark circles ringed Judith's eyes. Her high cheekbones had grown more prominent with age. Something was stealing her sleep, but she was beautiful. Funny that after eighteen years she hadn't remembered her teacher as so beautiful.

Judith moved first. "I've been here ten minutes," she said. "Do you remember that today is her birthday? You haven't even asked about her."

"What is there to ask?" Reese pulled her spine straight. "You took her from me. I don't know her and I don't know you."

Judith held Reese's gaze. Her eyes were stony blue and heavy lidded. "I couldn't give her over to Ray."

She took Reese's hand that was a claw in her lap and gently pulled the bent fingers. She stroked her palm. Reese let her do it for a long moment. Sister Judith's touch was soft and knowing. It could be a comfort to someone she loved. Then Reese pulled her hand back, her face burning. She felt as angry as if she'd been stripped of her clothes.

"Did you know what Ray did to Michael?" Judith asked.

Reese hated hearing Michael's name out of her mouth, but there was nothing Judith could say about him that would surprise her. She knew the whole story. She knew everything about what had happened in her old life, to her old love, to their daughter. It was obscene to talk about it aloud. "Why do you think I went off with Billy when I did? I thought I could protect Michael that way. It was all for nothing. I was so fucking stupid."

"So you know why I hid Crystal. You understand."

"I was just a kid. And you didn't visit me in prison, not once," Reese said, a tiny bead of spit flying from between her teeth. "You let everyone think I killed her."

"I knew you'd be acquitted."

"How could you have known? Ray said I did it. He had her bloody shirt."

"Once Ray and Billy were dead, it was over," Judith said.

"I was in there for months. How could you have known they'd be dead?"

Judith remained still in her gaze. There would be no games played between them now. No lies. It felt to Reese like racing a bike downhill without brakes. Pursuing the truth was a dangerous activity.

"I know," Judith said. "And in that time, you were safe from both of them. You got off drugs."

"You left me."

"I didn't even change my name when we left Eureka. We were only in Berkeley. It would have taken that lawyer five minutes to find us if you wanted him to. Be honest."

"You have no idea what it means to be locked up." The injustice was a burr in her throat, making it difficult to speak.

"I know more about that than you think," Judith said.

Reese gathered herself together. She reeled in the ribbons of longing and pain and jealousy and tucked them under her helmet. Judith could not hurt her anymore. No one could.

"Why are you here?" she asked.

"Like I said, it may be that it all comes out soon," Judith said. She was exhausted, her eyes sunken. "I'm here to offer fair warning."

"What does this have to do with me?"

"Teresa. Why pretend now?"

"I am not Teresa. You and I do not know each other."

"Okay," Judith said, "but we should agree on what to do if and when the truth comes out."

"I have no idea what the hell you are talking about." The ladies from the kitchen glanced over at the scene in the icy living room. Reese imagined what they were thinking. Wasn't that nice, a pretty lady coming to pay respects? It was more than a bitch like Reese deserved.

"You will. Everyone will, if it blows apart. Maybe it won't. I've protected your privacy up to now." A line formed in Judith's forehead. A worry line.

Where is my daughter Crystal? The question rested on Reese's tongue like a heavy black plum. She didn't speak.

Where is my daughter?

Judith stood. "I was fair to you. I never imposed on you while you made a new life. Please return the favor. Come forward and tell the truth if it comes to that."

Reese looked past her old teacher at the portrait of Madison on the wall. St. Madison of the killer smile. That girl would get whatever she wanted in life. *If* she lived. She balled her broken hands into fists on her knees. "You have not been fair. Nothing in my fucking life has ever been fair."

"I see I've upset you." Judith leaned forward, closing the space between them. "Listen, she may come here looking for you. You'll tell the truth if it comes to that. Let's agree."

"I'm not agreeing to anything," she said. She grabbed Judith's forearm and squeezed. "And if she comes looking for me I'll kill her for real this time. Do you understand me?" She shoved her away so hard she almost fell.

"You don't mean that," Judith said, putting her hand on the piano to regain her balance. She smoothed her hair, the worry line deepening between her eyes.

"Oh, don't doubt me," Reese said. "Maybe if I murdered Crystal like everybody said I did, Madison would be allowed to live."

"Absurd," she said. "You sound insane."

"Keep her the fuck away from me, Judith. What would I have to lose? Think about it. They couldn't try me twice for the same crime. Now get out of my house." She knew she sounded insane. She didn't care. She meant what she said.

The phone jangled and Jocelyn picked it up. Judith looked like she might try again to reason with her. Reese's hand twitched, aching to land a blow that would shut her up. Then Jocelyn ran between them, her face white. "Reese. It's the hospital. They need to talk to you right now."

Reese shuddered and felt cursed.

Chapter 9

October 21, 1989
Del Rio Beach, California

Judith

❦

IN FOUR DAYS Judith caught maybe a total of six hours of sleep in the back of one of the police cars parked by the rescue scene. It was more accurate to call it a death scene, when only one person made it out of the St. Francis shelter alive. But the one who made it was Angel. God forgive her, but Angel's life was all she cared about. She could not sleep or eat until they pulled her daughter out from under the bricks. If it had been possible, Judith would have stopped breathing until she knew Angel was safe.

The drive to and from Silicon Valley to see Teresa Hamilton, now Reese Camden, robbed Judith's body of the last drop of adrenaline. She planned to go straight to Angel's hospital room and ask for a folding cot so she could rest. Her stomach was killing her. She stepped off the hospital elevator onto the wrong floor and didn't realize it until she was halfway down the corridor and Dr. Henry grabbed her by the shoulders.

"Judith? What are you doing? You look awful."

"I must have come here out of habit," Judith said. She gazed at the ceiling with its rows of fluorescent lights. She hadn't been thinking straight.

"I need to talk to you," Dr. Henry said. He pulled her into his office. The window overlooked the parking lot. News vans crammed the curb. Judith's knees quivered as she sat down. By coming in one of the side entrances, she had missed the reporters. There were so many of them. It was so much worse than she had feared.

"I have your blood work from last week," the doctor said. He held a file open on his desk. "I've been trying to call you. Maybe with the earthquake your phone is down?"

Judith looked at him. He didn't know that the Angel on the news was hers.

He didn't know that while she was driving back from Palo Alto, a news story had broken about Miracle Angel Kelley that would put Judith in the sort of trouble from which not even cancer could excuse her.

"According to the samples, we're going to need to move quickly on this. Even sooner than I recommended last Tuesday." He pointed to the figures on the page. "Your platelets are way down. If we are going to ensure a good outcome we should start treatments as soon as possible." He frowned. "How are you feeling? You look fatigued."

Judith got out of the chair. If she left the hospital the way she came in, she would had time to get away before the police found her. "I need to go."

He took her elbow. "We should get you into a room right now," he said. "We'll keep you overnight for observations and get you started on the chemo tomorrow."

Judith pressed her knuckles into his desk. She fell against him. Before she knew it, she was in a wheelchair moving back down the hall, her head bobbing on the end of her neck.

"We have you, Judith," the doctor said.

Judith reached her thought toward Angel's room in a prayer to her daughter, for the past eighteen years her only god. *I'm sorry, Angel.*

I'm so, so sorry.

JUDITH OPENED HER eyes. An IV protruded from the top of her hand under a cross made of tape. Her head ached.

"Hello, Sister Judith."

She turned her head. A woman in a pantsuit and long black hair stood beside the bed. She flashed a badge from a lanyard around her neck. "Detective Laura Redleaf," she said.

Judith clawed at the cross of tape.

Dr. Henry came in already angry. "What the hell is this?" he said.

"Is this Judith Kelley, as registered to this room an hour ago?" Redleaf was all business. The tape ripped Judith's skin.

"Yes, and she can't have visitors now," Dr. Henry said. Certain of his control over the situation, he motioned to the door for her to leave. His overconfidence was astounding. He could save his patient from cancer, from the past, from arrest. Judith knew better.

Redleaf lifted her badge again. "We are about to put this patient in custody, Doctor," she said. "There are federal agents in the hall waiting for us."

"I won't release her," Dr. Henry said. He crossed his arms in front of his chest. "This woman will die without an aggressive round of chemotherapy and radiation." He turned to her. "Judith, I don't know what this is about. I can tell them that I don't authorize your release. They'll have to wait. I'm not exaggerating about your prognosis. You need to be in treatment. This is no joke."

"I'll say it isn't," Detective Redleaf said. She stood like a mountain rising. Judith stuck her hands under the blankets and tore out the needles. She eyed the window and saw the morning light dawning. She wished for the cover of night. Her hand dripped blood.

The monitoring machines exploded in alarms. Judith pushed the heavy cart that carried them into the doctor's hip. He stumbled forward, caught by surprise. Redleaf raised her arms to protect herself, and for an instant she and the doctor were dancing. Judith slipped out the door.

She headed to the staircase. She moved against the wall. They would not be able to catch her if she was fast enough to get down the stairs and out the building. She only had to run.

The elevator dinged and the doors opened. Two men in dark suits stepped out to greet her, and in their faces Judith saw the end of everything.

Chapter 10

October 22, 1989
Palo Alto, California

Reese

〜〜〜

IN THE MIDDLE of the night Reese lay on the king-sized bed she had shared for six years with Rod Camden. She wrapped a cashmere blanket around her shoulders as tight as a pupal casing. Her wet hair clung to the back of her neck. The warming effects of the long bath she had taken were wearing off. The hot earthquake weather had succumbed to cold rain. In the day since Rod's funeral, a chill had crept along the backs of her shoulders like a new ice age. She couldn't get warm unless she was in a scalding bath.

Reese cradled her bedside phone between her jaw and shoulder. The crisis from the day before had passed. Madison's heart stopped but they got it started again. Reese imagined her daughter's heart in her fist. Stopping. Starting. Out of her control.

The prognosis for Madison was still uncertain. She hated the words the doctors used—"critical" and "serious." Could they fix her or not? The doctor tried to be reassuring, but Reese hated the vocabulary of hospitals. The doctors had many different ways to lie. For days Madison dipped in and out of the mouth of death like a kid on a carousel from hell.

Reese kicked free of the blanket and spread her legs under the sheets. She was tired of talking to the doctors.

Travel brochures littered the bed. She wouldn't be followed this time. She wouldn't be followed or tracked. Dr. Hendricks yapped in her ear, continuing his report on Madison's day. Madison's second surgery went uncommonly well. She was a strong kid. "Quite a trooper you have there, Mrs. Camden." She was still in serious condition, of course. Pediatric Intensive Care.

The doctor acted like Madison's recovery wasn't a given. He was an idiot. Of course she would have a full recovery. Of course Madison would live through this. There wasn't any other thing that could happen. Madison was more alive than any person Reese had ever known.

"You can visit whenever you want, Mrs. Camden. I realize you are grieving your husband's death. But Madison is conscious now. It would help her to have her mother there."

Reese looked at her broken, badly healed hands. These were hands that failed to give care. She doubted they were capable of it. She had thought once that she could take care of Madison, but she was a person who hurt children. She had grown up with a person who hurt children so she should know. Maybe she didn't do it on purpose the way her father Ray Hamilton had, but children got hurt by her all the same.

Reese clutched her belly. She wasn't anything like Ray. It was important to remember that. She missed her daughter. The pain of it was too much. She got up and paced the floor.

"When can she come home?" she asked.

Madison would be able to leave the hospital in a month at the very earliest, the doctor said. There would be at least a year of physical therapy for her to regain full use of her legs. He tried to talk on but she interrupted him.

"Will there be scars?" Reese asked.

The doctor's voice became brittle. "There will be some scarring, yes," he said. "Her left leg is broken in no fewer than seven places. She's suffered internal bleeding from a lacerated stomach. Surely surviving all of that warrants a few battle scars, Mrs. Camden. Mrs. Camden, surely you can understand."

Reese turned on the television but muted the sound. Camden was a dribbling name. She couldn't wait to change it.

She wanted her daughter back, even knowing she was a poisonous mother, even knowing she was the reason the little girl was in the hospital in the first place. She had left her daughter with stupid drunk Rod and those awful people in that terrible house.

Scars on Madison's perfect legs pissed her off. She nursed the anger and rocked it like a baby that nothing could ever take away, not even death. Maybe she should leave Madison behind for good. Maybe Madison would be better off with somebody else forever. Crystal had been.

After getting off the phone, Reese turned up the television. Every channel carried earthquake footage, though it had been five days since it happened. Not as many people died as they had thought at first. In fact, compared to other disasters in other places and other times, it didn't amount to much, she thought. She lived only thirty miles away from the epicenter, and that area had been untouched. Everyone needed to calm down.

Then a face took over the screen. It was a photo of a girl who looked like a teenaged Reese, only with Michael's eyes, Michael's mouth. The room tossed around. She felt dizzy. The photo wasn't Reese. The girl on the television had wild caramel hair. It was much wilder than Reese's own ever was. It looked like she brushed it with blackberry brambles.

This girl was Angel Kelley. They called her Miracle Angel. In the video she looked dead, covered in gray white dust, on a stretcher lifted from a mountain of broken rubble and bricks.

There was Judith running alongside. She wasn't Sister Judith anymore. They called her Miss Judith Kelley. She'd stayed alongside the rescuers lifting bricks with her bare hands.

Miracle Angel Kelley. She once was lost and now she was found alive. So this was what her old teacher was talking about.

The rescuers and engineers had thought everyone in the building in Del Rio Beach had died. Then a dog trained to find corpses sensed a live person. It took them nearly two more days after that to locate her. Reese watched them lift her limp body from a hole in the rubble. They played the same clip over and over. With her hair and face white with dust, she looked like a ghost.

Reese wondered what the hell a person thought about for four days in the dark all alone.

But Angel was not giving any interviews at this time. She was sick from being under the bricks for so long, her body bent in thirds with no water. She suffered injury to the kidneys, the newscaster said, and nerve damage to her neck. A bacterial infection threatened her lungs. There had been episodes of crisis in the hospital with her breathing.

What unfortunate stars the girl must have been born under to be stuck in an old brick building on the day and time of the worst earthquake since 1906. Reese moved so close to the screen that the static tickled the fine hairs on her forehead. Baby Crystal had escaped her birth mom but landed in the arms of Mother Earth, who was, it turned out, even worse with her kids.

The lady with the microphone droned on. Finding Angel safe and sound was the answer to a community's prayers. The other people in the building had not been so lucky. More pictures. Two long-haired college girls. A man from the city council with round eyeglasses. A cop. A newspaper photo of homeless residents getting ready to sit down for the evening meal. Twenty-eight people died when beams fell on top of them and the floor gave way from below.

Up-and-coming rock star Sundullah was reported to have visited Miracle Angel Kelley. Someone had taken a fuzzy snapshot of a tall dreadlocked boy leaving the hospital. There was another one of him getting into a car.

Why was she working in a homeless shelter in the first place? How did she live through that when everybody else was crushed? Reese seethed with questions. The news didn't say. She cursed at the television. She needed to know things about this girl. The newscasters were focused on the wrong things. Who gave a fuck about Sundullah? Rock stars had nothing to do with her daughter.

Reese turned the channel. It was the story of the night. Angel Kelley's face appeared on every station that ran the news. They offered a few more flashes of the same two snapshots of Sundullah, and again the reel of Angel emerging from the ground as though the earth had been the one to give birth to her in the first place.

Angel's face flooded the screen. She had large brown eyes, light skin the color of a butterscotch candy, a pointy chin. The eyes were so much like Michael's. Her hair was crazy and stood about her small face like a shaken can of cream soda. She was one of those girls who could be pretty or sexy or plain or even invisible if she wanted to be. Depending on the girl. Depending on how she chose to play it.

So Judith had taken Crystal and renamed her Angel. It was the opposite of what anybody ever called Reese.

The story of Angel had the attention of the nation. Reese ran her hands over the glossy brochures strewn across the bed and thought of Detective Redleaf from the Eureka Police Department.

Reese wondered how much time she had. Not much. If Detective Redleaf ever watched television, then in fact it was already too late.

Reese opened a pamphlet featuring palm trees, white sands, and bright blue waters. She and Madison could live in a beach house in Fiji, or in a grand one somewhere else. Maybe Texas. They could learn to talk like Southerners. Austin seemed pretty.

Reese stroked her chin. Angel looked like Michael. Madison resembled only Reese—no trace of Rod anywhere on her face. It was possible to gaze at Madison and forget about everything in their prehistory. Reese craved forgetting.

She moved to the walk-in closet. Forget Texas. They would head to a tropical place. She decided right then that she *would* take Madison with her. She would have another chance to be a good mother. She could raise a strong girl. Anyone who had survived all that she had could at least show someone how to be strong.

She and Madison would land somewhere out of the country, where it was possible to get lost. Madison would tan and learn how to speak French from the locals. She loved to swim. She could play mermaid whenever she wanted. They would be queens of their island. No one would ever bother them. People would be nice and wave as Madison and Reese walked by, and then they would let them alone.

Redleaf would come knocking soon, or else someone else wanting answers. She was no longer safe in the Palo Alto house. But Reese couldn't leave without Madison. This was a problem with no solution. She folded some things and left them on the floor. A violent shiver sent her to run another hot bath.

REESE DID NOT remember falling asleep. In the morning she woke under a pile of blankets on the massive bed. The phone rang and she answered it before coming fully awake. Doctor somebody, a man's voice. It was about Madison. An infection raged in an internal organ. They needed Reese at the hospital. He advised her to drive carefully but to please get there quickly.

Reese dropped the phone and gagged. The doctor squawked out of the phone on the floor. She pulled the wire free from the wall.

Plans were card houses. The wrong kind of movement in the air brought them down. This was what happened when she thought she could have a second chance with Madison. Her daughter would not live long enough for Reese to reclaim her. This was the way life evened out. She'd lost one girl and now she would lose the other. The doctors and the fates were in charge. She needed to go somewhere where she could have some power over her life.

Reese grappled for clothes. She gathered her wallet and shoes and pushed them into an overnight bag without even looking. The only course of action was to run. This would save Madison; she was sure of it. Jocelyn could take care of Madison. Or maybe Judith could do it. She'd looked after Crystal so well that she had grown into a woman who could survive four days under a building's worth of bricks. No way did Reese have that kind of mothering power. Madison would be better off without her. She needed to get out of there. This time it would be Reese who would become the ghost.

The television blinked like a strobe light in the dim room. Angel Kelley's face. Breaking headlines. Baby Crystal Found. Crystal and Angel were the same person. News flash. Reese groaned, riveted, unable for a moment to look away as the strangers on the screen told the story of her life.

There was Judith from a recent picture, maybe a DMV photo, her hair so white she looked like a fairy-tale witch. Then a grainy picture of Teresa Hamilton. Terrible Teresa. Everyone thought she'd killed her baby. It was old news but some would perhaps remember. In her high school senior portrait her hair was parted down the center and hung on either side of her baby face. She was the maybe murdering mommy of Saint Angel Kelley, the miracle girl who cheated death twice.

To Reese, saints were bad news. Give her witches over saints any day.

Reese hefted another suitcase off a shelf. It was a small, old-fashioned rectangular box with a wooden handle that released a sulfur cloud when opened. The billowing pouch within the maroon sateen lining contained two keepsakes. She had forgotten about them. The suitcase held memories that were too painful to keep in her mind.

Reese's mother had brought this suitcase to her father's house when they were first married. The thought of her fragile mother as a hopeful young woman carefully folding her silky nightgowns to place inside it tugged at her heart in a dangerous way.

"Fuck," she said. She repeated the swear word like a talisman, hardening the web-like threads that covered whatever semblance of human feeling remained inside of her. It was so much easier not to love.

A teddy bear hung its head over the pouch's ruched edges. It was still lush. The child owner did not have it long enough to love it to destruction. The bear's velvet fur was the color of wine. Reese hugged its round soft head under her neck. "Fuck you," she said like a lullaby.

Beneath the teddy bear rested a piece of stiff brown canvas, folded like butterfly wings. She blew into one end so that it expanded like a boxy balloon. The sulfur from the lantern's fuel pack suffused the closet. Judith had an extra floating lantern that she'd kept from their prayer service by the sea. She'd brought it to Reese as a gift during her last visit to her garden shed home. She had not told her teacher a thing about her plan to leave with Michael and their daughter in the night. Judith needed plausible deniability when Ray questioned her later.

Reese put the lantern and bear in the pouch. She tucked the bank statements into the sateen lining and closed the suitcase. She lugged it down the stairs with the duffel over her shoulder.

On the other side of the closed garage door, a car pulled into the driveway. Doors opened and slammed. Reese stood silent as two pairs of footsteps clacked along the stone walkway. The doorbell rang.

Reese peeked out the dirty window. A man and a red-haired woman in navy blue suits stood on her porch. Cops, only worse. The woman wore a skirt with a badge attached to her hip. Reese crept across the floor. Rod had left a ladder leaning against the wall to reach the Halloween stuff in the attic crawl space. Reese scrambled up the rungs. She tucked herself in with the insulation and dust. A spider crawled across her hand.

They pounded on the door. "FBI, Mrs. Camden. You're not in any trouble. We just need to talk to you, please."

Reese made herself small. She covered her ears. They knocked and rang the bell again. "Mrs. Camden. You haven't done anything wrong. We just want to talk."

She had done so much wrong. Everything about her was wrong. They would take her and make her answer questions until they figured it out for themselves. They would punish her somehow. They would find a way.

Judith wanted her to tell the truth but if she did that, Reese would be left with nothing. All the power she had in the world was in being who she said she was and no one else. Besides, Judith had left her in the prison for months knowing nothing for absolute certain. When Reese had needed her, she wasn't there. It wouldn't kill Judith to know how that felt. Her anger beat in her chest with the iron hammering of a bird's heart. It sustained her. It kept the blood flowing through her veins.

They pounded harder. The vibrations shook the crawl space. There was a muffled conversation and then the rattling of keys.

She scooted into the farthest corner. She would shape-shift into a rat and escape through a crack in the wall. She would become an owl and swoop over everything in a night wind. She was who she said she was. The past did not exist if she willed it. She could be anyone she wanted. The doorknob turned and they were in her house.

Another spider skittered out of the shadows. Teresa studied its brown back and disjointed legs. *I am you*, she thought, and smashed it under her palm.

Chapter II

October 30, 1989
Berkeley, California

Reese

〜〜

I T WAS DEBORAH the thief hairdresser who taught Reese at twenty-one that the trick to getting what you want was to do the thing nobody could imagine anyone doing. She talked while she applied the purple evil-smelling dyes that kept Reese's dark roots a secret. Deborah and Reese had the same lawyer. During the two years that Reese lived with her lawyer after the trial, she had met many useful people.

Deborah knew who Reese really was and she didn't care. She didn't care if she'd killed Crystal or not, and she wasn't afraid to get that fact in the open first thing.

"There is only today to be concerned about," she said. "Nobody ever got anywhere by looking out the back window."

Deborah liked to do the talking. She believed in honesty. She told about nights when she would walk into suburban homes while the people who lived there slept and take whatever she wanted. She did this for over three years before she got caught. Nobody suspected her because she looked just like the people she robbed. She pilfered from her own neighbors. It was crazy how people didn't lock their doors. They were sleeping chickens in henhouses full of golden eggs, she said. The only reason why she'd been caught is that she got greedy and tried robbing a house in a neighborhood much more upscale than the one she lived in. She'd driven to another neighborhood with a gate and a guard. She scaled the wall okay, but the house had a silent alarm. The cops had it surrounded before she realized she was in trouble.

"It's when you get too greedy that you get caught," Deborah said. She pulled her long nails through Reese's limp blonde strands and it felt like heaven. "But other than that, do the thing no one else would do and take what you want."

Don't get too greedy. Take what you want. That paradox followed Reese around long after she graduated from high school at twenty-two. It was her lawyer's idea to change her name, lie about her age, and get a chance to have her senior year of high school. Re-entering high school at twenty-one wasn't as strange as she thought it would be. The public senior high in Ukiah was nothing like St. Rose Academy for Girls. She was not special in the public school. She was one drop in an enormous sea in the hallways. No one noticed her anywhere. There were young men with broad backs she could sit behind in the classes. The anonymity was the closest thing to a haven she had ever experienced. Her cheeks were still round enough, her body slim enough to pass for eighteen. Despite the facts of her savage past, time smoothed her face with the same power in which high tide rendered a corrugated beach as flat as a concrete sidewalk.

She passed through the days unnoticed, her story a cipher no one suspected. She sat alone in a corner of the cafeteria to think during lunch hour. Every day she bought a milk, marveling anew at the simple design of the small carton. Cartons of milk were such hopeful, pure things. They were the realm of wholesome childhoods. She drank down one a day while she observed the groupings and couplings of her classmates. The kids lived in a kind of Garden of Eden. She liked the way they claimed their space in the world without ever dreaming of the possibility of men like Ray and Billy. In this world there was no such thing as a man who forced his will by breaking his daughter's fingers. Here no one would imagine that love was fragile and could be murdered or stolen away.

Teresa wanted a place in the world too. She would claim for herself a new story. She decided that she was a fresh-faced teenager named Reese and so she was. She could become whatever she desired. No one questioned it. The lawyer had been right. The plan worked in her favor. She posed as his niece and lived with him and his wife as a pseudo family. School was even easier the second time around. Her grades were good enough that she attended college on scholarship right after.

She couldn't remember what her own mother had looked like but she would never forget Deborah's long nails raking rows down the back of her head and neck, her smoky voice full of facts and knowing. *Take what you want.*

Her lawyer Jack Warren was the only decent man she'd ever met besides Michael. Jack was the hub of a wheel spoked with criminals he had helped stay out of jail. Through him she met lots of helpful people. Besides Deborah, who kept her hair curly and honey blonde, she met Rick, the forger who created her identification documents. With their help, Terrible Teresa Hamilton the baby killer became Reese Warren the high school honors student.

As Teresa Hamilton, she had been a skinny, filthy, drug-addicted piece of garbage. People thought she'd killed her own kid. Everyone knew her name and hated her. With Jack's help she went from an irredeemable monster to a pretty honors student who maybe didn't smile enough but had a bright future.

After her year in the high school in Ukiah, she went to college. She worked an accountant job. Then she met Rod and became Reese Camden, his wife. She hadn't invited Jack and his wife to the wedding. She didn't know if the Warrens were dead or alive. It wasn't that she wished them ill, or even that she didn't care. Reese was careful about her emotional energy. It was important to her survival that she not care too much about anyone once they became part of her past. The hairdresser had been correct. The most necessary thing was to look forward, always.

Now her husband was dead. Her daughter was in the hospital and maybe she would live, maybe she would not. Reese didn't have a man anymore to give her a different identity. This time she would mutate into a new incarnation through other methods.

Since moving into the Berkeley house she took nightly scalding baths in bleachy water. For long days she sat quietly on the hardwood floor, thinking. She watched the sun stretch across and then disappear from its white walls and waited for an idea. It was on a walk up Solano Avenue that she found a flyer for a channeling in Santa Rosa. She took the drive and bought a fifty-dollar ticket to be a part of the crowd in an old movie theatre in the downtown area. A woman named Isabel walked on the stage. She said hello and bowed to the audience. When she straightened, she said a strange word in a language Reese had never heard before. The woman's voice was changed. Her body contorted and the crowd gasped. Isabel had changed into a thousand-year-old Miwok shaman named Aditi.

Isabel was a beautiful woman, older than Reese but not by too much. When Isabel channeled Aditi, her voice rolled and pitched. She told the audience that each of them were on a "vision quest." She said that they needed to be aware of the spirits encouraging them on the way. Everything they wanted in life was in their grasp. They just had to believe that the power and the money and the love were already theirs and then soon they would be.

Afterward Isabel let people approach her and she spoke to them privately in a hushed voice. She was tall with long red hair. She was unusually beautiful, like a model or a movie star, but what fascinated Reese most about the performance was the crowd. Fewer than half of them were the dreadlocked, hippie sort she expected. Most of the audience were people like Linda and George. The crowd was filled with people just like the one Reese used to be. If Rod were alive he would have loved this. He would have pretended to be jaded at first but he would have been into it. Aditi sounded like the self-help tapes he paid too much money for and listened to in his car.

No one in this audience appeared jaded. This audience wore expressions of pure rapture as they walked away from Isabel/Aditi. She'd made them happier than cocaine.

Reese waited until the lines for Aditi tapered off. A much younger woman, maybe a teenager, tended to the channeler. She poured a glass of water from an earthen pitcher and placed a shawl over the older woman's shoulders when she asked for it. Pure theater. Reese knew how to put on an act. She recognized a liar when she saw one.

Isabel/Aditi sat in a large chair fashioned from redwood burls. Red silken cushions padded the seat and her legs were crossed like a comic strip version of a mountaintop guru. Reese waited behind an overweight woman who gushed over Isabel and held her hand in her own two hands. Some people were too stupid to be believed.

When the fat woman stepped aside and made room for Reese to have a turn, a strange thing happened. Isabel shook her hand and to Reese the entire planet jolted to a standstill.

"Hello, sister," Isabel said. She did not flinch or even look down at the feel of Reese's accordion fingers.

Reese tried to end the handshake, but Isabel held on. She looked into Reese's face with the objectivity of a microscope's lens. Reese's cells opened and became transparent under this stranger's singular, focused gaze. Reese's hair stood on end and she felt a sense of rushing backward through time. She felt she was a child, standing before this redheaded sorceress who could tell what she was thinking. This woman knew everything inside of Reese, and everything she saw she accepted and loved. Reese stood paralyzed in the light of Isabel's attention.

"Why haven't you had those fixed?" she asked, patting Reese's palms. Isabel raised two fingers like a saint on an icon and then stroked Reese's hands with them. "The healing would be painful but complete," she said. "You would be whole again."

Reese yearned to run out of the decrepit theater but she forced herself to stand her ground. She was learning something here and she would be still for it. This woman was like the hairdresser, like the forger. She had survival skills Reese needed in order to keep going forward.

"How do you do that?" Reese asked. If she expected the woman to plead ignorance, she didn't. Instead, she smiled.

"Nobody notices anyone, nobody listens," she said. "We are all children lost in the snow, ready to die from the cold."

"Yes," Reese said.

"Every human being just wants to be seen." She placed her cool, dry hands on the sides of Reese's head. A screaming panic stirred in Reese's throat but she stayed. She stayed while Isabel looked into her eyes and showed her the big trick of reaching a brazen hand around her dead heart and squeezing.

"I see you," Isabel said.

Reese grit her teeth at the horror of it. Because the stranger did see. She saw everything.

After what felt like a thousand years, Isabel's teenaged attendant moved just slightly. She held in her arms an Indian woven basket full of paper money bunched together like fallen leaves. Isabel dropped her hands and turned her head to speak to the girl in a whisper.

Reese wasn't leaving any money. She backed away from the throne, already puzzling over what to do with this information. Isabel leaned in to say something further to the girl and Reese watched their intimate exchange with fascination. She yearned to stand and watch them longer, to hear what they said when alone. Perhaps they dropped the masks and counted their money like poker players after a big win. Maybe they were true believers. Or maybe Isabel's powers and Aditi were real.

On the drive home Reese brushed questions about Isabel's veracity aside. It didn't matter—no more than the true story behind any religion mattered. Reese worked the puzzle over so that by the time she returned to Berkeley she knew her next steps. She stopped on the way home at the used bookstore and purchased a New Age Baby Name Book. She ruminated all night on her new name.

Jin. "Superexcellent" in Japanese. Jun. "Truth." She would change her name to Jin Jun. Superexcellent Truth would be the channeled spirit flowing through her on a five lane highway.

Razi. Short for Razilee, which was a Hebrew name meaning "secret." When she found Razi among the R names, she felt a quiver of understanding. Teresa, Reese, Razi. The names flowed in a river of women's faces, lives, and modes of survival. Teresa and Reese were dead. Razi bloomed from their corpses.

She closed the baby name book and pulled a white shawl around her shoulders. She sat on her porch and watched people walk by on the street in the early morning. It was as though she had been blessed with a whole new way of seeing. There were a few homeless adults wearing packs, eyes clouded by schizophrenia and drugs. The students carried different kinds of backpacks than the homeless, and they walked with purposeful strides. Some of the students were young men whose strides expressed less urgency. They were the ones who questioned the meaning of their lives in the very way they carried themselves. She could see their need so clearly.

There were also teenagers with furtive eyes and hungry faces who weren't students, who were varying degrees of homeless. One or two of those would be useful to her as well.

Then there were her neighbors. The type who walked for the exercise, wearing leggings and athletic shoes, their elbows swinging to burn extra calories. That type was the money.

Roses and bougainvillea bloomed in the manicured yards of the houses on the street so close to the human carnival of Telegraph Avenue. The people with the money looked out their windows and sat on their porches and took their fitness walks. The façades of the homes on the street were well maintained and pretty. Reese peered into those façades from her own porch. She knew better than anyone the loneliness that could be hiding inside a cute house. Everybody needed something.

Everybody needed to feel seen.

Chapter 12

December 23, 1989
Berkeley, California

Razi

⌒⌒⌒

Teresa Hamilton, Reese Camden, now Jin Jun Razi, poured boiling water from a steel teakettle into the deep, old-fashioned bathtub. The steam pillowed off the surface and touched her face. The kettle clanked against the white floor tiles as she stepped into the scalding water.

The drops of bleach she'd applied to the bath sharpened the steam in her nose. Her eyes felt like they were bleeding. This ritual left her skin silky as slime when she got out, but then as the water evaporated, the skin on her legs broke into hexagons like a desert in drought. She wanted to see how much she could take. She wanted to see if she could peel herself away to a molten core.

The whole house was white, except for dark-brown exposed hardwood floors that gleamed with polish. The walls were painted in the chalky wash of a California mission. Dark-brown Craftsman beams crossed the ceiling. The wide sheepskin rugs on the front room floor were expensive, but she didn't buy much furniture. Her house with Rod had been full of useless things. She would not make that mistake this time.

Her body pinked in the hot water as though she were feverish. After a while she stepped onto the white bath mat and she sloughed off layers with a cheap rough towel. The ends of her hair would split like burned branches when it dried. She'd dyed it the lightest blonde she could find on the shelf at the drugstore. The peroxide so damaged her hair that she was surprised it didn't fall out in clumps. Long, corn-silk strands swirled around her scalp.

As the mist receded from the small mirror above the sink, it was clear that the blonde hair suited her. Her eyes looked even larger and bluer with her nearly white hair and articulated thinness. She looked like a being from another world. Just like Jin Jun Razi should.

She had moved to Berkeley in order to create this new woman. She'd invented Razi to get clean from the inside out and to transform herself into someone whose power was untouchable. She dyed her hair white. She bought colorless clothing to wear. She ate so little that her collar bones jutted out. Her breasts flattened and her wrists extended from her cream-colored sweaters like spindly branches.

The meeting would start in an hour. The house was ready. She swept and scrubbed until every inch was hospital clean and no sign remained that any living thing resided there. The house was dead and quiet and bathed in cold afternoon light. She applied a towel to every surface in the bathroom until they were all dry and gleaming. She padded naked into the bedroom, where her few clothes hung in an otherwise bare closet. Her tunics and pants were ethereal garments in white and cream cotton on blond wooden hangers.

Razi thought of Deborah the hairdresser as she lit the cream-colored candles on the windowsills and hearth. She'd had good teachers in her life. Judith, Deborah, Isabel/Aditi. Even Ray was her teacher. He'd taught her the power of giving people exactly what they wanted. He'd taught her the power of fear.

She needed purification, but she also needed income. She needed a new start, a new self. She needed a complete breaking away from Teresa and Crystal, and from Reese and Madison. Those failed motherhood personas were funguses on her heart. They rotted her from the inside and made her soft. She was incredibly foolish to think she could redeem herself for losing Crystal by having Madison. She should have known better. She'd taken what she wanted when she married Rod. She had another baby out of too much greed for love.

Now Rod was dead, but he deserved to be. He'd had a cruel streak that other people didn't see. Because of him, Madison was attached to wires and tubes. The doctor had high hopes for her full recovery. She'd called once around Thanksgiving to see if her daughter was still alive. "Your little girl would love to see you," the doctor said. "She asks for you every day."

She cried herself breathless after hanging up. Her crying sounded inhuman, like the grunting of an animal. Her arms ached with emptiness for Madison. She wrung the bed sheets and inhaled their chlorine smell. She ached for her little daughter in an urgent and physical way that felt like holding her breath underwater. She couldn't come up for air. There was none there to breathe.

She had to pretend Madison was dead. He had to have lost her daughter because if she went back to trying to be her mother it was only a matter of time before she lost her again, and the next time maybe Madison wouldn't survive. She could not imagine she would be allowed two resurrected daughters.

The doctor said Rod's sister Jocelyn spent long hours at Madison's bedside.

He was full of good cheer the last time they spoke. Eventually Madison would be as she was before the earthquake day. She had strong legs. Even at five years old, she had the physique of a tiny athlete. She was a fighter.

Jocelyn would be a good mother, Razi thought. She would be the kind of mother who didn't lose track.

Razi peered down the street from behind the gauzy curtain. A woman starting her own religion needed followers. She glanced at her watch before unbuckling it and slipping it in a drawer built into the wall. Time was of no consequence in her house. She'd created a nucleus of peace in the center of the world.

Razi cleared her throat. "Aksana Jin Joooon," she said in the rolling bass words that hurt her throat to utter.

During the readings she channeled an ancient being named Jin Jun to growing audiences willing to pay up to twenty dollars apiece just to sit on the floor and hear her speak. She'd started in a New Age bookstore downtown but since the beginning of December had moved to her own house. She'd found the money in their joint accounts for a down payment. This evening was free of charge, a special treat in honor of the Winter Solstice. A few days late, but not in conflict with other more established events in town. *Don't get greedy,* Deborah would say.

It was easier than she would have thought to start a religion. All she needed was followers and a god. She invented Jin Jun out of the air and the believers were growing in number.

As the sun slanted in the winter haze, people wandered up the walkway in groups of two and three, checking the address against the cheap neon green postcards Razi had dropped in every café and bookstore in town. They advertised a special free reading from Razi's home. She'd sent a couple cards to Judith, but she couldn't say why. If she was afraid people wouldn't come to her spiritual party, she shouldn't have been. They flowed in like water.

She stood in the foyer with her hands in a prayer position under her breastbone. She bowed as they entered and whispered the names of the ones she'd met before as she greeted them. The act was so good that she fooled herself. She always believed her own lies. It was one of the secrets of her success.

The reedy women and goateed men expressed gratitude that she remembered them. But of course she remembered them. They were her salvation.

Chapter 13

November 1, 1989
San Jose, California

Angel

⌒⌣⌐

ANGEL'S EARLIEST CHILDHOOD was a primeval forest. It was perpetual night. Creatures slunk behind the trees. Their eyes winked in the darkness but they did not make themselves known. Detective Redleaf wanted answers about the things that lurked there. She asked questions about people, but Angel never knew the answers.

What do you remember about a man named Ray Hamilton? Did you call him Grandpa? Do you remember the sound of gunshots? A car wreck? Angel tried to be polite for the first hour. She didn't want to make her mother look bad. But after the third round of the same set of questions, she'd had enough.

"I don't know," she said. "I don't remember. You asking me again does not make me recall the answer." She gave Detective Redleaf, sitting across the table, a level look. An FBI agent man stood against the wall with his arms crossed. Angel sensed that he was impatient with both of them. He watched the conversation with the air of a person at a slow-paced movie waiting for the climax.

Angel and her mother had done nothing wrong. She held on to the certainty of their innocence like a buoy in a rocky sea.

"Do you recognize this man?" The detective paid no mind to the agent behind her. She slid a black and white photograph from a folder. It was a man in a shirt and tie, his hair slicked back. The man in the photograph smiled in the manner of a kindly grandfather, but something in Angel went cold.

"No," she said, "but he looks like an asshole." Her kidneys were on fire. She rubbed her lower back.

"Help us figure this out, Angel."

"I'm not trying to make your life hard. I don't know that guy."

"We have invited a special therapist to speak with you," the man in the suit said. "He may help you remember things that your conscious mind has chosen to forget."

"Not happening," Angel said. She headed for the door. The ceiling felt so low, she fancied that the hairs on the top of her head touched the fluorescent lights. She would never get used to being inside buildings again. Every cell in her body yearned to be out of doors, despite the cold and the impending rain. It so happened that Jerry had more smarts than anybody. Ceilings were treacherous. She could not imagine the day when they would not make her nervous.

"Have a seat, Miss Kelley." The agent uncrossed his arms.

"You can't keep me here," she said. "And hell if I'm letting you put me under hypnosis."

"Who said anything about hypnosis?" A female agent entered and gave the detective the stink eye. She had curly red hair like Botticelli loved to paint. It undermined the badass image she was obviously aiming for, with her suit and badge and unsmiling expression. Angel was sick of all of them.

"Take me to my mom," Angel said. "Or let me go." Detective Redleaf sighed and bent her head.

"You were almost four when Sister Judith took you," Redleaf said. "Kids that age do remember things."

Don't ever say Michael's name. Ray will kill him and he'll kill us too. The sting of a hard slap on the face. A voice with black feathers and hard and bony wings.

Angel felt lightheaded. "She didn't *take* me," she said. "This is all such bullshit. Take me to my *mother*."

The agent led her down the hallway chattering the whole time, pretending she didn't notice Angel's frustration. She wanted Angel to know that they weren't talking about hypnosis exactly. It was more like a relaxation method. She'd done it herself a couple of times. It was good for stress. Angel should try it.

They ended in a smaller room with an even lower ceiling where Judith sat with her left wrist handcuffed to a chair bolted to the floor.

"Really?" Angel said. "Handcuffs?"

"Don't argue with them," Judith said. Angel kicked the table leg. The metal rang from the hard tip of her new boots.

The agent raised her eyebrows then ducked out. A wide mirror took up one wall. Angel bent to hug Judith and an electric pain charged down her spine into her kidneys. She knelt to embrace her waist. Judith wore her own clothes but she smelled different, like the wrong kind of soap.

Angel rested her forehead on Judith's knee. "What the fuck is all of this?"

"They can hear you. They're watching us right now."

"I don't give a fuck," she said. The curse words burbled out of Angel's mouth like toads and snakes. Since the earthquake, once she started talking she couldn't control what flopped and slithered out of her mouth, starting with her confession to Sundullah. It was better to be silent, she knew this, yet seeing her mother in handcuffs was so absurd that she couldn't help it.

She moved to the other chair across the table.

"Like my new boots?" Angel stuck her foot out above the tabletop. Judith tilted her head to get a look.

"You and those boots," she said. "I can't believe they don't hurt your feet."

"They're the only shoes that don't," Angel said, smiling at the familiar conversation. For a second she saw a flash of her mother's regular strength behind the worried, disconcertingly pale mask.

"What kinds of things did they ask you?" Judith asked. Her smile disappeared. She raised her hand as if to brush her hair out of her face. The cuff clanked against the armrest. She used her right hand instead.

"They want to know what I remember."

"What did you tell them?"

"Nothing. Because I remember nothing." She gave the mirror the finger.

"Don't," Judith said.

"Why not? This is so bogus. They say you kidnapped me."

"That is what they say." Now it was her mother's turn to smile, and that smile was a weird squirmy thing on her dry lips.

"This isn't funny, Mom." Angel needed her to be serious. "This is a violation of your rights. Do you have a lawyer?"

"I was hoping it wouldn't be necessary."

Angel leaned backward and stuck her tongue out at the mirror. She immediately regretted the mini backbend. It took a minute to straighten out. She kept forgetting about her injuries.

"Stop the antics, Angel. We need to talk."

"Then talk," Angel said. She rubbed her lower back with both hands. "Why don't you have a lawyer? Why aren't we out of here right now?"

"I was hoping to hear from someone who could set this straight today," Judith said, "but she isn't answering her phone."

"Who?"

"Your mother. Your real mother."

Angel pressed her palms into her eye sockets. Her own life story shimmered like oily heat off of a long road. "I thought she was an anonymous person," she said. "I thought you got me from an adoption agency."

"You know now that I lied about that. Stop playing games. You need to listen to me, Angel. Are you listening to me?" Angel nodded but still hid her eyes. "Remember the fairy tales? The Good Lady of the Woods who saved the changeling from the monster and the sad witch?"

Angel could feel the FBI people straining on the other side of the wall to hear. This was going to be the good stuff. She hated them.

"Those stories were the truth," Judith said.

Angel hid behind her hands. Her tiny fairy hands. She wasn't stupid. She'd seen the news reports. She knew all about Crystal Hamilton, the Lost Girl. It was supposed to be her but she couldn't believe that anyone expected her to deal with this revelation after everything she had just been through. *Just take me home*, she wanted to say. *Stop all this bullshit and let my mother and me go back to the cottage.* Her own home in the shelter was missing; her entire world was missing. Now, come to find out, she was missing too. She dropped her hands. It was all still there. The pale room. The metal table. Her mother looking frail and strange.

"The woman who was your mother is out there, Angel. She knows what's happening and she's choosing not to come forward."

"Why? Why did you steal me?" It was an absurd question to have to ask her mother.

Judith—or the Good Lady, or whoever she was—shook her head. "I rescued you, my love." Angel shivered and hugged herself tight. "And you saved me too. I need you to believe me. I know you believe me."

Judith wasn't pleading. Angel knew her mother well enough to accept the plain truth when it was finally told.

"I believe you," Angel said. For the first time since the visit began, she felt comforted. She was never missing, not really. Angel knelt before Judith again. They put their foreheads so close that their breath mingled. This was home, this space they created based on mutual rescue. Wherever they were together would be where Angel belonged.

"There is more for you to know, but not much more," Judith said. "Teresa, your real mother, knew I had you. She knew I would keep you safe. And for a long time that is just what I did."

"She knew?" The ground trembled, and the walls creaked. She wondered about the seismic safety of the building. Aftershocks at irregular intervals reminded her that the earth would never be a good place again.

"She knew all along," Judith said. "She knows where I am now. I think we've always been aware of each other."

"What the hell are we doing here, then?" Angel asked. "We have to find her, right? We have to make her come here and explain." The warm relief of her mother's assurances gave way to confusion. Her mind, sluggish since the earthquake, reeled with what Judith was saying. Angel looked around the bleak room. There must be something she was missing, some piece she was forgetting that could help her mother, Judith, get free.

But Judith's eyes darkened and her next words chased all remnants of comfort away. "Leave me, Angel," she said. "Don't worry about me. Let me handle this. Go to your life."

Her life. That was funny.

"Where is she?" Angel asked. "My *mother*."

"I don't know. When she disappears it can take quite a lot to find her again."

"Well, if she's the one who can get you out of here, we need to find her."

Judith lowered her voice. "Leave me, Angel. What if you go to Sundullah for a while? When he came to the hospital he told me he wanted you to recuperate at his house in L.A. What about that?"

Angel sat back as if burned. She opened her mouth. *I killed our baby.* But nothing came out. She had lost her taste for confessions.

"Sundullah is beside the point," she said instead. "You're going to federal prison, Mom. Let's focus on that fact."

"Leave me, Angel. Go to your life."

Angel struck her fist on the table, and it rang like a bell. "Stop saying that," she said.

The male and female agents rushed in. All business. They had more questions, more they wanted to say. More ideas to get to the bottom of this. They barked and drowned each other out like untrained dogs.

Angel's kidneys burned and her head went swimming apart from her body. The ceiling bore down. Angel remembered what it felt like to be dying. Her childhood was a primeval forest where the Good Lady reigned. In this room the only mother she knew was a falcon in a cage. She was small and matted and gray. A thought in Angel's head said that it was her mother Judith who was dying.

Her mother bowed her head as though praying for grace. Angel reached across the table. "Mom," she said. Her hands opened and closed. "I love you, Mom. Say it back."

"I don't want you to have to deal with any part of this," her mother said. "It's absurd that you should have to bear a single bit of what happened when you were just a child. Leave this place, Angel. Don't come to see me anymore."

"I love you," Angel said again. "Now say it back."

Judith didn't hear or pretended not to.

"Say it back," Angel said.

Judith would not raise her eyes. The agents uncuffed her and took her away.

* * *

JUDITH WALKED BETWEEN the two armed FBI agents down the hall to her cell. They were the cherubim and seraphim of her new life in the jail, ushering her through transitions. The meeting with Angel had left her hollow inside and so deeply sad that she could barely breathe. She found herself grateful for the agents' stoicism. There was peace in their silence.

Their reason for keeping her behind bars shifted from kidnapping to suspicion of foul play in the disappearance of Reese Camden. They thought she kidnapped Crystal Hamilton and raised her as Angel Kelley, and most of that was true. Now they thought she had something to do with Reese's disappearance, which made no sense. No wonder they never found Crystal Hamilton. No one in authority had the imagination required for ferreting out the truth.

Judith spilled the name of Reese Camden before she left the hospital, but the betrayal meant nothing in the end. Judith allowed herself to hope that when confronted, Reese would admit to being Teresa Hamilton and tell the truth—that she had known since her release from prison that Judith had Crystal. She had let her keep the child because it was for the best. An argument could be made that Teresa knew that Judith had Crystal even during the trial for her murder. Judith had promised to always look after her and the baby. She had simply fulfilled that promise. Teresa knew she would.

But of course the woman now known as Reese Camden had disappeared. She'd left her daughter fighting for her life in a hospital, alone. But it was unfathomable that a mother would abandon her child while she clung to life in the Intensive Care Unit. The agents Judith spoke with weren't convinced that Reese and Teresa were the same person. They had no idea what Judith had really done, but they weren't totally incompetent. Detective Redleaf and the FBI knew she stank. They just couldn't figure out why. Judith sat on the knowledge of the crimes she had actually committed like a bird guarding a rotten egg.

When Reese was Teresa, she'd run when those who loved her needed her most, and lost her daughter because of it. She lost Crystal's father back then too. The authorities didn't know her the way Judith did. Running away was Teresa Hamilton's style.

Still, Judith had hoped Teresa would come forward with the truth. Judith often believed in people more than they deserved. She also often made the mistake of thinking that she deserved redemption that never came. Judith recognized her own comeuppance. The situation had a neat symmetry. Why should Teresa come forward to the FBI at this point when Judith had remained hidden during Teresa's trial for the murder of Crystal? Teresa had almost lost that case, and would have if Ray hadn't been murdered before he could testify.

Ray had hinted to prosecutors that he had seen Teresa take Crystal from her bed the night she went missing. *The liar.*

The agents led Judith into her cell and locked it. She rubbed the raw places the cuffs had left on her wrists. Hysterical laughter formed a bubble in her throat, and she popped it at her larynx. She'd been suppressing it all day. If she let it out it would never cease.

The agents kept her in bland rooms that washed the world in dirty chalkboard colors of pale yellows and grays. Everything was neat but not clean. A film covered the floors from inadequate mop rinsing. She didn't know how people could stand the grime collecting in corners. She expected the FBI to know how to clean.

She craved a rag and a bucket of hot, soapy water. She could get the hallways or at least her own cell clean. She thought that maybe the claustrophobia wouldn't be so bad if the place were really clean.

Depending how things turned out, she might be in this place or somewhere like it for the rest of her life. It wouldn't be too long—the rest of her life. The cancer sentence outdid the feds. That fact was the one thing that could make her once again believe in God.

She washed her mouth with water from the sink and stretched out on the narrow bed. Closing her eyes, she willed herself to forget that she was in a small room connected to the whole world with a door she could not open. She thought of her last group home in the foothills a hundred miles east of Bakersfield. Trees with orange leaves bordered the yard. The backyard paths connected with hiking trails into the rocky blue-green canyons, and she was allowed to go outside whenever she wanted.

A couple in their fifties named Bob and Robyn ran the home with strict rules of conduct, but it was their kindness that was most shocking. Robyn took the time to iron Judith's blouse on the first day at her new high school. Bob taught her to drive. They gave her a charm bracelet when she turned sixteen. Bob and Robyn invited her to church. When she asked, they taught her everything they knew about God. Thinking of them brought Judith something like joy. After so many years of brutal placements, her last home had been heaven.

Judith thought about the St. Rose Academy. She recalled Arcata and the long road through the green flats where she unlearned God. The forest loam spiced the air that night four years later when she heard the car crash on the highway. The next morning she left Angel sleeping and took a walk toward the road. She couldn't have said what she was looking for, but what she found was a pool of blood congealed in the duff at the base of a tree. Propped on the other side of the trunk was a book. Teresa's favorite one, the *Children's Tales.* The stories were the old versions of Grimm's and Andersen's fairy tales, and

Sister Judith privately thought they were too grisly for a child Crystal's age. Little ones didn't need to hear about talking horse's heads and bleeding loaves of bread. But when she touched the book, still tacky with blood staining the edges of the pages, all doubt left her mind. A warm calm infused her middle, the way it used to after she'd taken the Eucharistic wine at Mass. It was a sign.

Making Crystal her daughter wasn't just the right thing to do. This was what she was supposed to do. It didn't matter anymore if there was God or no God. This bloody story ended with the little girl safe in her arms, and that was what mattered. She took the book back to the convent, and the next day, she and the child were far, far away.

Judith fell asleep remembering the feel of the child's heavy head against her shoulder as they drove south. "You're the good lady," she had said, and Judith had felt blessed and reborn. She let the memory take her to sleep.

She was the Good Lady. It had to be true if an angel said it was so.

In the morning a guard brought breakfast. She escorted Judith to a private shower. Real prison wouldn't be so easy. She should have been grateful. Gone was the fleeting peace of the night before. Despair crusted over panic in an uneasy scab.

Another room—this one with water-blue walls, metal table, gray floor. She waited. It felt like waiting for a tsunami rising. No cuffs this morning. She wondered why. She was already so tired, and it couldn't have been later than nine a.m. She probed the soft tissue under her jaw to feel the hard buckshot of tumor growing there.

Detective Redleaf entered unattended by the federal personnel who were Judith's keepers. Judith gripped her chair to keep herself from flailing her body against the door as the detective closed it.

Redleaf's face was as blank as the wall. She opened a folding file and flipped through a sheaf of papers. "I know what you aren't telling the feds," she said.

Judith's cheeks prickled with heat. It was not possible that Redleaf knew. She matched the detective's fathomless calm with her own silence.

"I was there, Sister. I was one of Teresa's arresting officers. You could say this case has been my hobby since then."

Police cars crowded the side of the road the night that Michael died. The police did what Ray said. They reported the poor kid dead from multiple injuries sustained in the accident. There was nothing in the news about the gunshot. Nothing about the child who had been in the car with him.

It was likely a cop who shot Michael. She only heard him calling Crystal's name, telling her to run, and then the shot that ended him. His blood might have been on the hands of this cop sitting across from her.

"You must have been a friend of Saint Ray," Judith said. "The police generally were."

Detective Redleaf tossed her head as though she had bitten something sour. "You St. Rose people called him saint but Ray Hamilton was no saint. You harbored a monster, and do you know what I think, *Sister* Judith? I think you knew it."

"You know about Ray Hamilton."

"I know about the things he did," Redleaf said. "I know about the drug dealing. I know that he shot Michael Lopez, or had someone else do it for him. A couple of guys on the force filed a false report saying he died in a car wreck. The accident was real, but that wasn't what killed him."

"How do you know?" The detective was a goose laying golden eggs. Judith yearned to gather them all at once without giving up a single piece of her own information.

"Hamilton put a spell on everybody and I was the only one immune," the detective said. "Let's just say I have a low tolerance for bullshit. I knew something wasn't right. It wasn't any big deal to take the guys on the force drinking one night. I kept paying for shots until I got the story." She looked as though she might spit on the floor. "Did you know that they were chasing Michael? Ray told them to run him off the road. He told them Michael Lopez was a dirty Mexican who had stolen his grandbaby. Did you know they bashed his face with a hammer to hide the hole in his head from the gunshot? They mutilated him. They had to have a closed coffin funeral."

Sweat formed a sheen on Judith's face. *That poor sweet boy.* A landside of fresh grief.

"I see that bothers you," the detective said. "Let me tell you what bothers me. You let that girl think her baby was dead. You let her go through a trial for her baby's murder in front of the whole country while you were off somewhere acting like that baby was yours."

Judith picked at her cuticles and kept silent.

"I think that you and Ray had an arrangement. I think you were his lover."

Judith ripped a wedge of skin from the side of her forefinger until it bled.

"And then when he was killed you kept the baby for yourself anyway."

The blood pooled next to the fingernail before running down her knuckle. Her stomach rebelled but she kept still. Her true sins could squat behind this ugly story until the day Teresa emerged from hiding to save her with the truth or Judith died and found freedom that way.

There would be no chance for freedom if she told the truth. The real story would condemn her to prison forever.

"Wow," Judith said. "In some ways it's a relief, you know? I was so tired of running." She sucked on her finger, tasting the copper of cooling blood.

"There is more to this," Redleaf said. She leaned forward and talked right into Judith's face. "I never once let this case go. I used to walk the woods alone for hours looking for her body until the best I could expect to find were her bones. I never forgot Crystal Hamilton, not for one day. Because it isn't right that somebody takes a baby girl and does anything she wants with her. When I saw her picture and then yours on the news, I left my own family and got in my car. I drove right down here to arrest you myself."

Judith would not hold the detective's gaze. She dropped her eyes.

"So why do I feel that even now I don't have the whole story?" Detective Redleaf asked.

"You said you knew what I wasn't telling the feds."

"What more haven't you told me?"

Judith rubbed her fingers together where a Rosary would be if she still had the faith. She didn't need faith to take another sort of vow of silence. She would talk no more to anyone, not even Angel. Least of all Angel. She would push Angel off from her shore, force her to go sail toward her own life. Hopefully the girl would go to Sundullah, but even if not, Judith would not have her daughter's life interrupted any further than it had been already. Angel needed to move on. Judith had nothing left to offer her. The past could only hurt them both.

Judith's life was ending now, and that was not such a terrible thing. When she died, so would the story of Ray's car and all of the death that happened inside of it. In many ways her death had occurred there, as well as his. Judith had spent eighteen years shielding her daughter from Ray's bloody grasp. He was dead, and that was good. With her silence the damage he did would stay dead too.

Detective Redleaf was a patient woman, but Judith was a volcanic mountain holding tight to her own story. The secret of what she had done was the only freedom she had left. They would keep her for a time. Then, if Teresa did not choose to set her free, she would disintegrate, turn to ash and blow away.

Chapter 14

April 20, 1967
Arcata, California

Judith

❧

S ISTER JUDITH WAS in the middle of the long run she enjoyed every Sunday after Mass. The flatlands of Arcata were endless green fields and farms. The sky hung low and purple where the ocean lay past the dunes.

She had been thinking of Buddhist monks praying without ceasing. Their certainty in the power of faith was something she wanted like she used to want things she saw in store windows, the way she used to want a family. She knew the words of all the prayers. She said them every morning and night with the other sisters in the convent. Sometimes during prayer a wave of surety that God was present rose in her, only to go away again like a retreating tide. She tried on her runs to conjure absolute certainty that God was real in such a way that it stuck. She prayed every day for unshakable faith.

She had expected a life of service when she'd entered the convent after high school. She had expected sacrifice and obedience and prayer. She longed for the safety of rules, boundaries, and routines. She never dreamed of the freedom to take long afternoon runs that filled her with such contentment. She never dreamed of living in such a beautiful place. With every stride her body hummed a gratitude prayer. After a childhood of mostly bad foster homes, her new life in Arcata offered nothing short of redemption.

It had been easy for Ray to pull up alongside in his gray Cadillac and get her in the car. He asked her to stop so that he could speak with her about urgent business of the school. She only hesitated because she didn't like the looks of the young man in the backseat. He had long hair with bad skin and a pointed nose. The way he stared made her wish for the shield of her habit and cassock in place of her sweatpants and t-shirt. She knew the young man's type. She had dealt with his kind enough times as a girl to know a bad fellow when she saw one.

Ray Hamilton left the engine idling and walked around to the passenger side. She stepped into the ditch and eyed the small farm a quarter mile away. An urge to dash across the pitted field of weeds as fast as she could spun inside of her like a hurricane. The wind shifted and carried a whiff of hay from the chicken coops at the side of the white farmhouse. Her legs twitched.

"Please excuse the unorthodoxy of this request, Sister," Mr. Hamilton said. He was nearer, holding open the back door like a gallant in a movie. He smiled in that way that made the mothers on the PTA swoon. The silver cross around his neck flashed in the hazy sunshine.

Ray Hamilton served as the president of the school board. His financial contributions kept St. Rose Academy running. Without him, the school would not have been able to afford her job teaching Honors Chemistry to the girls. A job she loved. A job she would lose if she ran away from him like a madwoman. She could have nothing to fear from Saint Ray Hamilton, Knight of Columbus, Vice Chair of the Chamber of Commerce.

"This is a matter of some delicacy. Please don't deny me," he said. His ring finger tapped against the window glass. It was strange that he would approach her here, in the middle of the flats. It was odd that he wanted her to sit in the backseat with a strange man. Her stomach fluttered an urgent warning.

But her first impulse was always to distrust, especially men. The internal warnings were phantom pain from an old wound. Her past was done. Ray Hamilton was a married man, the father of one of her students. She should be grateful that he valued her opinion. She was still unused to living according to God's plans amid good people. If she were ever going to have the peace of faith, she would have to learn to trust.

She ducked into the car and gazed toward the farm across the field. Ray walked back around to the driver's side and got in behind the wheel. The smell of his cologne coated the back of her throat. She yearned to roll down the window for fresh air but was afraid to appear rude. The man next to her smiled and shook his head at a private joke.

Saint Ray Hamilton gunned the engine and the car squealed down the road to a remote lot by the Mad River Beach where he and the man in the backseat took all hope of faith and peace and gnashed them between their teeth like bones.

It began with the sudden violence of Billy's elbow like a battering ram bashing her head against the window glass. She blacked out for a moment, then awoke in pain so acute it confused her. She forgot where she was. Her sweatpants were balled on the floor. This wasn't happening.

The cold air on her bare legs sparked her into action. "Hail Mary, full of grace …" she began. This was a Catholic man. He could be reminded of shame. But Ray clamped his hand over her nose and mouth when she prayed aloud. His ring scraped her gums as she bucked. She couldn't breathe. She couldn't breathe. Then he flipped her over, smashing her face into a seam in the backseat. He entered her from behind. She yelled in a voice so guttural it was strange. *No.* As she bled, there was nothing but panic, and the noise of Ray Hamilton grunting. She was caught between tectonic plates grinding her into dust, and something ripped inside of her with a searing pain. She struggled to focus only on her own papery gasps, each one taking her to the next until they formed a prayer of their own in her head.

Live through this. Live through this.

After Ray, then Billy. Billy was quick, nervous. Then Ray again. He moved on top of her like a lover this time, missionary style. He slapped her to consciousness when her eyes rolled into a blackout. He leaned in close as he tore her in two. She breathed the smell of yeast, her own sweat, Ray's cologne. She swallowed a flume of vomit because releasing it would mean he would surely kill her, and she meant to survive this. This annihilation of her body was familiar in the way it hurt, in the chaos of pummeling fists. She knew her old enemy, helplessness, as Ray bent her like a doll so that her knees spread above her face. Over the hours, panic soured to numbness. She clung to the knowing that she'd survived this before. She would survive this again. Where prayers had hummed before, now blew a much more certain wind. She would survive this. She would do whatever it took to live. She turned her head, her cheek slimy against the vinyl.

Her faith in her own survival was unshakable.

Chapter 15

November 17, 1989
Del Rio Beach, California

Angel

~⌒~⌒~

A NGEL AND RUSSELL stood at the lip of the giant mouth carved into the ground by bulldozers. The tires gouged crisscrossed tracks in the mud.

A winter wind blew from the west smelling of kelp and brine. Angel's toes were so cold in their boots that they felt stubbed. Down the street other earthmovers roared as they scooped away other collapsed buildings. The machines left behind scoured holes.

A square-shaped maw in muddy ground was all that remained of the shelter. The earthquake had eaten her job and her home. She truly was kin to Jerry. Sometimes she ran into him, wandering the streets with his finger pointed at phantom offenders. The worst had happened as he had warned them.

They pretended not to notice the tabloid reporter lurking a half block away, but Russell kept an eye on the guy. They had ducked into an alley and lost him for a while between crumbling buildings. No one knew the wrecked city better than Russell and Angel. They wandered the ruined streets in the long days and often the nights too when they didn't sleep.

The lives lost here had left no evidence. No blood in the dirt. The earthmovers had scraped it as clean as the hole left behind a pulled tooth.

The heat of Russell's body warmed her back. They had built a daily routine out of visiting the shelter site. It was like the edge of a dead volcano. They stood and paid homage to a cold and silent Pele who never answered back.

Thank you that I lived, Angel prayed. *Fuck you that I might as well have died.*

Every day Angel approached the pit with a pearl of hope that the prayer would work this time. She really wanted to feel something. Judith had kidnapped her. She'd been a missing person up until a month ago. Angel waited to feel mad or sad or even relieved. She waited and waited and it never happened. The story had ruined her life but it still didn't feel like it was hers.

The first tabloid headline read Murdered Girl Found Alive. One of Russell's roommates brought the cheap newspaper home and Russell balled it up and set fire to it in the backyard. "It doesn't make sense," he said. "You were never murdered."

Angel stood at the side of her almost grave where the shelter used to stand and felt murdered.

If she felt like talking, she would have suggested they stop the daily pilgrimage. It didn't do them any good. But Russell seemed to want to keep going on the long afternoon walks. Visiting downtown just served to remind Angel that for her the earthquake had been an apocalypse.

Not only had the earthquake destroyed her job, her home, and the people in her care, but it had also stolen her mother. If it weren't for the earthquake and the television press, her mother wouldn't have been arrested. The deepest pages of her story would have remained unopened and nobody would have cared.

Without the earthquake, Angel would not have known where she came from. Knowing who her real mother was meant nothing to her. She'd never met Teresa Hamilton and now no one knew where she was. The earthquake stole the mother she knew and left her with a shadow stranger who was everywhere and nowhere. Nobody could stop talking about Teresa Hamilton, but no one knew where she could be. Judith had said she was living under the name Reese Camden, but nobody could find her either. Angel had a hard time keeping the names straight in her new old life story. Only guilty people changed their names so often. She could only remember ever being Angel Kelley. The name Crystal Hamilton didn't fit her. Now she would never know for sure who she was anymore.

As for Russell, Angel couldn't tell what the earthquake stole from him because he wouldn't talk about it. They could not breach the long silences between them. They clung to each other like drowning people who had to conserve their energy. She craved talk but maybe words were as much a waste of air now as they had been under the desk.

She did know that Russell was a different man since the earthquake. The laugh lines on his craggy face drooped. No one would guess he once baked for a living. He no longer smelled of vanilla cake.

He gripped her hand as they walked west. This wasn't a place for humans. This was bad land. Metal chain-link fences bisected the streets where college student buskers used to sing Bob Dylan songs in lovely voices trained in suburban musical theaters. The only music left downtown was the Holy Cross

Church bell ringing a five o'clock Mass nobody attended.

"He's there," Angel said. She meant the reporter. His camera clicked behind them like an insect scuttling on metal. But Russell was looking ahead.

"Jerry," he said. Sure enough, Jerry rocked along the sidewalk right toward them. He was a sailor on a rolling ship. If he recognized them it didn't show in his hooded eyes peering from beneath his hair's wiry fringe.

Angel blocked his path. "Do you remember me, Jerry? It's me, Sweet Angel."

Jerry halted in place and gazed at the sidewalk. Russell tried to draw her into the street but Angel wouldn't move.

"It's me, don't you remember? Say you see me." She needed him to know her. If he recognized her then maybe she did exist in the world. She was tired of being a ghost. She shook free of Russell's hand and lifted her palms to Jerry's face. He let her touch him, but his eyes stormed. He looked over her shoulder at the approaching cameraman.

"The manifestation of suicide kings is the shotgun conspiracy," Jerry said. "It's the way of the world and the world of the way."

"Yes," Angel said.

"You think you know," he said. He smelled like old piss and skunkweed. "There is a man there with an eye of a mechanic and a mechanical eye," he half growled.

"Yes," Angel said. "He's bothering me, Jerry. He means to take my soul."

Maybe Jerry knew her and maybe he didn't, but he barreled after the tabloid guy, wagging his long and terrible finger. The reporter called for help but he shouldn't have bothered. The police weren't cracking down on the homeless these days. They had bigger fish to fry now that the ground beneath the city's feet turned out to be the real felon.

"You shouldn't have done that," Russell said. He led her through an alley.

"Do you think Jerry knew me?"

"It doesn't matter," Russell said. "He's dangerous. You shouldn't touch him."

Angel kept silent. She and Russell linked hands again and walked into the wind toward the water. At the end of the street, the Pacific Ocean spread to the horizon like molten steel in the gray evening.

On the pier the air was thick with fried clams and cotton candy. According to the Del Rio Beach Boardwalk, the earthquake had never happened. Seals barked in the water among the pilings. Men in dungarees and beaten-down field hats held poles off the railing. They used small live fish for bait. Angel peered into a bucket of the doomed, their tails and fins flapping against one another in dirty water.

Tourists huddled together for warmth. They trailed in and out of stores that sold waffle cones, souvenirs, clam chowder in bowls made of bread.

Angel and Russell only had to walk fifteen minutes to escape any sign of the gaping holes in the ground. The lonely church bells didn't reach as far as the sea. Across from the beach was the Ultramat Laundry with its rolling dryers. There on the corner was the Los Palmas Taco Bar and a line of people out the door chatting and laughing. People were living as if nothing had happened.

Angel liked it better downtown, with the broken buildings and chain link and mostly empty streets. She liked talking with the National Guardsmen who stood at the fences surrounding the rubble. This wasn't peacetime, Soldier. This was not Ordinary Time.

A man caught a fish on the line and as he reeled it in, Russell enclosed her in his arms. She tucked her hands under his flannel shirt. She faced southward. Just five hours down the highway in that direction Sundullah would be waiting for her when his tour was over in January. He'd invited her to go, but she hadn't said yes. She hadn't said no. The problem was that everything was broken, including herself. It was hard to imagine rebuilding in the negative space. If she went to Sundullah now, she would be like the gaping hole where the shelter once stood. She was an empty place where once there was life. Maybe that was all she would ever be again.

Russell wasn't Sundullah. She didn't love him and she doubted that he truly loved her. But as they walked down the pier toward town, they held each other as if they were children left alone in a forest with no trail of stones to mark the path home.

Home was a room in the house Russell shared with three college guys. They went in through the back window in case any more reporters hid in the bushes along the street. Russell didn't talk about their evasion tactics anymore. She just followed him and trusted. They snuck through backyard gates. They climbed through the windows of Russell's house like thieves.

Jane's Addiction whined from one of the bedrooms. A lumpy party gathered in the space that would have been called the family room if a proper family lived there. Angel found a place on the floor. A cold black light illuminated neon paintings on the walls. On the canvases, red bulbs and blue stalactites pushed through yellow skies.

The artist, one of the roommates, never painted unless he was on acid. He sprawled on a couch. He had blond ringlets like a child in a Victorian photograph and wore overalls and no shoes. He passed her a water pipe. Angel's t-shirt glowed blue in the fluorescent light.

Angel passed the bong without partaking. The invisible feeling in the warm darkness was nice. She could be anyone with her glowing shirt and silence. The pot-smoky conversation jumped from worthy professors to good campus bands to the cheapest burrito stand. Another roommate named Mike had provided the night's weed for everyone as a gift. He sat on the La-Z-Boy chair cross-legged, a frog king on a throne.

"Aren't you that girl from the news?" The conversation in the dark turned to her.

"Drop it, man," Russell said. His voice had the authority of a grown man in this blue-black room of boys.

"We're your friends here, man. It's cool," Mike said.

"I heard about this guy in Uruguay who lived for two weeks under a building after an earthquake by drinking his own piss," another voice said.

"Is that what happened to you, Angel?" Mike said.

"Watch out, man," the coil-haired painter said in a stoned drawl. "The *Enquirer* offered us like twenty thousand bucks if we got anything on you. More if we took pictures. Mike's being a douche."

Russell hoisted Angel off the floor by the elbow. "Give me your keys, Mike," he said. There was a jingle and a muffled apology. Russell grabbed her coat off the kitchen table on their way through.

The moon was a stingy sliver in the sky. A white van was parked across the street as it had been every night since Angel got out of the hospital.

"We need to get out," Russell said. "What are we staying in town for?"

"You have that new job at the machine shop."

"I'm no good at work right now," he said, shaking his shaggy head. "I can't stand having a roof over my head and all that heavy shit on shelves. Freaks me out."

"One of them has a telephoto," Angel said. The camera's lens was a round eye in the van window. They weren't after her. They were interested in Crystal Hamilton Lopez, the lost child of the north. Angel knew the story by heart. They wanted the murdered daughter of Terrible Teresa. They had never found Crystal's body but everyone had been so sure the mother was guilty. Teresa's own father was about to testify that she took the girl out of the house in the middle of the night and never returned. She hid the body so well that nobody could find Crystal's remains.

Angel thought of the photo of the smiling man with greased-back hair. Her grandfather, or so they said. The FBI agents showed it to her several times, as if the repetitive questioning would shake loose a memory. The picture gave her a vague sense of dread, but she had no memories of the man or the events. Someone shot Teresa's father, Angel's grandfather, dead in the street the day before he was supposed to take an oath and testify in a court of law against her. The open and shut case against Teresa died with no body and no evidence of a crime. They had to release her in the end. She left town with her lawyer and nobody ever saw or heard from either Teresa or Crystal again.

Until now.

Because Teresa didn't take her daughter into the woods and kill her. A young nun who was Teresa's high school chemistry teacher took Crystal and ran away with her. The teacher changed Crystal's name to Angel and made the child her own. Some reports suggested that Sister Judith was involved in an illicit relationship with Teresa's father. Anyone who knew Judith would know that was bullshit, but the strangest part of the whole story was that Judith wasn't denying having an affair. In fact, she wasn't saying anything to anyone anymore.

Such was the story of Angel's life and death and life again. Though it was her story, it had nothing to do with her. The story of Crystal was as removed from her reality as the stories in the book of fairy tales her mother read to her at night. In reality, she was Angel who suddenly knew fear and who now had no mother and no life. She had crumbled into a pile of rubble that machines scooped out and turned into an empty hole.

She had shadowy memories of an angry first mother but that didn't make her feel as though she were truly Crystal Hamilton. She was a nothing girl now. It was incredible that someone would pay so much for a photograph of her. The joke was on them. After it was developed there would be nothing in the frame.

Now Judith refused to see her or even speak to her.

"Judith doesn't want you involved in this any further. She says you've been through enough as it is. She says to go to your life," Detective Redleaf had said the day before when Angel made another trip to the FBI headquarters in San Jose to visit her mother. She waited in one of the interrogation rooms where the furniture was screwed to the floor. "That's all she wants to say to you, I'm afraid. She won't see you."

The detective didn't like her mother, Angel could tell. Yet she wanted Angel to stay. She offered to take her to lunch to talk away from the others. But Angel pushed the woman's hand off her shoulder. She drove her mother's truck back over the Santa Cruz Mountains alone.

As much as the rebuff hurt Angel, she understood her mother's strange logic. Judith thought she was doing the right thing. Since Angel had learned that she was Crystal Hamilton, she felt out of place in her own life. She was moving around in an unreal purgatory of someone else's memories. Judith wanted her to get out of town and leave the whole mess behind. Without knowing the whole story, she counted on Angel to go back to Sundullah.

They ducked to avoid the photographer. Mike's motorcycle was parked in the driveway. Russell passed her a helmet but Angel refused it. She climbed behind him and zipped her jacket to her chin. Russell jumped on the starter. As soon as the engine rumbled underneath their legs, the van started.

"I'll lose him," Russell said. He seemed to enjoy this. Evading the press was a game that got his mind off things.

On the back of the bike her hair whipped around her face. They cruised toward the Boardwalk. Drug-addicted wraiths loitered in the dirty haloes of streetlamps. The roller coaster towered above the quiet park, a white dinosaur in the slight moon. Russell wove through the dead streets past dark houses and closed motels. Angel tightened her hold on him. His stomach had a layer of softness over a granite core. She held him and thought that comfort was easier than love.

On the freeway toward Monterey she squeezed her eyes shut, and the world was nothing but the thunder of the wind and sea. Russell accelerated into the fast lane. They exited the freeway and rode along a frontage road. He turned off the engine in a dark parking lot. They waited in the silence. No one followed.

"I can't believe you lost them," Angel said.

"I told you I could take care of you." Russell swung off the bike. The front of her body felt the shock of cold. His hulking form disappeared over the dunes.

"Follow me," he called out.

On the other side of the hill, Russell sat in the sand like a child, taking off his boots and socks.

"Have you ever done this?" he asked.

Angel knelt beside him. "What are we doing?"

He pulled her onto his lap. He took off her boots and socks.

"Follow me," he said again. He tore off toward the water in his bare feet. Angela ran, knowing that she would never be able to catch him. He was testing her bravery. It was fun at first but the cold in the sand began to seep up her leg bones. She stiffened and ran in marionette jerks and hops. Russell hooted in the shadows. The foam of the waves shimmered in a distance that grew longer with every painful step.

Powerful cramps gripped her muscles from the bottoms of her feet to the backs of her knees. She stumbled and cried out, her calves like rocks. She forced herself to keep running but in a few more yards she fell.

Russell veered back. He swept her into his arms and barreled down the beach. She clutched his neck, praying that her own would not snap.

His feet slapped wet sand as they neared the waves. He set her down and she braced for icy water, but after the brutality of the cold sand, something else. The ocean was warm and soft as a caress.

Russell kicked up foamy arcs. Angel jumped over a low wave and considered immersing her whole body in the tepid tub the ocean had become. Things weren't as they should be. The earth insoluble under their feet, the

Pacific Ocean warm on a cold night. All of life had entered a dreamscape.

"Let's head back before it gets cold again." Russell put his arm around her shoulder and guided her past the reach of the tide. He motioned for her to climb onto his back. She tightened her thighs around him as he humped up the beach. He was the giant in one of her mother's stories whose seven league boots allowed him to traverse a mile in a single step. Angel could go anywhere with a giant like Russell. Her bravery passed the test.

Sand blew in their faces as he trudged toward the dunes. He stooped so she could spill off his back. While patting around for their boots, their hands met in the cutting sawgrass. Russell nudged Angel, searching for her lips in the darkness. She let him find her. He tasted like salt. Angel cupped his jaw in her palm. This was the face of someone mighty. A man this size and strength could protect anyone.

The cold settled in. When her teeth rattled, he held her against his chest as if he could still her shivering by force.

THEY RETURNED LATE that night, soaked with seawater and exhausted. Despite the kisses on the beach, they did not have sex; they hadn't since the earthquake. They held each other for warmth and so chased off the cold and horror. Since Sundullah's visit, Angel felt like a traitor sharing Russell's bed even to sleep. But solitude would have meant oblivion. Her heart shrank into a petulant stone at the thought of being alone. She shouldn't have to face the nights by herself. She closed her eyes, her ear pressed to Russell's chest, and thought that Judith was right about one thing: she had been through enough already.

ANGEL WOKE HUDDLED in a corner of Russell's dark bedroom. A three foot-long grasshopper picked its way across her arm. She opened her eyes wider to unsee it but it continued to crawl, impervious to her waking.

Russell thrashed on the bed across the room. He banged the headboard. She yelled at him to wake the fuck up, praying to God that she would too. She refused to blink, refused to look away from the giant insect that crawled toward her face. She yelled, though great wads of bunched spiders fell from the ceiling, ready to land in her eyes and mouth.

The walls reverberated with the housemates' fury. Angel groped for the light. She crawled across the floor until she found the nightstand lamp to pull the chain.

Russell groaned like an animal, his arms cutting the air like scythes. She shone the lamp in his face. The grasshopper crawled across her back, his pincer feet catching on the fabric of her t-shirt.

Russell lifted his hand against the light. She ducked to avoid getting hit and dropped the lamp. She swatted at her back with desperate hands. Her shoulders lifted to her ears in fear and disgust. The spiders would crawl into her ears.

Then the spiders faded. The grasshopper too. Russell's chest heaved. His eyes were wild. Angel slumped on the floor to catch her breath. She knew better than to touch him until he was fully awake. She had a bruise on her shoulder from making that mistake a few nights before.

Russell's ragged breath turned to sobs, as it did when he was snapping out of it. She smoothed the blankets and shook the sand out of the sheets. The walls shook with one last pounding from a housemate. Russell made a fist to return the message but Angel took it in her hands and shook her head. They sat until the house settled around them. There would be hell to pay from the other guys in the morning.

They kept the light on. Angel lay staring at the ceiling, not daring to close her eyes. Russell's back was hot and wet with the vinegar sweat of fear. When he began snoring, she crept out of the bed and rifled through her backpack for the book Sundullah had returned to her. She had not looked at it since leaving the hospital. Feeling its weight in her hands made her wonder if Sundullah was gone from her life for good. She pressed her nose into the edges of the pages. They used to read the fairy tales together when they were young. It seemed like a dark forest of time ago.

She padded into the kitchen and sat at the wobbly thrift store table. Opening the book unleashed the deepest memories of childhood. A brown stain stiffened the first pages. She ran her fingers over it. Maybe Sundullah had learned how to grow armor and could fend for himself without a memento of Angel for help. The thought made her hopeful and sad at once. There were days when they were in high school that it took her so long to talk him into going into the building that the teachers had to mark them late for class. There were nights when he visited her at the cottage and she had to talk him out of anxiety attacks so that he could return to Los Angeles in time for a recording session.

"Don't make me go back alone," he had said after their last visit together before she knew she was pregnant. They stood at the gate in the airport. He clutched her waist, his face buried in her neck. "Those people are alligators chewing on me. My parents, Uncle Eli, everybody. I'm only safe with you."

He was supposed to be in Amsterdam in the week before Thanksgiving. She looked at the time, wondered if he was on stage at that moment. Maybe he was in a hotel bed with a groupie. She shook away that thought. She had no right to be jealous. He seemed a lot less needy in the brief, morphine-addled time she'd had with him in the hospital room. He was the same but different. He said he would be waiting for her when he returned Stateside in January.

As she did now in private moments, Angel turned over the possibility of traveling to Los Angeles in a few months. She handled the idea of a new future with Sundullah as she would a perfectly intact seashell found on the beach. Anything beyond consideration for the moment would crush the delicate shelter. It would be a much different relationship than before. She was not the strong girl she had once been. Now she knew how it felt to need, and the only other friend she had was an out-of-work baker worse off than she was. Nature had arranged a brilliant revenge against her for having refused the life she and Sundullah made inside her.

In the quiet kitchen she realized that it was a good thing that she could not run to Sundullah now. If Sundullah had forgiven her, then she would need to forgive herself and she couldn't yet. She wasn't sure of anything. Like Sundullah, she was chased by people who found her fascinating for reasons having nothing to do with who she really was. She needed to get out of town and hide for a while. She needed rest, a quiet mind, space to figure a few things out for herself, or else she would just be running broken into Sundullah's life, begging him to fix her. It hadn't worked when he was the broken one. It wouldn't work now.

Angel made a cup of tea and read stories until the sky lightened. She'd decided what to do. Russell moved around in his room. By the time he joined her in the kitchen she had his coffee ready. "We're getting out of here," she said. "Today."

He ran his hand over his face and nodded. "Yeah. Okay." There were now five news vans on the street. Russell stood at the side of the window to study them.

"Motherfucking Mike," he said.

"They're offering a lot of money," Angel said. "I'm his ace in the hole."

"We better go now before I kick his head in." He gulped his coffee, baring his teeth as he swallowed.

"Only problem is I have no idea where to go," she said.

"I do," he said, as she'd known he would. "Pack your stuff. We're leaving."

He left first and drove to the parking garage where she kept her truck. By the time she met him there, splinters studded her palms from scaling backyard fences to evade the alligator reporters and their telescopic lenses.

"Did they follow you?" she asked. None had. She started the truck. Through the speakers a crushing Led Zeppelin guitar riff echoed the thrill of flight. She was getting out. She was stepping off the page. She drove out from under the parking garage ceiling into the cold morning light, grateful for the freedom of the open sky. In his own truck ahead of her, Russell bobbed his head to his own music. She followed him out of town.

This wasn't love. She was not yet ready for love, for the responsibility of anyone's heart but her own. This instead was a great pair of Seven League Boots standing in for love. This was Angel and Russell's Great Escape Part Two, leaving marshy land and nightmares behind. This was a girl Tom Thumb finding a good broad shoulder to ride on, and if that wasn't what she'd always dreamed of, it was good enough for the end of the world.

Chapter 16

October 1, 1967
Arcata, California

Judith

~~~

SISTER JUDITH RAN into the chapel for the lanterns. The students waited with Sister Joanne in the bus. They'd blessed the folded pieces of canvas in a ceremony in the chapel on the Hamilton estate. Then Sister Judith left them on the altar by mistake. She made absent-minded mistakes a lot lately. Forgetting her glasses, misplacing a stack of exams. Each stupid error spun her deeper into hopelessness.

She kept an eye on the big house for any signs of Ray. He had not been home during the afternoon. She was relieved he was gone, but she never relaxed. The whole day felt like playing at the mouth of a dragon's den.

The chapel was dark. She had just gathered the lanterns when Ray jumped out of the gloom. Judith started, her heart hammering so hard it hurt.

"Don't touch me," she said.

"You came back hoping to find me here," he said. He moved in front of the only door. Ceramic statues of Jesus, Mary, and St. Joseph guarded the altar. They held silent testimony. The statue of Mary smiled in submission. She would be the one Judith grabbed to break over Ray's head if he came any closer.

He caught her wrist. She sucked in breath, tasted his cologne. She'd been in such a hurry when she'd run in, but God, how could she not have detected that smell? His grip tightened. With a twist her wrist would splinter like the dry bones of a dead bird.

His eyes shone. She struggled against panic.

"You're breathing funny," he said. "Am I making you sexy, Sister?"

In an instant of violent revulsion she freed her arm. He laughed. "If I wanted you again, I'd have you, Judy. There would be nothing you could do to stop me."

Rage filled her mouth and throat and she wanted nothing but to be the dragon. She would breathe fire and turn him to cinders.

The girls and Sister Joanne waited, the older nun surely ready to scold Judith for her absentmindedness. The bus was as remote as the farm across the field the day Ray found her in the flats.

"Stand aside, Mr. Hamilton," she said. She hated the betrayal of her wavering voice.

He made an exaggerated sidestep as though she were the crazy one. "Until next time then," he said. She ran past him into the blessedly cool evening. The gravel popped under her shoes. Maids cleared away the dishes from the deck where the girls had eaten supper. Mrs. Hamilton gave her an odd look as she bolted past.

"Where were you?" Sister Joanne said. Judith didn't answer. She sat in the empty seat beside Teresa Hamilton—Ray Hamilton's daughter. She was one of Judith's favorite students, and always had been. Maybe now even more so.

Judith and Teresa sat together in silence as the bus driver headed away from the Hamilton's sprawling estate and barreled down the hill toward the ocean.

Judith was going to throw up. She lurched down the aisle. "Please sit down, Sister." The bus driver frowned into the mirror above his head, yet when he met her eyes he pulled over without saying anything further. The doors hissed open on their levers.

She retched in the ferns on the side of the road. Sister Joanne was at her elbow but Judith warded her away.

"I'm okay," she said. Sister Joanne made a clucking sound with her tongue. The driver turned off the engine. The bus bellowed and went quiet. Judith spit into the bushes. The students' eyes were on her. They would be worried. They would be laughing. There would be as many reactions as there were girls watching. Judith wiped her mouth. She walked straight into the forest.

There was no path here. She walked for several yards until the thickness of the trees hid the road. Prairie Creek rushed at the bottom of a ravine about five hundred feet deep. She understood right then that she was going to jump into it. She covered her mouth against the urge to retch again.

Limestone jutted from the sides of the bluff under a lush evergreen canopy. Dripping ferns draped the rock walls. A northern flicker called from the trees, a sound that echoed Judith's loneliness. She stood on the edge of the cliff, her arms spread as if she were a bird testing her wingspan. Suicide was a sin, if sin existed anymore. Lucky for her there was no sin and there was no God.

She had no parents, no family. She just had Sister Joanne and the other nuns she lived with in the convent and they didn't want her anymore. She would decompose in the duff and rise up as one of the trees, her branches reaching from her sides, her face turned toward the sun. There would be no more lying awake at night thinking of the baby she would have had in her arms if it had lived. There would be no more nightmares recalling Billy's hand on the back of her neck, and the stench of Ray's cologne as first he then Billy broke her in two.

She closed her eyes. She imagined how freedom would feel. She would fall with the heaviness of a stone. The filth of what Ray and Billy did and the filth of her baby's blood would fall away and die with her. She would finally be free.

Because the truth was that nothing that happened in the back of Ray's Cadillac killed God. Prayers had not protected her, but she had survived, after all. She had learned from childhood the trick of removing her spirit from her body to keep some semblance of one and survive in the other. When it was over, Ray dumped her off where the nightmare had begun. She squatted in the ditch across the field from the pig farm in the flats until she regained her feet. She limped home and made it to her room and to a hot shower without anyone seeing her. She knelt beside Sister Joanne at evening prayers same as always, her forehead burning and her jaw clenched in shame and hatred, but there was still God.

Six weeks later she felt the heaviness in her uterus and soreness in her breasts that told her she was pregnant. It could have been the child of either of the monsters who had raped her, but from the very start she didn't think of it that way. She would have to leave the convent and that was sad. She would have loved to raise a baby in such a beautiful place, but it didn't bear thinking of. Sister Joanne would reject her soundly when she found out. Nobody would believe that Ray Hamilton had done this to Judith. Not Saint Ray. The Virgin Birth would be more plausible than to believe that their own Ray Hamilton would attack a nun and get her pregnant. Still, this was a miracle. Judith had never dreamed of a baby of her own. Now that one was coming, she understood what the prayers had been for. She understood what the Buddhist monks meant—to pray without ceasing. Her baby would have a heartbeat by now, a tiny, murmuring, constant miracle.

As the baby grew, Judith made quiet plans. She walked to town to make phone calls from the booth in front of the library. There was a friend from Bob and Robyn's foster home in Kern River Canyon. Her name was Betty, and she lived in Bakersfield with her husband and child. She'd be happy to have Judith stay with her. She would need a job but she had a master's degree and a teaching credential. She could find a small home and a babysitter and a church where they could go to Mass. Judith could already feel a little girl's hand in her own. She would never be alone again.

Hiding under the nun's robes, she knew it would be months before anybody saw what was happening to her body. Maybe she'd be able to get through the entire pregnancy without anybody noticing. God had not abandoned her. He was watching from farther away than usual, but she felt His grace. God saw her love for this child despite how it came to be.

God saw her essential self. She wasn't a victim. She wasn't a pure young nun. She was the quiet orphan child watching and waiting and accepting food and shelter when it came to her, knowing to leave no trace and to be no burden. She was the young girl learning to shove a dresser in front of her bedroom door against the older boys, locking herself in for long nights for her own safety. She still hated enclosed spaces.

She was the grateful straight A high school student in Bob and Robyn's group home in the hills, so glad to finally have a good place to live. She was the young novitiate in college and the teacher in the idyllic north woods of Arcata.

Judith was the sum of all these parts of her cast-aside life and more. She was a child of a God who knew her. He had a plan for her. He was the Father who never abandoned her, not once. Not even on the acrid summer nights she'd suffered at the hands of damaged and merciless boys. Not even on the terrible Sunday afternoon in the back of Ray's Cadillac.

It wasn't until she was five months along—when she woke in the night to knife-sharp cramps in her gut and white sheets drenched in blood—that she knew God had died. She bent over while sitting on the toilet, a steady stream of thick fluid dripping from her body. The gem she'd been holding inside of her and cherishing and planning for and loving now clouded the toilet water and gripped her body in horrifying spasms.

No pain she'd ever endured under the rough treatment of other human beings had been anything like this. This was a hot Pentecostal wind scraping her insides bare. This was burning and damnation and none of it made any sense. It was the pure absence of intelligence and grace.

In a few weeks her body healed, but her soul never would. The only thing she could hope for was release.

A wind that smelled of bay leaves came up from the bottom of the ravine and lifted her hair from her face. She wanted so badly to feel clean. She wanted to be nothing but bones and air. Even the birds were quiet as she willed herself to let her body fall. She lifted her chin and her heels and her stomach dropped as she pitched forward.

There was a snapping of twigs and someone squeezed her upper arm with hot fingers and jerked her down. Judith's neck popped with whiplash as she fell on her butt. Pain shot down her arm.

Her first thought was *Ray*. He'd followed her. He didn't want Judith to have the power even to kill herself. But it wasn't Ray. It was his daughter Teresa, holding onto a low-hanging branch for leverage in one hand and a fistful of Sister Judith's sweater in the other. She yanked her back once more so that her head hit the ground with a soft thump.

"Sister. What the hell are you doing?"

Judith pushed herself to sitting, annoyed and embarrassed. "Nothing. Just getting some fresh air."

"At the edge of a fucking cliff?" She leaned over, her own balance precarious at the top of the abyss. "Jesus Christ, that's far down."

"Come back from there," Judith said. "Did Sister Joanne send you to get me?" She rubbed the back of her head.

"I sent myself," Teresa said. Judith could imagine how that went. Teresa wasn't the kind of girl who waited for permission. "So, let's go back already. Okay?" She held out her hands to help Judith stand.

Judith stayed down and looked away. Then she covered her face in her sweater. Teresa stood to the side for a while. Then she sat in the dirt, close enough to extend a scrawny arm across Judith's shoulders. Judith didn't cry but neither could she speak.

"Whatever it is, it can't be that bad, Sister," Teresa said. Her hair smelled like cigarettes. Judith wished for just an ounce of Teresa's toughness. An ounce of her strength. "I mean, come on. You're a nun. How many problems can you have?" She continued to speak as if this was some kind of normal conversation.

"You don't know everything," Judith said.

Teresa fumbled in the waistband of her uniform skirt for a crumpled pack of cigarettes and a lighter. She offered one to her teacher. Judith shook her head so Teresa lit it for herself. Judith should have told her not to smoke but the girl had just rescued her from suicide. She supposed that earned her a pass.

The ember of the cigarette glowed. Soon it would be so dark they would have a hard time finding their way to the bus. Teresa let out a long, smoky sigh. "Well, let me tell you one thing. It might make you feel better to know that someone has it worse than you, okay?"

Judith thought of starving children in Africa, of the Chinese and the Russians with no God, of people dying of cancer, of people in wars. These were the intentions they prayed for with the students every day at St. Rose. Judith didn't want to hear about them. They prayed for millions of faceless people who suffered while no one prayed for her. She moved to stand.

Teresa grabbed her arm again. "You're the only one I can tell this to," she said. "I'm pregnant. What do you think about that?"

"Pregnant?" Judith was shocked. "Are you sure?"

"Yep," Teresa said. She thumbed a flake of tobacco off her lip. The bus honked from the road. Pretty soon the driver would come in after them.

"Whose ...." Judith thought of Ray and his beatific face as he commanded her to do his will in the back of his car. Did he act on his own daughter that way?

"It's Michael's," Teresa said. She stuck her chin out like she was ready to take a punch.

"Michael who?"

"Michael Lopez. My boyfriend."

"Does your mother know?"

Teresa huffed a laugh. "Nobody knows but you, Sister. I haven't even told Michael yet."

She ground the cigarette on the bottom of her saddle shoe. Then she stood and lifted Judith by the upper arm. She had amazing strength for a skinny kid.

"Now we know something about each other, Teacher," Teresa said. The bus driver laid on the horn again and Teresa cursed him. "If you think I'm ashamed of it, I'm not," she said. Her voice was as powerful as her hand pushing Judith away from the ravine and through the brush. "Michael and I love each other. It isn't a sin, I don't care what you say."

"I never said—"

"The problem is my dad. He'll kill Michael. You think I'm exaggerating? I'm not. He'll kill him."

"What are you going to do?" Judith asked. She knew Teresa wasn't exaggerating. Maybe she knew better than most what Ray Hamilton would do.

"I'm going to make sure you get on the bus in one piece. Then we're going to do this prayer thingy at the beach. Then we're all going home."

"But I meant the baby."

"I know what you meant." She poked Judith in the back to keep her going.

The din of girl talk and laughter poured from the bus. When the driver saw them he strode forward in case they decided to run away again. He took Judith's arm and guided her over the ditch like she was an invalid.

"No more stops," he said.

Sister Joanne chattered admonishments, but Judith slid past her to sit again beside Teresa. Teresa reached across and opened the window for her, even though the driver had said not to. No one objected. The air blew cold and sweet on Judith's face and she felt different than before.

The girls talked around them. Judith and Teresa sat alone in a space held by their secrets. By the time they got to the beach, the horizon glowed in purples and reds. Judith led everyone by the rising moonlight to the water. In the cold breeze the girls lined up to take the lanterns out of Judith's hands.

"Say prayers, girls," Sister Joanne called. "Then let them free so that our special intentions fly to heaven."

The girls stopped their noise during the lighting of their lanterns. Teresa and Judith held lighters to the fuel packets at the mouths of the canvas balloons until they burned on their own. The students held them in two hands as the stiff material billowed with the heated air. They glowed like fireflies running across the sand toward the churning surf.

Eighteen girls said their prayers then let the lanterns rise. Teresa stood still as the foam of the sea licked her shoes. She bent her head over her light. She looked so young. Judith's heart filled like the lanterns she had sewn late into the nights when sleep brought nothing but a void. She placed a hand over her chest to feel it beating.

The umber lights danced on the cross breezes over the water in the dark. The word *haunted* came to Judith's mind as though someone had whispered it in her ear. The sky lanterns were eighteen glowing, lonely messengers floating over the Pacific. They began together but headed to sea on solo journeys.

Teresa kicked her shoes up the beach. She waded into the water past her knees.

Sister Judith said nothing but took off her own shoes and followed alongside the girl. Maybe Teresa meant to walk in too far and let the waves make her decisions for her.

But Teresa wasn't the suicide kind. The water surged above her knees. Teresa gazed into the flaming lantern. Her face glowed in the fire. Her lips moved in a secret prayer.

Judith closed her eyes to say her first words to God in months. When she opened them, Teresa had let go of her lantern and moved to her side. They grabbed for each other as a wave knocked them unsteady. The receding tide sucked at their legs as they walked backward, out of the surf.

Teresa's lantern danced above their heads. They retreated to where the foam fizzled on the wet sand. Judith watched the lantern, her whole heart pleading to a probably empty sky. She prayed for the baby inside of Teresa. She prayed that the young mother would be okay. She prayed that the baby would live and that Teresa and her young man would find a way to be happy together with their family of three. It was a holy trinity of the most sacred kind. No god could hope to meet its magic.

She would help Teresa with this baby. She would advocate for Teresa at the school and provide advice and kindness. This would be a new purpose and a reason not to die. The long moment at the top of the ravine would recede in her memory. She would make herself forget it. She was a part of the life of a new baby.

Sister Judith let Teresa drag her on a run. Their bare feet splashed in the water and they were laughing. They were powerful together. Here, with the ocean and the wind on their side, Ray Hamilton was a puny thing.

"Everything is going to be okay," Sister Judith whispered in Teresa's ear. They sat side by side on the way home with sand in their hair and Sister Joanne too angry at them for getting their clothes wet to speak.

Teresa turned her face to the window. Her eyes reflected back at Judith in the glass against the black night.

"Everything is going to be okay," Sister Judith said again.

Like a child, Teresa grasped Judith's hand, but she remained silent and would not agree.

Chapter 17

Angel

⌒‿‿⌒

THE DRIVE TO Creekside traversed the Santa Cruz Mountains, Silicon Valley, and miles of oak covered hills on either side of the Central Valley. The mountain sentinels of the Sierra Nevada emerged from a blue haze. Snow covered their tops and ridges in the far dreamland at the end of the long road.

Angel followed Russell, though he drove too fast. Her truck's engine block rattled with the exertion. They never talked over directions or made a decision over a map. She had to stay with him or be lost.

The radio newscasters broke in between songs and barked her story. The mountains would be a good place to hide until she was forgotten. The mountains would block the public from view. Maybe in a geological age people would forget about the earthquake and the ghost daughter. Maybe she would forget herself and be able to start a new life in a house in the woods.

When she switched the channel, a Sundullah song leapt like an ambush from a local station, and she switched it off for good. The radio dial was a minefield. She would never not love Sundullah, but love didn't protect her from anything. Her love had been a bad shelter. It didn't protect their baby. She didn't need his hopeful love songs reminding her of what she had lost.

She put in a cassette from a stack borrowed from Russell. The rest of the way she listened to Led Zeppelin, Janis Joplin, Creedence Clearwater Revival. Russell liked oldies so she did too and that was fine.

Granite made up the tectonic underground in the mountains. She'd learned in Geography and Landforms in her freshman year of college about prehistoric glaciers carving rivers and canyons out of pure rock. Solid granite held the dirt together here and that made it safe. There were fewer earthquakes in the mountains than by the sea.

The valley rose into foothills and then inclines so steep her ears popped. The road twisted through a glacier-cut canyon of sheer rock. The Feather River roiled over jagged boulders parallel to the highway. Russell's backlights glowed, and he pointed right before turning to cross a wooden bridge, slick with rain.

The bridge gave way to a narrow and muddy trail. She trundled behind Russell until a rectangular mobile home appeared through the trees. She parked alongside his truck. With the engine off she could hear the gurgle of the river down the bank. Trees surrounded the property and shielded it from the highway. With a surge of good cheer, she got out and ran to Russell. He pulled her close. The wool of his red plaid shirt tickled her ear. He smelled like cigarette smoke, diesel, and anti-freeze. She breathed him in.

"I love it," Angel said. The damp piney air felt like home more than any place she had ever known. She was overcome with a strange feeling of nostalgia. Strange because she'd always lived in towns, never in woods.

Russell peered down at her face. "You okay?" he asked.

"Yeah," she said. She rubbed her face in his scratchy wool shirt. They would make a life here for a little while. A long rest was enough for both of them to hope for. It wasn't much to ask.

Later that night Angel tucked sheets and blankets around the king sized mattress that took up nearly the entire smaller bedroom. The master bedroom was on the other side of the trailer jumbled full of boxes and broken furniture. The trailer belonged to Russell's uncle, who used it in the summer for fishing trips. Pale-yellow Coors cans were piled in the sink, but one of the burners on the stove worked. The oven worked. They turned it on to chase away the mildew and cold damp, and smoke billowed from it. The next day Angel would clean the oven and then make cookies to fill the place with the smell of warm baking.

The wind whistled through the treetops and rattled the trailer. Only an inch or two of flimsy metal wall separated them from the outside. They could not even be called walls. They seemed as thin and light as the Coors cans. In the event of collapse, she and Russell would pop from underneath with no problems. These walls didn't offer much protection, but they also couldn't do any damage.

Maybe Russell was thinking the same. They were survivors. They had survival in common. The earth herself had tried to kill them and they both escaped her terrible reach alive. They lived when everyone else around them died. Angel watched Russell brush his teeth and felt exhilarated. The newspapers were right about her survival being a miracle. In this dumpy trailer in the middle of nowhere, she was gripped with a sudden gratitude for being alive.

Angel pressed her back into Russell's body in the bed. He was as substantial as a wall was supposed to be. He would be her shelter, at least for a while. He put his arms around her from behind. He kissed the back of her neck and moved his hands over her hips. He was not Sundullah, who knew her body. He was not Sundullah, whose lips were full and generous and sweet-tasting. She craned her neck to kiss Russell and his stubble was rough on her cheek.

Russell was with her in the real and the now. She turned to face him. Angel had to think as a survivor if she were truly going to survive. She had to forgive herself for everything she had done, for everything she was about to do. She wore sweatpants that he easily slipped off of her still-sore hips and legs. The bruises were the last souvenirs of her time under the desk. He ran his fingertips over the fading blotches that marked her skin like an animal pelt. She was sad to see them fade. She wished they were permanent tattoos marking the disaster on her skin. They were proof that she had been beaten by the earth and lived. After that kind of fight, it didn't matter what she did, or who she did it with. She was only responsible for herself. The only true moral obligation was to live.

Angel shrank into a Thumbelina-sized woman under Russell's hands. The calluses on his palms scratched at her back, and for a moment she forgot her own name. His mouth covered hers and tasted of toothpaste and tobacco and whiskey. He lifted her so that she rode him, his fingers gripping her hips, guiding her rhythm. He brought her down again and again until he shuddered and cried out. She ran her fingers through his long hair and thought of dreadlocks. Exhilaration gave way to sadness.

Russell threw his arm over his eyes and lay in silence. She climbed off him and went to the bathroom. In the cold light she filled the sink with water and splashed it on her face. She watched it swirl down the drain. She grasped for the careless happiness that she had felt when they arrived, but it slipped away, leaving a hollow place inside of her. In the mirror, her eyes were purple with exhaustion, her cheeks sunken. When she returned to the room, Russell was already snoring. She molded herself to his back, measured her own breaths to his.

IN THE MORNING, a light rain ticked on the aluminum roof. Angel arched her back in a painful stretch and listened for movement in the trailer. When there was none she got up and pulled on her clothes. Her jeans, which had been snug before the earthquake, hung off her hips. Her stomach stretched like a canvas. She never wanted to eat since getting out of the hospital. When she tried, she smelled the meaty stench coming through the bricks. Maybe that would fade here in the mountains, along with her nightmares.

The air in the trailer was cold and wet as a bog. Russell had left a note on the metal-ringed kitchen table. *Gone for supplies.* She flipped through the cupboards in search of coffee or tea. The shelves held a dirty Crock-Pot and a mason jar full of cigarette butts. Russell had turned on the electricity and hot water when they arrived. The refrigerator was filthy but cold. The wall heater banged alive when she turned it on. The coils reddened inside the grate like the eyes of a demon.

She rubbed at her own sore eyes. Everything could be cleaned. She was good at cleaning. As long as the water and electricity worked, she could make this shack a home. While she was growing up, she and her mother had transformed a few "in-law units" that were barely glorified garages into cute places to live.

Her mother. Angel stood still for a minute in the tiny kitchen, caught on the barbed wire of the word *mother.* If Judith were there, she would clean the place and make it livable. Angel began moving, tossing beer cans into a garbage bag. She could get a belt to hitch up her pants later that day. They could drive into town together to see if there was a thrift store where she could buy some new things. They would get through the days, comfort each other in the nights.

A tour of the trailer revealed shaggy carpet the color of a ripe avocado in the main room. The trailer wasn't as small as it looked from the outside. In the wide main room, a mirrored wall marbled with golden-colored veins faced another made of false wood paneling. Cardboard boxes and broken chairs were stuffed in the larger bedroom, also paneled in mirrors and fake wood. She turned on a light, then switched it off. It was too much like the bare light bulb in the basement office of the shelter.

She picked a path through the boxes to the master bathroom. A huge whirlpool-style tub overlooked a stained glass window depicting orange fairy-tale mushrooms. The window cast the bathroom in an amber glow. She swished water in the tub to rinse out the dust. This was the only room in the trailer that wouldn't give Sundullah an anxiety attack. If she were here with him instead of Russell they would have to sleep and eat in this bathroom.

She turned the hot water on full blast. There was ginger soap and oil in her bag. She fought her way back to her things in the other bedroom and returned to a full tub. In the hot water her joints softened and became pliable. She palmed her hipbones like handles. She would stay this thin forever. She wanted no sign of her former self, that naïve girl in cowboy boots thinking she was queen of the shelter. Thinking that she could atone for her sins through good works. Redemption was impossible in a story where so many innocent people died in the end.

She sank to her chin. Her love for Sundullah and their baby was a ghost haunting her ribcage. She was tired of the cold drafts they made inside her.

She sank under the water to fill her ears with its roaring.

The front door creaked opened on its springs and bounced shut. Heavy footsteps sounded through the trailer as though they were in the same room with her. She waited for him to call for her but he did not. She stepped out of the water and into a man's flannel robe that was hanging on the back of the door. It smelled musty. She didn't have a towel. Russell would have to direct her to where she could buy the things they needed cheaply. Towels. Soap. Fresh-smelling cleaners. A vacuum. More garbage bags. It would be good work, making this home for them. She could make it into a place where they would hibernate and heal at least for a couple of months. She pictured them taking walks in the afternoons, playing cards at night until they were sleepy and fell together into bed. They would create their own world, their own amnesia. It wasn't a forever solution, but she was grateful to be there, even to have the work to do fixing the place for them to hide in. If she believed in prayers, she would see this random trailer in the woods as an answer to one.

Russell unloaded groceries from a bag. He did not look up. Angel rested her hand on his forearm. He stopped unloading.

"We're having someone over for dinner," he said. His voice sounded strained.

"Who?"

Russell sighed. "My wife," he said.

Angel sat down hard in a cracked vinyl chair. The country motif pattern of the kitchen wallpaper crawled the walls in brown and yellow and white. Flour sacks and honey jugs and stalks of wheat.

"I didn't know you were married," she said.

"I'm not … really," Russell said. He resumed putting away milk, butter, bread. He pulled out a six-pack of beer bottles clattering in a cardboard holder. He wasn't supposed to be drinking. He was an ex-drug addict two years clean. He brought Narcotics Anonymous meetings to the shelter. She watched him put the beers in the moldy refrigerator like it wasn't any big deal.

"Okay," she said. She would ask him about the beer later. She would. "Do you want me to cook?"

He turned from the refrigerator and rushed her. She lost her balance and smashed her nose against his sternum. She breathed through the wool of his shirt, the cigarettes and fuel and outdoors and sweat. She wrapped her arms around his waist as though he were her anchor, her desire a traitor rising in her body.

Sundullah smelled like clove cigarettes. He smelled like soap and clean laundry. His lips were soft and his eyes were always kind and he told her everything he was thinking. He never had secrets from her. Secrets were Angel's undoing, not his. She squeezed her eyes shut.

She let Russell and his secrets hold on to her. His need for her was the flesh on her bones. It was the gravity that kept her from floating away.

"You are so sweet," he said. She held him and let him believe that she was somehow comforting him. She held him in the cold, brown, and yellow country kitchen. The wind rattled the trailer so that it bobbed like an earthquake but it wasn't an earthquake and for that one last moment, it was enough.

Chapter 18

October 3, 1971
Arcata, California

Teresa

～～～

FREEDOM CAME FOR Teresa at midnight. It rapped on the window by the bed where she slept with her daughter. She lay on her side curved around Crystal's back like the shell of a sea snail. The sound that woke her could have been a scratch from a branch in the wind or an owl flying between the trees.

She unlocked the bolts. Even in the moonless dark, she knew it was Michael. He had been in the liquor store on 3rd Street when she'd stopped to buy her father's cigarettes. He turned his back when she came in but she knew him. Her heart filled at the sight of his lanky scarecrow shoulders in his sheepskin-lined denim jacket. His hair spilled over the collar same as always. Her hands shook as she peeled dollar bills from the roll her father made her carry for errands. Michael stood only a few feet away. She could be in his arms in seconds.

Their eyes met sidelong as the man behind the register told her to give her father his regards. He would not have been able to tell that Michael and Teresa knew each other. It took every ounce of Teresa's willpower to leave the store.

He waited outside the bakery the next day as she bought Crystal a donut. He watched them through the window. He was gone by the time they headed to her car. That afternoon Teresa visited the library and headed straight for the children's section. As teenagers they had met there after school. It was the only place they felt safe. She knew he had to be waiting in the library for her and he was. Michael sat in a small chair reading the same ancient edition of *Children's Fairy Tales* that they'd read from as love-struck kids.

She trembled as she set Crystal down in a beanbag chair with a picture book, though Teresa knew she wouldn't look at it. She would sit quietly for as long as Teresa asked but she would keep her eyes on her mother. At nearly four years old, she knew to watch for trouble.

"She's so beautiful," he said. The book of fairy tales lay open on the round table. In the wooden chair made for a child, his knees were higher than his chest. She couldn't talk. Engine grease blackened his fingernails, but his hands were clean. They spread over the yellowed pages like the hands of a giant. All she'd wanted to say twisted in her throat.

She read the title at the top of the page. When they were teenagers they'd loved the stories of girls kept hostage by evil characters only to be set free by acts of bravery. "Rapunzel." "The Three Little Men in the Forest." Now he read another story. "The Youth Who Went Forth To Learn Fear."

"But of course she's beautiful," he said. "She's ours." He reached for Teresa and stopped. His face paled as he stared at her fingers.

She hid her hands under the table. "You're not safe," she whispered. The librarians puttered together behind their desk. They acted like they didn't notice the two big people in the kids' area. Maybe they didn't, but she couldn't count on that. Ray had spies everywhere. Just the dread of him was enough to control her.

"I'm not afraid." He slipped the book inside his denim jacket. "I'm coming for you tonight," he said. He kissed her head. He left her at the low round table with their daughter on her lap as quiet as a doll.

So when Michael came knocking on the window, Teresa left the shed and followed him into the cover of the forest. They collapsed in the duff as Michael covered her face with kisses. When he noticed her shiver he put his hooded hemp sweatshirt over her head. He gently guided her arms through, tracing the bloody Braille of pinpricks on the inside of her arm. He explored her badly healed broken fingers with the rough tips of his own.

"What happened?" he asked.

"Don't ask that. Never ask that."

"I shouldn't be surprised that he forces you to live in the shed," he said.

"It's better than living in the house," Teresa said. "It was what I wanted."

"Please don't defend him," Michael said.

She wasn't defending him. She had more right to hate her father than anyone. She wanted Michael to understand that she had arranged this safe place for them herself. She wanted him to be proud of her.

Michael was doing the talking now. They could escape Teresa's father and never look back. He hid his car in the brush up the road. Michael had an apartment and a job fixing cars in Oregon. He had friends at the college where he was taking classes. He could support them now. They could change their names, he said. They could get married. It was time to set the beautiful hostage princesses free.

"We'll get you off drugs," Michael said. "I'll help you. You'll never have to be alone again." His tracing of the scabby tracks on the inside of her arm gave her chills.

"I'm not really on drugs," she said.

"Teresa, you're so skinny. You have these scars."

"It's just a bump once in a while to get over. You have no idea what it's like for me." It was true that he didn't know. He couldn't accuse her while he built a life with friends and a job in a whole other state. Rage flashed inside of her from a hot place she had a hard time controlling.

"Let's get Crystal and go right now," he said.

She almost went. He was so good. He was so strong and she was almost convinced. But she was afraid he was not strong enough. As much as he hated her father, there was much Michael did not know.

He kissed her again and it was the taste of clean mint and fresh air that she always loved. Michael was the best person she ever knew.

"I'll carry her. She won't even wake up. My car is only a half mile away."

Her whole body broke out in a clammy sweat. A half of a mile was not far enough. Her father's night guards patrolled the roads. She wished Michael had learned more fear, not less, in the years since Ray had run him out of town.

"I can't leave tonight," she said. "Give me two weeks. Two weeks from tonight, come to my window again and I will be here waiting."

She told herself that two weeks would be enough time to get some money. She didn't work this hard in her Cinderella life to leave with nothing. Ray kept cash hidden in different outbuildings on the property. The religious statues in the chapel alone had tens of thousands of cash in bills rolled inside of them.

"I don't care about the money," Michael said. "I have enough money for us, Teresa. We'll never be rich but we'll always have enough. I'll take care of you."

"Two weeks."

He kissed her palms and led her carefully in her bare feet back to the converted shed. He bent over Crystal where she slept in the bed she shared with her mother. Michael stared at his daughter for a long time. He reached inside his jacket and pulled out the clothbound book from the library. Placing it beside her head on the pillow, he kissed her smooth round cheek.

"Tell her I'm your prince," he said. "Tell her that I'm coming to the rescue."

Teresa embraced him one last time. His tears dripped onto her neck. He vanished into the trees and her mouth was full of his name. She ached to call him back and hold him on the braided rug on the floor beside the bed while their daughter slept. If she could be with him for a few more minutes then she could carry his hope and confidence inside her for strength.

But her father had hired men with guns and dogs to protect what was his. If they caught Michael in the woods, they would shred their dream of freedom to pieces. Ray Hamilton was a natural force. He was a violent tornado that ripped homes from their foundations and the skin off of bones.

Teresa stood in the doorway of her shed, listening to the forest. *Don't defend him,* Michael had said. He thought the story was still of the evil father and the good captive girl. He had not seen her in a while and things were not as they used to be.

She was not Michael's girl anymore. She was not even her own girl. She was her father's partner in the secret business the good people of Humboldt County knew nothing about. Teresa ran bags of pills and heroin and marijuana. She monitored sales out of the back of her father's restaurants. She delivered heavy bags in the evenings and stayed up late counting his money.

Only Teresa, Crystal, and Sister Judith entered the converted shed. Her father let her have it when Crystal turned two and then pretended it didn't exist. It was the last place that felt pure.

Teresa wasn't pure. She wasn't the girl she had been. She wasn't the in-love schoolgirl in the plaid skirt stealing Michael's kisses behind the convent school when she was supposed to be at Mass. That crazy love was the one Michael remembered and the one he wanted returned. She didn't blame him. She wanted their love magic too.

Maybe she could be that girl again. In two weeks she could hoard some money, clear her bloodstream, and shift her shape back to the Teresa Michael Lopez loved enough to risk his life to rescue.

There was so much sweetness in Michael. Four years had not left the mark on him that it had on her.

Teresa breathed deeply to calm the panicked thumping in her chest. Her bones shivered like water. She used to be as brave as Michael. She used to be as blind. She trained her ears to hear something as subtle as a twig snap, or the brush of owl wings too soft to alarm a doomed mouse. The night was quiet. Michael had come and gone and no one knew but her. Maybe it had been a dream. With her fingertips she touched her mouth, the warmth of her lips the sole proof that he had been there.

Teresa locked the bolts on the door. Her arms hurt for missing Michael. She wrapped them around Crystal instead. Her daughter's cheek was silky against her own. Crystal would be her lucky charm. Their child would stand in for courage until Michael could be her strength.

Hope swelled in her chest and made her sick. She wanted a bump in her veins. Just a tiny one.

She should have gone with him. But it was too sudden. She was used to watching and dreading. She wasn't used to kindness. She wasn't used to love. He had surprised her. The loving was too much. Raw feelings rankled her insides as though she had swallowed a cactus with long spines. She wrapped a blanket around Crystal and lifted her off the bed. She stood at the window. She could run after him. There was still time.

The trees seemed to shift positions. Ray's men could have been moving in the shadows. Perhaps it would be that pointy-nosed Billy or it could be Ray himself. She yearned for just the smallest hit. If she had just a taste of the warm sugar through her veins then she would have the courage to leave.

Go! her brain screamed. The realization hit her with the force of falling bricks that if she were going to survive then she had to unbolt the door and leave right then. Panic shrieked through its iron beak. Her thigh muscles quivered and then were still.

She wasn't strong enough. She couldn't do it. She lay on top of the bedcovers in agony.

Before the sky lightened in the morning, she skirted the property through the trees and slunk into the outbuilding that Ray had made into a chapel. It stank of funeral incense and her father's cologne. Porcelain religious statues as tall as Crystal lined the walls, staring sightlessly at the seven rows of empty pews. St. Teresa, St. Raymond, St. Catherine for her mother. Their painted half smiles hid a secret only Teresa knew. Teresa grabbed St. Mary around the neck and stuck her hand in the hole at the bottom. She extracted a wad of hundreds and twenties and shoved them in her pockets.

She'd more than earned her share of Ray's blood money. St. Mary went back to her place and Teresa ran to her daughter, sleeping under the protection of the trees. She couldn't leave when Michael first came for her, but she would leave in two weeks. She would be ready. She slipped into the shed and bolted the door. Crystal did not stir as Teresa took her sewing kit from under the bed and her pea coat from over the chair.

The heft of the money in her pockets and the smell of its filth on her hands was as good as courage. She ripped a clean hole in the heavy lining of her coat and spread the bills between the wool layers so there was no bulge. With every stitch of the seam she pulled the needle through and whispered a single-word prayer.

Freedom.

RAY KNOCKED ON the shed door in the late morning. Teresa sat at the card table sipping tea with Crystal while she colored. She'd listened for his approach through the grass. The walls of the shed were thin. He jangled his keys.

"Would you mind coming with me while I run some errands?" he asked. "Your mother can watch the baby."

Teresa nodded and hurried her daughter into her sweater. Ray enjoyed acting as if he was making a polite request. It was one of his tricks.

"Better wear your coat," he said. "It's cold today."

He held it for her to slip her arms through. He patted her back as she locked the deadbolt. The hairs on the back of her neck stood on end. Crystal was silent and stared at her shoes. Teresa took her hand and ran with her across the lawn to the big house. Teresa's mother waited on the back porch, clutching her arms in a thin sweater. The only time Teresa's mother smiled now was in the moment that Crystal ascended the steps. Crystal leaned her thin body against the older woman's hip and the two formed their own private world. Teresa remembered the softening of her mother's eyes and her welcoming smile from when she herself was very young. Yet by the time Teresa was twelve, her mother, exhausted by her father's cruelty, had sunk beneath the foam of the pills Ray provided. The memory of Teresa's mother's love was as fleeting as a memory of a dream. The memory awakened, if only for a few seconds, on the mornings when Teresa left the little girl with her grandmother.

In the driveway, Ray held the passenger door of the Cadillac open for her to ride in front. He was whistling. Teresa flipped through the steno pad she kept in the glove compartment. Anxiety coiled in her stomach and shook a heavy rattle.

Ray was in one of his expansive moods. He wanted to give advice. "You're the only person in this world I truly trust, Teresa. You know that?"

Teresa nodded. She knew better than to interrupt him even to answer a question.

"I'll tell you what the secret to my success is. Are you ready? Here it is. I read people."

They waited at the long stoplight at the intersection by the liquor store her father liked. A homeless man trudged across the crosswalk, his back bent under an enormous pack. Ray jumped the accelerator as the man passed the fender. The man stumbled to his knees, his eyes wide with terror. Ray waved at him while he staggered to the sidewalk like a beetle with a shell he could hardly carry.

The light turned and Ray drove. His face had returned to serious business.

"I know what people want and I give it to them. The thing with me is I can read what it is that people want in a second." He snapped his fingers. His watch flashed from under his suit jacket. "I can tell what you want just by looking at you. I know you better than you know yourself."

Goosebumps sprang over Teresa's arms. She did not dare move. Her cheeks grew hot, and she took a silent breath to cool down. He would notice that she was afraid. He noticed everything.

They stopped at the house where Billy Stamm stayed. If Ray noticed Teresa's fear, he didn't show it. He looked over the flats toward the dunes.

"Here's the thing. This town needs me. I keep the balance. The junkies get what they want. The chamber of commerce gets what they want and so does St. Rose. So do the nuns. So do the kids. I provide for everybody. Just what they want. Write that down."

Teresa didn't know what he wanted her to write exactly. But she wrote anyway. *I know you better than you know yourself.*

"I know things so that other people don't have to. I stay guilty so that the good people of this town can stay innocent. Nobody can hide from me. I know everything."

He knew about Michael. This was what he was telling her. The atmosphere inside the Cadillac was the low heaviness of clouds before a funnel dropped to the ground. Her face tingled. He would bash her head in this time. He would cut out her tongue. He would make the scene in his workshop when he found out she was pregnant look like a tea party.

But his face remained pensive and his eyes stayed focused ahead. "You're the only person I trust," he said again. "You are my legacy in this town."

The idea of being the legacy of Ray Hamilton stunned her. He thought she was a robot that did his bidding. He was positive he had beaten her down badly enough that she would obey him even after his death.

"Uh-huh," she said.

He cut his eyes to her. She should have known better than to speak. How is it that she didn't know better? His mouth moved in a smile she couldn't read. Her misshapen knuckles turned white around the pencil.

Billy emerged from the house and Ray raised a finger to him. Teresa gave Billy a half-wave too. His hair was so greasy she wondered if he ever washed it. She could not imagine him clean. Ray told her to stay still. She did—as still as one of the chapel statues.

When he returned, he looked around but he shouldn't have worried. Nobody was watching them. There were no cops in this deserted part of the flats, and even if there were, the police were her father's friends in this town. Nobody would think to ask what was in the brown paper sack he had just taken from one of the biggest scumbags who ever lived.

He settled in the driver's seat with the package on his lap. "Here's the thing, Teresa. Here's the thing I always say. Are you ready for it? Are you listening?"

Teresa knew better than to make any noise or move.

"Okay, here it is. The universe craves balance. Where one thing is lost, another takes its place. A life for a life."

Ray fished around in the sack and with a crinkle of cellophane tossed a gift to his daughter. The packet landed on the notebook. She regarded it with cold dismay. It contained twice as much as he usually gave her. A moustache of sweat coated her upper lip. The heroin was a scorpion with a dripping tail. It was also a glorious magic genie that could grant her any wish.

Ray kept his eyes on the road as they headed to town. The packet crackled in her hooked fingers.

This time she could read his smile very well.

Chapter 19

November 19–December 10, 1989
Creekside, California

Angel

❧

ONLY TWO OF the burners on the stove worked, but they were enough to make a meal. Angel stirred a pot of bubbling sauce. At a grocery and bait store down the highway less than a quarter mile, they had bought canned tomatoes, an onion, and a dusty jar of dried oregano. There was a refrigerated meat section with cables of red ground beef in white Styrofoam packages. Spaghetti. A wilted head of iceberg lettuce.

Judith always said that with enough love, any meal could be made special. Angel supposed she felt a kind of love for Russell. They were veterans, bound together by calamity. She wished more than anything that he did not have a wife coming to visit. He said they were separated but she had a baby daughter. He had doubts that the baby was his.

Judith would think this situation was absurd. Angel wished she could call her mother. Talking with her would give her a sense of what to do. Her mother always knew what to do.

Meatballs bubbled in the pot. She wondered if the baby would need different food. The oven door hung ajar in order to let out the heat. Though her shins burned, cold air still crept along her shoulders like a yoke. If she were alone she'd take another hot bath. She craved time to think.

Russell hauled boxes from the master bedroom to the storage shed past the trucks. The trees thickened in the falling gloom. Angel wasn't sure exactly when Sheila the wife was coming and she didn't feel like asking. She and Russell were storm-weakened people shoring up for more rough weather on the way. Russell would not meet her eyes nor respond when she touched his back. Only two days earlier, he had promised to take care of her. The thought of finding somewhere else to live was an impossibly heavy burden to bear.

She breathed in the oregano sauce to quiet her yo-yo brain. She and Russell were both haunted by children they weren't ready for. Russell had married Sheila when they were just out of high school. It didn't mean anything, he said. He was wrong about that. Babies meant a great deal, even the unwanted ones. They had a way of coming back to take what they were owed, one way or another.

She turned the heat to low to let things simmer. In her mind's eye her child would have had delicate hands and caramel skin. She would have had her father's green eyes and talent for music. Her fantasies formed around Sundullah by habit. She couldn't picture having children with anybody else.

A gray Camaro grumbled as it pulled in between their trucks. Tree branches reflected in the windshield. Angel wiped her hands on a towel and found she couldn't move. She could only stand at the window and watch while Russell stood, also frozen, at the entrance of the shed.

The car door swung open. A woman with long hair the color of straw got out. Russell held an ax in one hand. The woman strode forward, pulled him by the back of the neck, and kissed him hard.

This woman was trouble. She would be the end of hope for a little peace and quiet.

"Say no," Angel said to the window.

But Russell's back bowed as he dropped the ax. He melted into her kiss and with all of his being said yes.

ANGEL WAITED ON the front steps with the book of fairy tales Sundullah had returned. Teeth clenched, she reread a few of the stories. This was mean, serious cold. Denim was no protection against the icy metal of the trailer porch. The weight she'd lost since the earthquake left her bare to the alpine chill. She wished she could go inside, but she didn't dare.

She read the story "The White Snake" and wished for an apple of life to cut in two and share with Russell to make his heart whole again. Real life didn't offer such easy solutions, let alone magical ones.

She hated it when her teeth chattered. Chattering teeth was a sound from under the desk. She'd have to go back inside soon, no matter what Russell and his so-called wife were up to.

The aluminum door screeched on its hinges, slammed shut. Sheila wore Russell's leather jacket over one of his flannel shirts. The shirt flapped open as she hopped down, revealing a curve of breast.

"Were we making too much noise?" she asked. She held a smooth wooden pipe like a kazoo in one hand and a lighter in the other. She lit the weed so it crackled while she inhaled.

Angel shook her head. Her stomach felt queasy.

"Sorry I was rude when I first saw you," Sheila said. She blew sweet smoke from kiss-shaped lips. "It's not like I can have my husband living with another girl."

"It's okay," Angel said. The dinner hadn't gone well. Sheila had screamed profanities when she saw Angel standing in the kitchen. Then she banished her to the porch so that she and Russell could "say hi."

"But he explained everything." She passed the pipe along to Angel. Angel took it. Getting high was something she'd only done with Sundullah once in a great while, but she thought that she might like some of that fire inside of her lungs. Anything to warm her up.

"Oh, right," Sheila said, grabbing it before she had a chance to toke. "He said you don't partake."

First invited. Then uninvited. Sheila wore the smell of wood smoke like perfume. Her hair hung in bleached ropes down her back. She was as skinny as Angel but bustier. She must have been so much prettier naked. Jealousy twisted in her stomach.

"I'll leave in the morning," Angel said. She closed the book and wrapped her arms around herself.

Sheila wore silver rings over big knuckled hands. "Don't be so hasty," she said. In the trailer Russell stomped in his heavy boots. The refrigerator door opened and closed. There was the tinkling of a fallen bottle cap.

"Russell told me everything you guys went through, you know? He told me he sees you like a sister after he saved your life."

A wind blew the treetops. Angel wondered how often it happened that one fell. The trailer would be light enough in an earthquake but no protection against a falling lodgepole pine.

"Yeah," Angel said. Though it wasn't true. Not even a little bit. Russell hadn't saved her life. No one had. She had simply refused to die while being killed. It wasn't even the first time, if the Crystal Hamilton story had any truth to it. She was the hard-dying kind. The thought warmed her like nothing else had all day.

"So I trust you, okay?" Sheila said, picking bits of residue from her tongue. "I know you won't try to sleep with him."

Sheila had to have noticed that the master bedroom didn't contain anything to sleep on except the one bed. There was no way to miss Angel's things strewn across the room where Sheila and Russell had just had their big reunion.

The porch light gleamed off the ring on Sheila's middle finger. "It's cold as fuck out here," Sheila said. "We're going inside." She stood, held the door open. Russell grumbled about letting the heat out as Angel followed her.

"You tell her your idea?" Russell asked. He sat at the table, his legs crowding the entire kitchen. He was too big for this place. He could outstretch his arms and legs and they would pop through the siding. He could wear the trailer for a hat.

"Not yet. I was too busy freezing to death."

"Smells like pot," Russell said. "I thought you didn't do that shit anymore," he said.

"I don't, baby. I told you."

Angel felt dizzy. She didn't need a call to Judith to know a bad story was unfolding right there. "It's just a little pot," Sheila said with a wave of her bird-talon hand. "So Angel, this is it. We have a kid, right? I'm sure Russell told you we have a child."

"She knows," Russell said. He crossed the living room, disappeared into the master bedroom, and turned on the light. There was the sound of rustled boxes.

Sheila looked after him with her face pinched. "Well, it's fine with me if you stay here, Angel," she said. "Stay as long as you want. For rent payment you can watch Tawny during the day."

"Tawny?" Angel imagined a cat with lots of neck fur and copious whiskers.

"The child," Sheila said. She talked as though Angel were the dumb one between them.

"You want me to babysit?"

"In exchange for room and board. You can be our housekeeper," Sheila said. Her laugh sounded like a window breaking.

Angel shrugged. "Okay," she said. "For a couple days until I figure out what to do." Russell entered the middle room, embracing a television. He plugged it in and turned it on.

"Do you know anything about kids?" Sheila asked. Her eyes narrowed as though she had caught Angel trying to steal something she hadn't earned.

"Do you?" Angel asked. Russell kept his eyes on the screen. Fiddled with a dial.

"Do you have a problem?" Sheila leaned into Angel's face.

This was the moment when a reasonable person would pack her bag and leave. A reasonable person with anywhere else to go would tear into the night before a tree fell or the creek flooded or Sheila tore her heart out of her chest and ate it raw. Even in fairy tales people ran from witches.

But Angel didn't have anywhere else she wanted to go. Things happened fast in real life. There were no enchanted apples. She wasn't ready to leave Russell. She needed time to think things over.

"No problem," Angel said. "For a few days."

"She's almost two," Sheila said. "Think you can handle that?"

"Sure," Angel said. She looked at Russell, his face aglow in the television screen's light. He just shrugged and looked miserable, big in stature only. Inside he was a very small man.

"Fine," Shelia said. She shook off Russell's jacket. "I'll go get our stuff."

She grabbed her car keys off the counter and with another slam of the door was gone.

"You okay?" Russell asked.

Angel shrugged. She was afraid she would start crying and she didn't want to do that.

"I thought she was out of town already, I swear," he said. He lowered to the sagging couch. "I don't need this shit right now."

"But that's your daughter," Angel said.

"Yeah well. That remains to be seen," he said. "Meanwhile, there's that bedroom if you want it." Angel went to see. The mattress was still there, covered now with a brown comforter pocked with cigarette burns, a flat pillow. She stood in the doorway and felt sick.

"You should know that she never stays in one place long," Russell said. "I'd give this a week, tops. Then we can have the place to ourselves again. Think about our next move."

She didn't want to wait. Their next move would be out of there. She had avoided Judith's cottage because it had been rifled through by investigators. News vans with their awful cameras flanked the cul-de-sac outside the bigger house on the property. She had stopped by once to pick up some things, and it was awful to be there without Judith, with reporters crouching in the geraniums outside the window. But they had a lease through December. Maybe the news people had given up. She could cut the police tape crossing the door. The FBI considered it a crime scene. It was better to live in a place where a crime had already been committed than in a place where it felt like one was about to happen.

"You sure you're okay?" Russell asked. She swallowed bitterness when he kissed the top of her head. She left him at the television as she closed the door on the room that was now hers. She huddled under the comforter and woolen army blankets and stuck a tape of Sundullah in her Walkman. The headphones made his voice as intimate as a whisper. She ached for him. He'd never have given Sheila, a girl who looked like she might bite somebody, the time of day. He liked gentle people.

Sundullah had loved Angel. Better still, they had loved each other. She cradled the Walkman in her hands and yearned for a crimp in time so she could pull her life back from the moment she'd ruined it in a single act of cowardice.

She'd lost everything the day she walked into the clinic to get rid of their baby. Barely twenty, she was overwhelmed with taking care of Sundullah.

She was as thin and pulled apart as cobwebs. How cruel that the baby was impossible to imagine until after it was gone. She went into the clinic numb, but she woke from the anesthesia wracked with grief. As she rode the bus home, bleeding, it hit her that after what she had done she could not return to Sundullah.

After the earthquake he had said that he wanted her still. For her part, she never stopped wanting him. These two truths—her yearning for him and her knowing that she could no longer take care of him—formed the fence that encircled her life. Maybe in the past three years he had grown past his own embryonic stage so that she could have needs too sometimes. Maybe enough time had passed for her to forgive herself, to allow herself to desire things, to come to life. But maybe not, and she was too brittle to risk her own safety any further just then.

Angel turned the volume high enough to drown out the sound of howling wind knocking thin metal, and to fill the hollow echo where once she'd trusted love.

IN THE MIDDLE of the night, Sheila came to Angel with a screaming child in her arms.

"Here," Sheila said, dumping the baby on the mattress. The baby looked like a fat wild animal, something dangerous that might have wandered in from the surrounding woods.

"Earn your keep, Angel," Sheila said, and slammed the door.

Angel pushed off the blankets in the freezing room. Tawny's pajamas were soaking wet and worse. There was an eye-burning smell of urine.

Angel tried to gather the girl in her arms but she twisted away, crawling toward the door after her mother, her nose running, her face a soggy mess.

Angel knocked on the smaller bedroom door. "Go away!" Sheila yelled. Russell stuck his head out, his hair in his face like a kid.

"Diapers?" Angel asked.

"I'll get some in the morning," Sheila said from the musky darkness.

Angel backed off before Russell could shut the door in her face. She returned to the screaming thing writhing on the floor of her bedroom. She moved quickly. Action in the face of human need was her way. Angel lifted the child to the bathroom that looked like a church and ran a warm bath. Warm but not too hot. She would get supplies in the morning. Diapers. Wipes. Milk. Cleaning sprays for the kitchen and bathroom. Air fresheners. She could take care of a baby for a few days. Somebody sure as hell had to do it.

She took off her own clothes before stripping the baby. Tawny's skin flamed with rash. She wiggled dangerously in Angel's arms as she stepped into the Jacuzzi-sized tub. In the warm water Angel sang a Sundullah song until Tawny rested her head against her shoulder. The baby peed against her stomach.

It was a good song. They'd written it together when they were very young, inspired by one of Angel's favorite stories. It had never appeared on an album. That song was just for them.

Rubies from your lips, my love, flowers on your toes. Share your bread with me, my love, and you'll find berries in the snow.

After the bath, Angel patted Tawny dry. She hummed the silly song while she wrapped the baby in a towel she'd found in one of the boxes. Angel curled herself around the little one. She would be a protective shell. She would be a temporary home.

In the morning, Sheila paced the yard with a cigarette dangling from her fingers. She stopped and took a long drag. Angel tried to pass unnoticed with the kitchen trash. She dumped the bag in the can by the shed. Sheila followed Angel's return path to the trailer. Silver bracelets jangled on her arms like weaponry, and the end of her cigarette burned in the foggy gloom. She wore acid-washed jeans and shiny red high heeled shoes plastered with wet leaves, gathering snow.

"It's so beautiful here," Angel said to make conversation.

Sheila snorted. "This is a hell hole."

The cigarette smoke bothered Angel's lungs but in a respiratory game of chicken she refused to turn her head to avoid it.

"I know what you're thinking," Sheila said, tapping her ash. "I can tell by how you look at him." She nodded toward the trailer. Angel followed her gaze as though there were answers there. "If I thought you had a chance, I wouldn't let you stay."

Angel knew girls like Sheila in high school, with their tight jeans and sharp, wicked eyes. These were girls who lurched from crisis to crisis, burning everything they touched. A few of them went for Sundullah but he deflected them by rounding his shoulders and pretending they didn't exist.

Yet while Angel judged her, Sheila had her baby, and Angel had rid herself of hers. At least Tawny had a chance at life. Looking at it that way, Sheila was the better mother.

Small birds flitted from tree to tree. Sheila raised an imaginary rifle and shot them down.

"Like you said last night, Russell is sort of my brother," Angel said. The lie slithered between her lips. She missed sleeping with Russell. Sheila was a thief of comfort and it wasn't fair. Russell had said she would leave soon, but it seemed she intended to stay.

"Then we'll be sisters," Sheila said.

Angel assumed she was being sarcastic but she wasn't smiling. Her mood swung on a wide and dangerous arc. "Most girls are bitches," Sheila said. "It's nice to find someone I trust for once. Now that Russell and I are getting back together, my life is on track." She bounded ahead and held the door open at the top of the stairs. Angel climbed the steps like an obedient prisoner.

"What are you looking at?" she asked. "You look funny."

For something to say, Angel replied, "I've never had a sister before."

"You're stupid," she said and let the door close on its loose springs, leaving Angel in the cold.

Tawny's rash eased after a few days of baths in the giant tub. Her personality settled along with her skin. She allowed herself to be distracted by Angel's songs and limited games of hide and seek. The world became the mossy inside of the trailer and the packed gravel yard. Once she put Sundullah's tape in the boom box she'd brought, but his voice sounded wrong in the trailer.

Angel had meant to leave after three days. But on the fourth day, Russell came into the warm kitchen from shoveling the driveway with a layer of snow dusting his shoulders. Sheila and Angel brushed it off together. Sheila hung his coat on the hook while Angel sliced lasagna she'd made in the rickety oven. She served Russell first. Sheila handed him a cold beer from the refrigerator and perched on his knee.

"This lasagna is so fucking good," Sheila said through a mouthful of food. She raised a glass of red wine in a toast to Angel the cook. Angel took a sip. It burned in her stomach as a substitute for warmth.

I've never had a sister. She didn't have one now, either. But it didn't seem impossible to go through the winter this way. It wasn't home, or even playing house. It wasn't what she'd wanted. But she was better for Tawny than her own mother. This was the story that might get her through a few months of winter, anyway. The deprivation of the thin mattress she shivered in alone sucked, but she could survive. It was a place to heal until January, until she could decide about Sundullah.

There were worse fairy tales than this. There were worse endings.

Sheila came home one Friday evening in early December with her face pink and her eyes glittering. Russell and Angel sat at the table while Tawny sat in the high chair. Angel had made Irish stew for dinner with provisions Russell had bought in Quincy. Angel was afraid at first that Shelia would grow angry at the domestic scene—the three of them under the glow of the hanging kitchen lamp. But she didn't seem to notice.

Tawny reached for her mother. Sheila grabbed her out of the high chair without loosening the tray so that it scraped against the baby's belly. Holding her tongue, Angel served Sheila a bowl of stew. Sheila pushed it away and lit a cigarette. She flicked ashes into the gravy, at least pointing the smoke away from the baby's face before putting her back behind the chair's tray.

Russell had temporary work at the lumber mill and left hours earlier than Sheila got out of bed. Most of the time she was gone to the bars before he got home. As far as Angel could see, Sheila and Russell hardly ever crossed paths. It had been several nights since she'd heard them having sex.

It was almost possible to imagine that Sheila didn't exist. Angel could perhaps learn to love Tawny in time. She could smooth over her crankiness the way she had smoothed over her skin, with gentle bathing and ointments. At the moment Angel had to admit that her true feelings toward the baby weren't love. What they shared was a camaraderie. They were both shunted aside with a fuzzy television and a faulty heater in a stinking trailer. The sort of purgatory they had in common didn't breed love.

She dabbed at Tawny's face with a cloth. It felt like shit to be unwanted.

"I bought a truck today," Sheila said. She blew smoke over Russell's food. Russell craned his neck to see through the window, but wouldn't go outside to look when she asked him to. He shook his head when she invited him for a ride.

"Come on, Russ. I'll let you drive." She dangled the keys in front of his face, but he shook his head again. He was too tired from working, he said. Somebody had to buy the groceries and the diapers.

Sheila ignored the bait. She was terrifying in her good mood. "I got a bunch of stuff added onto it," she said. "It's black but it glows underneath with these pink lights and it has pink windshield wiper thingies too."

Russell put down his fork.

"Hot pink," she said. She shook her hair over her shoulders.

"How'd you pay for it?" Russell asked.

"Wait, I'm not done telling you. I got fuzzy zebra seat covers too and dice to hang off the mirror. Isn't that funny?"

"Hilarious," he said.

Sheila snapped her head to face Angel. "What are you staring at?" she asked.

Angel went outside. Bay leaves and pine scented the air. Sheila's new truck had tires so big that it had to be difficult for her to climb in. Neon-pink plastic clips on the windshield wipers glowed in the moonlight. Angel walked away from it down the long gravel driveway.

The narrow bridge over the creek was slippery. The offshoot of the Feather River dashed in white peaks over boulders and swirled in eddies of sticks at its banks. Soon the surface would freeze, but beneath the cover of snow the water would still run fast. Russell had told her about it during the one night when they were alone. In the snowmelt the river sometimes washed over the road. If they were caught on one side or the other, they would have to stay until they dammed the weir upriver.

Angel kicked a stone into the froth. If she jumped off the bridge she would be crushed on the boulders. Any death she could imagine would be an anticlimactic coda after the earthquake. A muscle spasm snaked in her spine just at the memory of the universe's worth of time under the desk. A part of her was under the desk still and always would be.

Sheila's truck popped gravel down the road on its fat tires. Angel plastered herself against the rail. Megadeth blasted through the open window. The underside of the truck glowed in pink neon as though Sheila had run over a girlie UFO and never stopped to detach it from the axels.

The window hummed as it rolled down. Sheila's hair was wild, her face twisted in an angry mask.

"I know what you're trying to pull," she said, jabbing the air with a long finger sheathed in silver. "Do not think for a *second* that I don't *fucking* know what you're trying to pull." She gunned onto the road, cutting off a Land Rover and yelling obscenities at the other driver before squealing off in a glow of pink and red.

When Angel returned to the trailer, Russell sat amid the dirty dishes holding a beer. Tawny sat in the playpen, clawing at the dirty netting. Russell gave no indication that he heard her crying. The places Sheila went at night didn't exactly welcome toddlers, but Angel had been hoping that she would have the evening for herself. She picked the baby up, holding her outward the way she liked. She swayed back and forth to calm her down. The effort, after her walk in the cold air, made each breath slash her lungs like razor cuts.

"We got together in high school." Russell took a long sip from the brown bottle. "What the hell does anybody know in high school?"

Angel didn't answer. She looked back at high school as the time when things made sense. Sheila's cigarette tottered on her plate, still trailing smoke. Angel dragged the playpen with Tawny inside to sit in front of the television. The flickering screen reflected in the baby's eyes.

"If I were you I would leave, Angel," Russell said. "Get as far away from here as you can. Pretend you never met me." With that he walked out. She listened to him drive away. By doing as he suggested, she'd leave Tawny alone in the trailer with no one to look after her.

As Angel gathered plates and ran hot water in the sink, the baby started the creaky pre-crying sound she always made before throwing a fit. Angel gave her a bottle of milk to make her quiet. She doused Shelia's cigarette under the faucet.

Angel finished the dishes and wiped down the counter. She felt like an interloper, but she went into Russell and Sheila's bedroom to look for something else for Tawny to play with besides the same old things in the playpen. The room stank of funky sheets and garbage. Neither had unpacked their bags or hung anything in the closet. Under the bed something glittered. With a careful index finger and thumb she pulled it into the light. It was a crinkled sheet of aluminum foil with a burnt smudge in the middle like a dirty eye.

She dropped it, knowing that if she looked deeper she would find a glass tube, a lighter, probably a set of works. She sat back on her rear end like a kid falling hard at the end of a tall slide. *Well, then.*

After bathing Tawny, Angel walked around with her while singing Sundullah's lullaby. After the child fell asleep, Angel covered her with a heavy blanket on the mattress they shared. Tucked it under her wet chin.

A stick of incense from a street vendor in Del Rio Beach was strong enough to overpower the mildew smell. Angel ran her hand through the smoke ribbon of the nag champa and reread the last chapter of *One Hundred Years of Solitude.* She'd read it for the first time at seventeen. She thought she'd known what it meant to be so consumed with passion that she could die while making love and not even realize it. She always put herself with Sundullah in that picture of undying devotion back when she was a whole person. Back when things made sense.

Angel brushed Tawny's hair from her face and kissed her forehead. Angel thought she could be whole again. It took being needed to be whole. She saw that now. The snow fell past the window. She made plans to leave the trailer and take Tawny with her.

Chapter 20

October 17, 1971
Arcata, California

Teresa

⌒﹏⌒

WATCHING SISTER JUDITH sitting on the braided rug with Crystal, Teresa thought her little house looked like what it was—a tiny, shabby converted garden shed that still smelled like machine oil from the lawnmower once stored there. Crystal held her plush burgundy teddy bear for the nun to kiss. Teresa wished Sister Judith would leave.

"How did her appointment go?" Sister Judith asked. She made a big fuss over giving the bear a hug. Teresa couldn't figure out how to muster that much fake excitement over a toy. She both admired and pitied her old teacher for the effort.

"Fine. She got her shots," Teresa said. The walls felt too close. She wanted to be alone with her daughter.

Crystal extended her arm to show off her Band-Aid battle scars. Sister Judith praised her bravery. "I got her the teddy bear after because she didn't cry," Teresa said. Jealousy pooled in her chest to see her teacher admiring her child, giving the little girl all of the attention. She knew it was dumb but she couldn't help it.

"You didn't cry?" Sister Judith echoed. Crystal shook her head. "What's the teddy's name?"

"Angel," Crystal said. "She flies."

"We've got to go," Teresa said. She gathered their teacups and saucers and dumped them in the sink with a crash.

"Where?"

"To do stuff for my dad."

Teresa made a show of making her bed and then putting things in a bag for her daughter. She pulled on the Mexican hemp sweatshirt Michael left with her two weeks ago. It smelled of him still. Sister Judith could not know that they were leaving that night. Teresa had to protect her from Ray, because as soon as he realized they were gone he was going to make hell for everyone left behind until he was satisfied that no one knew where she was.

Besides that, she didn't want to answer the one hundred questions Sister Judith would ask if she knew. Sister Judith saw herself as Teresa's protector sent by God. The fact that she wasn't a very good one just made her more desperate.

"You're getting sick," Sister Judith said. *Sick* was her euphemism for the track marks and the shaking.

"Don't worry so much," Teresa said, trying for a smile. Her lips were dry.

Sister Judith washed the cups and dried them properly. "You can't keep on like this," she said. "What do you think you're teaching Crystal?"

"I know. Don't worry about it, Sister."

"Let me help you," she said. "Please. I'll get you out. Just say the word. We could take off right this minute if you wanted. I know people who live far from here who would hide you until it was safe."

Safe. That was a foreign word. A Holy Grail. It was a thing that never happened.

But it might happen. With Michael. Michael was her only real hope for safety. Sister Judith would be no shield against anything, even if she did have friends who would help. It wasn't just Ray whom Teresa had to fear, as if he weren't bad enough. Teresa was going to get fully clean with Michael. She would never touch any drug ever again once she was free from Ray's power.

Teresa loved Sister Judith. She did. Sister Judith was her only friend besides Michael. Sister Judith was kind but she could never give her what Michael could. Her teacher was a part of her past. Michael was her future.

"I'll see you tomorrow and we'll talk about it more," Teresa said. She opened the door.

"Just promise that you won't take anything today. Just try one day without it."

"I'm not an addict," Teresa said. "Have a little faith in me."

"Then you can do without it for one day."

Sister Judith lifted Crystal to her hip. They looked natural together while they waited for Teresa to lock the deadbolt. Annoyance joined the jealousy pricking the pincushion of her insides. She wished Sister would stop talking about the drugs that would smooth her over as sweet as pie. It was like talking about food to a starving person.

"I don't do it every day," Teresa said. A lie. In the past two weeks she had shot up every day. The inside of her elbows were so sore that she'd moved to the soft tissue on her ankle.

She could become a clean person with Michael. She would.

"I have something for you," Sister Judith said. Reaching into the satchel she carried over one shoulder, she extracted something that jarred Teresa with a memory as painful as a needle jab. It was a floating lantern made of stitched brown canvas, folded and unburned. Teresa took it in careful hands as though it might break.

"I remember that night," Teresa said in a choked voice.

"I remember it too," Sister Judith said. "I remember what I promised you. I'll look after you and Crystal. Maybe I haven't done the best job so far."

"No. You've been my friend."

"He's a monster. What he did to you, Teresa," she said, shaking her head. "Let's get out. We can do this together. I'll go with you. You never have to be alone."

"Let's talk about it later," Teresa said. Her secret about Michael bubbled behind her lips but she did not tell it. Her former teacher's only safety was in her ignorance.

"Yes, later," Sister Judith said. "I'll call my friend, let her know to expect us at some point soon. In the meantime, I found this left-over lantern in the campus ministry things. I want you to have it."

"Thank you," Teresa said. Sister Judith enclosed her in a half-hug, Crystal wedged between them. Teresa did not like hugs. She hated social touching in all forms. Her badly healed fingers collapsed together like a paper fan in handshakes. Embraces felt like attacks. Sister Judith knew this and normally respected her space. Teresa did not pull away but she did not relax either. She tilted like a doll while slipping the lantern in her shoulder bag.

Sister Judith put Crystal down and looked as if she wanted to say more. Teresa took Crystal's hand and hurried to where her mother waited at the big house. Anything else that she said would have to be the truth.

"Tomorrow," Sister Judith called. "I'll be here."

I won't, Teresa thought. She tightened her damaged grip on her daughter's hand and she didn't look back.

TERESA PARKED IN front of Billy Stamm's house. The two-story Victorian gazed at the road and green fields through thick cataracts. Gray mildew mottled the windows. The place may have appeared abandoned, but Billy squatted inside with the silence of a tumor. On collecting days nobody wanted to be home.

She knocked with stony knuckles. Her pea coat was heavy on her shoulders. Her bony wrists made her hand look like an old woman's, like the hand of a woman close to death.

The house swallowed the sound with no response. She rested against the railing. The road stretched long in either direction. In one direction lay the town of Arcata and in the other, the world ended in a fog-shrouded ocean. There were no neighboring houses along Mad River Road. The ocean roared beyond the dunes. A mist-laden breeze brushed against her face and promised something better than this. Michael's apartment was in Oregon, in another coastal town. They would have speed freaks there too, and they would have the mellowing pills and Horse she preferred. There would be work to do in the first few weeks. Getting clean would be hard. But she would do it and she would never think on her parents or her hometown again.

She wouldn't need to party once she was with Michael. She wouldn't want to. She never had before when they were together. She was tough and she ran around with boys sometimes, but she'd never so much as drank a beer before Michael left under her father's threats. Before Ray ran Michael out of the state, she'd never dreamed that she'd try any kind of drug. Drugs were for hippies in San Francisco. She didn't know they were something you could get right in town from awful men who worked for her father.

There was a lot she didn't know before she got pregnant. She ran her thumb along the crooked length of an index finger. Dropping the cigarette she'd smoked to a butt, she ground it under her heel into the wooden plank porch. It might be better just to let it start a fire.

There was no one in Humboldt County she'd miss but Sister Judith. Besides Michael and Crystal, she was the only good person. Teresa took a deep breath of the clean, misty air, and it filled her with a resolve she hoped she could trust. This was the last time she'd ever make a pick-up for her father. Something was making her bob on the balls of her toes. It was hope and she wasn't used to it. It was the same happiness she felt at sixteen when Michael whispered promises in the library, where they felt safe. She willed the sea air to rush through her, to clean her insides. She would leave the flimsy garden shed in the shadow of her father's house. She and her daughter would start a new life free from Ray. It never seemed more likely than it did in that one certain moment.

Go now. A frantic voice inside of her urged her to get into the Dodge Dart her father let her drive, gather Crystal from her mother, and hit the road out of town. Her father was Ray Hamilton. His reach was wide. But he couldn't reach the whole world. He was not a god. She stepped off the porch.

An oily reluctance squirmed to life, stopping her feet. She would do this last job. Better not to make him suspicious. Better to act like everything was normal. Better to leave under the cover of night just as she had planned. She and Crystal had been practicing taking walks in the woods to look at the stars. Their walk into the woods tonight would seem like just another stargazing adventure for a child.

She would do this last job. That was all.

The doorknob turned but the door would not open. Sea moisture swelled the wood in the jamb. It needed a hard kick. She swung back and jackhammered the door with the bottom of her sneakered foot as hard as she could. It gave with a crack. She scratched the inside of her elbow. Kicking the door in was one thing. Crossing the threshold was another.

Billy's house was a piece of hell. A broken curtain rod hung askew over the front window. The floor was a dirty beach of paper plates, old food, empty cans, and half-smoked cigarettes. A couple of sets of works were scattered across a card table in the middle of the front room. The air was thick with butane, mildew, and the more immediate stench of rotting garbage.

"Billy," she called, "come on out." She slapped at a pinch on her ankle. Fleas. She flexed to her tiptoes. She didn't want to bring home fleas to Crystal. Crystal and Michael.

The house bore the heaviness of occupants. A floorboard creaked.

"Hurry up, man." Her watch read nearly five. Ray liked the money home before dark. It was one of his rules. If she didn't get back soon, he wouldn't want to hear about slow-moving junkies out in the flats. Disappointing him would call attention to herself, and that was dangerous.

Her heel crushed an empty beer can. If Michael knew she ran drug errands for Ray to secure a place to live and food and clothes for Crystal, he would hate it. She imagined his broad hands balled into fists. He was a strong guy. His fists could do real damage if he wanted them to. He never fought as long as she'd known him, but he would to protect their little family. She knew he would.

She couldn't think about Michael yet. She couldn't think about the cash sewn into the lining of her pea coat like quilting. She had to act tough and bored like always. The thought of escape made her feel like she was walking on unstable ground. Everything would fall apart under her feet if she wasn't careful. By this time tomorrow she would be free. She would be happy, or at least on the way to the possibility of happiness.

Teresa kicked the can across the floor to make some noise. It seemed impossible to believe her life could be different. Michael would make her believe. She just had to get through this one last pick-up and then hand the money over for Ray to help him count and hide it. He couldn't suspect anything because she never left any signs. His trust in her obedience was the only power she had.

"Billy, hurry the fuck up. Ray's waiting." Heavy boots shuffled down the hall. Ray's name tended to reanimate junkies stuck in slow motion. Even stoned people knew enough to fear.

But it wasn't Billy coming down the hall. It was one of the small-time boys who loitered around the Arcata Plaza when he should have been in school.

She didn't know his name. He looked sick, his face shiny with sweat as he shambled forward.

Billy moved behind him as close as a lover. He held a gun to the boy's back. It was a small thing, just a black handgun. A game of stick-up or cops and robbers.

"Tell Billy I'm good for it, will you?" the boy said. Terror squeezed his voice into a whine.

"Too late for that," Billy said. The boy started to cry. He looked maybe eighteen. He could have been a dropout from another town, drawn north by the rumor of cheap drugs. There were more of those kids every year, Peter Pans looking for something they weren't getting where they came from. The north seemed a fantasy world with the redwood groves and misty beaches, but Ray Hamilton ruled this town and it was no Neverland. At least not for this poor kid at Billy's mercy.

"He's got the picture. Let him go," she said. She rubbed her eyes with the thumb and forefinger of one hand. She didn't have time for games. If Sister Judith hadn't dropped by, she could have had a hit before she started running Ray's errands and she'd feel better. She wished she could have taken a last hit.

"Don't worry, kid," she said. "Just get Ray the money you owe by tomorrow. You'll be okay." She raised her eyebrows at Billy. Time to get this show on the road. Another flea bit her ankle.

Billy didn't say anything. He looked straight into her eyes. In one movement he lifted the gun to the side of the boy's head and shot him. The explosion burst in her eardrums. She fell to her knees, covered her head with her hands as though she were caught in some kind of drill in elementary school. Earthquake, tsunami, fire, bombs. Stop, drop, and roll.

The boy collapsed like a marionette with cut strings. His head turned to the side and his eyes were wide and sightless. This was no drill, no false alarm. The expression on Billy's face was deader than the boy's. Billy's eyes were cockroach beady above a pointy nose and a thick, drooping mustache.

"He wanted you to see that," Billy said, wiping the snout of the gun against his wheat-colored bell bottom jeans. A spray of blood and tissue dripped down the moldy wall. "He wanted you to learn a lesson is what he told me."

A lesson. That meant he knew. That meant she wasn't getting away with anything. The smell of the kid's brain matter was too much and she threw up on the floor.

"Your job is to help me get him into the back of my van," Billy said when she was done. He was already grabbing the legs. He swung the body around.

Teresa gagged again. The boy's Chuck Taylor sneakers flopped. Billy's arms were long and cabled as an ape's. She went ahead, her flattened eardrums muffling every sound. She climbed in the back of Billy's van to pull the body in by the feet.

Billy drove them high into the mountains. Sunset passed with no fanfare. The overcast sky turned purple. The time passed beyond when the night held any trace of the daylight. After Billy parked on the side of a deserted road, she waited in the passenger's seat. She listened while he opened the back over the edge of a cliff that dropped into a deep ravine. The body slid over the floorboards and then she heard crashing brush and then nothing.

On the return to town, she held her face toward the open window. The wind whipped her long hair about. The girl on the porch with the hopeful feeling—the one who'd knocked on Billy's door—was an ant under her shoe, destroyed beyond recognition. She had no memory of the certainty that she might learn to be alive.

"Am I taking you home?" Billy asked. When he spoke, toads and worms flopped out of his mouth. His was the epic evil of legends. A simple, loving boy who knew no fear would not recognize the monster within a Billy Stamm. And because of his blindness, Michael would never be safe. She shook her head.

He reached across the seat, tucked her under his armpit.

"Then where we headed, darlin'?" he asked.

She shrugged. Her hearing still wasn't great. The gunshot echoed in her head, her throat, her mouth.

The sky was ink. Michael would wait outside her window. He would wield a hopeful branch scratching at an empty shed. Crystal would be in the bed Teresa's mother kept for her in the big house on nights Teresa worked late.

Billy palmed the back of her neck and she shuddered. His cold hand slid down her shirt and settled at her breast. She let him do it.

Of course by now Michael would be gone. He would not wait long before figuring out something had happened and she wasn't meeting him as they had planned. Maybe he thought she didn't want him anymore. Poor hulking Michael with his sheepskin denim jacket and his kind hands would leave hurt and angry. He wouldn't be careful enough. Her father would do to him what Billy had done to the boy in the ravine. Her only shred of hope was the chance that Ray would be satisfied that Teresa had forsaken Michael. She imagined him driving north to Oregon on the highway and prayed that he would be safe.

She prayed that she would never see Michael again. She was poison to kindness. She was Michael's biggest danger. The wrenching in her chest was a physical thing. It hurt worse than birth. She felt an internal implosion like the collapse of a building built on mud.

"Take me nowhere," she said to the darkness.

Billy cackled. He drove one-handed so he could squeeze her tit. It didn't matter. She was anti-matter. As long as Michael was safe and gone away from Billy and Ray, then hell was good enough for her and she would disappear into nothingness.

Chapter 21

November 20, 1971
Trinidad, California

Teresa

❧

TERESA PUSHED HER face into the window screen. The rot of the camper trailer was death's chin digging into her shoulder. Billy's camper perched on a bluff in an abandoned campground posted with signs warning of erosion. Below her the ocean rolled toward the shore. She was more afraid of looking into the belly of the trailer than she was of falling down the bluff into the sea.

Her wristwatch was dead. Waterlogged. The band itched. Funny that she still wore it. She unfastened it and flung it to the floor on top of the clothes and trash. It landed beside a blanket of flies moving over a chewed-on chicken leg. She knew she shouldn't have looked.

Billy had been gone a long time. She needed him to come back.

She crunched the ends of a piece of her hair between her fingertips. It was still stiff from a dip in the ocean. Maybe two nights ago. Maybe last week. She licked her arm. Salt. She licked it again. The trailer shuddered in a light wind. She pulled the hood of Michael's Mexican sweatshirt over her head and inhaled the air blowing through the screen mesh. The gray weather ate time. All the days looked the same except early morning and night.

She needed Billy to come back. Her skin crawled. She scratched at her scalp until blood caked her fingernails. She dug for a hold under a scab so she could imagine the sensation of pulling the skin over her face and down her neck. She longed to peel her outer layer to the bottoms of her feet and step out of it, raw and bleeding but clean.

She tried counting to sixty. Made it to seven.

For weeks Billy kept her hidden and supplied with drugs. She wore Michael's Mexican pullover the whole time. She still imagined it smelled like him. The night he shot the boy, Billy drove her to the trailer and she stayed there to hide and forget.

Teresa had stuck her hand up the bottom of a statue of St. Mary in the chapel and stole a wad of Ray's money the night Michael first came for her. She'd sewn it into the lining of her coat. The money was supposed to be for going away with Michael. She'd wanted it for Michael, not for Ray's needle-nosed thug. But she cut it out with Billy's knife and in exchange he brought her drugs. Her world shrank to the drugs and the trailer and Billy, who she hated, until she got high and it didn't matter.

A car approached the campground. Her heart thumped but the car drove past. She might have tried to sleep, but her eyes wouldn't stay closed. Nothing about her body was under her control. Every second was like being dragged naked on concrete. She knew this was hell when her savior was Billy Stamm.

Billy Stamm. Teresa would never forget the night they met. That morning after church she told her parents she was pregnant and that she and Michael were going to get married. She wore her pink skirt that hung past her knees, the white blouse her dad liked. She'd given a lot of thought to how she'd tell them, how she'd act. She and Michael were ready if they kicked her out of the house, if they sent her away, even if Ray tried to go after Michael. They thought they'd considered all possible scenarios.

Her mother cried. Her father smiled. Her first gut reaction when she saw Ray's smile was to run for her life.

Instead she tried placating him. "I'm sorry I've disappointed you," she said. "I'm sorry I've embarrassed you." She said these things for survival. She didn't mean them. She was proud of the baby that moved inside her. Nothing about her love for Michael was disappointing or wrong. She knew this the way her parents knew there was a god, and saints, and heaven and hell. She believed in Michael.

But she would say what she had to in order to survive.

"You mistake me," he said. Just that. And the smile.

"Michael and I are going to do the right thing," Teresa said.

"Yes you will," Ray said. "Now off with you. You've upset your mother."

Chastised, Teresa left the parlor. She sat in her room for hours, looking out her window, worrying. She wanted to believe that her father's cryptic remarks meant he supported them getting married. He wasn't happy, and he would see a wedding as an apt punishment. *Let him think that*, she prayed. *Let him think that marrying Michael would be punishment enough.*

She stayed in her room past dinnertime. Hunger brought her downstairs in the night. She would grab a banana, a glass of milk. Since the baby, she was plagued with hunger she couldn't ignore.

Ray must have heard her in the kitchen. The door to the basement workshop stood open. The light was on. He called her name.

Billy sat on a stool next to Ray at his workbench, holding a beer. Teresa took a few steps, unsure that her presence was what her father had wanted. Ray waited, giving no encouragement. He watched her descend. His face was a mask. Billy wasn't watching her. He was watching Ray.

By the time Ray's mask fell, it was too late to get away. The kitchen might as well have been in another world. It was as remote as heaven.

"Meet Billy," he said. "You'll be working together. For me. I'm taking you out of school, of course." He took her wrists between his forefingers and thumbs with an intimacy that repelled her. He tucked her between his thighs. "We can't have a girl as nasty as you among the other students."

Teresa's face burned. She could endure the things he said. She had already imagined the terrible things he would say. Her eyes shot to Billy. His expression was hungry, expectant. She could see through his jeans he was excited. Her stomach fell.

"You'll work for me. You'll do as I say," he said. "Billy will be your colleague."

"That's right," Billy said. He was disgusting. His pointed nose made her think of a rat.

"You'll keep your skirt down from now on, however," Ray said. "Remember tonight the next time you go into heat."

"Daddy, I ...." She gasped in shock as he tightened his grip and used his thumb to bend back her wrist until her palm lay flat upon the table.

"No more out of you," he said. His tools hung with precision on the pegboard above the workspace. There was not a shred of sawdust on the floor. He reached for a gleaming hammer with a clawed head, testing its heft and weight in his hand. Her right pinky finger was still crooked from the day when she was little and he took her hand in his for no reason. He had bent her pinky back with the idle speed of someone breaking a twig collected from the ground. He looked out the window while he did it. Listening for the crack.

"Spread your fingers," he said. Billy had something caught in his throat. He coughed, and Teresa couldn't look at him. She stared at her hand, so small and white in her father's hairy grip. "Spread them wide," he said, his smile growing.

What about Michael? It was her only thought. She did not dare say it aloud. When she saw the madness in his eyes she tried to pull free, though she knew that would make it worse. She could not help but try with everything she had to get free of her father and his shining hammer raised above his head. His legs held her in place like a vise.

What about Michael? Until he brought the hammer down again and again. Until she was an animal with no questions or thoughts or love or anything but pain.

Teresa opened and closed her hands at the memory. She'd stayed in her room for days, looking out her window just as she was doing now. Ray would not take her to the doctor. He would only allow bandages and alcohol for the cuts and contusions. Her mother stayed away. She sent the housekeeper with food and fresh gauze. Later Teresa learned that he had not killed Michael as she told Sister Judith she feared he would. Billy beat the shit out of him and ran him out of town. Ray threatened to kill him if he ever came back. Not killing him was a gift to show his power. Ray could give pain. Ray could spare it. That knowledge and the increasing doses of product kept her nicely under his control.

Yet in the trailer she was in Ray's control no more. She was in no one's control except Billy's as long as he kept her in smack. That morning less than twenty dollars remained. She gave it over and he left to get more. After this she would have to pay with something else.

She would pay it.

She would pay anything. Real life was a horde of scrambling beetles, edging in, hungry for her flesh, her ears, her heart. The only point was to keep from feeling anything. The thought of stepping off the bluff flitted around for days like a butterfly with wings of black velvet that had now finally landed for her to observe. She'd once caught Sister Judith about to jump off a cliff on the way to a prayer service on the beach. Sister Judith was sad and freaking out and she tried to hide it, but Teresa could see what she had been meaning to do. In exchange for knowing that private thing about her teacher she had told her about being pregnant and from that second they were friends. Maybe knowing that Teresa needed her did the trick for Sister Judith. God by Himself wasn't a good enough reason to live, even for a nun.

Teresa climbed her fingers up the camper window screen. Her hands looked like nightmare spiders with their broken digits bent sideways at the knuckles. There were other ways to die besides jumping. An air bubble in the syringe or too much dope too fast and that would be the sweet, warm honey end. She deserved the rocks and the battering waves, but it would be the honey she'd have the balls for.

She would miss Crystal. Maudlin tears popped in her eyes. She would be dead and Crystal would go on living with her mother and father. Maybe she would fare better than Teresa did or maybe she wouldn't, but either way Teresa couldn't keep anyone alive—not even her own self.

Gravel crunched under tires. Teresa closed her eyes and sucked in a sobbing breath of relief. Billy with her drugs.

Car doors slammed and someone banged on the door. Police pushed in. One of them cursed the bad air. Sure hands grabbed Teresa and pulled her off the narrow bed and handcuffed her wrists behind her back.

"You have the right to remain silent …" a policewoman said. They dragged her out of the camper and into the gray day.

"Where is she? Where is the body?" the policewoman said. "Is she alive?"

Teresa didn't know what the woman was talking about. Maybe she meant her. She looked down at her own body, the filthy hemp sweatshirt and the skinny naked legs pocked with sores. Her knees knocked together like a pair of grapefruit and then buckled. The policewoman held her tightly around the shoulders with one arm. Teresa had thought she was alive. Maybe not.

The policewoman had long black hair in a braid. An Indian lady. Yurok, Hupa. One of those. She squeezed Teresa's face in her hand and made her look up.

"Where is Crystal?" she asked.

Teresa's throat closed. The question didn't make sense. They banged things around in the camper. The policewoman lowered Teresa to the ground.

More sirens. Car doors. The spit and buzz of Walkie Talkies. The sun pierced Teresa's eyes through a hole in the clouds. More police walked in a horizontal line through the grass up the hill toward the forest. They called Crystal's name.

"Trailer's all clear," one of them said. He came out, followed by two others covering their noses.

The Indian cop crouched to Teresa's level. She cupped Teresa's face again in her strong hand. "We need to find Crystal," she said. "Where is your daughter?"

"My mother," Teresa said. Her mouth was so dry. She tried to remember the last time she drank water.

"No, she is not with your mother. Where did you take her, Teresa? What did you do with your daughter?"

This had to be a trick of her father's. Teresa looked around. The ground shifted under her butt. The bluff was collapsing beneath them. They would slide into the ocean if they didn't get away, but the cops didn't notice.

"I didn't …" Teresa began. Then she stopped. It was Michael. Michael saw she wasn't coming and rescued their daughter without her. Teresa's heart leapt in its filthy cage.

"What is it?" the policewoman asked. She pulled Teresa aside. She put her face right in Teresa's air. "You know something," she said. "Say it. Let me help you."

Teresa's lips bled as she pressed them together. Michael and Crystal were safe and so far away that even Ray Hamilton couldn't find them. The Boy Who Did Not Know Fear foiled the dragon after all. Teresa's head pounded. She was sick to the marrow yet full of a pure and sudden joy at the realization that Michael had Crystal and Ray couldn't find them.

"I know you work for Ray, Officer. Tell him he can kill me if he wants. I don't give a shit. I'm not talking."

Michael had gotten away with Crystal. Now it was her job to be quiet about it. All she had to do was say his name once and then every cop in the county on her father's payroll would be on his trail. Teresa would never say a word, not to this cop or to any of them.

"Miss Hamilton, you have the right to remain silent," the policewoman repeated. Then Teresa stopped listening. Sweat ran in rivers down her sides. She tried to hook her brain on a memory. She tried to recall the scent of Crystal's hair after a bath. The silk of her cheek when she was sleeping.

Teresa ran her tongue over her sticky teeth. She had the right to remain silent. Silent she would remain. In the back of the car the policewoman slid in beside her. The other cops lingered outside. The officer kept a watch on them as they walked away from the car. Then she turned to face Teresa. Her eyes were steely. "My name is Officer Laura Redleaf. Teresa, I am your friend." She reached around to undo the cuffs in a gesture that was so close to a kind embrace that tears spilled down Teresa's cheeks.

With her newly free hands, Teresa wiped her face. She picked at the scabs of her cuticles. She wasn't saying another damn word. She knew her father in a way no one else did in the world. He wanted her to be the one to betray Michael. Her whole life had been twisted by Ray's games. She'd go to jail for the rest of her life before she'd say Michael's name and whereabouts to any cop.

"Teresa. Michael Lopez is dead."

A game. Another part of the game. Ray told the police to say this to get her to admit that she was going to run away with him. She knew all his fucking tricks.

"Did you hear me? There was a car accident. The reports state that Michael died of traumatic injuries due to a car accident the night that Crystal disappeared."

"Was Crystal—" Teresa slapped her hands over her mouth. Officer Redleaf grabbed her shoulders.

"Crystal wasn't with Michael. We need to find her, Teresa. And listen, I do not work for *him*," she said. "Talk to me. I can help you." The voices of the policemen grew louder.

She let go and gave her head a quick shake. *Stay silent.* The driver settled in and closed the door. Redleaf's face was stern. Teresa could almost believe that she hadn't said the terrible thing. Then the woman reached over and placed one finger on Teresa's forearm, pointing to the cop in the driver's seat. She gave a tiny nod.

Redleaf didn't work for Ray. The cop driving did.

The driver turned on the siren. The wail seared napalm into Teresa's brain. She swallowed a geyser of acid panic. Because if this wasn't the worst joke her father had ever played then it was the worst thing that could happen.

Teresa thought of her parents' two-story Cape Cod-style house that looked so innocent and grand. She had left Crystal to grow up in that evil place the same as she had. Sideways and bent. Now maybe her child was dead.

And, she thought, maybe it wasn't the worst thing if Crystal was really dead.

A cavern ripped open inside of her and into it fled any purity or joy or true courage she would ever feel again.

Chapter 22

November 22–December 5, 1971
Arcata, California

Teresa

A NURSE BROUGHT A cup of pills. "Water," she said.
Teresa obliged. She swallowed the pills with lukewarm water that tasted like the paper of the cup it came in. Something moved in her intestines like a living thing. It would chew its way out of her body. She smelled the junk pouring from her skin. It soaked the gray sheets. She was poisoned and poisonous. She was dying and it was taking too long.

But she didn't die. She slept and woke and flailed against the mattress. She threw up in the bucket they left by her bed. She scratched the walls until her fingers bled. She took the pills and lay her head on the wet pillow.

Her prayers for death only rose so far. They collected against the ceiling in floating lanterns and bounced against each other. She wasn't surprised. Her prayers were never answered. The lanterns burst open and spiders spilled from the burnt canvas, raining upon her face as she screamed.

TWO WEEKS LATER, after a sleep longer than most, Teresa opened her eyes. She flew upright and slammed her back against the wall. Ray. He sat in a chair across from the cell. She squeezed her eyes shut and opened them again. It wouldn't be the first time in the past couple of weeks that she saw a nightmare image that wasn't real.

The metal chair he sat on creaked under his weight. "Are you feeling better?" he asked.

He put his elbows on his knees. "You smell like a pig."

Teresa pulled the dirty sheet to her chin. She coiled in on herself and glanced at the barred door.

"No one is going to save you from me," Ray said. "I sent the guard away."

She pressed her sheet-wrapped fists to her mouth. She couldn't catch her breath. She squeezed her eyes shut and prayed to God for a shot to the head rather than something more inventive. The boy that Billy killed couldn't have felt anything. Ray would have to act fast. Even Ray Hamilton couldn't order the guards away forever in the county jail.

He chuckled. "You're afraid. But you needn't be. I'm not going to hurt you." His voice was suede. "But you should know I saw you."

"Saw me?" She thought of Billy's camping trailer and the filth she lived in for nearly a month while she shot up every day. He was lurking outside and looking in the windows? Maybe he saw her swim naked in the ocean. Funny if he thought that would shame her at this point.

"I saw you take Crystal out of the trundle bed Mother and I kept in our house for her," he said. His slicked-back hair was thinning. "You took her the night you disappeared."

"I never went back home," Teresa said.

"Oh, but you did," Ray said. He smiled as though he were a kind man. "I'm going to be testifying in court. You took her. Your mother and I were worried sick but we stayed out of it. After all, you are her mother. Were her mother. We thought you would have Crystal's best interests at heart. We really thought you would."

He bowed his head like a penitent and cried into one of his hands. Then he stopped and looked up. Smiling. That horrible smile.

"Do you know where she is?" Teresa asked.

"No," he said.

"You know and you won't tell me."

"No," he said. He looked at his watch. "I'm assuming you killed her just like they said. You always had to have things your way." He whistled for a guard. There was the sound of steps hustling from a far end of the hallway.

"I didn't," Teresa said. It hurt to talk. It hurt to breathe.

"But you did," he said. "You killed your own daughter, you witch. Now you'll die in prison where you belong."

The guard couldn't meet Ray's eyes. She fumbled with the keys and dropped them. Ray stood silently as she finally opened the door. Only Teresa saw the dangerous twitch in his jaw. If she could have spoken, she would have warned the guard to hurry. She would have warned her to run.

A cloud of cologne remained after Ray was gone. She bent over the empty bucket and turned her body inside out to fill it.

Chapter 23

December 25, 1971
Arcata, California

Teresa

⌒◡◞

ON CHRISTMAS AFTERNOON Teresa sat alone in a cell in the county jail with a tray of warmed-over turkey dinner. The overhead lighting had the direct glare of an operating table. She stabbed the rubbery piece of meat and flung it onto the wall and it stuck.

She had a small television. The *Lawrence Welk Show* played through the fuzzy reception. The ladies sang "America the Beautiful" and wore red dresses that made them look pregnant. Ray loved Lawrence Welk. To tell the truth, Ray looked like him with his greasy hair and square-shaped smile. The women on the show all had the eyes of stoners. Maybe that was the secret of Lawrence Welk's success. Give them all enough smack so that they'll wear and do and say whatever stupid thing he asks.

A cluster of grief nested in her throat but she had to survive this. She had to get out of jail and find Crystal. She would survive one night at a time without going insane. The drugs were out of her system now. She was exhausted and depressed but at least she was alive.

Teresa's mother never came to visit. Since before her teens her mother had turned into a shell-shocked sailor, adrift in the big house. She took fat Valium pills with glasses of water and did whatever Ray said. Teresa's mother wasn't strong enough to protect her from Ray's brutality. Yet in the cold desert of her days in jail, Teresa saw that she was no better a mother than her own. In fact, she was worse. At least Teresa had lived to adulthood. Crystal was lost at four years old with no one to even try to protect her.

She felt Ray everywhere. She would have told the guards not to let him visit if she thought that would keep him away. When Ray wanted to see her, he would do so. No one would be able to stop him.

Sister Judith never visited either and that stung way worse than being ignored by her cowering mother. Her lawyer said that Sister Judith had left the convent, moved away before the new school year started. She must have thought that Teresa was beyond saving. There was no reason to continue to bother with a former student the police found wasted and half naked in a drug dealer's trailer. She must have believed what they were saying, that Teresa had hurt Crystal in some way and hid the body so nobody could find it.

She focused on the television. Lawrence Welk called all the grown women on the show "girls." Teresa hated that. She observed her hatred and filed it away in a corner of her mind that she was cultivating for later. Someday she would get out of that jail cell. When she did, she would be a woman who would never let anyone call her "girl."

"Merry Christmas." Officer Laura Redleaf stood outside the barred door waiting for the potato-faced guard to find the right key and let her in. Teresa was so glad to see her she almost cried.

"What are you doing here?" Teresa asked.

Officer Redleaf smiled but her eyes were hard. She held a plastic bag filled with gum and candy and magazines. Bobby Sherman grinned on the cover of the latest *Teen Beat*. Since her arrest, Redleaf came to visit Teresa once a week, asking questions about school and Michael as though they were friends. Teresa accepted the Bobby Sherman magazine and hoped Redleaf didn't notice the gray slab of turkey stuck to the opposite wall.

But Officer Redleaf wasn't paying attention to the wall. She held Teresa's gaze. She sat down on the bed and leaned in close.

"I'm going to tell you something and I need you to keep cool," she said.

Crystal. She knew something about Crystal. But Redleaf must have read it in her eyes and she shook her head.

"Not her. Michael," she said.

She whispered the news, her lips brushing Teresa's ear. Teresa didn't have to ask why the secrecy. Ray Hamilton had friends everywhere.

There had been a car crash the night Teresa and Michael were supposed to run away with Crystal. But Michael had not died in the wreck. He had run from it. The police found him in the woods a half mile away from the crash site with a gunshot through the back of his head.

"He was running," Redleaf said, glancing out toward the hallway, rubbing her hands together as if in a frantic prayer. "They found him near the convent off the old highway road."

Teresa looked at her food. "Take a bite," the officer said. Teresa obeyed. It tasted like chalk but she chewed and swallowed. The guard strolled past in the hallway. "They're hiding evidence. Sons-of-bitches I work with. They're all in on it, up to the top."

Teresa glanced sidelong at the earnest woman who thought whispering would keep her safe from Ray. Redleaf took the boys from the precinct out for drinks, paying for round after round. It wasn't so difficult to get them to tell the story of dragging the boy's body through the woods. What they did nagged at them, despite Ray Hamilton's assurances that Michael was a rapist, had raped his daughter and deserved swift justice. They'd bashed in his head to cover the gunshot and falsified their reports.

Redleaf's breath was hot against her face. "What can you tell me, Teresa?"

"My father killed him," she said. Ray had to be behind Michael's death. No other force was strong enough to do it, not even a car wreck. Not even the laws of physics could kill someone as good as Michael, but Ray could. She realized that Redleaf's story did not surprise her.

She'd known it was Ray from the moment she learned of Michael's death.

"He'll kill you too," Teresa said, speaking to Officer Redleaf's broad knees. "Whatever you did to get this information is no good. It will get back to him."

"I don't care," she said.

She would care, though. If she was ever caught alone at the mercy of Ray Hamilton, she would care.

"You seem like a nice lady. Why don't you get lost?" Teresa pictured her smiling at her superiors, looking innocent with her round face while sneaking into evidence rooms at night. Taking the other cops out for beers and facing their bleary-eyed suspicions the next day.

"You let me worry about me," Redleaf said. "Now think, Teresa. Where could Crystal be? If your father has her stashed somewhere, then where?"

Teresa raised her fingertips to her eyes. *Where is Crystal.* Everyone asked that question. Crystal floated above them like Sister Judith's floating lanterns. Out of reach. Fading from view.

Back when they slept in the garden shed, she held Crystal close to her in bed every night. In those long nights the little girl felt as solid as the earth itself. It was impossible that she was gone. Thinking about it was like touching an infected tooth with her tongue. It might explode and release enough toxins into her brain to kill her.

Redleaf rubbed her chin. "This has always stunk. From the beginning. You may not know where your daughter is but you know some things you're not telling me."

Down the hall someone yelled. They kept Teresa away from the other prisoners. She knew the others only by their night terrors and their yelling. She rarely saw anyone besides the guards, her lawyer, and Redleaf. Teresa's hand shook and her plastic spoon rattled the tray. Officer Redleaf seemed so solid, so good in her slightly too tight uniform and long black braid.

"You think it's because I'm trying to protect myself that I'm not telling you all I know," Teresa said. Her voice was so low she could barely hear it herself.

"I don't know who you're protecting," Redleaf said. "But I do know you're wrong to do it. Any detail might lead us to her. Even something you think isn't important. What if she is still alive? Every minute counts."

Teresa bowed her head. Sister Judith had taught them that God heard them better when they bowed their heads. It showed God that they knew how small they were, how great His love.

Redleaf mistook her quiet pause for weakness. "Your father isn't getting away with what he's doing much longer. I've been working on this on my own. All the narcotic traffic in the entire county leads straight to Ray Hamilton. He can't buy off everybody forever. You'll go down too if you lie for him now."

Teresa barked out a laugh. "You think I'm trying to protect Ray?"

Redleaf put out her broad hands. "Who else, then? Who else is involved in this? Was it Michael? Is that why your father had him killed?"

"Michael was dead from the day we met," she said. "Michael was shot for loving me. For loving our kid."

"Well then, why not tell me all you know?"

"There is no point." She moved the five whole steps to the other side of the cell.

"And what happened to your fingers, Teresa? Who broke them? Was it your parents?"

Teresa leaned against the wall and studied the bitten tips of her broken fingers. She couldn't think about what Ray had done with Crystal. She had lost track of her own baby daughter. And though Ray was a monster, Teresa was the guilty one. She was the one who'd never returned home. She was the one who left her baby alone in that house with her own broken mother and her father who looked like a man but who was in no way a human being.

"Why won't you talk to me?" Redleaf asked. Her frustration was barely audible over the humming of the building.

"Because he'll get you too, Officer."

Officer Redleaf sat as still as a tree.

Once again Teresa thought back to the time she'd caught Sister Judith standing at the top of the ravine in the woods on the way to the beach, standing there with her arms extended like she was playing a game of Jesus Christ. She didn't know why Sister Judith had been depressed. Maybe there didn't have to be a reason besides the fact that life sucked. Judith hadn't even bothered to say goodbye before she moved away.

She couldn't lose Redleaf too. She couldn't get one more person killed. Michael and their daughter already rested on her soul. She couldn't take on the weight of Officer Redleaf too.

"Forget about me," Teresa said. She climbed back onto the bed and hid in the shadowed corner under the bunk. "You should leave now and never come back."

"Let me do my job."

Teresa didn't answer. She lay quietly until the officer sighed and called for the guard.

In the filthy half-light of the jail at night Teresa waited for the grief and despair that were her sleep companions now. They didn't come. Inside of her was nothing. She forced herself to remember Crystal's bow-shaped lips, her silver-bell laughter. She made the movie in her head replay the warmth of Michael's sheepskin-lined denim jacket as he hugged her. They'd destroyed his beautiful face to cover their crime. How lovely was the scratchiness of his cheek and jaw under her fingers and against her lips. All destroyed.

Ray and his bad men had destroyed her whole world. Yet tonight there was no grief or despair, no longing. Her sadness fell away in an internal erosion, leaving the kind of void that could suck in whole galaxies. Hers had grown to be a heart that felt nothing.

The kind of nothing that consumed whole worlds.

Chapter 24

December 20, 1989
Creekside, California

Angel

⁓⌣⁓

T HE CLOUDS LOWERED their ceiling, threatening snow. Angel tried to catch the plot of a soap opera through the revolving static. She'd been sick for over a week. It hurt to breathe through lungs that felt thin as paper. The doctors had warnings about infection, pneumonia. She'd skipped three or four scheduled checkups since running away to Creekside.

Tawny snored in a fitful nap. The TV provided jangly reminders of Christmas. Angel couldn't get motivated to do anything about the holidays. She hadn't driven her truck once in the entire time she'd been living in the trailer. The key hung on a hook by the door. She meant to take off with the baby but every morning she felt worse than the night before. She shivered and sweated at the same time under a wool sweater of her mother's that she never removed except to bathe. Dizziness struck whenever she got off the couch. While the trailer sank into its original squalor, she and the baby fell into a kind of rhythm with each other. She came alive when Tawny needed something, and sank into static lines when she didn't.

Angel before the earthquake would have left the minute Russell announced that he was married. Angel before the earthquake didn't need a place to hide. Before the quake she was a misfit who lived and served among people who took being a misfit to the extreme. She was happy there, atoning for the thing she'd done to Sundullah and their baby. She was a killer of love, but at the shelter she could at least feel the possibility of redemption, and that made her bold and incisive and the champion of the homeless people who needed her.

Now she lay with her face in the mildewed upholstery, a roll of toilet paper in her hand for when she needed to blow her nose. When she coughed, her lungs rattled like maracas.

She felt the tugging of an inner voice. She should get out, with or without Tawny, at once. Angel could barely hear it. The fever melted her drive. Without the shelter and without a home, she had no purpose and nowhere to go. Without Sundullah and without her mother and without her own baby she had no one and she was no one. She was the cinder girl now. She did a few chores and she cooked the meals and she shut the fuck up.

Angel coughed gluey mucus into a tissue. Tawny slept in the playpen under cozy blankets. Angel wished for a remote control so that she could change the channel from the couch. A storm brewed, the wind louder than the television. She eyed Tawny sleeping every time a howl whistled through the windowpanes and prayed she wouldn't wake up cranky.

Sheila stormed in with a gust of wind and twisted the deadbolt. She was out of breath. "Don't let anybody in," she said.

Angel shuffled to the window. Sheila must have been on foot. Her truck was not in the driveway. "What's going on?" she asked.

Shelia slammed her bedroom door and locked it.

Then Sheila's new truck spun to a stop in front of the trailer. There was a man at the wheel Angel did not recognize. He left the driver's side open. He had a shaved head that looked blue in the cold air. He pounded on the flimsy door.

"Shelia!" His throat clotted and he hacked and spat before yelling her name again.

Angel rushed to turn off the TV. She crouched by the playpen. The aluminum walls shook with his pounding. The man's face was in the window. "Tell Sheila to come out here now," he barked. "I can see you on the floor."

"Sheila isn't here," Angel said. A piece of carpet fiber stuck on her tongue.

"Lying bitch." He kicked the door with what was surely a steel-toed boot.

"I'll call the police," she said. "I don't know you." Her voice wavered. She was afraid she might cry. He cursed again but left in Sheila's truck.

"He's gone," she said to the closed bedroom door. "You can come out now."

There was no answer. Tawny started crying, which Angel hoped would melt Sheila or at least annoy her into coming out. She flattened her ear to Sheila's door to try to hear what she was doing.

"Are you okay?" she asked. Still nothing.

Angel wrapped Tawny in a blanket and patted her on the back. She sat at the window until the child pushed to be let down. Angel followed her around, her heart thumping. She prepared her a snack of cereal and juice, always keeping watch for the bald man. She had to get them out of there, no matter how sick she was. Tomorrow would be the day. For sure.

She ran a bath. Every breath hurt. She was light-headed. Tawny grabbed at her jeans with both fists and Angel had to brace herself against the wall to keep from falling over. She wished for thicker walls, a real roof. The trailer was no protection against the man looking for Sheila. Shelter residents had called her bitch before and other names too. Gene had a few choice ones the times she evicted him for being a bully. The city council hated her for defending the shelter they wanted closed down. There was a time when this bald loudmouth would have been no threat to her. There was a time when she would have welcomed the fight.

Before. This was the word that ruled her life. Before the earthquake she had a home, a mother. Before the abortion she had love. Before she had memory she had a real mother who lost her in the woods.

Angel placed a shaking hand under the faucet. The bald man didn't know her. If he did know her he would realize that they had a few things in common, starting with a shared dissatisfaction with Sheila. He didn't seem the type to listen to reason. The tin deadbolt would not be enough to keep out a crazy man in heavy boots who wanted in.

Tawny screeched on the floor. Angel was a raw nerve pulled as tight as sinew. She shrugged off her sweater. She was freezing. She was always freezing. Russell had said that morning if she'd thought it was cold in December then she should just wait until January. Just wait until the pipes froze.

Angel sank into the water. The baby blinked at the ceiling as Angel held her in a back-float. In the bath was the only place the child didn't want something she didn't have. It was quiet except for the sounds of water and the fierce wind. If she could stay in the tub for the winter then she would emerge in spring rested and ready to live again. Ready to make decisions about her life and her heart.

There was noise at the stained glass window. Two bloodshot eyes appeared at the bottom of the long rectangular pane. "What the hell you doing? Taking a bath with a baby?"

Angel startled. Water sloshed on the floor and Tawny's eyes widened as her face submerged. Angel lifted her to her chest and stepped out of the tub.

"I know you are in there!" It was the bald man. She hadn't heard the truck.

"Go away," Angel said. The baby slipped in her arms as she grabbed for towels. The man laughed. He was watching her. Angel struggled to keep Tawny from falling as she tried to hide her body.

"Are you some kind of pervert in there?" he said.

Sheila had to hear what was happening. She was only ten yards away on the other side of the trailer.

The man whistled. She hauled the wailing little girl into her bedroom. The man jumped and peeped into those windows too. Angel pulled the shades down. He thundered at the exterior walls with his fists and boots.

Angel pulled jeans onto her wet legs, wrapped Tawny in a blanket. She raced through the trailer, holding her close. Sheila's door was still locked. Angel kicked at it. The bald man was hammering the front door with his boots. It would break down soon. It was in fact bizarre that the thin metal and plastic were holding against him so far.

Angel shouted Sheila's name. Tawny cried, yanking fistfuls of Angel's hair. When Sheila didn't answer, Angel scrambled for the phone. She held the baby in the crook of her elbow and shuffled through an outdated phone book for the police department, if Creekside even had one. Maybe the police would have to travel all the way from Quincy. That would take forever. She tried the Plumas County Sheriff Department's number. She misdialed. Tawny slapped at her face. The doorframe cracked, which encouraged the bald man to kick faster.

He swore he was going to kill the bitches. All the bitches. Angel's hand was slimy on the receiver as she dialed again. The phone rang and rang and nobody answered. The door swung inward and the man charged through.

Sheila burst from her bedroom with her arm held straight down her side. Angel huddled on the floor with Tawny while Sheila lifted her arm and pushed a handgun against the man's nose.

The man stumbled down the stairwell and off the front porch. He scrambled backward on the ground while Sheila chased him with the shiny black thing pointed at his face. Her arm formed a perfect straight line. She was an isosceles triangle come to life in sharp edges and uncompromising points.

"The truck is yours," she said. A freezing wind blasted through the trailer, carrying her voice. "Take it. That more than makes up what I owe you."

"You barely made a down payment. You're not giving me shit."

"So break it down for parts and sell them. I don't care what you do." She flipped the hammer with a click that echoed in the forest. "Take it and leave me the hell alone, Frank."

"You're crazy," he said. But he scurried to the truck. Sheila kept the gun raised until he boomed down the road. Only when the creek was the only sound did Sheila return to the trailer.

Angel stood in the kitchen holding the baby, who cried in ragged sobs and reached for her mother.

Sheila met Angel's eyes. "You were a whole lot of help back there, thanks," she said, her voice flat. Before Angel could answer she backward-kicked the front door closed again. It hung loose with a six inch gap, letting in the cold.

Sheila set the gun on the table and took her daughter. She whispered against her cheek in an act of tenderness Angel didn't think possible. Tawny stopped crying. She nestled against her mother and clung to her neck.

Sheila grabbed the gun and took Tawny into her bedroom. With a click of the lock they were gone behind the closed book of the bedroom she and Russell shared.

Angel went into her own room and sat on the flat mattress for a while. Then she put on her socks and boots and two layers of flannel shirts. She needed to get out of the trailer. Now it felt like the most unsafe place in the entire world.

She tromped into the forest, wheezing for breath. She cut through the trees that lined the driveway but stopped after a few yards. There was no trail. Her breath made small puffs of cloud in the freezing air. She'd be lost in less than five minutes if she kept going this way. She headed back.

Her mother would say that this was the part of the story when the girl got lost in the forest. The girl was lured by a promise of love that was as fleeting as cotton candy on the tongue. It fed her nothing. And then it was gone.

Sheila and Tawny sat together on the couch with the television on. Sheila talked on the phone, playing with the long coiled cord while a cigarette dangled from her fingers. Angel wished she had a habit like cigarette smoking to calm herself. Something to do with her hands that made everything else look like a secondary distraction and not important enough to warrant her full attention.

But Angel was never cool. It felt like a real lack in her personal make-up to be so uncool. As much as she resented Sheila, in her presence she felt like half a person and wished she could be more like her. It was a hell of a spell.

"What's for dinner?" Sheila said, tucking the phone under her chin. "And don't say that leftover stew crap. I hated it."

There was an electric feeling in the trailer. Sheila ignored her to agree on the phone that someone was an asshole and deserved what happened. She bounced her leg and lit another cigarette with the end of the one she'd just finished. Her freshly washed hair hung over one shoulder. Without eyeliner her face was startling in its prettiness. Her nose and chin were as fine as a porcelain doll's.

All that was left in the freezer were a couple of bags of pheasant parts Russell's uncle had given him earlier in the week. Stalagmite frost collected along the top of the compartment. Angel pulled out the pheasant pieces and clunked them on the counter like cold stones.

They needed groceries. Angel inspected the breasts and thighs through the plastic. Black feather stubs stuck out of the white flesh and curled like pubic hairs. Maybe in a roasting pan with some potatoes and broth she could make this not gross. It couldn't be much different than chicken. She dumped them in a pan of hot water from the tap to defrost. She could walk across the highway to the Bait and Shop and see what she could find to add to it.

The wind from a speeding car whipped her hair in her face. The lights of the grocery played through a prism of fine snow. Bits of rain fell on her eyelashes and stuck in frozen beads.

The store was warm and smelled like wood floors and produce. She chose a few apples, some cinnamon. The man behind the counter had a peppery beard and kind eyes. "Careful out there, miss. Storm front's coming along now," he said. He patted change into her open palm and Angel stood looking at the quarters and pennies through tears.

"Why, what's wrong?" the man asked. "You don't look so good." Angel gathered the grocery bag to her chest. She could not bear his kindness. A man threatening to kill her made more sense than a man treating her with kindness.

The unforgiving wind fought her as she trudged along the side of the highway. She stopped to cough and spit. One fairy tale in the book told about a young girl abused by her stepmother and stepsister. They sent her out into the snow in her bare feet to find strawberries. The girl was blessed by good dwarves who gave her gifts of berries, and the magical power of gold coins spilling from her mouth whenever she spoke, and the love of a prince at the end. The dwarves cursed the bad stepsister with toads and snakes spilling from her mouth with every word, and in the end a dunking in the river.

Angel always imagined that she could be as good and brave as the girl sent into the snow. She still wanted to be that good. She concentrated on walking as the snow fell harder. The earthquake tore open the surfaces of her life and through the cracks oozed a kind of mud she never knew was there. On the dividing line of good and evil she had thought she was good. Despite everything she had done, she had thought redemption was possible.

The wind blew spikes of snow against her cheeks. She wiped her nose on her sleeve. Wet patches spread along the fronts of her thighs. Crossing the highway, she scrambled down the road toward the bridge. The river sloshed at the wooden planks. She wished for a flashlight to cut the snowy night so she could see the path.

She thought of the day she learned she was pregnant. She'd bought a pregnancy test from the drugstore and used it in a bathroom at school. She tossed the result in a trash can before sitting through a sociology lecture. It had been idiotic to go off the Pill. She'd been taking it since high school. Those days she would sometimes go eight weeks without seeing Sundullah. It had seemed like a good idea to get her body into its own natural rhythms without chemical hormones, and to try other methods of birth control.

The last time he visited had been a surprise, and while the danger of a baby lurked in the back of her mind, she dismissed it as they lay together. She didn't have the heart to ask him to wear a condom. She didn't even tell him she hadn't been taking her birth control pills.

Her actions were stupid, but not entirely a mistake. If she were honest, she would have to admit that along with the fear of conception, she'd hoped for it too. Sundullah's career and his absurd fame were taking him from her. They were in a strange doldrums of unhappy phone conversations and scribbled postcards. The phone calls were worse than silence because she could not help him long distance. Through the phone his anxiety and loneliness swallowed everything good between them. A baby would force the kind of change she wasn't brave enough to make herself. A baby would ask for the things she wanted.

Now that she had seen the two blue lines for a positive test, Angel felt as though someone had pressed the pause button on her feelings. She was numb. As the professor spoke about cognitive dissonance, she drew hearts in her notebook. She didn't feel happy. But she wasn't unhappy either. When Sundullah heard about the baby, he would be happy, purely. This she knew for sure.

Baby. She mouthed the word in silence.

The campus was quiet after dark. On the way to the bus stop, Angel passed a commons room filled with yellow light. A single voice wavered over murmurs of encouragement and the popping of finger snaps. She wandered into the poetry reading, at first standing in the back and then helping herself to cheese and crackers. Though meaning to stay for only one poem, she stayed for two. Someone unfolded a chair for her. She accepted a cup of sparkling cider. The room was warm and patchouli hung in the air, the scent of college. Angel lost herself in the strings of words, and afterward talked with a couple of the poets, congratulating them. She knew the things to say to make artists happy.

When she returned home hours later, Judith waited by the fireplace, worry lines dug between her eyes. "Sundullah's been calling," she said.

The glow from the poetry reading evaporated. Angel looked at her bedroom wall as Sundullah wept into the phone. He was in New York that night. There were back-to-back shows and he was so tired. They were pulling him apart like dogs. His mind was racing in a million directions. He couldn't turn it off to sleep and it was one a.m. where he was. Where was she when he tried to call before? Why hadn't she been there? No one could help him but her. Didn't she love him anymore?

Angel remembered pressing the phone to her ear, her feelings undammed as Sundullah called her name. Disappointment. A river of dread. A breathless need to escape that made her think of a panicking bird caught in a too-small cage. The dread didn't leave her until the moment she woke from the abortion procedure. In its place rested cold, leaden guilt that stayed with her still. It made each footstep heavier than the last, even now.

By the time she returned to the trailer her feet were painful frozen hooves in her wet boots, her hands red claws clutching the disintegrating grocery bag. The trailer was empty. She turned to the window. She hadn't noticed at first in the driving snow but now it occurred to her something was missing.

Her truck was gone.

AT TEN O'CLOCK Russell entered and shook his boots. Filthy snow puddled on the linoleum where he dumped them. White snowflakes, bigger than the tiny pinpricks that fell in the beginning of the storm, dusted his eyebrows and shoulders and crowned his shaggy brown hair.

The candles she'd lit on the counter flickered at the end of their wicks. His eyes dashed around the trailer as though he was not sure where he was.

A Dutch oven sizzled on the table. She'd plucked out the feather stems and roasted the pheasant with apples. It smelled like Christmas dinner. She took his coat and he let her do it.

"Listen, a guy came by today. He said he was going to kill us," she said as soon as he sat down. "Sheila chased him away with a gun. She keeps a gun, Russell. With the baby in the house."

He raked his fingers through his hair and rested his head in his hands. It seemed eons ago when they were friends, running along the alleys of downtown Santa Cruz, clinging to each other for warmth. They were still at least that, friends. Old war buddies. She wouldn't leave him to this. She wasn't the kind of person anymore who left people who needed her. She had to try to make him see that they were dying there. If they stayed, then surviving the earthquake was a moot point.

She pushed his plate toward him along with the knife and fork she had placed together on their napkin bed.

"Eat," she said.

"I'm not eating this. I had dinner in town with Sheila and Tawny."

Russell rolled his fork and knife in the napkin she'd folded just for him. She was a ghost in the room.

"She took my truck," Angel said. "Without asking. She's mean to me all the time. The baby had a horrible rash, did you know that? Sheila didn't keep her clean. The rash is gone now but only because I bathe her every day. Twice a day sometimes."

"Angel, wait." He rose his hand like a crossing guard.

"We need to get out of here, Russell. I'm serious. We can go back to the way we were before Sheila."

"I don't think we can," he said.

"The crazy bald dude has her truck, did you know that?" She could keep talking. She could make him see. "He broke the door. I thought he was going to kill us."

"Sheila's accusing you of molesting Tawny," Russell said. He pointed his face to the table as he said it.

Angel shut her mouth. The overhead lamp buzzed. The tea light candles she'd set on the counter wavered in the draft hissing through the broken door. Bird pieces swam in gravy on Russell's plate. She'd gone to so much trouble and had made something out of nothing. She'd found the strawberries in the snow just like the girl in the story and it had not mattered.

She kept quiet as Russell said that Sheila was thinking of pressing charges. But he didn't think she would. Either way Angel needed to stop taking baths with the baby.

"It's not like I think you're doing anything wrong," he said.

"The baby cries all the time. The bathtub is the only place she's happy." Her skin warmed even in the chilled trailer. What Sheila was accusing her of was beyond belief.

"Do you have to get in the tub with her? You can at least see why Sheila was wondering about it."

He poked at the carcass of the bird that his uncle had shot from the sky. A bit of buckshot had worked its way to the surface and stained the skin in a blooming bruise. If Russell bit into it he would break his teeth. Her fingertips were raw from where she'd plucked the ends of feathers from the skin. They hadn't come out easily. She'd half expected the flesh to bleed from the empty holes.

"I think I can keep her from calling the police," Russell said.

She saw him suddenly for what he was. He was no old friend. He was a lost and drowning man who would pull her down to die along with him.

"She's not calling the police," Angel said. The flesh on her arms erupted into goose bumps as she took corporeal form. She turned on the light, blew out the candles. Under the blue overhead lamp, she was struck with the sudden absence of longing.

"She was really pissed," Russell said.

"She's not calling the police because she knows damn well I haven't done anything wrong. But she has," Angel said. "She's stolen my truck."

"I need a beer," he said. He opened the refrigerator. Angel kicked it closed.

"Get my truck for me, Russell. Get it and bring it here within the hour so I can leave or I'm calling the police."

"What? You can't drive the pass tonight without chains."

"Then you will need to get some and put them on my tires," Angel said. "Take an hour and a half. If you aren't here by then I'm calling the sheriff and telling them she stole it. I have a couple of things to tell him, actually. Maybe he can take a look around. Under the bed."

Russell looked at her as though he might argue. She looked him straight in the eye and did not blink. Standing up for herself was like riding a bike. Not so bad once she got back in the swing of it. He put on his coat and left.

Angel turned off the oven. She felt lighter somehow. She went to the bedroom with the bathroom like a church and packed her things. It didn't take long. This was the part of the story when the girl found her way out of the snow.

Chapter 25

April 27, 1972
Arcata, California

Judith

~~~~~

IT WAS ONLY a matter of patience. Judith drove into town in a car borrowed from her friend Betty. Teresa had talked about her father's night business with the liquor store on the corner of First and Humboldt Avenues. The owner laundered money for Ray. Teresa had explained some of the operation during Judith's visits to the garden shed. He spread his drug profits between the restaurants, the liquor store, and the saints in the chapel. For Judith's purposes, the liquor store made the most sense from a logistics point of view. At night, deserted. No bystanders.

She parked and hid and waited.

The Cadillac idled by the curb for thirteen minutes during her first night of watching. Billy left the store, carrying a package. He and Ray sat together in the Cadillac with Ray in the driver's seat. She couldn't see what they were doing. It wasn't important. She timed them. Nine minutes with the front-seat business before they drove away.

She prepared beforehand until she knew how to do it. Betty's husband taught her on the range. She practiced for weeks. She was no expert. She knew enough.

The second night they passed a bottle back and forth for seven minutes and thirty seconds before they left. She almost followed them. *Patience*, she thought. It was a virtue.

They returned an hour later, bumping to a stall with the front wheels on the sidewalk. The drinking had done them in. Billy staggered into the dark liquor store.

He exited with another package, she assumed of money. She waited for them to go but they didn't go. Teresa had once told her that Ray loved to count his cash. It calmed his nerves.

Judith ducked across the street, praying the backseat would be unlocked. It was. She slid across the shiny leather. The smell of the inside of that car made her throat close with the memory of the hell that happened there. She didn't look to see if her blood had stained the floor. She didn't stop to think or feel.

Billy and Ray were pickled in alcohol. Her face was sweating behind the laboratory safety goggles she wore to prevent splatter from getting into her eyes.

First Ray. Then Billy, before he had a chance to react. Bang bang. They were so drunk. Large bills fluttered in their laps as they hunched over, bleeding. She left the money there, blood roses blooming in the dirty green.

Judith's ears hummed. She was deaf as she ran to Betty's car. She didn't stop driving until morning had dawned and she returned to Angel, waiting on Betty's porch. Watching the road for her return. Running to her with open arms, begging to be lifted.

Chapter 26

April 27, 1972
Arcata, California

Teresa

❦

THE LIGHTS FLIPPED on and Teresa started awake in the prison cot, fearing Ray. But it wasn't Ray. It was Redleaf.

"Teresa, I'm sorry to say I have some terrible news for you about your father," she said. But she didn't sound sorry. Her voice was carbonated with excitement. Dread crashed against the walls of Teresa's heart. Whatever it was she was sick of surprises.

"Is he coming here?" Teresa whispered. As she rose, a muscle in her neck snapped in whiplash and blue spots of pain danced in her vision.

"No, ma'am," Redleaf said. "Nothing like that. He was found dead tonight at an intersection south of town. Nobody saw who shot him."

"Oh my God," Teresa said. It was her first mention of His name in years.

"Any idea who might have done it?" the officer asked. She wasn't happy exactly. But she was excited.

Teresa waited for the revelation to sink in. No more Ray. It could have been another test. Redleaf didn't know about how tricky he could be.

"If he's really dead, then I'd bet it was Billy Stamm," Teresa said. She touched the side of her neck where it hurt. "It's Billy you want for it." It was likely her father's partner was making a play for the big trade routes in the Redwood Empire. Strange that she should have to explain that to a cop.

"Not Billy Stamm." Redleaf shook her head. "He's dead too. They found them together in Ray's Caddy stalled at a red light. Both shot in the head."

Teresa couldn't blink. Both of them gone. It was too much to imagine. "This was me," she said. "You might as well say I did it."

"That's crazy," Redleaf said. "You've been stuck in here."

"Not crazy," Teresa said. "Don't call me that." She knew that somehow she had a part in putting the bullets into the heads of two of the worst men who had ever lived.

"Tell me how this happened, then. Anything could help me," Redleaf said. She watched Teresa as if she expected the killer to pop from Teresa's forehead, whole. "Any detail can mean more than you think."

"You always say that. I've told you everything."

"And you always say you've told me everything when you've told me nothing." Redleaf pounded her fist on the table.

Teresa jumped. "I'm not crazy," she said. Ray was gone. Redleaf wouldn't say it if it weren't true. No one was tricky enough to get out of a shot to the head. Not even Saint Ray.

"They had bags of pills and grams of heroin on them. There were literally rolls of cash in a bag on Billy's lap," Redleaf said. "They were driving around with thousands of dollars in cash and drugs. It was still in the car when the police found them, Teresa. This wasn't a robbery. This was revenge."

Teresa's lips played with a smile. Her father always liked to touch money. He liked having it around. He filled flour sacks with money like a robber in a cartoon. He rolled it in coils and stuck it up the bottoms of the religious statues in the hypocrite's chapel he built in the garden. None of it would do him any good now. She massaged her knuckles.

"You know so much more than you're saying. Why won't you trust me?" The officer's hair shone like obsidian even in the grungy lighting of the prison cell. Her eyes were intelligent and their dark-brown depths seemingly limitless. "You're thinking something right now," she said. "Tell me what you are thinking." Her voice carried a hint of an accent. Officer Redleaf carried secrets of her own, Teresa could tell.

"I killed them," Teresa said.

"You didn't."

"I feel like I did it," Teresa said. "Somehow I know it."

"You didn't do this. You may be rejoicing and nobody would blame you for it, Teresa. But trust me, this was not you." She grabbed onto one of the bars and called for a guard. "Go to sleep. We'll talk in the morning."

The hall went dark again. Teresa whispered the word *freedom* in the hollow quiet of her room.

She said a silent prayer of thanks as Sister Judith had taught her to do when something good happened. It had been so long since she'd had occasion to be thankful. "You could be thankful for the sight of a beautiful tree in nature or the kindness of a friend," her teacher had said. Teresa remembered that advice now. Say thanks when something good happens and more will come.

Steel bands unloosed from her ribcage, her head, her wrists, her heart. She clutched the mattress to keep from floating to the ceiling in her lightness. The prosecution had nothing on her now. Ray was dead. Teresa was free.

"Thank you," Teresa whispered into the prison darkness. It felt funny to say it to nobody. She didn't know who deserved the thanks. God. St. Mary. Whoever murdered Ray.

And with that, suddenly Teresa knew. She knew who killed her father and Billy. She knew what had happened to Crystal. Redleaf was right. She knew so much more than she was saying, even to herself.

She knew everything.

Her prayer broke through the prison ceiling and into the starry sky, burning at its base with the agony of her broken fingers, her grief over the death of Michael, the numbness that had gripped her since the loss of Crystal.

The knowledge of what had happened and what this meant opened in her chest like great wings expanding. She lay on the bed and touched just the trailing hems of happiness and freedom. Maybe her life could have meaning. The mirage of hope shimmered so that she could almost remember what it felt like to have it.

But self-hatred and shame wriggled to life, then grew to a swarm of hot and buzzing memories of a life defined by humiliation and pain. She was the reason Michael was dead. She had left Crystal alone in the dragon's lair. With Crystal present, she had shot up many times in the shed, only telling her daughter to close her eyes. Then she'd fallen into a dead sleep when she was supposed to be looking after her. When she was supposed to be loving her.

She was every bit as much Ray's servant as Billy had been—more in fact. She knew what passed between her and Ray the night he broke her fingers. He'd taken more than her freedom in that basement workshop. He'd stolen her belief that love could save anyone.

"Thank you," she said once more. And it hurt too much to be loved enough to be saved, so she never said it again.

Chapter 27

May 20, 1972
Arcata, California

Teresa

~⌒⌒⌒

THE CEILING OF Teresa's cell contained a universe. She knew every hole in the plaster, every crack and ripple. It had its own constellations. She made predictions based on patterns in its markings. There was the shape of a gun. A pointed finger.

She wouldn't forget the ceiling, though she would want to. In the same way her back memorized every roll and bump in the rusted springs of the bed and she knew through her peripheral vision just how much distance stood between each of the four walls.

The guard came to fetch her for the final time. The uniformed woman walked her down the long hall, touching her elbow as though she were blind and Teresa the leader. The colorless linoleum reflected the overhead bulbs in the labyrinth connected to the courthouse. Teresa met her lawyers in front of the elevators. As the guard dropped her grip and left them, Teresa didn't say goodbye, though that one had always been kind. Teresa didn't say goodbye to anybody. It was one of her new rules.

They rode to the top floor. Teresa needed to sign papers with the lawyers. Her patience was a deep well. Above everything Teresa had learned how to wait.

When Officer Redleaf entered, she charged the air in the room. Murmured conversations ceased. The other officers found places for their eyes. They looked at the walls, the ceiling, the floor, anywhere but in the round, serious face of Officer Redleaf.

Teresa realized that she would miss Redleaf. She'd never called her Laura. She'd never told her anything she wanted to know. But over the past nine months Redleaf had been Teresa's friend. She sat close enough to share the faint cloud of the officer's jasmine perfume. It was a scent for a much more feminine woman. In the long hours spent in her cell, Teresa had wondered about it . She'd noticed Redleaf's flower perfume, her engagement ring. She turned the facts of them over in her mind to study their facets. Redleaf had a life outside of her obsession with Teresa's life. She had a romance, a man who gave her a diamond, albeit a tiny one.

"Just so you know, I will never stop searching for Crystal," Officer Redleaf said.

Teresa's bitten cuticles were as sharp as spines. She made fists to hide them. Nothing mattered but going forward and pretending none of it had happened until it was possible to believe that none of it did. She would pile the objects of a new life like dirt over the swamp that was her old life. She was already in the process of forgetting her addictions and her parents and Billy. She planned to keep only a few pieces of evidence of her life before the moment she walked out of the county jail. After today she was not going to think about any of them. Even Michael. Even Crystal. Love was the final habit to kick.

"Ray's dead," Teresa said. She hadn't known she was clenching her teeth until she tried to speak. Her jaw ached. "That's all that matters to me."

The lawyer stood at the long window in the hallway and hooked his finger for Teresa to come observe. A crowd seethed below on the wide concrete stairs. A camera crew jostled for space at the top. A newswoman held a microphone in her hand on shaky ground in front of the cameraman.

From Teresa's vantage point the crowd looked like a swelling tide. It knocked the newswoman off her feet. They held her aloft. Teresa locked eyes with her for a second before the crowd set her upright.

"That isn't all for me," Teresa said.

"Afraid it is," the lawyer said. He put his hand on her shoulder. Teresa willed herself not to cringe. He seemed like a good man. He had not asked for anything in exchange for helping her. At least not yet.

The courthouse building had secrets too. Redleaf led them through an underground maze that spit them out into an empty alley. The lawyer's assistant waited in a sedan. A cigarette wobbled in his fat, nervous fingers. The lawyer did not give Redleaf a chance to speak a last word. He hurried Teresa into the car and slammed the door.

He slid into the passenger's seat in front. "Let's go," he said.

Teresa cranked the window to escape the driver's smoke and to smell the air. She'd been outside for an hour a day but it wasn't the same. Free air was different than jail-yard air.

"Put your head down," the lawyer said. But she disobeyed. She watched the crowd's backs as they waited for her to come out the front. A woman accused of killing her daughter drew a bigger crowd than she would have expected. The driver nosed past them. People spilled off the sidewalk into the narrow street, and the driver had to brake to keep from mowing someone over. She watched the crowd as though she were on a driving safari. They were dangerous to her, these people.

Then she saw Sister Judith.

The woman stood on the fringes. She looked different out of her nun's habit. Her hair was cut as short as a boy's. She wore jeans and sandals and a sweater. She looked barely twenty.

She held to her belly a clothbound book and a burgundy teddy bear made of velvet plush the color of blood. *Children's Fairy Tales* and Crystal's Angel Bear. She saw Teresa just as the driver stopped short in front of her. Protesters blocked the way. Sister Judith let the crowd push her closer and she shoved Crystal's teddy bear into the narrow space of the partially open window. It tumbled from the seat to the floor. A lady standing next to Sister Judith saw her do it and yelled, "Terrible Teresa!"

Teresa slumped in the seat, cranking the window closed as fast as she could. There was a great collective shout like the roar of a rogue wave. Teresa pulled the jacket over her head. There was a bump and a curse. The thump of a hand hitting the hood.

"I just ran over a foot," the driver said.

"Just keep going, for Christ's sake," the lawyer said. The car rocked. They would be rolled in the street with the tide of people who hated her. "Baby killer!" someone yelled. "Where is Crystal?"

She peeked from under the coat, but Sister Judith wasn't there anymore. There was only a crowd of people's middles pressing against the car, their belt buckles squeaking against the steel and glass. It didn't matter that she had been acquitted by the court. If the people got a hold of her they would tear her apart.

Crystal's teddy bear crumpled under the driver's seat. The men were too focused on the front to see what Sister Judith had done. Teresa picked the thing up from under the tent of the lawyer's jacket and kneaded its head.

The driver accelerated and the crowd fell away. He pointed the car toward the freeway. South. They would go south to a place far from the land of Ray Hamilton. Teresa tossed the jacket aside in order to watch the crowd recede. Soon they were past the town itself, the paper mill, the sea. With the threat of the crowd behind them, the men argued over which ball game to listen to.

Teresa dropped the bear. Her heart would split open from her ribcage and she would die of loss in the backseat of the lawyer's sedan. Blood loss, love loss, loss of a child.

She forced herself to stare at the back of the men's heads in the front seat. She had only to go forward. There was power in survival, much more than in love. Love could be lost. Wherever found, it could always be lost again. Survival was the one constant. Her survival was the only certainty in the world.

Chapter 28

December 23, 1989
Del Rio Beach, California

Laura

RED GERANIUMS RELEASED their pepper scent under Laura Redleaf's shoes as she hid in the side yard of Judith's cottage. She hoped that the guy who lived in the big house fronting the street wouldn't happen to take a look into his backyard right then. If he came out asking questions, she could flash her badge, claim police work. Hopefully he wouldn't call anyone to check her veracity. She was woefully out of her jurisdiction.

Laura had been parked outside Judith's house for two days. Before leaving San Jose she called home from the motel. Her husband's voice sounded far away.

"Christmas is the day after tomorrow," he said. "You're missing everything."

"Angel is coming back."

"Who?"

"Crystal. The missing baby," she said. He knew who. "She's twenty-two now."

"When is she coming back?" he asked. His quiet response told her everything he was feeling. Patient. Not happy. Not buying it that the case was soon to be resolved.

"If not today I'll drive home tonight."

"Don't promise that," he said. Static buzzed through the wires.

"I know," she said. He knew she had to see this through, despite the cost.

On Christmas Eve their daughter and son would collect evergreen boughs from around the property. Her husband had already hung the white lights around the fireplace in their house in the woods inside the boundaries of the reservation. She loved them so much. Away from her family she was not whole. Her longing for her husband and children felt like dying for lack of air.

But the fact was that Angel did appear. First she roamed the four rooms of her mother's rented house. She sat on the couch for a minute. Then she disappeared into one of the bedrooms. Every few minutes she let loose a hacking cough that sounded like bronchitis.

Angel was almost four when she went missing. Laura's twins were fully conscious human beings at four. They carried on conversations at that age. They had wants and desires. They had fears. They referenced things from their fourth year even now that they were nearly teenagers. Her son remembered the trip to Disneyland they took that summer. Her daughter at four couldn't be told what to wear. She always insisted on the same cotton dress with jeans.

Angel at four would have understood that her mother had disappeared from her life. She would remember later what had happened the night she and her mother separated forever.

The ocean boomed below. How Judith could stand living at the edge of a bluff like this, Laura did not know. With one good storm it would topple into the sea. Inside the house Angel stood at the kitchen table. She sifted through papers and found a neon-green postcard. Flipped it over then flipped it back. Laura Redleaf would have loved to know who it was from.

Laura took a deep breath before entering through the kitchen door. Angel dropped the mail in her hands. For the first time since she'd seen Angel's face on the television after they'd pulled her from under the bricks, Laura faltered. She waved a hand as if to say hello.

"You," Angel said. She braced herself against a chair for a bone-wracking cough. "You going to arrest me?" She avoided Laura's eyes as she grabbed the cheap advertising mailer that dropped on the floor.

"I just want to talk to you," Laura said. "Judith has been worried." She indicated that they might sit together but Angel remained standing.

"My mom won't see me," Angel said. "So you're a liar." A glassy sheen reflected in her eyes. She looked terrible.

"I knew your mom," Laura said. "Your real mom—Teresa Hamilton. I want to know what happened to her."

"A lot of things happened to her," Angel said.

When Angel spoke, it was clear that this was a grown woman. Though she should not have been, Laura had been startled by the sight of Angel when they first met in the FBI office. Every single day for eighteen years she'd wondered about the baby Crystal. She had not expected a young woman with a spine as strong as rebar.

"I'm worried that she's hurt or needs help," Laura said.

"You think my mother—Judith, I mean. You think Judith hurt her."

"I just want answers, same as you do."

"Judith couldn't hurt anyone," Angel said. "She didn't hurt Teresa, that's for damn sure. Teresa isn't missing. She doesn't want to be found. The Good Lady didn't do anything wrong. She doesn't belong in jail and you know it."

"The Good Lady?"

"My mother. Judith. She told me stories. It's too hard to explain." She covered her forehead. Sweat shone on her face despite the cold house. Laura guided Angel into a chair.

"You're not feeling well, are you?" Laura asked. She didn't wait for an answer but moved around the kitchen. She put a pot of water on boil and started opening cabinets. "How long have you been sick?"

"I don't know," Angel said. She rested her head on the table. "A week, I guess."

"How about you go to bed."

Angel didn't fight. Laura didn't know what she would have done if she had. She had no legal right to be in the house or to tell Angel what to do. She was relieved when the girl went into the bedroom still clutching a few pieces of mail.

The refrigerator contained rotten vegetables and spoiled milk. She dumped the garbage in the can outside. While the water boiled she searched for food a sick person could eat. Judith had some crackers and aspirin in the pantry. Canned soup. She went about making a tray.

Angel was fast asleep on the bed, even thinner than when they'd last met. In a closet, Laura found more blankets and piled them on. She took off Angel's boots. She swept through the house, wiping the surfaces of shelves and tables. Angel had a lung infection in the hospital. The musty air in the closed-up house wouldn't be good for her. Laura cleaned the dust and mildew that had accumulated in the two months of neglect.

When she was finished, she stood at the picture window. A glorious view of the ocean sunset twinkled before it. It was a cute place, despite its wear and tear. There were overstuffed bookshelves and white walls. Sisal rugs covered the wood floors, and seashells and sea glass lined the windowsills. Laura collected wood from a pile by the geraniums and lit a fire in the white brick fireplace.

The rocking chair by the hearth was a good place to rest while going through Judith's mail. The landlord must have been bringing it in for her daily. There were neat stacks of bills, notices, and paychecks from the textbook company she wrote for. Letters from addresses all over the country. Laura opened a few. A woman accused of stealing another woman's child got a lot of hate mail from strangers. These were just the first droplets of a deluge. There were more at the FBI headquarters.

Around midnight Angel called out. Laura ran into the bedroom to find her sitting in bed with her eyes wide open, staring at the ceiling.

"Angel?" Laura waved a hand in her face. Angel blinked, then flopped onto the bed.

"Damn," she said. "I'll never get used to the fucking spiders."

Laura's shoulders hunched near her ears and she looked up, expecting the worst. But there were no spiders. She swatted the bedcover, looked under the bed.

"I don't see what you're talking about," Laura said.

Angel held a pillow over her face. "Don't bother looking. They aren't real."

Angel's hair was a nest of tangles. Laura suggested they move to the front room. The young woman was still in a compliant mood, too sick to protest. She sat on the couch and let Laura serve fresh tea, soup and crackers. Laura tried to rest the back of her hand to Angel's forehead to check for fever.

"Don't touch me," Angel said.

"Sorry. I'm glad you're alive. Part of me doesn't believe you're real." Fatigue rested heavily on her shoulders. She settled into the rocking chair. "What was that about the spiders?"

"Hallucinations," Angel said, "courtesy of Mother Nature. I was sleeping through the night in Creekside. Thought I'd kicked them."

"Post-traumatic stress syndrome from the earthquake?"

"Yeah. Sure," Angel said. Her voice was gravelly. "Can I ask *you* a question for a change? What are you even doing here?" She coughed.

"I want to find your mother. Your birth mother." She added another log to the fire, wishing there was central heating.

"I don't know where she is," Angel said. She looked into the fire. Her face revealed the lie in the way that all faces did. Human beings thought they could bend the truth to their will, but Laura could almost always tell. Her heart leapt but she kept rocking, holding her own face still.

"Then she's alive," Laura said. She held her breath. Angel shrugged.

Laura shouldn't have been surprised enough for relief. Survival was Teresa's great talent.

"Where were you the past month?" Laura asked. Maybe she had been with Teresa. She resisted the urge to brush Angel's hair from her eyes. To rock her back to sleep.

"Creekside." She lifted her eyes over her mug. "It's sort of a town. Ever hear of it?"

Laura shook her head.

"You should be glad. It sucks."

"Who were you with?"

"A guy I know." Angel sighed. "I'm an idiot, did you know that? Put that in your report. Angel Kelley is a fucking idiot."

"I doubt that very much," Laura said.

"You shouldn't. I stuck around for weeks for no reason. I wasn't in love with him. After a while I didn't even like him."

"There must have been some reason you stayed," Laura said. She had no idea if what she was saying would be helpful. She felt like she was swatting around for a light switch in a dark room.

"You wouldn't believe the whole story if I told it to you. You wouldn't believe anybody could be so stupid."

Laura let Angel sit in her unhappiness without pressing for more detail. At Teresa's trial, Laura had to cross lines of angry people holding signs that said "Terrible Teresa" and "What happened to Crystal?" The words were slashed letters written in the red of blood.

This was what happened to Crystal. She grew into a person. Her life had gone on in another woman's care, built over her true mother's sadness like a new city over a ruined village. There was a resemblance to Teresa in her sharp jaw line, full lips, and intelligent eyes. But she had a strength and grace that came from being cared for properly and loved. However bad Angel thought it had been in Creekside, Laura would never find this young woman nearly dead in a drug dealer's RV, her arms ravaged by bleeding sores.

There was a birth certificate for Angel Kelley with the parents' names blacked out. It was a forgery, of course, and a good one, but Angel Kelley didn't really exist. This was Crystal Hamilton grown and feeling miserable.

Over the years of working on her case, Laura fantasized about what she would do if she found her. In the beginning, she dreamt of leading a search party through the woods, finding her hurt but alive. Laura could feel her little arms encircling her neck as she lifted her from the ground.

Over the crackling of the fire, the ocean roared from below the bluff. The pounding of the waves was not constant in its rhythm. It whispered, and exploded at irregular intervals. The lives of her own children were constant. They got out of bed, went to school, played sports, came home. Every day they depended on a daily flow of kindness from adults. They didn't know enough about what it felt like to live without love to understand how lucky they were.

Laura had built a career in law enforcement, even though there weren't many Indians or women when she started. It was hard but she kept on. She married the best man she knew, a man with a deep capacity for love. They had steady incomes, integrity, small but purposeful lives. Kids thrived in homes built on such foundations.

Her own childhood was more like the waves of the sea. Relentless. Sneaky.

"Why don't you tell me about Creekside?" Laura asked. She wanted to stare at Angel. Instead she watched the blue spirits inside the flames. "It might make you feel better."

"I don't want to talk to you. I kind of hate you," Angel said. The firelight danced on her face and in one instant she was a baby with blankets tucked under her chin. In the next she had an old woman's hollows in her cheeks and under her eyes. "You took everything away from me."

"Is that the way you see it?"

"That's the way it is, Laura Redleaf, Detective. If it wasn't for you, nobody would have cared who my so-called real mother was. I'd be sitting here with Judith, not you. I really need her right now and there's nothing I can do about it."

"You could tell me where Teresa is," Laura said. "We could see about straightening this out."

Angel rolled her eyes. "My mother's lease only goes through the end of December, did you know that? I'll have to be out of here in a week. And now with Russell gone I have nowhere to live. So the truth is you ruined my life, and even if I did know where Teresa was, I wouldn't tell you." She started hacking, and stumbled to the kitchen sink to spit.

Angel returned to the couch, clutching the blanket tight. "Then again, my life was already ruined. Sundullah visited me in the hospital when I was so stoned on morphine that I thought it was a good idea to tell him what I did."

"What did you do?" Laura asked.

"I killed our baby. But don't worry, it was legal. I didn't break any laws. It was all done in a doctor's visit." She was an old woman again. A very old woman. Bitterness held her fast.

"You felt it was the right thing to do at the time," Laura said. "Maybe it's time to forgive."

"Would you?" Angel's voice sounded like she had a throat full of stones. "I'm asking. Would you forgive yourself that?"

"I would," Laura said. She hesitated. Thought of her twins. "I hope I would."

"Do you think a guy could really forgive a girl for doing that without telling him? I mean, say the guy might have loved having a baby and the girl just got rid of it herself without telling anybody. What kind of guy forgives something like that?"

"A good one," Laura said.

"I couldn't tell my mom I did it, you know?" Angel said. "I don't think my mom knows, unless Sundullah told her." She took as deep a breath as she could and squeezed her eyes shut. "I don't know why I'm telling you all this. I haven't had anyone to talk to in a really, really long time. I don't know what else to do."

"Tell me where Teresa is," she said.

"I literally don't know," Angel said, defeated. She wanted to keep talking about her love life. There were more important things to discuss that night.

"You literally do," Laura said. She retrieved her briefcase from the kitchen and opened the latches. "You want to know what I'm doing here? I thought you were dead. Every day I went to work wondering if this was the day we'd get a report from some hikers about a baby skull and bones they found in the woods. But that day never came and instead here you are, alive and beautiful."

"What do you want from me?"

"I'm here because it's wrong to take a daughter from her mother. You belonged to somebody and that Good Lady, as you call her, stole you away."

"She says she had a reason for it," Angel said. "Like you said, maybe it's time to forgive."

"It's impossible to forgive without knowing the truth. You know what I want. I want the whole story, Angel. I want to know what happened. I want to know where Teresa is now."

Laura passed a sheaf of papers to Angel. They were Laura's only ace. She prayed the information they contained would shake the ground enough to loosen the truth from its subterranean moorings.

Only the truth had the power to undo the damage of people like Ray Hamilton and Judith Kelley. Laura laced her fingers over her stomach and closed her eyes. As for the damage inside of her, standing up for Crystal healed those wounds too.

She listened to the papers rustle. Angel clicked her tongue against her teeth.

"Is this true?" she asked.

"I'm afraid so," Laura said with her eyes still closed. "Teresa is the only one who can help us. If only we knew where she was."

Angel coughed. The coffee table scraped the floor as she pushed it aside on the way to the bedroom.

The firelight danced on Laura's eyelids, taking ancient shapes. It flared from the air that blew in as Angel left through the front door. Laura's grandfather's drums and singing called from her memory. It was sacred music that turned his love for her into strength. The music was his hand holding hers as he led her from the courthouse the day when she was eleven and he took her home for the first time. The music was the tenderness in his eyes when he nursed her bruises and distracted her from her night fears with the long stories telling everything the old people knew.

"It's time to go home, Laura," he said. His words vibrated in her ear as though he sat beside her.

"I can't yet, Grandpa," she said.

She opened her eyes to the cold gray light from a sunrise behind clouds. A pile of white cinders swirled in the fireplace. Laura rubbed the back of her neck. The night in the rocking chair had left her stiff but rested for the first time in weeks. She made coffee, used the bathroom, took a shower using Judith's shampoo.

The landlord would have to extend the lease and let Laura pay for another month. The police chief in Eureka would have to extend her leave. Her husband would have to be satisfied with a lonely Christmas.

Laura took her mug to the picture window. When she sat, a wisp of mildew wafted from the cushions. She would wait right there where Crystal could find her when she was ready.

As for Crystal Hamilton, she was gone to find her mother.

Chapter 29

December 24, 1989
Berkeley, California

Razi

RAZI FLOATED THROUGH the hippie restaurant that smelled of incense and coffee and bread. She passed a table of young people in corduroys and peasant dresses. She passed a young family sleek in zipped fleece jackets and hiking boots. She felt them watching her.

The persona she'd created this time was not meant to blend in with the crowd. Her long corn-silk hair matched her silken layers in shades of cream. She walked as though across a promenade of light.

Tom Shepard waited at a corner table and smiled when he saw her enter.

"You look so pretty," he said. He rose from his seat to pull out hers. She liked the springy wires of his beard when he kissed her cheek. She liked his blue jeans faded from wear, not acid-washed. Unlike Rod, he knew what real work was. She slipped her hands into his to feel the leather of his calluses.

When the waitress came, she ordered white tea.

"Aren't you eating? You look like you could eat," Tom said. She waved his concern away. He ordered a full breakfast with eggs and sausage and biscuits. It might be a hippie diner, but they still served meat. The neighborhood patrons liked the looks of peace and love but they still wanted their pork and blood.

Her father had taught her to think this way. People with ideals were the easiest to control. They never wanted the truth. All she had to do was tell them that they were safe and correct while they were taking what they wanted. Once she'd made them feel special, they would do anything she said.

Everybody had twin desires to be special and to be safe. The channeler Isabel Aditi had just confirmed what she'd learned from Ray.

Jin Jun Razi gave her followers back Santa Claus and the Easter Bunny. She provided fantasy that elevated them from their banal lives. She gave people what they wanted. She'd been doing it her entire life, starting with her father. It was how she'd survived him.

"What are you thinking about, darlin'?" Tom held his coffee like he needed it for heat. She said nothing but smiled at him until he smiled too. "Something about you makes me happy," Tom said. "Where have you been all my life, lady?"

The waitress brought fresh tea. Razi closed her eyes to take in its aroma. *Who* had she been was a more accurate question, but she would never say.

"Where is your bus?" she asked.

"It gets problematic in the city. I park it by the marina and ride the Harley to work. You're not really supposed to, but I know one of the guys at the rowing club. He turns a blind eye for me."

Teresa watched him eat. Her stomach tightened in some kind of need. Maybe it was hunger.

"Sorry about this but, I've gotta eat. Hope you don't mind," he said. No food ever got stuck in his beard. He was a red pirate of a man and he looked rough, but he was neat and smelled good. She liked him. He fell for her tricks.

"Never apologize," she said.

He nodded over her two words as though they were profound.

Tom Shepard sat at the free reading at her house looking like a giant among dwarves. He fought to get into the crossed leg position, an unlikely Buddha in jeans streaked with motor grease. After the channeling session, she touched his hand. She knew what he needed. His was the most basic need of all.

The hot tea soothed her sore stomach. "Jin Jun's work is so important for this world but I'm just a vessel for her. I can take no credit for her wisdom."

"You're plenty wise," he said.

"I'm just Razi; that's the only person I've ever been. You were brought to me for a reason, Tom. I need you."

The waitress lingered over pouring his coffee. She looked over her shoulder while she walked away. That was the kind of attention Tom Shepard got from women. He didn't notice, or pretended not to, but Razi did.

"I'll tell you something. I felt a weird energy from the second I saw your card in the bookstore," he said. "It was like I had to go. I didn't know why, but I had to."

"You're nothing like anyone I've ever met," she said. That was the truth, and for the first time the breathiness in her voice that she sustained like a fake accent wobbled. She imagined Tom underneath her in bed.

He reached for her fairy hand in his bear's paw. "Your hands are cold," he said. She folded her fingers toward her palms.

Don't get greedy. Greed caused blindness and blindness caused mistakes.

He paid the check. Once outside she climbed behind him on his motorcycle.

He looked soft but he wasn't. She wrapped her arms around the hard brawn of a man who worked for a living and rested her head against his back.

She would take what she wanted. She wouldn't get greedy. They rode through the hills and then down the frontage road by the water. Her skirts whipped around her legs. She emptied her mind of everything but the wind.

THAT AFTERNOON TOM Shepard left her on a rumpled futon mattress to go to a construction job. She spent two hours cleaning. She stripped the sheets and laundered them, opened windows, scrubbed the bathroom and kitchen and took another long steamy bath. She dropped oils instead of bleach into the water. She anointed herself with the essences of sage and sandalwood. She ran her hands over her angry stomach, her jutting hipbones. Tom was a generous man. The memory of Rod's scrawny shoulders straining as he pumped himself into her was from someone else's life story.

If she thought of her life as happening to someone else then it didn't cause pain. Saint Ray and Michael and Crystal's histories were ruins crumbling to dust. They couldn't hurt her anymore. Rod and Madison's chapters had already begun to decompose. Rod needed a hot girl to tell him he was amazing. He needed her admiration and when he sensed that it had dried up then he went to find it in Linda. What did she care? He had never really seen Reese. In eight years of marriage he never suspected that she wasn't who she said she was.

Jocelyn would take Madison home from the hospital. Jocelyn had always hated Reese because she suspected something foreign slithering under the pretty façade. Her skepticism was a good trait for a mother. She would keep Madison safe. The ground never shifted beneath Jocelyn's feet.

Madison was hers, though. The feeling nagged. She wanted not to miss her but she did. She carried Madison with her every second. She was greedy for her. Love was always the big wrinkle in her master plans.

Razi patted herself dry with a white towel. She hung it in a precise rectangle and dressed. At the door she waited with her hair framing her face in perfect shiny curtains for her followers to arrive. Time to focus on work.

She rubbed the ring finger on her right hand. The bones lumped where she pressed on them. Ray had left his marks on her body. She'd inherited his strange blue eyes as well as his radar for where other people carried their weakness. She bore her broken hands, every single day reminding her of his power. Even dead he lived in her. She carried this truth like a toad in her belly through every seismic shift. So she was a drug addict and dealer and then a supposed child murderer and then a high school honor student and then a college girl and then a newlywed. A new mom, a suburban mom, a grieving widow, and frantic mother.

Just as easily, she'd shifted into a new age guru channeling an ancient spirit. The roses bloomed along the walkway. Their thorns snagged the first followers as they turned to enter her home.

"Welcome," she said in the airy calm of Razi.

The regulars bowed. Some grabbed her hands to kiss them. They took her ugly fingers as evidence of her specialness. She whispered greetings and touched people's faces and held their gazes for longer than was normally polite. One woman who looked like the suburban mom she used to pretend to be broke into tears. Razi patted her back. She feigned patience.

A girl wandered in among the last of the visitors. When she entered the cold white house, Razi stopped breathing.

She'd know her even without the news stories. She would know her blind.

She exhaled and resituated the Jin Jun Razi mask. "Welcome," she said.

"Thank you," her daughter said. She joined the others on the rug. Razi stared at the rounded curve of her cheek that was the same as always. Greed broke through with the power of a tsunami after a seismic event.

Chapter 30

December 24, 1989
Berkeley, California

Angel

⌒⌣⌣⌣

ANGEL SAT CROSS-LEGGED like a kindergartner while everyone else filed to the guru in a line. They talked about her while they waited. *She's so amazing. This is changing my life.* They kissed her hands.

A few non-believers in the beginning of the session huffed and puffed like steam engines before leaving early. They couldn't complain too much. There was no charge for the show. Yet Jin Jun Razi kept a hammered bronze bowl in the corner of the hearth like an afterthought, and people filled it with cash. When the guru started talking in her wild voice everybody in the room swooned. Many of them wore all white, just like her. They looked like ghosts.

Nobody noticed Angel except for one girl who stayed after to organize the money in the bowl. She counted the bills, noting the amount in a notebook before folding the money into a cloth pouch and handing it to Razi. The two spoke by the door in low tones so that Angel could not hear them. The girl's blond hair was twisted in messy dreadlocks. She wore white pants under a white eyelet dress with gold bangles on her arms like a hippie princess. She cut her eyes over Razi's shoulder to Angel but did not say anything. Finally she left, and Razi rested her forehead against the closed door for a long minute.

Then she turned around. Her power over the crowd emanated from fierce, light-blue eyes. Being alone in the room with her felt like sitting too close to uranium. Angel crossed her arms but let the woman stare. So the lapis blue eyes weren't an imaginary dream.

An engine rumbled outside and stopped at the curb. Razi dashed to the window. She turned to Angel with her strange hands in prayer.

"That's Tom. Don't say anything," she said. The raspy niceness was gone. As Angel nodded, a memory dislodged in her brain. It was a clot of memory loosened from its ossified place in a forgotten vein. This was something she'd done before. A silent nod to a direct and desperate order by this very same woman.

"Let me do the talking," she said. Angel nodded again. It was a reflex from an ancient place.

Razi opened the door for a large man with a red beard and wild hair. He wore dusty denim clothes. Though he hunched over, he could not reduce his size.

Razi rose to her tiptoes and kissed him on the cheek.

"This pilgrim needs me," she said. "There's food for you in the kitchen. Wait for me in the bedroom." He patted Angel's head on his way. She felt great weight and restrained power in his touch. It made her feel very young.

"Pilgrim?" she said. "This is crazy." She reached into her bag for her car keys. She was confused and didn't know what to do. The ceiling was too low in that house and she wondered about the safety of the foundation. Berkeley was on a big fault line and everybody knew it. She seemed to be shrinking in size and shedding years with every passing moment. *Danger Will Robinson.* Jerry's voice inside her head.

"Don't leave," Razi said.

"Why?" Angel asked. She waited for Razi to drop the mask.

"You are a pilgrim seeking answers," she said.

A door clicked shut as the man disappeared into a back room.

"No I'm not," Angel said.

"Are you sure?" Razi reached for Angel's face. Electricity sparked where the fingertips met her cheek.

"I know who you really are," Angel said.

"I am the great I am."

"Judith needs you to tell the FBI you're okay. And that you knew about us."

"Judith," the woman calling herself Razi said. "Sister Judith took my little girl."

"Which you knew about," Angel said. Her breath caught in her throat. Her real mother knew about her but never tried to see her, not once. This was important information to hang on to in this weird white house. "She's got cancer and she refuses treatment while she's in the jail. So you need to go tell them the truth or whatever. Maybe you could just make a phone call. I don't know. You'll probably have to go there and talk to them in person."

Razi took Angel's face in both her hands. "What about you, Crystal? Where are you going?"

She tried to twist out of her grip but the woman's birch twig fingers would not relent.

"My name is Angel. You never came to get me or see me, so my name is

Angel." She broke away to cough, and it felt like exhaling a fireball. "After this I'm visiting a friend in L.A. but that has nothing to do with you so don't worry about it."

"I'll take you," Razi said. "You'll stay with me here tonight and we'll leave tomorrow. We'll be together on Christmas."

"Just go to the FBI. I don't need you to do anything else."

"Let me take you to L.A.," Razi said. Her blue eyes were full of pure need. Needier than the St. Francis men. Needier even than poor Tawny.

"I might let you down," Angel said without thinking.

"Come with me and I'll do whatever you want. I'll go to the FBI."

"You better," Angel said. She had no idea what threat she could wield if the promise wasn't kept.

"You'll sleep here tonight. But never say a word to Tom or anybody about who we are."

"Why?"

"If you do, that's the end."

Razi's face was as smooth as porcelain despite the rough seas in her eyes. Angel wondered what she meant by *the end*.

She is dangerous, Angel thought. *She is dangerous to me.*

Razi led her to a white bedroom empty of furniture except a low pile of sheepskin rugs. She made a soft bed of the rugs with a sheet and blankets and left her alone.

Angel sat in the white room. Whatever she expected from the first meeting with Teresa Hamilton, this was not it. She closed her eyes and saw the woman's blue wolf eyes, her long pale hair. If she left, she would spend the night in a motel someplace and then maybe Judith would have to stay in prison until she died.

Her only luggage was a backpack. She fingered Sundullah's letter inside without rereading it. Lying on her back made it hard to breathe. The gunk in her chest turned to mud. With Tom and Razi murmuring on the other side of their bedroom door, Angel went into the bathroom and filled the bathtub with hot water. She craved steam to loosen her lungs.

The tub filling made her think of Tawny. She hoped Sheila would remember to change Tawny's diaper more often. She felt the pressure of Razi's fingers on her cheekbones from where she'd held her face. She'd remembered a woman's startling eyes, a voice brimming with fear. That was all. There had to have been more. That's how it was with little kids. Tawny had likely forgotten Angel's care already. She would never remember Angel. As for her own baby, she never had memories to begin with.

Angel stepped into the bath. A bleach bottle rested on the edge of the tub. She nudged it with her toe.

She'd taken two pieces of mail from the cottage. One was a letter from Sundullah, and the other the card announcing Jin Jun Razi's free spirit channeling event at her home. Sundullah's letter was a connection to a promise of home. It was a poem made of promises.

He learned how to look after himself more, Sundullah said. He took medication to help with the anxiety. He was in therapy. It was about learning to love like a grown man, he said. The music was going well. He was making a lot of money, but it didn't mean anything without love. And he loved her. The scene was too crazy for him and it always would be. The girls he met scared him and the ones he got to know just disappointed him in the end because none of them were his Angel. He'd be home by the first week in January, he said. Please come.

He'd written it in October, a week after seeing her in the hospital. He'd sent it to Judith's house and Angel only got it when she returned after being in Creekside for a month. Redleaf had surprised her and then told her to go to bed. Angel obeyed for the excuse to be alone. Reading it was like drinking water for the first time in days. She knew what that kind of relief felt like.

Then there was the postcard from Jin Jun Razi. The picture of the guru reached for her through the recesses of her own dreamscape and she knew exactly who Jin Jun Razi was.

As soon as Redleaf showed her Judith's doctor's reports, Angel knew what she had to do. Judith was dying and was refusing treatment while she was in custody. If it were Angel being so stupid, Judith would be furious.

Angel had more than one mission in this crazy house. Terrible Teresa, witch-mother, whoever she was, this woman was not okay in her head. So-called Razi needed help too and that was a fact. She needed Angel more than Angel needed her, in a fundamental way. Angel had to find out a few things about her so-called real mother and she had to save Judith. She would go to Sundullah clear about what was memory and what was myth in her own history. Angel would go to Sundullah knowing she'd done everything she could to save both her mothers. He was right about learning how to love like a grownup. She needed to do the same.

Don't tell. If you do, that's the end. It was a familiar song caught on a loop in her mind like a tune she couldn't quite recall. The words were as familiar as the voice that said them. Razi, Reese, Jin Jun. Teresa. Whoever she was, she'd promised to go to the FBI and set the Good Lady free. Angel had to see this through, though if Jerry were here he would call her out of the white steam. He would extend his jagged finger and point her to the door.

He would be right to be afraid. She knew enough to recognize mental as well as earthen instability. The ground under her so-called real mother was barely holding.

Chapter 31

December 28, 1989
San Jose, California

Judith

～ ～

O N THE WAY to the interrogation room another prisoner spit at her. "Baby-snatcher," she said. Judith stared at her own slipper shoes.

"Keep moving," said the guard.

Judith didn't see her accuser. She imagined a young Teresa with her blue eyes piercing through the bars. Judith had stolen that young woman's child to raise as her own.

Only a monster would steal another woman's child.

The guard led her to the windowless room with the metal table and bolted chairs. Judith spent her life these days seated at a metal table waiting for someone to try to make her talk.

Judith hated jail. She ignored the other inmates because to acknowledge those sad women would be to submit to their pain as well as her own and she just wouldn't do it. She averted her eyes and evoked other convent habits of keeping privacy in a crowded place. After so many years of living with Angel and then by herself she had landed in a community again. She and the other prisoners serving together as the sisters of lost souls.

She ate her meals in her cell. She kept custody of the eyes. She made a cell within her cell. A community of one.

She was thinner since the eight weeks of her incarceration began. She ate at monastic levels. Two spoonfuls of everything was what her appetite could stand. The cancer ticked the time out from under her.

Judith had options. She could tell the agents about Teresa's new incarnation. The advertising mailer Teresa had sent to the prison passed inspection, but Judith knew exactly who it was.

There was going to be a free session with Jin Jun Razi in her own home. She was going to channel an ancient spirit. It was bizarre, but not so uncommon. When she and Angel lived in Berkeley there were constant postings for meditation circles, channelings, and readings of past lives. People started their own mini-religions every day.

The prosecution and investigators could not think beyond the scenario that a young Sister Judith came in the night and took Crystal from her grandparents' home and then let Teresa Hamilton flap in the breeze for her murder. The reality was a whole other story, stranger than they could ever imagine. They didn't recognize it when it came in the mail.

When they searched for Reese Camden, the agents had found an empty house. She didn't want to be found. Well, Judith had promised to protect her too. She wouldn't send the dogs after her further, not just to save her own life. She only regretted telling Angel that her real mother was out there, knowing about them but never contacting them. Judith had given in to the desire to seek out Angel's favor. She had wanted her daughter to be on her side. With this piece of hurtful truth she solidified herself in the role of the Good Lady. Judith shook her head over her own avarice. If only she had sent Angel away a moment sooner, she would have spared her this painful thorn. The guilt weighed heavy on Judith.

That week, instead of forgoing her phone privilege, she'd made one call to Albert. She just wanted to hear his voice. He'd been the most ubiquitous part of her life since Angel went off to college. He was the kindly landlord, the spurned gentleman. The daily friend. It was funny how much she missed him. He talked with her for her full twenty minutes of allotted phone time. She could smell the lavender in his beach towels, see the oil paint flecks on his hair and skin. He didn't ask her if she was innocent or guilty.

"I am here when you get out," he'd said. "I am your friend. Always." His words broke her heart and mended it in the same moment.

The door of her cell had a square window to the hall just like her classrooms did when she taught high school. If she had known then how prison-like the school and convent were, she would have picked somewhere else to work and live. Now that her world had shrunk to the jail, she wondered why she had imprisoned herself in her young adulthood in a career of classrooms. Taking Angel freed her from teaching. The scrutiny of any kind of public service job would have exposed them. She took independent consulting jobs and wrote copy for textbooks. It wasn't great money, but it was a regular income. She supported them.

Yet Judith had lived eighteen years knowing that there were consequences for the things she'd done. She'd lived with the consequences over her head like a sword on a string. She'd made her own prison out of that knowing.

She needn't have been so careful. No one was asking the right questions.

She regretted having lived so small. They could have taken a tour of the world. No wonder Angel worked so hard to get a degree and then holed up in a cell-sized room in the upstairs of a homeless shelter not five miles away from Judith. Judith had kept her safe but she'd never taught her how to live.

In this narrow place she ran the reels of her life over in her head. Old questions posed themselves anew. When Angel loved Sundullah, the girl's life unfolded in such big ways. Angel loved Sundullah with his mythological hair, his heroic green eyes, his way of adoring her. He sang in a voice that made people think of first love. When his star rose, Judith looked forward to the adventure for both of them, but then Angel ended it and she would never say why. Maybe there was no reason. Maybe it was the natural death of a very young love, but it bothered Judith. She should have found a way to make Angel talk to her about it.

Detective Redleaf interrupted her thoughts by banging into the room with a briefcase. The woman had more energy than ever for the task today.

"Laura," Judith said, begging for relief, "I'm so tired."

The detective crouched so she was eye level with Judith. Her knees popped and Judith smelled strong coffee on the woman's breath. "You could tell me the story, Judith. Tell it to me. It's too much for one person to hold. It doesn't have to be that way."

Tears sprouted to Judith's eyes. They surprised her.

"I was alone once too. My mother …" she cut herself off and her knees crackled again as she stood. "Damn. I thought I would tell you my story and then you would tell me yours. This was my big idea. Twenty years on the job; this is what I've got. Stories. Fairy tales."

"Fairy tales mean more than you think," Judith said.

"You ever wonder why I care so much? Why I carried Crystal Hamilton with me all these years? Because nobody else did. I'll tell you that right now. As big a story as that was, when Ray got killed and Teresa left town, nobody wanted to talk about it anymore."

"I remember," Judith said. The story disappeared from the news after Teresa's release. Crystal Hamilton was a pebble thrown into an enormous lake, the ripples she'd made already forgotten.

"Just know this. The reason why I kept Crystal's case alive is because in some ways I am Crystal. I was that kid, if you know what I mean." Laura smiled in a humorless way that frightened Judith. She didn't want to know this. "The only difference was that my grandfather was a wonderful man and he finally got me away from my dad. Every kid needs somebody. Crystal and Teresa didn't have anybody."

"They had me," Judith said, anger flaring.

"I told Crystal you were sick. She knows."

Judith hung her head. "No." She could not say more. This woman saw her as Ray's accomplice. She supposed that to a person like Laura Redleaf, some cases justified torture.

"I did it for a reason, Judith. Crystal left four days ago. She went to get Teresa herself."

"She doesn't know where Teresa is," she said, telling herself not to panic but thinking of the cheap mailer on thin neon-green cardstock. "She wouldn't know where to begin to look."

"She does. I'm convinced she knows exactly where Teresa is."

Judith lunged at the detective. Redleaf raised her forearm, blocking her. "You don't know what you did," Judith said. "Where did she go?"

The detective's jaw twitched. "I don't know," she said.

"You better find her. Goddamn you! What if she finds her?"

"That's what I'm hoping. They belong together."

After the burst of effort, Judith was deflated by fatigue. She fell into the hard chair. "You're so stupid. You all are. You mean well but you lack imagination."

"How so?"

"Teresa said she'd kill Angel if she came looking for her. You have to find her today." Judith swallowed the bile rising in her throat.

"You spoke with Teresa? When? Why didn't you tell me that?" Redleaf rested her hands on her hips and looked at the ceiling.

"Why couldn't you just let me do what I'm supposed to do?"

"What you're supposed to do."

"I'm supposed to protect them," Judith said. Her throat constricted in fear. "I'm sorry you were abused or whatever it was, but I had a job to do too."

"For Ray," Redleaf said.

This was like trying to tutor an obtuse child. "For God," Judith said. "For those girls. Teresa and Crystal. I was the only person who could protect them."

"And Ray said he'd help you," she said.

"Fuck you," Judith said. She spit on the detective's shoes.

Redleaf threw up her arms. She called for the guards to take the prisoner out. Judith sucked in her cheeks to keep from screaming.

"I'll tell you a story," Judith said as they pulled her like a ragdoll. Her only thoughts were of Angel. She felt her mouth moving on its own. The story would come through as though she were the one channeling an ancient spirit.

The detective motioned for the guards to stop. They held her in the box of their uniformed bodies.

"I didn't kill Teresa Hamilton. I didn't kidnap Crystal. Teresa knew I had her. She knew from the beginning. I named her Angel because that is what she was to me. She saved my life."

The detective lowered herself into a chair. Her wrinkled shirt sported a stain on the front. She carried in her body the futility of the past eighteen years looking for a lost girl who reminded her of herself. This was a woman far from home. Judith would send her back there with a story that would be a bag of winds in her sails.

She would tell her the truth.

JUDITH ONLY AGREED to talk to Detective Redleaf. It took some time to convince the guards to leave. For the FBI agents to say yes to a room without mirrors and cameras.

It was Judith's turn to make demands. Turn off the recorders. This is between you and me. I'll be the penitent and you'll be the priest. But this isn't going to be the confession that you think.

* * *

"EVERYONE CALLED TERESA'S father Saint Ray but you're wrong if you think I ever did. All he cared about was money and what he could buy. Who he could buy. In lean times he was the savior of last resort. He supported the school and the church. He ran three or four businesses. The whole town loved him. I've never known a more powerful man.

"Meanwhile he sold drugs through the whole region with this horrible young man named Billy. Billy was a real hard case. They caught me one day when I was by myself in the flatlands. You can imagine how that went. You're going to have to imagine because that isn't the story for today. I will tell you that I see that you think you have a corner on pain. Well, I was a lost girl too. A foster kid. I thought I knew everything about the evil people can do to each other, but Ray and Billy had more to show me.

"He hurt Teresa too. Did you know that? When she was nine he took her pinky finger and snapped it in his bare hands for no reason. That was a forerunner for what he did when she told him she was pregnant. Oh, he was a soulless son of a bitch. True evil.

"I was in the woods the night they killed Michael. The car crash woke me. I hurried on the path toward the highway to see if I could help whoever it was. I didn't want to call the police. So many of you were Ray's pack dogs in those days.

"Crystal didn't make any noise when she ran to me. She was half naked and covered in blood. There were men in the woods and some kind of fight. A man yelling.

"I ran with her to the convent. There was a gunshot and I thought it was meant for us. I just kept running.

"I hid her in my room. She knew how to be quiet. That one knew how to hide and it wasn't me who taught her that. It came out in the papers that

Michael died in a car crash, but as soon as I read it, I knew the truth was something different. I knew who that gunshot I heard had been for.

"After a few days I bundled her into the car I'd driven from Bakersfield when I started at St. Rose. I drove away from those haunted woods and I only went back twice. Once to let Teresa know for sure that I had her girl. The other time, well. I'll get to that.

"They couldn't convict Teresa without a body and without evidence. But Ray planted Crystal's bloody shirt that his guys must have found near Michael's car. Those idiots in the courts just fell for it. You all did. I read about it in the papers, every day hoping one of you would get wise. But you never did.

"My friend Betty looked after Angel. I drove to Arcata and I waited for days. They had no idea. I was right behind them at a red light on a deserted street in the middle of the night. Ray had been getting just the tiniest bit sloppy, drinking a bit more, getting cocky. Making mistakes like going out drinking at night. They were both drunk and that made them slow. It was the easiest thing. I shot them both. You would think men like that would be harder to kill. After everything they did to hurt people it just took a couple of bullets and they died just like anybody else would.

"Judge me if that's what you will do. As for Teresa, if she ever doubted, she's known for a fact that I have her daughter since the day she got out of jail. I took that baby out of the hands of a murderer. Angel's grandfather was the most hateful man I've ever met and I've met a few. I can bet that you have too, Detective.

"Can you imagine what happened to poor Michael that night? He is the true saint of this story. The true hero. He sent her running, knowing she would be safer in the dark woods than with the likes of Ray Hamilton. That sweet, brave boy.

"The priests have it wrong, Detective. Redemption is not possible for everybody. There are such things as monsters in this world. There are monsters and they wouldn't want redemption anyway if Jesus Christ himself were offering."

Chapter 32

December 28, 1989
San Jose, California

Laura

～✧～

"Y<small>OU KILLED</small> R<small>AY</small>," Laura Redleaf said.

"He killed me first." Judith's eyes were dry.

"What makes you think Teresa would hurt Crystal now?"

"When Teresa was my student there was kindness in her, but she was also angry. It was like she contained a part of Ray's spirit. You would see his eyes looking back at you from her face. She hated that she was made from him but she was. I saw it then and I saw it this last October when I visited her. Trust me when I tell you this: Teresa is a dangerous person."

"Have you told anyone else?" Laura asked. "Does anyone else know what you have told me?"

"You're my first confessor."

"Let me be your last." Her heart raced. The walls closed in. She needed to get out, a familiar feeling. She imagined herself, a young girl locked in the trunk of a car and worse in the days before her grandfather won custody. Then there was baby Crystal as a grown woman, locked under several tons of bricks and plaster and broken beams.

"Detective?" Judith touched her hand. "Are you still with me?"

"Why did you say Crystal saved your life?" She wished she could grab Judith and pull her out of the room, out of the FBI headquarters, out from under the ceiling and into the daylight.

"You ever have a baby die inside you?"

"No," Laura said. She thought of Angel's secret pregnancy and how the loss of it had sent her spinning into such grief that she lost herself as well. She was such a young woman to carry such a burden of self-blame and Laura had said little in front of the fire to comfort her. She looked down at her hands, a feeling of uselessness making her angry at herself. An animal noise startled her into the moment. It was Judith, who was rocking and keening, the metal chair screeching under her weight.

"What ..." Laura began. But Judith put out her hand, as if to keep her from coming closer. She huffed for breath over the other hand pressed to her mouth. She shook her head.

Laura did not know what to do. Again, she found herself having little to say for comfort. Nothing came forth but questions that would injure the woman further. She had to voice them. They would spill from her lips of their own accord.

"Did you lose a baby of your own?" Laura asked. "Whose was it? I thought you were a nun ...." Every question had fangs and venom. She could not stop. She watched her own cruelty as if from afar.

Judith could not answer. A storm was passing through her thin body and they both had to wait for its end. Laura moved her chair to Judith's side and patted her back with a gentle, open palm. She waited. She'd been on the job long enough to know that truth almost always appeared in the aftermath of this level of grief.

When it was done and they had been sitting in silence for several minutes, Laura spoke one name. "Ray?" she asked. Judith shrugged.

"His or Billy's," she said, answering Laura's painful question with an answer just as ugly. "I wanted that baby. I swear to you I didn't care how she came to be inside me. We would have been okay. But God or whatever sadistic force that's out there took even that from me. As for Ray and Billy, they killed me first, Detective. They killed me first."

"I'm listening," Laura said. She held the squirming questions back. How did she lose the baby? She imagined a horrible scenario, blood on the bed sheets of a young nun, alone with no one to help her.

With a sigh, Judith rounded her shoulders forward. "I can't talk anymore. We're wasting time. Let's just say that when Teresa told me that she was pregnant it gave me a reason not to die." She stretched her arms, then folded her hands on the table as if in prayer. "There's a green postcard on the shelf in my cell. It's on top of my books. That Jin Jun Razi person is Teresa. Her address is on that card. I need you to find Angel."

"Don't tell anyone what you have told me," Laura said. Laura felt the ground falling out inside of her. She was a landslide on a slippery bluff that threatened to dash the people who depended on her into the sea.

"Find Angel," Judith said.

The detective called to be released. "We will," she said. Though surely Judith saw that she could not be so certain.

Chapter 33

December 29, 1989
Berkeley, California

Laura

THE AGENTS MOVED through Teresa's empty house. Laura followed as they rifled through the back bedroom. Soft rugs covered the floor in plush islands. The kitchen surfaces gleamed as if no one had ever used it for cooking. The scent of bleach from the bathroom permeated the house so that it smelled like a public swimming pool. The forensics team knelt at the tiles, swabbing the grout for evidence of blood. Bleach usually meant a clean-up after the fact.

The agents mostly ignored Laura. If they'd asked her, she would tell them she doubted Teresa lived in this house anymore. The bank listed Reese Camden as the recent buyer, but there was no furniture besides a mattress and rugs. The closets were empty as seashells.

"Any idea what this means?" One of the men found a page ripped from a *People* magazine under the mattress in the bedroom. In the photo, frantic rescue workers carried Miracle Angel Kelley on a gurney covered in white dust.

One word in black marker covered the miracle woman's face.

Ghost.

"It means we have to find her," Laura said. She stood alone in the bedroom as the agents scoured the house for fibers. There was only a flat mattress covered in a white blanket. On the single pillow rested a piece of brown canvas. She lifted the delicate, sulfuric thing with careful fingers. She chewed on her dread and prayed.

Chapter 34

December 31, 1989
Big Sur, California

Angel

～〜〜〉

THE TEENAGER WHO counted Razi's money climbed in next to Angel on one of the narrow beds built into the converted school bus. Behind a heavy curtain cordoning off the back end, Tom and Razi slept together on the large bed. The first time Angel met Fallon was the night she arrived at Razi's house. She took care of Razi, she said, though to Angel the girl seemed more like a slave. She was beautiful. Her favored status kept the men from coming on to her, but they watched her.

Fallon stretched her arms over her head. "I only care about poetry," she said. Like Tawny, she demanded attention.

"Only poetry?" Angel fumbled for her watch.

"That's right. I only care about poetry. And beauty. I only care about poetry and beauty." She rolled to her side. Angel smelled her morning breath. She kept her own body rigid. "What do you only care about?"

Outside, redwood boughs bustled in the wind like giant women wearing green. A line of five cars parked alongside them in the campsite. An overnight in Big Sur had turned into endless days among the redwoods and hot tubs.

"I only care about trees," Angel said.

"You just looked out the window for that information," Fallon said. "You're supposed to look inside. From when you first wake up. Your first thought. What do you care about?"

"I don't think that way," Angel said. "I don't sit around thinking about what I care about. I just do what people need. If people are hungry, I arrange for them to have food. If they have nowhere to stay, I work at a shelter and I give them a place to stay."

"You *used* to work at a shelter," Fallon said. "That shelter is gone now.

What do you care about? And don't say trees." She started playing with Angel's hair. It was uncomfortable but sweet at the same time to be touched with such kindness by someone she barely knew. Fallon pulled her hair through her fingers to work out the tangles. She made Angel sit up to brush her hair. Angel sat between her legs as Fallon straddled her. The sensation of having her hair brushed sent shivers down her neck. She closed her eyes.

"You're not answering me." Fallon rested her chin on Angel's shoulder.

Sundullah. I only care about Sundullah. But she couldn't say that out loud. She wasn't about to start wearing her love for Sundullah like a concert t-shirt. The hope she held that she might be so truly loved again in return belonged to her alone. She didn't want to share it with anyone, not even this beautiful girl who seemed to think they were sisters.

The air that blew through the open windows carried the promise of rain. Angel had awoken able to take a deep breath without pain for the first time in weeks. On the way out of Berkeley they had stopped at a walk-in clinic for antibiotics for her lungs. The doctor on duty advised her to go to the hospital, but Razi wanted to get going that night, and besides, Angel was glad to refuse. She was sick of the hospital.

Tom's bus was a good place to heal. It was cozy and it was clean. Bungee cords secured blankets, lanterns, and plastic bins to the upper and lower compartments. The whole place spoke to an aversion to clutter. Everything had its place in a scout-like neatness to which Razi only added blankets and pillows and jewel-colored fabrics. Tom already had the crystals and beads. They sat in front like a couple taking their kids on a psychedelic camping trip. Fallon gave Angel long Tarot readings in the back. Angel let Fallon play with her hair, weaving braids that took forever. She loved to undo them, one by one, until Angel's wild hair smoothed into mermaid waves.

"Love," Angel said. "I only care about love."

"That's a good one," Fallon said.

Angel thought about Judith and Sundullah, missing them. The three of them had been a real tribe, not like this ragtag bunch of seekers on a glorified party trip. The three of them now lived in a kind of exile. Sundullah on the road, Judith in jail. Angel traveling up and down the state with strangers. She thought about exile while watching the other followers move in their camps. She longed for the days at Judith's table with Sundullah eating vegetarian soup, listening to him play new songs on his guitar.

Razi and Tom sighed behind the curtain and spoke to each other in low tones. The curtain rolled back. Razi wore white, her hair lifted from her face in Fallon's trademark braids. Fallon wore white too, but Angel retained her own clothes. She waited for remonstrations to wear white with the rest of the group but none came.

Razi smiled at them with closed lips like she knew everything they were thinking. Her gaze cut like a laser, making Angel feel naked and shy. Razi kissed them both on the forehead in succession. First Fallon, then Angel. They were both her pick-up daughters, neither one more special than the other. With a pull of a lever, Razi went through the door to greet people. A hush fell on the camp as she moved among them.

"I only care about love too," Fallon said. She followed after Razi. This was her job, in case the guru needed water or something to eat, or a shawl to wear on her shoulders. At first Angel thought Fallon was crazy to work like that for no pay, but now jealousy tugged at her heart.

Which was bat-shit crazy.

Angel pulled on jeans. She crossed the muddy grounds. The wind mussed Fallon's work on her hair. She found Razi in the back of a van with a group from Berkeley. "Are we leaving today?" Angel asked.

Razi's eyes narrowed. "I'm glad to see you're feeling better," she said. "I'll talk to you later."

"We had a deal," Angel said. One of the other followers gasped. They didn't like her because Razi favored her for no reason that they could see. They didn't know anything about their history.

"We'll talk later," Razi said. The rest looked at each other like they were afraid something bad was going to happen. Angel didn't understand her own fearfulness whenever Razi gave a command. This woman was even thinner than she was, and not much taller. If anybody asked Angel what she was so afraid of, she wouldn't be able to answer.

The bus was a warm place to eat breakfast and watch the others from a safe distance. Fallon was sweet, shadowing Razi like a slave. Angel didn't mind it when Fallon combed her hair. It was a strange intimacy that felt enough like friendship to be soothing, especially after the cold weeks in Creekside. But Angel didn't want to get to know anybody else. The temptation to give in to the Jin Jun Razi crap and belong with people, even these goofy people, was stupidly seductive. Traveling with Razi and Tom and Fallon could feel like home if she didn't think too much. If she didn't remember a truer home with Judith and Sundullah.

Razi appeared on the stairwell. She pulled her long woolen fisherman sweater over her head, handed it to Angel.

"You're cold," she said. "Put on a sweater."

Their fingers touched in the pass off. Angel looked into the mirror above the windshield. They had the same pointy chin and the same sharp bone structure. Odd that no one caught on to the fact that they were related. They were mother and daughter. Alone among the group, Angel had been inside the living goddess. Angel had lived in the interior of her body like something swallowed whole.

"Did you ever have any other kids?" Angel asked. Maybe she hadn't been the only one. She had other questions for Teresa. Did she miss her? Why didn't she ever try to find her?

"It's time," Razi said. "We'll leave today." Razi never answered questions.

"Then you'll go to my mother? Tell the FBI the truth?"

Razi yanked the sweater out of her hands and pushed it over Angel's head. She jumped down the stairwell, called to the crowd that they were hitting the road. Whoever felt moved to come along was welcome. Tom waved from across the grounds and headed toward the bus.

"You need to tell the cops the truth about my mother," Angel said.

The ribbed collar of Razi's sweater smelled of sandalwood oil. Razi tugged it from Angel's face. She grabbed the back of her head and pulled her so close that Angel breathed her exhalation.

"I am your mother," Razi said and Angel felt devoured.

As they prepared to go, three young women in white said their ride had to head back to Berkeley. They asked to go on the bus. Fallon pushed past them on the stairwell and rolled her eyes. "Come on, my sister," she said. She grabbed Angel by the arm to save their place at the Tarot table.

As they headed toward the highway Fallon flipped over cards for Angel while the three newcomers huddled around Razi's back and questioned her about Jin Jun. Those questions she loved to answer.

"I'm the one who is dead, essentially," Razi said. "I'm a channel for Jin Jun's holy spirit. She is more alive than I am. I am just her ghost daughter."

The things Razi said to the followers almost never made sense, though they nodded and made noise as though they had just heard the smartest words ever spoken. But for once she made some sense.

Angel knew exactly what she meant by "ghost daughter." She felt the same way about herself.

Chapter 35

January 2, 1990
Eureka Valley, California

Razi

~~~

RAY HAMILTON METED out Old Testament-style justice like he was the God of Jeremiah and Job. He ordered killings and beatings, but like the Old Testament God, he reserved his most personal wrath for his own. He broke his daughter's fingers, and he made her his slave. Somebody shot him dead and that made sense. What goes around comes around. Too bad he couldn't die more than once.

Great golden sand mountains glowed in the lavender twilight. The four young men, boys really, scampered to the top. They looked like insects crawling the face of the dune from where she stood below. One turned and waved at her as though she were his mother watching him swim from the shore. She came alive the day Ray died; that was indisputable. Yet she wished some of these children could have met him long enough to see what she'd endured. They had no idea what evil was. They were totally untested. Their innocence made the rage inside of her pulse and glow.

Tom approached from behind and wrapped his arms around her waist. She stiffened at his touch until he dropped his embrace.

"Some of the kids brought drugs," he said.

"Yes." Sidewinder rattlesnakes had left divots in the sand with their roiling bodies. It would be wonderful to see one.

"Thought you should know."

She kept her eyes skyward. The moon was rising. "I know everything."

She felt him staring at her but she did not turn or move in any way. She had been able to hold it together with Rod for eight years before he died. With Tom it had been barely three weeks and already she could tell that he sensed the arctic wind it had taken Rod years to detect. Rod had known he was shivering but it took him some time to realize that his wife was the reason. Tom Shepard was a far less foolish man. She would have to be careful.

The Eureka dunes were supposed to sing at night when the wind blew the sand from the ridges. The young men had made it to the top. Their whoops and yells sounded as far away as the moon. She had no illusions about her power. She was a glorified camp counselor for people looking for diversions. Well, she was looking for diversion too.

She could say to Tom that she needed his protection. He only wanted a job to do, a way to be seen and loved. There were so many things she could do and say to warm him and make him forget for just a little longer the chill that blew from her dead heart.

But her throat closed over the words. He went away and she listened to him talk with Angel and Fallon as they cooked beans and rice on his propane stoves. He had a particular affection for Angel, she'd noticed. Big men liked small women and that was always the way. And there was Angel, pretending to want a ride to Los Angeles to be with her old boyfriend. If she really wanted to see him she'd have driven there herself. Instead her truck sat parked in front of Razi's house in Berkeley and Angel was in the middle of the desert with a fake family that had sprung out of Razi's forehead whole.

Angel thought she was so tough with her cowboy boots and her direct way of talking to people that was like throwing darts. When Razi tried to remember how Crystal's voice had sounded when she was a small child, she couldn't remember her saying anything. She remembered everything Madison ever said. She knew everything Madison liked to eat, the names of the children she played with at school, the names of her dolls and toys. Razi knew the contents of Madison's dreams.

They would spend one night at the Eureka dunes. She had been curious about the singing sand, but it was only a distraction. Insects buzzed in her head. Her thoughts were disorganized. They would head to Saline Valley over the mountains. One of her followers talked about natural hot springs, deep in the desert. There was a hippie encampment with running water, remote enough to elude the authority of park rangers and law enforcement. That was where the vision quests would begin, the tests these young people desperately needed. She would open her mouth and see where Jin Jun took her. Maybe Angel would not live through hers. It would be an Old Testament trade, a life for a life, and Razi could find her way to Madison again. Anything could happen in a desert wilderness.

Tom's laughter carried. He was a loud man when he wanted to be. Razi watched as he threw his arm around Angel's shoulders. If that girl really wanted to be with her boyfriend, she'd be with him by now. Angel wanted something from her. Her need for love emanated from her with a deafening sonar.

The day she had become pregnant with Crystal was the day Teresa lost everything. If she'd known, she would have found a way to get rid of her the moment she realized she'd missed a period. She was stupid when she was young. She was stupidly greedy for love. She hadn't realized the devastation that her greed had wrought until it was far too late to do anything to stop it. But still she'd insisted on this roundabout route south just to spend more time with her. The greed ran deep, despite a lifetime of evidence of its destructive power.

She hated Angel. She loved Angel.

The moon rose higher and took on more light. She knew the kids had drugs. She was the one who had sent Fallon with the money to get them. The boys ran in zigzags down the dune, landslides of sand falling from their footsteps. It was so beautiful with the moon rising and the sky darkening in purples and blues. Under what pressures, Razi wondered, would the entire mountain collapse and swallow every living thing upon it?

Chapter 36

Angel

Only stoned beyond reason could Angel climb naked into a mineral hot spring full of just as naked strangers.

"We should leave tomorrow or today," Angel said to everyone and no one. "My mother needs to go to the doctor."

"We will," Fallon said. She gathered her foot in her hands to massage it, her smile a rising sun across the water. The hot spring was filled with students from Berkeley, kids from Mammoth, a couple of old hippies. It might as well have been just the two of them, Fallon smiling like they shared a secret. Angel's heel rested against Fallon's breast. The Mammoth guys were snickering to each other but the weed and mushrooms obliterated Angel's caring. She rested her head. A military plane tore the sky in half. They covered their ears for the boom. Then Fallon was behind her, digging her fingers into her shoulders until an erotic charge unfurled and Angel sighed.

Razi called them from the bus. It was time for a meeting.

The warm air dried their skin as they slipped on their sandals and walked across the white sand. The long cotton shawls they used for towels flapped around their bodies.

Being born must have felt like this.

They dressed to join the circle gathered in the shade of the bus. The men strung ropes from the bus to stakes they pounded into the dirt. The women hung lean-to tents made of raspberry and lavender and turmeric-colored cloths. Tarps covered the rocky ground. Crystals and chimes dangled from the ropes and created clamoring rainbows. It was a cluster of beautiful forts, the kind children might imagine after reading about Aladdin in the *Arabian Nights*.

Razi sat in the middle of the circle, a sun-heated breeze moving her hair from her face. She looked so young she could have been Angel's sister. Fallon handed Angel a heavy ceramic cup of tea. The dirty sock stink of it turned her stomach, but she drank. It tasted milder than it smelled. She passed the mug of whatever it was along. It might make her feel sick or it might make her feel lit from inside, floating above the tents and campers. She could lie on the pillow and sleep or maybe just watch the rainbows and fabrics wave in the wind against the impossibly blue sky.

Judith waited in limbo on the other side of the mountains. Sundullah would be home from his tour, also waiting. Her tribe made the three points of a triangle. The mother of her birth sat in the shade, the fourth point. The weakest leg of the table. This was dumb. Angel was stoned, but she had enough of her brain capacity working to know she was wasting time. Razi would never give her answers.

Angel would end this after today—she would. She would insist. Make demands. Threaten to expose the truth. But for now, she sipped the tea as it passed under her nose again. She lay on a pillow as pain, anxiety, and guilt evaporated in the dry air. Her arm grew numb behind her head. The silk of the pillow slipped cool between her fingers. Sundullah would love this place with these people if she could make him understand. The drugs would scare him at first. They didn't have to do the drugs if he didn't want. If only he came back with her they could live in the desert. This was a good place to live. A rainbow danced across her torso like a wayward butterfly. There were no nightmares in the desert, no falling spiders. She reached for Fallon's hand and wished words were enough to tell her how much she loved her.

Jin Jun Razi knelt in front of the group of her followers. Her eyes rolled, showing the whites. It was time to hear from an ancient spirit born when tectonic shifts pushed the mountains skyward on the other side of the valley.

"We must be cleansed further," she said in the deep Jin Jun tone. "Each of us will go into the desert to be tested. In the heat of the afternoon, we'll search our deepest selves. You will each hear a message that you will bring back to the camp and then to the world. Jin Jun is only one of a great family of spirits. Razi is only one vessel. You have all been chosen."

Jin Jun Razi turned to Angel. "You will go first," she said. "You will walk into the desert and return with new light."

The hot tea bubbled in the back of Angel's mouth. Her stomach flipped over. *Danger sweet Angel.* Jerry's warning voice was as clear as the tinkling chimes hanging from the ropes. She turned and expected Jerry at her side instead of Fallon smiling like Angel had won the Miss America pageant. It was a smile for someone else's happiness.

"Don't be frightened," she said, squeezing her fingers. "You are so lucky to be chosen. I'm jealous but in a good way." She kissed her on the lips.

She pulled Angel to her feet and steadied her with her own body. Tom sat outside the circle on a lawn chair. He wasn't smiling. The chair creaked when he got up to whisper something to Jin Jun, but she shooed him away.

"This must be the sacrifice." This was Jin Jun talking, her voice a mad dog's growl. Not an angry dog. A mad one, out of her wits.

Then Razi slumped forward, her body bent over her folded legs. She was silent for a long moment and Fallon gathered the fabric of Angel's tunic in her hand, waiting for the next word.

Finally Jin Jun Razi stirred and moaned like a sleepy child.

She sat up, rubbing her eyes as though she had just awoken from a long nap. "Who is first?" she asked, blinking at Tom.

"Angel," Tom said, "which I believe you know." He frowned beneath his bushy mustache. He looked at Angel and shook his head. "You don't have to go."

Jin Jun Razi ignored Tom. "Get her ready, Fallon," she said. "This child must begin her vision quest." She wrapped a beige silk cloth around her head and shoulders and walked away from the raspberry and saffron tent city.

Angel didn't know what to do. She forgot for a second what was going on. Tom went around the back of the bus. The acrid smoke of his cigarette rose on the wind. Fallon hugged her. "Don't be scared," she whispered. "This is such an honor."

Angel stood like a scarecrow as Fallon fitted her with a backpack. It sloshed with bottles of water. Fallon and Razi must have arranged this beforehand. The bag with water bottles had been ready. Angel's muddled brain grasped at alarm but coherent thoughts slid around as though greased.

"She should have shoes." Tom came to the front of the bus and leaned against the hood. He crossed his arms in front of his chest. Razi stood in the middle of the stones and reindeer brush. At this distance, she appeared ghostly in the waves of heat. The other followers rested under the canopies, too high to move from whatever was in the tea Fallon had passed around. She had shown Angel her stash in the bus. Hash, mushrooms, peyote, weed, unmarked pills. The others lay under the prisms like preschool children during naptime, or like people who were dead.

Tom joined them. Fallon pointed to Angel's dusty feet in the cheap sandals they'd bought together. "They should be okay," she said. "She won't be going far, I don't think."

"You knew she was going to pick Angel." Tom's voice was matter-of-fact. Angel had noticed him frowning at Jin Jun in ways that carried over when it was just Razi among them. At first he'd seemed totally in love, but in the past few days, he'd spent more time away from the group in the tubs with the campers from Berkeley and Mammoth.

"Well," Fallon said. "Razi had a premonition."

"You must have worked it out," he said. "That's called planning."

Fallon bit her bottom lip. "I don't know what you are talking about," she said, "but it sounds like you are doubting Jin Jun Razi."

"I'm doubting why a young girl needs to go into the desert by herself," he said. "You're both baked out of your minds to begin with and have been since we got here. Sounds like a disaster waiting to happen, Fallon. Don't be an idiot."

"Get shoes," Fallon said to Angel. "And I'm not an idiot, Tom."

"Razi is just a woman. An ordinary woman. It's not right to make her into a god."

"You feel the same way as we do about her, or you did up until now. Don't deny the truth in your heart."

Angel left them arguing. She was stuck in slow motion. She found her backpack tucked under a seat in the bus and rifled through it. Her blue jeans and utilitarian t-shirts seemed foreign. She found her running shoes but no socks so she wore them with bare feet. Her head was a floating balloon.

Fallon waited for her under an emerald-colored sheet. Tom walked away from the camp toward the hot springs.

Fallon held out her hand. "Ready?"

"I just want her to tell me what to do," Angel said. "I don't even know why."

They hugged again, Fallon's sulfur and wood-smoked hair flying into Angel's nose. Angel watched over her shoulder as Tom took off his shirt and pants and slipped into the big warm pool with the Berkeley grad students. Someone handed him a beer. He laughed at a joke, the sound carrying over the breeze.

Water bottles were a great weight. Gripping the straps helped with the heaviness that dug into her shoulders. Fallon pressed her nose into Angel's cheek a last time.

"Everything is as it should be," she said, and while Razi watched from afar, pushed Angel toward the saltpan and stones.

Chapter 37

January 11, 1990
Saline Valley, California

Angel

〜〜〜

THE STONY GROUND flowed toward cliffs ever in the distance. The one full water bottle sloshed against the empties in the backpack, now light. The cliff was a place to head at least. Straight lines didn't exist in the valley of the bad sun.

Even in the cool of January it was a bad sun. There was nowhere to hide from it until enough time passed that it lowered in heavy degrees and hid behind a far mountain. The white sand reflected the pink sky. She turned her ankle but kept going.

The Jin Jun Razi game ended when her high faded as she huddled under the frigid stars. It was the darkest part of the night. A deep memory emerged of a lost child running through darkness. She felt that child's hopelessness as though it were her own. She was lost and it wasn't a new feeling.

The sun finally rose again. She walked. She took breaks on boulders and sipped small portions of the last of the water. She did not know how long she had walked the day before to get so lost. The red cinder cone mountain landmark that she and Fallon had climbed on the first day of their arrival in Saline Valley wavered in the distance, impossibly far away. Even if she had enough water to make it that far, she wasn't positive that it was the landmark she thought it was. This was a valley full of broken volcanoes and cinder cones. Better to walk toward the nearer cliffs on the off chance there might be a road or people.

The cliff face opened into a canyon. It was the end of another day. The quickening winter evening obscured the path. She picked her way into a slot canyon and found a sandy place to sleep. The stars appeared in layers, eons deep. The night fell to blackness prickling with rustlings and exhalations.

Living things skittered from hiding places in order to go about their hunger tasks. Stone falls trickled along the cliff. Angel meant to take just a last sip of water but couldn't stop drinking. She capped the empty bottle. Fell asleep in her own arms.

THE SUN ROSE like the eye of a remote god. The rays daggered her eyelids. Her tongue scraped the inside of her mouth as though it were barbed. The morning light glared on the walls of the canyon. The petroglyph of a giant bird spread its wings high on the wall. It had not been visible in the dark. Its simple lines looked drawn with fat chalk. Spirals and goats with short and jaunty horns danced around it, etched into the rock beneath a shiny patina.

She had slept in the middle of a circle of black rocks that stood as tall as men. Angel was an intruder here. She would have apologized to the stones if she had any spit in her mouth to form the words. She crept into the shadow of the canyon and waited for nothing.

A GUNSHOT RANG HER out of dozing. The sun warmed her head and shoulders. It wasn't high in the sky. Not overhead. Not noon. The noise came from a memory dream. Once she'd heard a real gunshot. Once she had been lost and afraid and it was as real as this.

She used the pack that had held her water as a pillow. Grains of sand tumbled against one another under her nose. A trail of fat black ants scuttled to and from a hole at the base of a barrel cactus. Angel was a higher life form but she could not figure out how to survive this hard winter sun. The ants could. They had a home and a purpose. They knew exactly what they were doing. They would probably have their way with her flesh once she died.

Angel forced her cracked lips together. She fantasized about a glass of purple Kool-Aid with ice cubes like Judith always made for her when she got the flu. She wanted to weep but had no tears. She was dry inside and out.

Ravens squawked over the ridge from the rock circle. The rocks wore their shadows like long trains at the ends of dresses. Everything in this nowhere place had a home and she did not even have one to yearn for. Her home had been a string of in-law cottages and converted garage studios. Home was her tiny room and bathroom above the homeless shelter. It was Russell's bedroom in the house of college boys, then the moldy trailer in the woods in Creekside where no one wanted her. For a short time the narrow bed in Tom's bus had been her home. She belonged in all of them. She belonged in none. In the end she belonged here clinging to the dry surface of an indifferent mother.

Angel's life was a teacher with a single lesson. There was such a thing as a terrible mother. Nature herself was a terrible mother. She would bring you into the world and she would rip you out. Angel pulled Razi's sweater over her hands and sunk her face into its neck hole. She inhaled the perfume of the woman who had sent her into the desert to die. She deserved no better than this. Her own baby hadn't made it past the subterranean stage.

Angel fell into an exhausted half-sleep. She tried to wake from it but it pulled on her and her eyes wouldn't open. She felt a weight on her belly. Then in her belly. Then small hands on her cheeks and a voice whispering forgiveness.

Chapter 38

January 10–11, 1990
Saline Valley, California

Razi

❧

Tom's flashlight swept the wash at the outer edges of the campground when the girl didn't return the first night.

"I lost her," Razi said when he returned alone.

"You pushed her out," he replied. "It's cold at night. She's got your sweater and enough water to be okay, I think. But we've got to find her."

He looked at her as if seeing her for the first time. She tried to head into the night but he wouldn't let her go. In the bus he looked over maps of the area and planned the next day's search. He borrowed two all-terrain vehicles from the Mammoth kids at the other camp.

"I didn't mean to kill her," she said when they met at the end of the long, fruitless second night.

"You didn't try hard enough not to," Tom said.

Let me find her, she prayed silently but had no idea who she thought was listening. She should have known better than to pray but it was a habit she never could break.

She waited while he siphoned gas from the bus for the ATVs. She wedged goggles over her eyes and headed for the wash without looking at Tom's maps for directions. She would either find Crystal or get lost herself and die of exposure in the middle of the desert. It would be a deserved death.

The ATV bumped over the stones, shocking the desert stillness with noise. The wind was freezing. That was something to think about. Crystal had spent two nights in the elements. She had enough water for at least a day and a half, but she may have already been dead of the cold.

Razi had strapped Crystal's backpack to the vehicle. If she found her dead, well then. When she'd thought of the idea of the vision quest she knew it was a possibility her child would not pass the test. Ray's bullying logic pulsed in her brain as malignant as a tumor. If she couldn't survive the desert, maybe she shouldn't survive it.

Tom was right that she didn't try hard enough not to lose her. At the Eureka Dunes she'd begun a long slide down. Since the earthquake her brain worked like the playground of a demented child, up and down on teeter-totters a mile long. Slides emptied into pits of fire. It created a world where someone like Razi could send a lost person like Angel out into the desert alone.

She wiped the surface of her goggles. Her own folly astounded her now. It was as though she was shaking herself awake from a long dream. If she found Crystal dead then she'd die right next to her. That would be life for a life enough for any demon dealmaker. Funny how with her it was always the children who were in peril, but the actual devil never was. Ray had been safe with her. He could always count on being one hundred percent safe with his daughter.

Let me find her. Another prayer, but not to God. She pictured God same as Ray: all-seeing, all-knowing, impossible to placate in the long term. Always making you choose, one thing or the other. You can have the baby but not Michael. You can have the baby but I'll hurt you first. You can have your freedom but not your child. You can have Madison but not a good husband. Madison can have life but you can't have her. Don't get greedy.

God could go fuck himself.

Let me find her. She squinched her eyes shut and drove blind. Of all the dearly departed saints in heaven interceding with a temperamental, psycho God, it was Michael she trusted to help her. Only her beloved Michael would be brave enough to persist on her behalf. He was The Boy Who Knew No Fear.

Are you there, my love? She sent her pleas into the sky. *Let me find her. Let me find our daughter.*

Rocks flew from beneath the wheels in the wash. She leaned forward to reduce the wind. She opened her eyes.

Chapter 39

Angel

A BLACK CURTAIN FELL and then receded. It skirted the periphery. Angel fought it with sandpaper eyelids. She should keep warm. She should keep moving. She didn't want to. This made more sense, to watch the ants in their tenacity and industry.

Through the spines of the cactus a distant figure wavered in the clear oil shimmering from the ground. At first it was a burro or a raven but then it was a lanky young man with brown hair falling over the collar of a denim jacket.

"Crystal," he said. His voice rumbled from a deep aquifer. He lifted her in his arms and dragged his scratchy jaw against her cheek. He smelled like rain. He wanted her to fight the black curtain.

"You need to live through this," he said. He set her on her feet and placed his hands on her back. She walked through the slot canyon, away from the ants and the etched birds and the goats and spirals and the condor who soared above them with outspread wings.

She stumbled on stones as the sun split her scalp. The world swam in a haze of blue and white. The man stayed behind. He wanted her to live. He wanted her to run.

"Michael," she whispered.

"Run," he said.

She clutched her arms to her chest. She had to hold the book. She wanted to keep it so badly but her hands dropped to stop her fall as she tripped on the uneven ground. She kept moving.

She fell again and rocks dug into her kneecap. She lurched bleeding in the direction the tall man had pushed her. Sandy soil shifted under her sneakers as she descended into an old wash paved in round stones.

He pointed her in the direction to go. *Run*, he said. So she ran.

DUST CLOUDS BILLOWED down the valley. Through them plowed a three-wheeler headed straight for her. The black curtain reduced the desert to a pinhole in her vision. She knelt on the ground, squinting through one eye. Goggles covered the driver's face but it was Jin Jun Razi. She bent over the handlebars, her white robes undulating like wings.

The engine cut, leaving them in silence. Angel's knees bled into the sand. The ends of her hair tickled her cheekbones in the breeze and reminded her of the ants. Razi disembarked from the three-wheeler. She ran with the purpose of a medic, rummaging in a bag. Water.

She held the back of Angel's head with one hand and a bottle in the other. She filled Angel's mouth. Water spilled down her chin. Razi forced her to take more. Angel fell against her.

"I was looking for you," Razi said.

Angel's stomach roiled. She dove to all fours and vomited. Long ropes of bile hung from her lips to the sand. Razi poured water on her face, using her hand to wipe Angel's mouth clean. She opened another bottle and made her drink. Cool water washed away the burning acid.

"You almost killed me." Angel's voice was as rusty as the croaking ravens.

"Almost," Razi said. The breathy tones of the guru evaporated. Her real voice was flat with an edge of sarcasm. "There is a world in *almost*."

Angel sat in the dirt while her mother wrapped her head in white cotton. She handed her a pair of big sunglasses. Razi helped her to the small shade the three-wheeler cast in the morning sun. She placed a soft white blanket around Angel's shoulders.

"Why did you come looking for me?" Angel asked.

"Why did you come looking for *me*?" Razi's reply. She kept her eyes on the horizon.

"So that you would tell the truth and let Judith go free." Angel's lips cracked. She drank more water, though her stomach felt its weight like a sack of stones.

"You could have sent the FBI after me if you knew who I was. You didn't have to come yourself."

Angel watched a handful of white sand blow through her fingers. Razi was speaking the truth. The time Angel had spent with her was a wasteland. She couldn't name what she had hoped for but whatever it was, she didn't find it.

"Judith stole you from me," Razi said. "She was right to do it. But she let me sit in jail for months. She kept you. She knew you were alive when everyone thought you were dead."

"Mom said that she let you know. She said you knew all along and that you never tried to get in touch with me. You never tried to get me back."

"It was too late. You were living but Teresa wasn't. The girl that was Michael's girlfriend and had you was dead by then. I killed her myself. It was me that died, not you." Razi's eyes bore into her with the intensity of the desert sun. "I have another daughter, you know. I killed her too."

"What happened?" Angel envisioned a stabbing, a choking, a drowning in the bathtub.

"I just lost track. I lost track. People want more than that. They want a bigger story. But the truth is that if you don't hold on tight, your daughter will slip from you and it will be your fault. You should have held on. You should have thought of her before you thought of yourself. But you didn't. You let go."

Angel's knees bled in clotting rivers down her shins. She felt the tugging of her own lost girl like a kick inside. She felt the baby's absence in her own dirty and aching arms.

"I thought if you died she would live. But Madison has another mother now. A better mother than me, just like Judith was." Razi extended her hands, showing Angel the lined monkey palms and the fragmented fingers. "I think crazy things sometimes. My hands aren't the only things about me that are broken.

"When Ray, your grandfather, learned I was pregnant, he acted like it was no big deal. He acted kind. Nothing on this earth was as dangerous as my father when he was being nice." Her eyes fixed on a point down the wash. "Ray called me to the workshop. Back then I still thought I could be safe. If only I showed enough loyalty, Ray would stay sane and we'd be okay." She sneered at nothing. "Ray spread my hands on the workbench and smashed my knuckles with a hammer. Every single one."

Angel reached for her. Razi tucked her chin into Angel's palm and kissed her fingertips. It was a gesture for a mother and her baby.

"I can't hold you, Crystal. I'll lose you again. I am not a safe place. I am not your home."

Angel looked over her shoulder toward the petroglyph canyon for the man in the denim jacket. He was no longer there. Her mother caught her from falling over.

"Are you passing out?" Razi asked. She reached for another bottle of water.

"I need to get to L.A.," Angel said.

Razi wedged herself under Angel's arm. "I promised I would take you," she said. "Consider it my last broken promise. I've arranged for you to go this afternoon with the Berkeley geographers … if I found you. They're heading south and they have room."

"What about Judith?"

"You let me worry about Judith. You let Judith worry about Judith. You worry about your own self. Keep your own self alive."

"We owe her. We both owe her."

"Go see after that boy. The rock star. Stop wasting time. Forget who you owe."

She let Angel lean on her for balance. Once on the three-wheeler, Angel rested her head on her shoulder as they roared down the wash.

After several miles, the palm trees and hot pools and camps appeared as apparitions and then solidified. Tom whizzed by in the opposite direction on another three-wheeled vehicle. His head snapped in their direction as they passed.

The people in white tunics were dispersed. There was no more jewel-colored tent paradise. There were no more chimes or rainbows. The followers poked around their camper vans, disoriented, like people at the end of a wild party after someone turned on the lights. Fallon wasn't among them.

Razi's hair stung Angel's face. Her waist was thin as a wraith's. Another day in the desert and Razi would disintegrate into ash.

Mud-splattered trucks and vans surrounded the lower hot spring pool. Razi rolled to the outskirts of the students' camp. She gripped the handlebars with the engine idling.

"Your stuff is strapped to the back," she said.

A man broke from the group near the pool and walked toward them, a hand raised in greeting.

"I don't know them," Angel said.

"You don't know me either."

"I wanted to," Angel said.

Razi squeezed the throttle. Then she turned it off and pushed the goggles below her chin. She grabbed Angel's face. Bony hands cradled her jaws. It was not comfortable but for once Angel felt the woman's hard reality, her physical strength. She felt her hardness and her coldness and why she had lived this long and would continue to live—maybe forever. This woman would live through anything. That's where Angel got it from.

"Be strong," her mother said. She bowed into Angel's forehead and breathed into her face. Angel breathed the air from her lungs. "You must live, no matter what. Survive me. Survive everything and find your way home."

She pushed her away. Angel cradled her backpack in her arms while Razi started the bike and thundered in the direction of the broken followers.

The man approached. "Are you Crystal?" he asked.

"Angel," she said.

"You need a ride to Los Angeles?" he asked. "We're headed to UCLA for a symposium." His eyes were green and gentle in his sunburned face.

She followed him into the camp of geographers. The professor with the green eyes set her up in a chair under a tarp and gave her an orange and water.

Later on she soaked in the tub and napped while they packed. The professor invited her to sit in the front seat of the van while they drove through the valley, but she preferred the back. She listened to the professor and his students tell her about the rocks and formations and massive desert pan. They knew the origins of the hot springs as well as hidden canyons and secret corners that held teeming life.

She rested her temple against the window. After forty miles of hard road, they reached asphalt and it hummed under the tires.

"Where am I dropping you when we get into town?" the professor asked. The gold wedding band on his finger rapped against the steering wheel, a talisman symbolizing a wife, maybe children. She imagined a woman with long hair who baked cakes made with raisins and honey. A man this kind would have children who clung to their mother's skirts but who ran to greet their father when he came home from trips.

She felt around the front pocket of her backpack for the letter Sundullah sent after her stoned morphine confession that she thought had ended his beautiful letters forever. But it hadn't. There was this one.

Her spirit will always be with us. Her beautiful ghost. You and I can bear our sadness together. We'll love her that way. I shouldn't have gone on tour. I shouldn't have left you dying and alone. I should never have left you alone, period. I should have fought for you. I should have made you tell me what was wrong four years ago so that you didn't have to grieve her by yourself. Let me grieve for her with you now. Forgive me, he said. *Come back to me.*

He left a forwarding address in Topanga Canyon. She handed the envelope over the back of the seat to the professor. He held it on the flat part of the steering wheel, glancing down and then back at the road.

"Is it too much trouble?" Angel asked. "Is it too far to drop me?"

"We'll figure it out," he said.

She unzipped the top of her backpack and a plush toy sprung from where it was crammed in with her clothes. It fell to her lap. It was burgundy and velvet and immediately familiar. Teresa, Reese, Razi, her mother, had put it there for her to find.

"Is that where you live, Angel?" asked the professor. "Topanga Canyon?"

Love bloomed out of compressional stress deep in Angel's core. It burst in her stomach and bloomed into her throat and broke through in laughter. Her voice was still creaky, her throat still damaged from infection and too many drugs and thirst. But it would heal. She would heal.

"Yes," she said. "That's my home."

Chapter 40

January 20, 1990
San Jose, California

Teresa

‹——~——›

S HE FELT NAKED in jeans and a t-shirt. She felt naked without a name. Her name wasn't Razi anymore; it never had been. Her name sure as hell wasn't Reese Camden. She waited in the FBI headquarters office and felt the eyes of the agents in the room. They stood like sentinels. She wore her hair in a ponytail that rested at the base of her neck. She fiddled with the ends, stiff as straw.

She'd found Crystal without a map and saved her life and brought her to safety. That had to count for something. She'd handed her over to a good person. Yet again. That didn't make her good but it did suggest a certain courage. It reminded her of the bravery she felt enrolling in high school masquerading as her lawyer's niece. If she could do one right and strange thing then she could do another. She'd built a life that way, brick by brick, and it led her to having Madison, the bravest thing she'd ever done. She could hold onto thoughts of Madison to help her get through this.

Detective Laura Redleaf rushed into the room, a flustered mess next to the cool agents. Detective Redleaf, still the one who cared most about the truth.

"I'm only talking to Judith," Teresa said before the detective asked a single question. No need to get her hopes up. "At least I'm talking to her first. So don't ask me anything."

Redleaf opened and closed her mouth, then ushered her into another room. "Well then, what are we waiting for?" she said.

They brought her into a room where Judith waited, looking sick. It took a long time for the room to empty. They hoped she hadn't meant it when she'd said only Judith. They hoped that she would forget. She waited in silence until finally everyone left.

"Tell me you didn't hurt her," Judith said.

"You know I didn't."

"I know she says you didn't. She called me when she got to L.A."

"I left her with you to save her life," she said, "and then she almost died anyway."

"I didn't kill her," Judith said. She looked exhausted.

"No. You lost her, though. I lost her too. It's what I do. I make girls into ghosts." Teresa bit a fingernail. "I'm telling them," she said. "I'm telling them everything. Then you're going to the doctor right after. Enough of the bullshit. A girl needs her mother."

"Oh, Teresa," Judith said in a voice so tender Teresa wanted to run. Judith reached for her but she drew herself in. She didn't want kindness. If she were going to do the right things in the right order she needed to stay focused and control her feelings. She didn't want to feel love. Love made her greedy and stupid. She could do loving things better if she didn't feel what it meant.

When the agents returned, Teresa told the true story. The agents had questions on top of questions. She answered them. She splayed her broken bones for evidence. She submitted to X-rays and lie detectors and questions that poked at her like a thousand needles drumming a tattoo into her flesh. She answered the same questions over and over again until the story itself became the drumbeat. *I left my daughter I left my daughter I left my daughter behind.*

I left my daughters behind.

She thought of the young men stumbling down the dunes. At some point momentum takes over when a person goes fast in one direction. At some point gravity has its way. She waited to feel the pull of inevitable action instead of the sensation of walking though cement in heavy boots, but it never happened. Not a single moment of it was easy.

"So at what point did you realize that Judith Kelley had taken custody of your daughter?"

"I always knew," she said. Which wasn't true. She knew the night Redleaf told her about Ray and Billy's deaths. That was when she knew. But she held on to that one lie. If they didn't know that the murders of the murderers were Judith's doing she wasn't going to be the one to tell them.

She met her old teacher one last time when it was over. They sat together in a questioning room but the questions were wrung out. Laura Redleaf wanted to speak with them both alone and she'd agreed to it but secretly planned to leave before it could happen. She didn't want a big scene. She didn't want to hear anyone talking about her life a second longer than necessary.

"I know what you did," Teresa said. "To Ray. Billy." She hated the taste of their names in her mouth.

Color spread across Judith's neck. Teresa felt uneasy as a kid catching her teacher in a vulnerable moment. It wasn't the first time. "Ah," Judith said.

"You probably feel guilty for it too."

"That's between God and me."

"God," Teresa scoffed. "He disappeared whenever Ray was around."

"Yes He did."

"You didn't disappear. You were braver than God."

She felt shy now that she had said so much. Judith's hands flitted like moths. It was obvious that the woman wanted to touch her, but knew better. Teresa was grateful to her for letting her be. She was grateful to her for so many things and the feeling was an overblown balloon pressing against her insides. Taking up all the air.

Teresa walked out without another word, without a new shape or a new name. She could have been anybody. Or nobody. She didn't have any ideas about who she was. Her only thought was for Madison. She had work to do to deserve her. It would take time. But she had one thought as she got in her car and drove away.

My daughter. I have to find my daughter.

Chapter 41

January 30, 1990
San Jose, California

Judith

❦

WHEN TERESA CONFESSED to the agents, there was a spark in her eyes that made Judith want to be careful. Madness lurked there like a flaw within an otherwise perfect marble. She was different from the hurt girl she knew in Arcata eighteen years before. But she was also not the polished suburban mother at her husband's funeral. Her cuticles were bitten. Her hair was straw. A frail thinness shook her limbs like a breeze rustles an aspen tree.

But she had thanked Judith in a way. And she had told the truth.

Judith walked out from under the ceiling and into the warm day. The sun shone cartoon-bright in an unreal sky. Laura had offered to be here for her but Judith refused. Laura Redleaf missed her family. Judith would not keep her a moment longer. There had been enough sadness already. Enough.

Judith walked across the parking lot filled with cars. There were no people anywhere. It might as well have been the end of the world. In her reflection in a sedan window she recognized a witch from one of her own fairy tales. She missed Angel with a loneliness that felt like a gutting. Without Angel she had no one, not even herself. How misguided she was to ever think she could live without love.

The cab rolled to the curb. She gave the address of the cottage behind the painter's house. The cottage was waiting for her, Redleaf had said. There was kindling in the fireplace, a stack of wood by the geraniums. Food in the refrigerator. It would feel like home, she said. Judith didn't argue, just thanked her. But she knew what it would and would not feel like without Angel there.

The cottage smelled like pine cleaner. The ocean outside the picture window stirred in a pre-storm boil. The tiny house stood perched on the edge of the cliff like a bird about to take flight. For the first time, Judith felt uneasy in the house. It was in a precarious spot for earthquake country.

Mail sat in piles on the kitchen table. She sorted through it. There was a postcard of a hillside dotted with oaks. The return address read Topanga, CA.

I'm home, Angel wrote. *Go to the doctor. Come see me when you're ready.*

It took Judith a few hours to pack her belongings. There were four boxes of mementos of Angel's childhood. There were locks of hair, photographs, drawings in crayon and marker. There was a drawing of her, the name *Mommy* scrawled across the top. A tall woman with silver hair and arms long enough to reach around a child and sweep her away from danger.

Aside from the boxes, a suitcase of clothing. Judith spent more time going through the drawings and photos than she had folding and putting things in the suitcase. She'd been born an unwanted child, a refugee in her own country. She knew how to hit the road and run. It was an easier thing than what she was about to do.

She jangled the house keys as she stood on the bluff and wondered at the expanse of sea below. The universe-sized space around her head felt strange. She'd grown accustomed to low ceilings in windowless rooms. But it wasn't the freedom and space that terrified her. She knew how to leave. It was more difficult to stay.

She knocked at Albert's door. She willed her heart to calm down. Albert would give her a ride to the hospital at least. The rest she could wait and see.

He traveled through his house with the bass of a heavy man's footsteps. When he opened the door, out washed a tide of turpentine, lemon polish, curries, and incense. His face registered surprise at first and then wrinkled into its regular good humor. He stepped aside and invited her in with a flourish of his arm.

"I'm glad to see you," he said. "Welcome home."

Chapter 42

January 30, 1990
Willow Creek, California

Laura

～⌣⌣⌐

Teresa looked nothing like the young mother in the pictures from eighteen years ago. Her hair was a torn white veil. She was beautiful in a way but also alien. When Laura had come to say a few last words to her, she was gone.

"We won't see her again," Judith said.

Laura swallowed her disappointment. It had meant so much to her to say goodbye, yet Teresa left early on purpose to avoid her. The objectives were met—that was the thing to remember. If not for Laura, the case would never have been solved. Yet the three women were never in one another's company at the same time.

Something had happened in the desert, Laura knew it. A new mystery.

Her bad feelings about Teresa's leaving sat within her like an irritant stone. She had invitations from morning shows and magazines to give interviews about the investigation. After learning that Teresa was gone, she took the list of producers and editors from her purse and threw it in the garbage.

Judith was polite, but glad to see her go. Everybody was glad to get their lives underway again. Laura thought on that as well as she drove the six hours north on the highway.

Once home she hoisted her duffle bag out of the trunk. Her son and daughter burst out the front like firecrackers. Her son took her bag and shouldered it himself. What a good man he was already. He searched her face, his brow knit in concern, his eyes looking for signs that she was happy to be home.

Her daughter bounced around, throwing herself into Laura's body and almost tripping her. She embraced her girl tightly. She buried her face in her hair.

Once inside, her son dropped the bag and hugged his mother too. He needed her physical touch as much as the girl did. They needed her but as she held them to her, she knew that she would always need them more. There was nothing more important than love.

Laura's husband waited at the bottom of the staircase. The smell of barbecue smoke from the backyard meant a special dinner. It meant a celebration. The table set with four places looked hopeful and complete.

She fell into her husband. She thought she had left her family but she had never really left. She had carried these three in her heart every minute away. She was a drop of rain falling back into the ocean.

Chapter 43

May 13, 1990
Pleasanton, California

Teresa

⌒⌣⌒

TERESA WAITED OUTSIDE the door of Jocelyn's house. It was one of those so-called ranch homes built in the seventies with the garage in front and a triangle-shaped eave over the porch. Jocelyn had never had any taste or style. It was a neighborhood out of a lower middle class nightmare.

Dread rested like a gray toad under her sternum. The doorbell was lit from within. It had a tiny lightbulb inside in case anyone needed to ring it in the middle of the night. She hated the thing for no real reason but she pushed it anyway.

A count of ten was all she'd wait. But she didn't have to wait past the count of three. Footsteps sounded from inside. Then the door opened and Jocelyn stood there, sturdier and tackier than the house itself.

"Come in," she said. She moved her great body to the side like a door within a door. She wore lavender pants with creases down the fronts and a pearl-buttoned sweater. It bothered Teresa that they were the same age. Jocelyn thought Teresa was younger by three years but that was just a lie her lawyer had helped her weave when she became Reese Camden. She and Jocelyn were both thirty-eight. It was the only thing they had in common.

Then she saw Madison. Madison standing in the foyer worrying her hands over her tummy. Every other thought went silent. Teresa fell to her knees.

Her daughter's arms were strong as she threw them around her neck. She shifted to sitting, rocking Madison in her lap. She pressed Madison's head to her chest just as she did when she was newborn. Madison clung so tightly that Teresa could not feel where she ended and her daughter began. They were one body. How had she ever drawn a breath without her daughter in her arms just like this? She smashed her nose into Madison's hair and drew her in.

Jocelyn left them alone while they murmured into each other's faces. Madison's cheek was satin. Teresa sucked the flesh between her teeth and gnawed gently, making the child giggle through her tears.

Teresa lifted Madison's shirt to trace her fingers over the white millipede scars crisscrossing her daughter's stomach and chest. Madison did not protest. She lay in her mother's arms, her eyes wide and watching. Teresa wanted to look her over just as she had the day she was born. But that would not be what her daughter needed, only what Teresa wanted. She pulled the shirt down and patted Madison's back over the soft cotton. Madison's feelings came first. Without Madison nothing mattered and despite everything that had happened, and everything she had done, Teresa wanted life to matter. She might not deserve the love of this daughter, but she could not live without it.

"Don't leave anymore," Madison said. She held a clump of Teresa's hair in her earnest fingers.

"I won't."

Jocelyn coughed and emerged from the kitchen with one hand resting on a mighty hip.

"Promise," Madison said.

Jocelyn looked down on them with a face like a prison door.

"Promise, Mommy," Madison said. Her voice caught on a hook barbed with grief. No one suffered like a little girl. Teresa knew this in her bones and marrow and blood.

"I notice you don't have luggage," Jocelyn said.

"I couldn't believe you meant it," Teresa said. "I thought you were just being nice."

"Promise," Madison said.

"Hush, Maddy," Jocelyn said. "Give it a rest." Teresa was startled by her harshness, but Madison's shoulders lowered from around her ears and she quieted down.

Teresa hated the name Maddy. Her daughter was Madison. Teresa stood, holding her daughter's hand.

"Where are you staying?" Jocelyn asked. Her eyes were hard and clear. She reminded Teresa of Judith. She didn't know why she hadn't seen the resemblance before. When she had hit Jocelyn in the face in the hospital, she had thought the woman was weak. She saw now that if Rod's sister ever decided to return the blow, she would be thrown flat.

"I'm not sure," Teresa said. She was still used to relying on a bully's shallow confidence. Jocelyn was strong for real.

"No more making promises to Madison that we can't keep," Jocelyn said. Inside the kitchen a teakettle whistled. "If you aim to leave again, let's make sure we're honest. It's getting the hopes up that hurts the worst."

Teresa nodded, because that was the truest thing ever said.

"Come have tea," Jocelyn said. "A cup of tea won't kill you. Then we can talk."

As Madison led her into the kitchen Teresa saw herself as Jocelyn must have seen her. She was a monster who did harm to innocent people. She was a child-eater, the unhappiest of witches. Part of her wanted to run away. Hide in a crawl space until the world forgot about her.

"My things are in the trunk of my car," Teresa said. Her mouth felt funny. It was hard to say any of the things she had come to say. "If you mean it, that is."

Jocelyn's back was straight as she poured water into cups. Tea bags puffed and fizzed. She told Teresa to sit, which she did. Madison pushed into Teresa's lap. She was a satellite between two planets fretting between her aunt and mother, searching for the pull of gravity.

"We have a room set up for you," Jocelyn said. "I wouldn't ask if I didn't mean it."

Rose bushes scraped against the window glass in the spring breeze.

"We haven't been friends," Teresa said. Jocelyn set down the cups then went to fetch milk and sugar and a plate of cookies. She'd gone to a lot of trouble and forethought. Teresa saw that this was meant to be a welcome tea. Jocelyn had planned this goodwill gesture to bridge miles and miles of bad water. The bravery of it made Teresa's face redden as though struck. She looked into her cup. It was the good china, and the delicate filigree was impossible and fragile under Teresa's fingers. Madison smelled like someone else's laundry detergent. She was solid in a way that she had never been before. Heavier. Teresa was expecting a delicate hurt kid. She did not expect arms of iron or such a comforting heft on her lap. Madison had thrived under Jocelyn's care. She didn't look much like the girl in the hazy glamour photo hanging in the living room of the Cupertino house.

"No, we haven't been friends," Jocelyn said.

"Be friends," Madison said. "Can I have a cookie?"

Teresa and Jocelyn both spoke at once but stopped before giving full answers. Madison kept her hand frozen over the plate. Jocelyn didn't even like Teresa. There would be these confusions and it would be doomed. Teresa put her hands on Madison's hips to remove her but she couldn't do it. She rested her head against her daughter's narrow back.

"Go ahead," Jocelyn said. "Don't forget to offer one to your mother first."

Her mother. That was Teresa. Teresa could take Madison right now and drive off with her. This was her right. It wouldn't be kidnapping. This was her child. Her daughter.

"Have a cookie," Madison said. "Please do not leave."

She took one of the sugar-frosted butter cookies and pressed it against Teresa's clamped lips. Madison thought Teresa meant to leave without her. It didn't occur to her that Teresa would take her along. She was so used to the idea of being left behind.

"Aunt Jocelyn's house is really good, Mommy," Madison said, leaving the cookie on the table. "Your room is nice."

Jocelyn sat and poured tea. Madison chattered between them as if she could weave the story that would tie them together. Teresa could not move or speak. She could only listen and hope along with her daughter that the story would be enough.

Carl entered from the garage. Jocelyn's husband. He called Madison to help him outside. Madison hesitated, clearly afraid that if she got up from her lap, her mother would disappear.

"Your mama will still be there when we get back," Carl said. He gave Teresa a stern glance, admonishing her not to make a liar of him. Speaking to Madison about a bird feeder project, he led her into the garage.

Once they were gone, Jocelyn leaned close and her words came fast. "Carl and I have it worked out. We want you to stay here, give Madison time to know you again. We love her like our own and we'd be happy to have her forever, Reese. But she loves and needs you. She cries for you every night."

"Okay," Teresa said. "But you hate me. Don't think I don't know it."

"I don't …" Jocelyn started to say then exhaled. "I don't," she said.

"Don't lie about it," Teresa said. "You think I killed Rod. You said so."

"I said unkind things," Jocelyn said. "I was in grief."

"I wasn't in grief. I didn't love him. But I didn't kill him." She would stick to the truth. No more silken lies.

Jocelyn sighed. "My brother was not a good man, I think. But I did love him and on that we'll agree to disagree. I will say this: I don't hate you and neither does Carl. Far from it. We hardly know you. We had no idea who you were."

"Nobody did."

"Well, you've got to admit you make it hard. You make it hard to love you." She tapped the saucer under her cup with acrylic fingernails painted fuchsia. They were her only adornment, a shiny carnival in a plain, wide valley. "We spoke to the doctor you're seeing."

"I told him to call you," Teresa said. "I needed you to understand what you were up against." She trusted Dr. Andreotti with the insects in her brain, the static lines, the radioactive core. She'd found him through the doctors who took care of Madison after the accident. Andreotti had a black and white beard and an air of calm good humor. She yearned for him at that moment, his knowing eyes behind thick glasses. He'd looked into her capacity to damage and saw a happy challenge in teasing out her ability to function.

"You love Madison and you want what's best for her. That's a good sign," Dr. Andreotti had said. Her love was just one brick over the cavernous maw that was her brokenness, but it was better than nothing. It was something to build on. Andreotti saw her for what she was and he still advised her to try living in Jocelyn's home with Madison. But she should tell the truth. He said it as if it were a simple thing.

Teresa had practiced truth-telling with him first, conjuring Angel's blunt way of talking for reference as she spilled her story, reporting all that Ray had done. She listed her own sins as well.

"He said that you can be dangerous," Jocelyn said. "He told me that we'd have to have ground rules. He told me to expect trouble."

"Why do you want me to stay here, then?" Teresa asked.

"You are our family, Reese. Teresa. Whatever you want to be called," Jocelyn said. She wiped her eyes with a dish towel, then studied the cloth. "You are Madison's family and she loves you very much. Stay here as long as you like. You'll help with the house and yard work and when you get a job we'll talk about your part of the expenses."

"Okay," Teresa said, relieved to be talking practicalities. "Did he tell you I might have to leave sometimes? I won't be able to explain it when it happens but it's like I break open inside. Sometimes I might need to leave to go for a walk by myself. Andreotti has been helping me with an action plan kind of a thing."

"I know. We'll figure it out."

"I might have a long way to go, though. Did he tell you that?"

"He did."

Jocelyn's shoulders were huge. She really was built like a linebacker. It was weird that she and Rod were related.

As if reading Teresa's mind, Jocelyn said, "Rod was my brother and I loved him, but he's gone and you're here. Madison is here. This could be your home and why not? It's too big for just the two of us, always has been. We love Maddy. We could stand in for each other like families are supposed to."

Family never meant anything good to Teresa. She mouthed the word to see how it felt.

"You think I never saw that you had problems," Jocelyn said. "You're not the only person in the world with anger inside because of what somebody did to you. Maybe we won't like each other, but it's not about us, is it? Maddy needs you. For heaven's sake, if you love her even a little bit, you won't leave her again."

"I do love her," Teresa said.

"She doesn't know it when you leave her behind," Jocelyn said.

"I do love her. I left her with you. That proves it."

Jocelyn looked down at her tea. Her lips trembled.

"That might be the first time you were ever nice to me," Jocelyn said.

"I didn't say it to be nice. I'm into the truth now."

"There's hope for you. That's all I'm saying."

Teresa was satisfied with that. The steam from the mint tea going up her nose felt nice and fresh. The roses squeaked against the glass. Teresa would stay here and drink cups of tea and watch the roses outside the kitchen window. She would brush her daughter's hair and marvel at her strength and oneness and separateness. She would help with the chores. She would accept kindness and try for faith that someday love would not make her feel afraid.

Madison and Carl came in with arms full of roses, their long stems stripped of thorns. Carl whispered to Madison, and she placed the flowers gently on Teresa's lap as though the bouquet were a baby.

"Welcome home, Mommy," Madison said.

Teresa tore off a bloom's head and tucked it behind Madison's ear. She pressed her nose into the petals. The rose was already dying, deprived of its ground. It would only look and smell pretty for a short time without its connection to the earth that made it.

She took her daughter in her arms. She held onto her small body for her own gravity and weight and earth and ground. She held onto her in gratitude for not dying and for forgiving her and for loving her.

She held onto her daughter for life.

Chapter 44

June 28, 1991
Topanga Canyon, California

Angel

⌒◡⌒

THE SMELL OF Topanga summers reminded Angel of the desert. Cousins of desert sage curled into the hillsides in the heat. In the evenings, coyotes talked to one another through echoing ravines. Sundullah loved the animal noises and the spiced air despite the hint of ozone from the valley. They kept the windows open to help him sleep. Under the morning sun the scents of the canyon brush blew in on cool breezes and hinted to Angel of even wilder places. The smell reminded her of desert canyons, and a valley of a much harder sun.

Her three-month-old daughter's cheek pressed against her chest. Angel sat at the window to watch the sunrise turn the hills pink, then gold. From another part of the house, a teakettle whistled and then ceased. She turned from the view to check that her husband was still sleeping. He'd been resting better lately. His therapist had recommended meditation. It was helping.

Still, Angel worried about Sundullah in Los Angeles. Sundullah's depression was a dragon that together they kept whipped in a corner. She knew better than to turn her back on it. His anxiety required vigilance. Making music and performing made him happy. He even liked the long video shoots. He liked the camaraderie and sense of purpose on the set. But she saw the hungry way the tour organizers pushed him to do more than was good for him. So often she wished for her old St. Francis authority to kick out people who weren't good for the house. Bullies were the same everywhere, whether they were men and women in suits or guys like Gene from the shelter. She didn't trust the producers who issued Sundullah's royalty checks. They would wring him dry if she weren't there. Even now, when things seemed to be going okay, she worried that the company executives were trying to get something for nothing from Sundullah. She kept a constant eye on them too.

The baby rubbed her face into Angel's neck. Angel left the room to let Sundullah sleep. Downstairs, Judith stood in the kitchen pouring tea. The grandmother oak growing outside the windows moved stiffly in the Santa Ana wind. The branches groaned in their heaviness. The arborist they'd hired called that tree the ancestor of every oak that grew down the hillside. She had a healthy trunk, and many years left. Her roots and the roots of her daughters reached deep and kept the land steady. It was the deciding factor in keeping the house rather than moving into something smaller. Property was an investment. They had to think long term. The old Craftsman had solid bones, a sturdy foundation, and good ground. No threat of landslide here.

Judith took Michaela from Angel's arms. Angel's skin felt cool where the sweaty baby had been. Judith brought Michaela to the window to point out the chaparral and oak, the birds, the clouds passing in the sky, the Pacific Ocean beyond the city.

Angel sat to eat the breakfast Judith made. It was hot whole-grain cereal and peppermint tea. She wished for sugar but Judith would fuss as if Angel were trying to eat poison straight out of a can. It wasn't worth it anymore to argue with her about nutrition.

A tiny white cotton dress lay across the broad plank table next to Judith's sewing machine.

"Is it done?" Angel asked.

"It's done," Judith said. "I'm happy with how it turned out. Are you?"

"It's perfect," Angel said. She watched her mother over the teacup steam. Her face lightened when she held Angel's daughter. She looked younger in those moments when she was happy.

Sundullah came down the stairs in his bare feet and no shirt. His dreadlocks hung down his back, burnished with threads of gold. He put his hands on Judith's shoulders and kissed her cheek.

"Hello, Mother," he said.

Michaela turned her face toward her father. He gathered her in one arm and danced across the floor.

"There's too much flaxseed in this oatmeal," Angel said.

"It's good for you," Judith said.

"Listen to your mother," Sundullah sang. Judith poured him a cup of coffee and then took Michaela back from him. Angel would have had coffee too, but Judith said caffeine was bad for the baby. While she was breastfeeding, she drank herbal tea only, at least while Judith was visiting.

"Baby Michaela," Judith said, kissing the space on the baby's forehead where her curly black hair met her eyebrows. "What are you going to call me?"

"Grandmother," Sundullah said. He grabbed the acoustic guitar that leaned against the wall. "Grandmother or grandma or Judith or Judy," he sang. Angel laughed and Michaela started the noises that meant infant hunger.

The housekeeper Ingrid bustled through the front door, carrying groceries. She was the only one to survive the Wrath of Angel, as Sundullah called Angel's paring down of his payroll. His Uncle Eli had assistants that Sundullah had never even met. Angel had helped him fire Eli, get new management, and let the hangers-on go. Ingrid, however, was one to keep. She was a good mother to anybody who was in the house, especially Sundullah. Angel noticed how she kept the refrigerator stocked with fresh vegetables, and how she made him dinners he liked. There was no question in her mind that Ingrid would stay.

"Good to see you, Judith," Ingrid said. "I'm making tacos pescado tonight. Albert's favorite."

"He'll love that," Judith said. When she spoke of Albert, her face softened as though someone was playing her favorite song. Thank God he was coming today.

Angel rolled a flaxseed around on her tongue. Angel had never thought they ate unhealthy foods before, but now Judith was all about green smoothies, fish, and flaxseed in amounts that took some getting used to. With Albert around, Judith would be too distracted to notice Angel sneaking a cup of coffee. He made her laugh, and when she laughed it was easier to believe she was in remission.

Judith gave the baby over to Angel to feed. Sundullah finger-picked a rambling tune Angel didn't recognize. Always with Sundullah something new. He leaned in for a kiss. Angel let herself relax into the nursing despite a pang of sadness that rose in her every time the baby latched on. She was no longer haunted except in these moments of private, almost gentle grief. Michaela did not replace her ghost daughter. Yet Angel's devotion to her living baby was a powerful natural force. This was love with a geologic age. This was love with the power of redemption.

She met Judith's eyes and they shared a smile. They had the day to prepare for Michaela's baptism party. The to-do list was long. Sundullah's recording studio friends were coming, as were the Sisters of St. Joseph who ran the homeless shelter where Angel volunteered. They were hoping it would be a peacemaking time with Sundullah's uncle. He couldn't stay angry once he saw how happy Sundullah was.

The baby flailed her hand against Angel's chin. She kissed the little fingers and pretended to bite them. Michaela grinned, milk running down her cheek.

Suddenly the hair on the back of Angel's neck prickled. She cried out a warning.

The house shivered. The glasses in the cabinets answered in a tinkling then a rattle as the shaking grew. Ingrid braced herself against the counter. Sundullah's guitar dropped as he lurched from his chair. He threw his body over his wife and child, covering their heads. He extended his arm to Judith and pulled her closer. Angel froze, her head bent under the cave of Sundullah's chest, unable to breathe, waiting for the crashing.

But the rumbling faded as if at the end of a short, rhythmic song. Ingrid rushed about, tucking plates and glasses into place from where they'd shifted to the edge. She turned on the radio to hear the news. The epicenter must have been nearby, she said. That felt strong.

Angel, Sundullah, Judith, and Michaela stayed in their clustered embrace for long minutes, holding their places, whispering promises. It was just an earthquake. It's over now.

Michaela watched them, her fingers spread on her mother's breast. Her eyes were wide with alarm and reflected the fears of the three people who were her whole world. Their arms cradled her. They embraced her and made for her an unshakeable ground that would never give way, no matter what happened.

They laughed at the racing of their hearts. There is no need to be afraid, they said. Look, how the baby is smiling. They marveled at her, this baby who knew no fear. What a strong child. What a brave baby girl. Even through an earthquake as big as that one, she is not crying.

Michaela's face froze in the moment before it crumpled into squinting eyes and hard cheeks, her mouth opening in a great wail. Her lungs expanded, her tongue shook, her breath smelled like milk. Her cry was so loud it drowned out the radio.

She howled over their cooing and teary laughter. She wouldn't be quiet. *I am here*, cried the baby, as they held her close and made their noises to calm her.

I am here.

MAUREEN O'LEARY IS a writer and teacher living in Sacramento, California, with her husband and daughters. She was at work in an old brick building in downtown Santa Cruz when the Loma Prieta earthquake hit, sending her ducking for cover under a big oak desk. She loves writing, teaching, public speaking, and hiking in redwood forests and desert canyons.

Her fiction has appeared in *Esopus, Blood and Thunder: Musings on the Art of Medicine, Prick of the Spindle, Xenith, Fiction at Work* and in an anthology from Shade Mountain Press. *The Ghost Daughter* is her third novel. In 2014, she published *How to Be Manly* (Giant Squid Books) and *The Arrow* (Geminid Press).

You can find Maureen online at: www.maureenolearyauthor.com.